WINGS OF STEELE
The Series

EPIC SCIENCE FICTION ACTION-ADVENTURE NOVELS

1

"A wonderful story, a great adventure. Full of excitement and action. Good guys vs bad guys, and yes very much like COWBOYS IN SPACE! What a hoot! Go where no man - woman - dog has gone before!" K. Caid

"Combining military and scifi into a fun adventure, Jeff Burger hit this one out of the park! I look forward to the next in the Wings of Steele series." B.K. Foster

"Best armchair adventure, ever! I haven't had so much fun reading a book in a very long time! Wings of Steele is an awesome, incredible story. I loved the characters... I loved it all! Thanks for writing this story - it should be a movie or a series..." Jolene E.

"Into the wild blue yonder... and beyond! Steele is a regular guy that gets in a jam and is forced to take on the FBI, CIA, the KGB and even a drug cartel...and that's before he even gets to the Bermuda Triangle! Imagine Indiana Jones morphing into Hans Solo with a little Captain Kirk thrown in... enough action to have been TWO books." John C.

"Spend the money and be prepared to have the wife tell you to turn off the light and go to bed already. Ignore her, go to the other room, and it will be well worth it! I'm not saying this actually happened but..." Stahl

"Suspense, drama, space ships, kick-booty humans - everything necessary for good space opera. Can hardly wait for the sequel!" Gary W.

"A cool new hero struggling to follow his moral compass. Keep a round in the chamber and be ready to go, because you aren't gonna be prepared for what's coming around the bend. Some great twists and turns." J. Grace

WINGS *of* STEELE
DESTINATION UNKNOWN

A NOVEL BY
JEFFREY J. BURGER

Other books in the series...
Book 2 - WINGS of STEELE - Flight of Freedom
Book 3 - WINGS of STEELE – Revenge and Retribution
Coming in 2016 - WINGS of STEELE - Dark Cover

www.wingsofsteele.com

Print Edition 2.0 - November 2015

Published in the United States by Templar Press. Templar Press and the mounted Templar Knight colophon are registered trademarks and may not be reproduced.

TEMPLAR PRESS

Wings of Steele – Destination Unknown
Copyright © 2012 Jeffrey J. Burger

Registered with the Library of Congress
ISBN-13: 978-0615692883 (Templar Press)
ISBN-10: 0615692885

Cover artwork, copyright © 2012 Jeffrey J. Burger
WINGS of STEELE logo, copyright © 2012 Jeffrey J. Burger
www.wingsofsteele.com

DEDICATION

I want to offer my thanks to all those who helped, offered their support, sat to listen to my story and ideas - and in some form or fashion helped make this, my first novel, a reality. And thanks to my parents for convincing me as a youngster that anything I put my mind to, I could do... even more so when someone told me it couldn't be done.

A big thank you to the folks at DAW Publishing - the only publisher that not only took the time to actually read the entire manuscript, but also took the time to review and positively critique it, encouraging me to move forward with it as well as a follow-up book.

I am most grateful to Fran Milsop... for her dear friendship and copious amounts of encouragement. The hours and effort she put into reading, and reviewing my work, her advice, technical and professional expertise, went well above and beyond the call of duty. Thank you Fran, for helping me to pursue my dream and move forward to completion - even though it took a little longer than we thought.

Convention seems to dictate that I should select one person to dedicate this novel to, however this is proving difficult, because he did not have a great deal to do with the physical process of writing, editing, or completing this book. But his influence in my life affected not only the production of the book, but the very story itself... my German Shepherd, Fritz. And yes, you're right, he isn't a person... but then again, you couldn't convince him of that. His companionship, friendship, comic personality and devotion were key to keeping me grounded while I worked on this project. Thank you buddy.

TABLE OF CONTENTS

Copyright © 2012 Jeffrey J Burger 5
DEDICATION 6
PROLOGUE 8
CHAPTER ONE 10
CHAPTER TWO 18
CHAPTER THREE 28
CHAPTER FOUR 49
CHAPTER FIVE 52
CHAPTER SIX 56
CHAPTER SEVEN 65
CHAPTER EIGHT 68
CHAPTER NINE 94
CHAPTER TEN 120
CHAPTER ELEVEN 127
CHAPTER TWELVE 132
CHAPTER THIRTEEN 140
CHAPTER FOURTEEN 155
CHAPTER FIFTEEN 167
CHAPTER SIXTEEN 182
CHAPTER SEVENTEEN 203
CHAPTER EIGHTEEN 214
CHAPTER NINETEEN 237
CHAPTER TWENTY 247
CHAPTER TWENTY ONE 268
CHAPTER TWENTY TWO 284
CHAPTER TWENTY THREE 303
CHAPTER TWENTY FOUR 313
CHAPTER TWENTY FIVE 321
CHAPTER TWENTY SIX 347
CHAPTER TWENTY SEVEN 352
CHAPTER TWENTY EIGHT 356
CHAPTER TWENTY NINE 370
CHAPTER THIRTY 385
CHAPTER THIRTY ONE 390
CHAPTER THIRTY TWO 403
CHAPTER THIRTY THREE 415
EPILOGUE 427
ABOUT THE AUTHOR 432

PROLOGUE

CHICAGO, ILLINOIS - SUMMER

Eleven year old, Jack Steele, laid back in the lawn chair on the grass in his yard, staring up at the star-flecked night sky. Even the city lights did not diminish the brightly twinkling specks of light visible in the patch of deep, inky-blackness exposed between the neighboring houses and overhanging maple trees. The yard smelled of warm, freshly cut grass and sweet lilac from the neighbor's bushes. There was a soft, even breeze that rustled the leaves of the trees adding a quiet hush to the darkness. Crickets chirped incessantly. His mother would have a fit if she knew he was out there. It was well past midnight and he was in his pajamas... supposed to be fast asleep in bed. Who cared? He was on summer vacation, there was no school to worry about, no homework, no extra credit assignments. But the dreams, he could not forget the dreams. Unsettling... but strangely exciting.

He reached down and felt for the huge Rottweiler sleeping on the grass beside him. Luke. Good old Luke... over a hundred pounds of pure muscle and willing to use it. They were the best of friends, inseparable. As black as the sky above, the dog was invisible to young Steele, blending in with the shifting shadows around him. Luke huffed softly, reassuringly, feeling the small hand of his young friend running through his smooth coat. Jack felt better for it, his strength and courage were contagious.

A police siren wailed mournfully in the distance, heading farther away, fading. Someday he would be a policeman... just like his dad. Maybe that was the siren on his dad's patrol car, he *was* on duty tonight. Jack wasn't worried, his dad was a big guy. The biggest. And a good shot too, performing on the police department's pistol competition team.

He listened intently until the siren was gone, then leaned back and stared up at the night sky again. He sighed, the stars winked at him. Someday he would be out there too... after he was a policeman. He didn't know how he knew that, but he did. And not like Neil Armstrong the astronaut, walking on the moon... But out there. Really out there. Maybe as far as Andromeda... he learned about that one in astronomy this year. It really didn't seem that far, it was like he could almost reach out and touch those stars.

Maybe it was the dreams, those weird dreams... and the Dream People. Well, at least that's what he called them. Cool, smooth, featureless gray-green skin, large ebony eyes... and their silent voices that talked in his head. He was afraid the first time, terribly afraid. But they never hurt him, or Luke. Besides, like his dad said, "A real man isn't afraid of the dark or the boogeyman. That the only thing to fear, is fear itself." *Well, maybe. Maybe not.*

Jack decided he pretty much had it figured out... he was sure, well, reasonably sure, that despite their dreamlike appearance, the Dream People weren't really in his dreams at all... but real. But how could you explain that to your parents? You couldn't. It wasn't going to happen. At least not with *his* parents. They'd either patronize him and admire his vivid imagination, or put him in a rubber room somewhere. He heard Tommy Brooker's mom went to a shrink and ended up in a crazy ward for a while. Tommy said she didn't like it. Jack figured he wouldn't like it either. Eleven was too young for a straight-jacket, whatever that was.

The stars blinked and sparkled, Jack's eyelids grew heavy. The crickets grew quiet, the breeze shifted and Luke huffed, his nose pointing into the wind. Jack suddenly grew more aware, paying closer attention. Luke moved his bulk to a sitting position and whined inquisitively, pensively. Jack squinted and could see the vague silhouette of the dog's massive head and shoulders just a foot away in the inky darkness. The Rottweiler made strange little whining noises, more insistent than before. Jack felt it now too...

Along with the tart, electric smell in the air, enough to make your mouth water, was the buzzing of his skin, like pins and needles all over his body. His eyes grew heavy again, heavier than before. Luke laid back down again, his head on Jack's thigh, quiet now, breathing easy.

The eleven-year-old knew the feeling. They were coming... somehow he had known they would come tonight. The Dream People. They would speak silently to him in his head and take him out there, but just for a little while... he was always home before it got light.

WINGS of STEELE - DESTINATION UNKNOWN
CHAPTER ONE

FT. MYERS, FLORIDA: *CAN'T TOUCH THIS*

Beside the king-sized four-poster bed, soft jazz floated quietly from the small clock radio on the nightstand. The heavy, hand-carved antique oak bed was scalloped with ornate scrolls and leaves. On the wall above the stately headboard, hung a large black, medieval shield, emblazoned with a golden silhouette of a winged horse against a red rising sun. Angled to the right of the shield hung a gleaming two-handed English broadsword. It was obviously a man's room, filled with dark wood and strong furniture but everything was in its place and the room was meticulously clean.

The wafting Sunday morning jazz began to reach the lone sleeping occupant of the great bed. Jack Steele was becoming vaguely aware of the music invading his sleep and struggled to maintain that last final bit of dream as it dissolved and faded away into waking awareness. He could also feel the warm Florida coastal breeze drifting lazily through his open window and smell the fresh tang of salt in the air. For a moment, he hoped the music was coming from outside and not the clock.

Jack propped himself up on his left elbow to look at the clock perched on his dresser next to the black lacquered rack holding a set of Japanese Katana and Wakizashi swords.

The clock confirmed what he dreaded, it was indeed morning. 7 A.M. Late for some, too early for others; like Jack Steele. *Crap.* Jack had never, *ever*, been a morning person, not by the wildest stretch of the imagination. "How bakers do it I'll never know..." He let himself flop back to the mattress, perturbed at the early arrival of morning. Gazing absentmindedly at the dancing patterns of sunlight playing on the ceiling that filtered through the vertical blinds, he gradually cleared the morning cobwebs from his mind and began reviewing the day's checklist of things to do.

Before Jack could finish his review, he caught movement in the shadows out of the corner of his vision and suddenly was acutely aware of everything around him. The low, dark figure which had entered the room so silently, sprang without warning over the foot of the bed, the two combatants wrestling on the bed, entangling themselves in the linens and blankets, fighting for whatever advantage they could manage. Abruptly, the tussle stopped. Jack poked the obscured form he had successfully wrapped in the sheets like a mummy and the form squirmed violently. With implied ferocity, it emitted a muffled snarl, then sneezed. "Give up?" Jack inquired. He carefully peeled back the sheets. Out popped a black, shiny nose, drawing deep huffing breaths, patiently awaiting another onslaught.

Since none came, the long-legged German Shepherd tossed his head, throwing off the sheets revealing a handsome, expressive face, with deep brown twinkling eyes. His name was Fritz. Not a particularly imaginative name, but it was given to him as a pup and Jack felt it somehow seemed to fit the dog's curious intelligence and personality. Fritz gazed up into the eyes of his human partner. Giving a defiant *harumph,* the dog half crawled, half wiggled, out of his cocoon of sheets to reveal a strong, lean physique. His coat was long like a Collie but mostly chestnut in color with a small black saddle, an ivory bib and a narrow, tapered black mask across his shining brown eyes. Fritz shook himself to settle his coat and bounded off the now thoroughly messed bed. He barked a taunt as he trotted through the house, his nails clicking on the polished maple floors.

Jack swung his feet over the side of the bed and pulled on a pair of beach shorts. He stared at the bed for a moment, the maid was going to hate this... she always did. Strolling through the house barefoot and shirtless, he stopped to pick up a dog leash off the kitchen counter which he knew he wouldn't need. Pausing at the refrigerator he snatched out a carton of orange juice and took a swallow, drinking straight from the container. It was a bad habit, but Fritz never complained.

The duo stepped through the sliding glass doors and onto the warm planks of the sundeck that lead to the fine golden sand of the beach facing the Gulf of Mexico. As Fritz dashed across the fifty yards of sand to meet the incoming surf, Jack took pause to survey the expanse of scenery spread before him. The sky was already a turquoise blue without a trace of cloud and the breeze shushed through the palm trees and played with someone's wind chimes up the beach. Planting his feet firmly, he stretched his six-foot-two inch frame, arms extended towards the hot Florida sun and reveled in the glorious weather.

While he was not overly muscular, his body was extremely well-defined. Choosing speed and flexibility over sheer mass, a lifetime of sports and selective martial arts left his physique lean and hard. While Jack proceeded through the stretching routines he did almost every morning, Fritz ran belly deep through the breaking waves. The Shepherd stopped momentarily to eye a woman jogging past. Jack noticed her too and admired her trim bouncing form as she trotted by, waving a friendly hello.

Yep, gotta love Florida, thought Jack, smirking crookedly. He waved back then leaned on the railing with his elbows to watch the dog slosh in the gentle blue-green waves breaking on the rippled blonde sand. A squadron of four pelicans flying single-file along the shore glided easily past, an occasional stroke of their wings to maintain formation as they played with the ocean breeze.

Shuttling new and used airplanes for delivery had become quite profitable. And for the first time since his painful divorce four years back, Jack was doing well. Buying and renovating the beach house was his reward to himself after the long, hard road of financial and emotional rebuilding. The house wasn't big, like so many of the others along that area of the shore, but it was very comfortable. Another buyer probably would have knocked it down and built some multilevel monstrosity, but Jack had genuinely liked it for what it was. The three bedroom, two bathroom house, was solidly built, a throwback to the late fifties and early sixties where quality and durability came before the excesses of bigger is better... and then later when it became ostentatiously huge is better than simply bigger.

Life's slippery slide downward began a year before his divorce, back when he was still a cop in Chicago. While recovering from the emotional scars of losing a close friend on the police department during a shootout with gang members, Jack took up flying. He found it profoundly exhilarating and relaxing at the same time. Unfortunately, his wife did not. She didn't like him being a cop either. She said one made him hard the other made him distant. At a time when he was forced to completely re-evaluate his life, she left him and took with her almost everything he owned... everything except the '66 Shelby Cobra he'd built. He was convinced the only reason she didn't pursue the car was the fact that she hated the thing. She liked luxury cars, and the Cobra was not ladylike enough for her. She considered it brutish with all its power and noise, while Jack considered the sound of the naturally aspirated 427 big block music to his ears. On reflection, there were a lot of things they didn't have in common, it was a wonder the marriage lasted as long as it did. Shortly thereafter, he realized the only things that made him truly happy, were the Cobra, flying and Fritz.

So after pulling a few strings and calling in a few favors owed him, he got a job flying and left the department. He and Fritz spent the next three years living like nomads, flying anywhere a job would take them. The freedom was spectacular and welcomed, but he finally realized the need for roots once again. Jack was good with his hands and thoroughly enjoyed refurbishing the beach house. Now self-employed, his time was his own, allowing him to tinker on the house whenever he had the inclination. But the house was pretty much finished now, and it was time to go back to work, in earnest.

Jack glanced at his watch then checked on the antics of his waterlogged canine, "Hey fuzzball!" he waved, "let's go, we got a plane to deliver!" Tongue lolling, kicking up sand as he ran, the dog raced from the surf trailing saltwater from his sodden coat. Steele figured the crazy dog loved to fly almost as much as he did.

They paused on the deck and Jack thoroughly rinsed the dog with the fresh water shower attached to the house, Fritz shaking himself violently, dispersing droplets over the deck like a lawn sprinkler. Steele was always amazed how much moisture he could shake from his coat. Smiling to himself he finished the carton of orange juice as they entered the beach house. Toweling Fritz off in the kitchen, Jack began to think ahead, talking to the dog like most people do with their animals, "This is gonna be a sweet run, dog..." Fritz cocked his head quizzically. Sometimes he paid such close attention, Jack could swear the animal actually understood every word. In the middle of drying him, the phone rang and Jack snatched the receiver out of the charger. "Steele, talk to me..."

"What time do we take off?" asked his copilot, Brian Carter.

"We should meet at the strip at about nine, I guess. I would think we'd be wheels-up by about a quarter to ten, doncha' think?"

"Yeah, sounds about right. How long did you say we were staying out there?"

"Don't quote me on it, but we should be back in about four weeks," replied Jack.

"OK cool. I'll pack a few extra things then. See you at the plane."

"Roger." Jack dropped the phone into the charger, gave the waiting canine one last rub with the towel, then headed back into his bedroom to continue to pack the bag he'd started the night before. Though he had never been and could never be confused with a Boy Scout, he preferred to be well prepared... part of being an Alpha personality. In his clothing bag, he

13

included his favorite protection; a satin stainless Kimber 1911 .45 ACP semi-automatic pistol. Since the magazines only held eight rounds, he tossed five extra mags into the bag, along with a couple boxes of fresh 230 grain +P ammunition, a shoulder holster and a right-hand, leather thigh holster that had a quick thumb release. He zipped the bag shut and on his way to the kitchen dropped the bags in the entry hall by the front door. Though it was legal in the state of Florida to carry a concealed weapon, it was not terribly legal to carry it when leaving the country... in fact, it was highly illegal. But Jack tended to be a somewhat of a survivor. His opinion was that he'd rather be standing in front of a judge explaining why someone else was dead than standing in front of Saint Peter explaining why he was dead. That's not to say that he was a violent person, he wasn't... unless he had to be. In which case you didn't want to be playing on the wrong team.

He picked up a pen and notepad to leave a quick message on the fridge for his maid Nina, apologizing once again, for the destruction of the bedroom. "Sometimes I think she just likes to complain," he told the Shepherd. Fritz barked a short confirmation while Jack hung the note with pizza restaurant magnets.

The phone rang again, and he snatched the cordless out of the charger on the kitchen counter, "What'd you forget buddy?"

"Hi, it's mom..."

"Oh. Hi, mom! What's up?"

"Your dad and I are planning to come down around the end of next week... wanted to check and see if you had room."

"Really? Crap, I'm leaving to deliver that plane I was telling you about..." Jack had hoped to spend some time with them this summer, maybe get them to look at a few homes in the area and move out of the cold.

"Oh..." her voice dropped in disappointment. "How long will you be gone?" she asked, sounding brighter.

"About four weeks I think. They need someone to fly the plane during filming, so we need to stay till they're done with the plane. I can try calling before we head back... but I'm really not sure what the service will be like."

"Oh, OK. Well then, we'll postpone for a few weeks..."

"Don't do that," interrupted Jack, "come down when you're ready. If you get here before I'm back, just call Nina and she'll come and give you a key... she's only about ten minutes away."

"Are you in a hurry Jack?"

Jack glanced at his watch. "Well yeah, kinda... we've got a schedule to keep." Mothers have an innate capability to make a grown man feel like an eleven-year-old kid again. "Uh... can I bring you and dad back some kind of souvenir or something?"

"How about a new *daughter-in-law?*" she mused.

Open palm, insert face. "Mom!" he groaned, "Can we please not go there?"

"Alright, just kidding. You be careful."

"Always..."

"Promise?" she prodded.

"Promise." Like the dutiful son he was, he told her he loved her and they said their goodbyes. He looked forward to seeing his parents when he got back, he didn't get to spend as much time with them as he'd like to.

"Let's go buddy!" Fritz followed obediently and eagerly to the front door. Jack paused at the mirror in the foyer, checking his image. His dark hair was neatly cut, combed back with a loose curl hanging on his forehead, his mustache full but trimmed. Steele's sharp features came from his father; tanned skin courtesy of the Florida sun, and blemish-free skin from his mother. Long dimples on each side of his mouth deepened when he smiled, but his most striking feature were his eyes, dark and piercing. He decided he looked pretty decent for thirty-something. "You my friend," he told his reflection, *"loook marvelous."* Fritz danced impatiently in circles in the foyer his nails clicking on the foyer's floor tile. *"Oooh* my friend, *you* look marvelous too!"

The gregarious Shepherd was as excited for the car ride as Jack was about this trip. Before Steele made it to the back of the Cobra sitting in the driveway, the dog was through the convertible's open passenger window and sitting in the front seat. With a wild roll of his eyes, Jack tossed the bags into the trunk and closed the lid.

At the driver's door he was confronted by an unlikely motorist. "Get outta my seat you clown, unless you think you can drive..." Fritz happily relinquished the seat, jumping back to the passenger side. Jack opened the door and entered the car the normal way, releasing the clips for the convertible top and folding it back one-handed. Strapping the dog into his harness and pulling on his own 5-point harness, Jack started the Cobra which shuddered to life with an aggressive rumble. It loped at idle, the side-pipes burbling, the engine producing a distinct vibration in the wheel and stick shift. Backing out onto the street he didn't bother with the stereo. Shifting into gear, the Cobra rolled down the short side street to Estero Boulevard, the main road running down the beach.

Jack made a left on Estero and headed toward the bridge. It wasn't exactly clogged with cars, but beach traffic always seemed to move slower than anywhere else - maybe it had something to do with the beach lifestyle frame of mind. It always seemed by the time you had crossed the bridge to the mainland, things started moving faster. He couldn't really hot-dog on Estero, the traffic was too close with too many sightseers, he'd have to wait till he hit Summerlin Road. Steele had learned to just be patient and enjoy the view on the beach. *Thank God* for bikinis.

The dark sedan a few cars back never caught Steele's eye, it rolled on anonymously with the flow. As the traffic crossed the bridge to the mainland, boats scooted past on the water below, their owners enjoying the glassy emerald water of the intracoastal waterway. As always, when the bridge fell away in the rear-view mirror, traffic picked up the pace. There still wasn't a lot of room, he'd just have to wait.

Jack could see the intersection ahead and the steady flow of traffic. Finally, a place to hustle. Glancing at his watch, he turned right to go South on Summerlin and accelerated hard to jump into the traffic flow. To maintain his balance, Fritz leaned into the turn, his harness holding him securely in the seat. The pipes snarled viciously and the meaty rear tires broke loose, the rear end of the Cobra squirreling sideways. Jack felt the shudder in the seat with the slack in the wheel almost before it happened and instinctively steered the wheel into the break, feathering the accelerator to give the tires a chance to bite. In a split second, the tires hooked up and the car launched, snapping straight. A blink later, shifting through the gears and accelerating hard again, the pipes singing their big-block combustion engine harmony, he was looking for openings and a place to let the Cobra run. Flipping on the radar detector and laser jammer, a nice hole opened up in the traffic and he shot through, running free. Fritz sat quietly, watching the world go by in a blur.

■ ■ ■

"C'mon, *c'mon!* Step on it! *Don't lose him...*"

The driver checked his blind spot as he hammered the accelerator on the Crown Vic and swerved into the next lane. "He couldn't have seen us... could he?"

"I don't know, but he's sure driving like he did."

"I wonder what triggered him..." The driver checked his mirror and changed back, weaving his way through the slower cars. "Jesus Christ, that thing is fast..."

"Next time *I drive,* grandpa..."

"Yeah, like I'm putting my life in *your* hands... that'll be the day." He hammered the pedal and the police interceptor engine launched the heavy sedan ahead. *"Holy crap,* we're coming up on ninety and he's pulling away like we're standing still..."

The other agent was pulling out a map, "he should, that thing's got like six-hundred horsepower..."

"Holy shit - *really...?"* The driver let off on the accelerator, "Dammit I can't even see him anymore... he must've been doing a hundred-twenty at least. I'm not sure how we're going to explain how we lost a bright blue car with white rally stripes on it..."

"The guy is driving a car that's bullet-fast, we're driving a sled. No real mystery there." The passenger looked up, "You can't tell me you've never seen a guy drive fast before."

"Yeah, but that was more than just fast, I've never seen anyone drive like *that* before - makes me wonder if he's a pro."

"I suppose it's not impossible, a street racer maybe. You've read the file, what do we know about him?"

The driver shook his head, "Apparently not enough. I'm still not sure how to report this..."

"We might not have to..."

The driver glanced over at the other man, "How so?"

"I'm pretty sure he's headed to the municipal airport," he said, pointing at the map, "Just stay on this, I'll tell you when to exit..."

CHAPTER TWO

FLORIDA, WHEYLAND MUNICIPAL AIRPORT:
WILD BLUE YONDER

The powerful Cobra made the drive easy and exhilarating, especially since he got to break a few laws. Steele pulled into the gravel service road at only 9:05am, minus his sedan shadow and followed the service drive around the back of the airport toward the private hangars. Slowing his speed to reduce the dust off the road, he listened to the steady crunch of gravel beneath the car's tires. A twin-engine Cessna taxied past the fence to his right on its way to the main runway. He thought to stop and watch the takeoff, but continued rolling. As the roadster rumbled toward the far side of the airport near the private hangars, Jack began to look for Brian's pickup truck. He smiled to himself, the truck was nowhere to be seen, he had beaten him there. Jack turned through the gate and pulled up onto the tarmac.

Driving past the first two hangars, he slowed the Cobra at the third, a well-kept aluminum building, larger than the others in the row. The doors had been rolled open all the way, the segments looking like an accordion folded against the wall. Jack let the roadster roll to a stop and peered into the hangar. Inside sat a beautifully restored B-25D Mitchell bomber from World War II. She looked stunning sitting in the shade of the hangar, looking as mission-ready as the day she rolled off the assembly line in 1944.

Brian strolled out from under the left wing grinning from ear to ear. "Where ya been Skipper?" Five-foot-ten and solidly built, Brian was a man with a ready smile and healthy sense of humor. His wavy, sandy brown hair, although a bit longer than Jack's, was neat and trimmed.

Miffed, Jack ignored the question. "I didn't see your truck, where'd you park?"

Brian was still grinning but not wishing to press the issue... "All the way in the back," he replied, pointing to the back of the hangar. "With the security system, they'll be safe inside."

Jack put the roadster in gear and rolled past his amused copilot without saying a word. Brian knew Steele's competitive spirit - he hated to lose at anything. As the Cobra rumbled slowly under the wing of the B-25, the echo of the car's low burble danced around the inside of the expansive hangar. Jack scanned the left side of the fuselage, his eyes pausing on the artwork of the reclining blonde pin-up girl who had been expertly repainted, her colors bright and crisp. As he passed under the tail and pulled up next to Brian's pickup truck at the rear of the building, Jack unlatched the dog's harness one-handed. Fritz disappeared out over the passenger door and hit the ground at a run before Jack had the Cobra at a complete stop. The pilot stepped out of the car just in time to see Fritz crash into Brian's open arms.

"Hey you big, overgrown hamster, ready to go flying?" Barking an affirmation, the Shepherd bounded around the inside of the hangar his voice ringing off the metal walls.

Jack marveled at how perfectly the old plane had been restored. As he lovingly tucked-in his prized roadster with its cover for its four-week nap, he thought about the first time he saw the plane... if you could call it that. Jack had met Stephen Miles, the owner, a year ago through the shuttle service when he delivered a replacement plane to Stephen's commercial seaplane business on short notice. Stephen took an immediate liking to the charismatic young pilot and was eager to share his most impressive project to date... the *Sweet Susie*. At that time, the B-25D had only been in the hangar about three months. The engines had been removed, the fuselage looked like hell, and the control surfaces were simply worthless. Jack couldn't imagine her surviving a stiff wind much less ever becoming airborne.

The B-25 "D" model was one of the later versions of the Mitchell Bomber series. A formidable aircraft, she incorporated some improvements with the combat proven standards. While retaining the twin 50 cal. turret on top of the fuselage, four 50 cal. guns were mounted facing forward. These four guns were fix-mounted forward below the cockpit on the fuselage, two on either side, in single mount pods. Two 50 cal. guns in the tail, one in the nose for the bombardier, and one on each side of her waist capped off the B-25D's armament. *All the good it'll do her,* Steele thought, *the only battle this plane is likely to fight is with the rust creeping across her airframe.* Jack figured Stephen probably wasn't rowing with both oars in the water but decided to humor him anyway. He thought, what the heck, when you work with unlimited funds, you can accomplish almost anything. And they did. Stephen's enthusiasm was severely contagious, and the next twelve months transformed the old wreck into a masterpiece.

Jack found out the reason for Stephen's desire; his father who had passed away prior to Susie's purchase was the plane's pilot during World War II. Stephen had paid Jack well for all the time devoted to the project and even gave him shuttles to do during times when they waited for parts. The young pilot became very fond of the B-25, as if it were his own and was extremely pleased when the Sweet Susie rolled out of the hangar for her first flight in over sixty years. All her systems had been completely finished, but the paint work had not yet begun. The B-25 was a patchwork of colors; red primer, zinc green and new, shiny silver wing and fuselage panels, not to mention remnants of her original camouflage scheme. Both Stephen and Jack flew her on the maiden rebirth run to test the systems and try out her new power plants. The hardest thing was to get used to the layout of avionics that had been added to supplement the original and updated gauges. As oddly as she looked on the outside, the Sweet Susie flew like a dream, lighter and faster than she had been when originally built. The engines were completely rebuilt and tweaked to wring out every last horse the power plants could provide thanks to Stephen's master mechanics and engineers. If Jack hadn't seen the remarkable transformation step by step, he wouldn't have believed it was the same plane he saw the first time he had walked into the hangar. The finishing touch was the paint, and that had been completed about a week ago.

Jack, bags in hand, strode towards the waiting copilot. "Damn, this place looks so empty."

"I was thinking the same thing," replied Brian, thinking back. "It looked so much smaller when all that equipment was in here."

Only a few months prior, scaffolding surrounded the plane, the engineer's office was filled with blueprints and plans, the machine shop, welding equipment... and of course, all the people filled every corner of the hangar. Crews worked independently on their own assignments, but together as a collective with the common goal to totally restore the historic B-25 to nearly factory-new condition.

"Is Susie ready to go?" Jack's voice snapped Brian back to present reality.

"Yeah, for the most part. She's fueled but I'm waiting for our weather report, and George is going to check all her fluid levels."

"OK, great, let's get George to move her out onto the tarmac skirt and we'll warm up the engines." Brian trotted off to find George.

"Where's the cooler?!" Jack shouted, as the copilot departed.

"I put it in the plane already!" Brian shouted back, as he disappeared into the hangar.

Can't afford to forget sodas and sandwiches, thought Jack. While he waited, he tossed his bags up into the belly hatch, then began a preflight inspection of the aircraft. Just as he finished, Brian returned with George. The mechanic climbed into the seat of the tow tractor and started its engine, Jack calling Fritz to his side. Brian handed his skipper a copy of the weather report and the two airmen studied their paperwork while George towed the Sweet Susie into the warm Florida sun. The B-25 and her crew were going all the way to Brazil; getting a good handle on the weather was an important part of a safe flight. Sweet Susie and several other existing B-25s, all from the U.S. were headed to Rio De Janeiro for the filming of a new movie. The planes would rendezvous in Rio then move further South near Sao Paolo to meet the film crew and begin filming.

Jack motioned his copilot to the chart table. "I think we ought to skirt this weather here," said Jack, pointing to the tip of the Florida Keys. "We'll head east, pass Miami, and halfway to the Bahamas we'll swing back south. We'll stop in Puerto Rico to fuel up the tanks and take off in the morning."

Brian pulled on his lower lip, deep in thought. "Could we stay..."

"An extra day? " interrupted Jack, finishing Brian's sentence. "No." He watched the copilot frown. "Besides," added Jack, "where we're going, the scenery, both geological and female is stunning..."

The copilot's expression brightened quite noticeably, "No kidding..."

"Scout's Honor," said Jack, crossing his heart and giving the Boy Scout salute. Jack knew, because he'd been there the year before to deliver a plane and was simply inundated with women. He wasn't sure if it was him that attracted the women, or the simple fact that he was an American. Being the kind of man who found it difficult to turn down a beautiful woman, he didn't think about it much.

"I gotta call bullshit on that one..." challenged Brian, "you were never a Boy Scout." Jack gave him a dirty look. "OK, OK, I believe you, so where do we go from Puerto Rico?"

"Maracaibo or Caracas in Venezuela, where we'll stop for fuel again. We'll have to see how the fuel holds up. We have an estimate on her fuel consumption, but it's not carved in stone."

"Are all these places safe?" asked Brian with raised eyebrows.

"You got me, as far as I'm concerned, we sleep with the plane. Oh, and I sleep armed... just in case." Steele's face had become momentarily serious,

21

and Brian wondered whether he should be concerned or not. The copilot hesitated, then lost his train of thought as he watched George unhook the tow tractor from the nose gear of the B-25. He disconnected the mechanism free with almost motherly care. Jack and Brian exchanged glances as they quietly watched the mechanic. He gave the warbird a loving pat on the fuselage, wiped an unseen smudge off of the starboard engine nacelle and strode toward the tractor without looking back. Without words, the two airmen turned back to the chart table to finish their flight plans. As they resumed reviewing their notes, the reclining Shepherd jumped to his feet and woofed softly, but loud enough to get the attention of the two fliers engrossed with their paperwork. A white pickup truck had pulled through the gate and was headed straight toward the Sweet Susie. Jack could see Stephen's company logo emblazoned on the door of the truck as it slowed to a stop in front of the right wing of the plane. A burly young man stepped out of the truck on the driver's side, while Stephen exited the passenger door.

"I couldn't let you leave without saying good luck and bringing you a going-away present," shouted Stephen.

"So, what did you bring us?" the two pilots queried, almost in unison, grinning widely as they strode out to the tail of the truck.

"Come see," chided the owner. At the back of the truck sat two long, skinny wooden crates and fourteen small metal military ammunition cans. Fritz jumped into the truck and gave all the containers a close examination. The dog stared blankly at his human partner.

"Well it's not drugs," said Steele candidly with a smirk.

"You know me better than that," Stephen injected with a hurt look. He opened a wooden crate to reveal twelve neatly packed M1 carbine rifles. "They're for the movie, so is this stuff," he waved at the metal boxes. Brian opened two of the metal containers, one containing ammunition for the carbines, the other, for the .50 cal guns of the Sweet Susie.

"Hey, this is *live* ammo..." Brian exclaimed, looking concerned. "What are we doing carrying real ammunition *and* real guns?"

"Relax, relax..." waved Stephen attempting to quiet the copilot. "All this stuff is for the movie company. That..." he said, pointing at the ammo boxes, "we could only get one way. It will have to be converted by the ordnance technicians on the movie site before filming begins." Stephen handed Jack a bulging sealed envelope. "All the proper documentation for this stuff is in here. If you have any customs issues, hand them this." Jack took it and left it sealed.

"OK, so let's load it up already, we're burning daylight." Jack slapped the apprehensive copilot on the shoulder to punctuate. "Quit worryin' will ya?" The pilot looked at his watch. "Let's go, *let's go*, it's after ten already!"

"Give him a hand, Kevin," prompted Stephen. The burly driver of the truck, who had stood by silent and unmoving, hefted a crate of carbines to his shoulder, in one clean motion. Brian grabbed two of the metal ammo containers. The two men carried their burdens to the open bomb-bay doors of the plane. Jack knew that carrying that type of cargo was illegal in most circumstances but dismissed the concerns, trusting Stephen's preparations. Besides, with as much as he had invested in that plane, Jack couldn't see him taking such a foolish risk as to do something that would jeopardize it. But he promised himself he would open the envelope and check all the paperwork while they were in the air before they left U.S. airspace. Jack and Stephen walked back to the shade of the hangar and the flight plans on the chart table. Fritz chose the shade under the wing of the B-25 so he could more closely watch the loading of the plane.

"These look just fine. Your fuel will be arranged and waiting, I'll see to it personally." Stephen handed the pilot another envelope, "There's ten thousand dollars here... just in case. Use it if you have any... needs," he said with a shrug.

"Cash? Thanks, I'll be sure to keep receipts..."

"Don't worry about that," said Stephen with a dismissive wave, "just take good care of Suzie and I'll see you in Rio." The two men shook hands.

"Well, I guess we'd better get going," said Steele, as he gathered up his flight charts and logs. "C'mon! We're outta here!" he announced as he strode toward the plane. "Let's get this show on the road and this bird in the air!"

"You got it, Skipper," called Brian as he jumped off the tailgate of the pickup. The reclining Shepherd rose to his feet and spun in a circle, excited about their departure.

The copilot disappeared up into the belly hatch, and Stephen's young driver climbed into the truck to move it off the taxiway skirt. Before getting into the passenger side of the truck, Suzie's proud owner stood at attention next to the open door and gave Jack an A1 military salute. "Clear skies, Skipper, see you in Rio."

The German Shepherd by his side, Steele turned, then saluted sharply. He watched as Stephen climbed into the truck and it pulled slowly away. "Yep... definitely a rip in that man's marble bag..." mumbled Jack. Spinning around he moved to the belly hatch followed closely by the dog and passed the charts with flight logs to the hand extended through the opening. "You're next," he told the waiting dog. Fritz stepped forward and Jack lifted him, boosting him up through the hatch by his rump. The pilot took one quick look around and lifted himself through the hatch, the inside of the aircraft smelling like fresh paint, oil and metal. It smelled like history. Locking the hatch he glanced at his watch producing a wince. "Damn, ten forty-five, I hate being behind schedule," he complained, dropping himself into the command seat.

"Quit worryin' will ya?" retorted the grinning figure sitting in the copilot's seat. The two men exchanged glances and began laughing. They continued laughing during the pre-flight check, neither really sure why. But it was a new adventure and it felt good, almost electric.

Jack watched the control surfaces respond as he tested the controls. "Bomb-bay doors closed and locked..." he glanced back. "Check. OK, ready?"

"Yep," Brian nodded, checking his instruments and switching on the magnetos.

The engines primed and all systems checked and ready, Jack pushed the starter switch for the starboard engine. The starter whined, turning the large, three blade prop over slowly at first, then faster. A cylinder fired off with a pop, and the engine roared to life with a small puff of smoke from the exhaust pipes. He cranked the port engine, watching the prop spin. It too roared to life in similar fashion. He listened for a moment, then adjusted the fuel mixture knob for each engine. "That's better..." He knew he'd be adjusting them again after the engines reached their proper temperatures.

"While they're warming up, call for clearance, I want to check our cargo." Jack rose from his seat and made his way through the plane, leaving the capable copilot to monitor the gauges and obtain clearance from the airfield's control tower. The bomb-bay box that normally contained the bomb racks would have restricted movement to the rear of a wartime plane, but had been removed during the renovation. A walkway was installed over the working bomb-bay doors from the front to the back. In the back, a cargo net held the crates of carbines securely in place. The ammo boxes fit neatly in places provided just for that need, all around the B-25's interior.

"Jack, we're cleared!" called Brian from the cockpit.

"Just a sec!" replied Jack. He climbed into the seat of the upper gun turret and working the foot pedals, rotated the turret to face the rear of the plane. Electric motors whirred as it spun smoothly around. Satisfied, he switched off the power, climbed down and returned to the cockpit. Dropping into his seat, he quickly surveyed the gauges and belted himself in. He released the brakes and increased power, just enough to begin a taxi roll. Fritz, wearing a tethered harness for his safety, laid on the cockpit floor knowing what would come next. Jack fitted his headset as the plane rolled slowly along the taxiway, Brian holding the controls. When they neared the end of the taxiway, Steele took the controls, adjusted the flaps partway down and edged the throttles forward. A small crowd had gathered at Sweet Susie's hangar, and several cars had pulled off the street and onto the grass that bordered the outer fence of the airfield. One was a dark sedan... the same dark, unassuming sedan that had attempted to follow Jack through traffic. It went unnoticed, maintaining its anonymity.

Jack decided to give them something to see. Edging the throttles up, he swung the left hand U-turn, from the parallel taxiway, onto the runway without slowing. The shining B-25 tracking smartly around the corner. Steele smoothly pushed the throttles forward as the plane straightened on the runway, creating a sling shot effect from the momentum of the turn. The crowd in front of the Sweet Susie's hangar cheered as the B-25 roared by on the runway at nearly full throttle, the new turbochargers kicking up the boost. Neither of the two men in the cockpit could hear the cheers, but they could see the waves, bidding them well. The B-25 raced down the runway, building speed. When she began to feel light Jack eased back on the control yoke and the plane separated itself from the concrete. "Gear up..."

"Gear up..." Brian pulled the levers for the landing gear as he said it. At an altitude of twenty-five feet, the hydraulic motors hummed steadily, and the gear clunked solidly as they locked into the up position. The gear doors closed, the indicator lights winking out one by one. "Up and locked," he announced.

Jack let her climb gently over the runway. "Retract flaps."

Brian slid the lever for the flaps. As the pumps whined, Jack glanced out over the wing to see the flaps slide neatly back into place. A final bump indicated they were all the way in. "Flaps in," said Brian. He glanced up at the approaching airport fence beyond the end of the runway. "Now might be good, Skipper..."

Jack had a wry smile as he eased the control yoke back toward his stomach. The Sweet Susie leapt upwards unhindered by wartime weight, her powerful new engines chewing up the sky. She climbed steadily at a rakish angle, and the stall warning light flickered momentarily but Jack eased his pull on the yoke before it was of any concern. Brian let out a long, slow sigh and inhaled deeply. He hadn't realized he was holding his breath. It was then that Elvis spoke, "Thank yew, thank yew very muuch. Yew bin a wonnerful awdience. Elvis has left the building..." The pilot curled his lip and sneered.

"Holy crap that's horrible," laughed Brian.

Jack decreased their angle of ascent, swinging slowly to a South-Eastern bearing which would take them over the middle of the state, over Miami and beyond. About thirty-five miles from the Bahamas, they'd swing south toward Puerto Rico.

"I think I could use a soda," said Jack, beaming.

"Yeah me too," piped Brian as he wiped the perspiration from his forehead.

"You weren't nervous, were you?"

"Oh no, not at all," he lied, "it was just a bit showy for my taste." He rolled his eyes as he made his way out of the cockpit.

Jack chuckled, "Quit worryin..." chimed the two men simultaneously, laughing.

Aahhh... thought Jack, a good dog, a good friend, a soda, and a great plane. What more could a man want? *How about a good woman?* said the little voice at the back of his mind. It had been nagging him lately and he'd been ignoring it. He wasn't quite ready for that yet. *Go away,* he told it.

Brian returned with two cold sodas and plopped into his seat. "Man, is it me or is it hot in here?"

"It *is* pretty warm," agreed Jack, taking the soda handed him. The pilot reached behind him and felt for the knob that controlled the air conditioning. It was decided during the renovation, that cold AC would be a must. He found the control by feel and dialed it up, the air sending its wash of cool air over the two men. The relief was well received as the small crew of the B-25 settled in for the long flight.

At 300 mph, the B-25 cruised faster than her wartime service speed, cutting briskly through the warm Florida air. With most of her armor removed, faster power plants and no bomb-load to carry, she felt more like an overgrown fighter than a retired bomber. However, the Radial Wasp engines were new and needed gentle breaking-in, so Jack throttled back and let her cruise considerably slower than she was able... there was no sense in pushing the new engines, their service life would be greatly extended with care. The lush green patchwork of the Florida landscape passed slowly beneath the plane and its occupants, later giving way to the crystal blue of the Atlantic Ocean. A few puffy white clouds played across the vivid blue sky, creating a movie-perfect scene. Almost. "I'm glad we decided to go around that..." Brian commented, thumbing Jack's attention out over the starboard wing, "It looks pretty nasty." Hovering over Cuba and the southernmost tip of the Florida Keys, the blackness of an angry storm front was noticeable, even at this distance. The towering clouds were swept and foamy looking.

"Looks pretty active too," Jack added. Dark, heavy streaks of rain fell away at an angle from the swirling sky off in the distance. The friendly puffy clouds, gave way to windswept, wispy pale-gray clouds, stretching out across the horizon to the right, spin-offs of the storm attacking Cuba and the Keys. As it descended, the afternoon sun was illuminating the spin-off clouds a vibrant pink, creating a strange, hand-painted, surrealistic look.

The two pilots took turns at the controls to prevent fatigue, switching between actually flying and sitting at the navigator's station, positioned behind the cockpit, which contained communication, navigation and radar equipment. The radar unit had been added, during the B-25's refitting. Brian stepped over the snoring Shepherd on the cockpit floor as he made his way to the copilot's seat from the navigation station. "The radar screen is almost completely blank ahead of us, but those poor bastards in the Keys are really catching hell." Brian was shaking his head in sympathy.

"Hope it doesn't grow," said the pilot, wincing mentally.

Jack clenched the bridge of his nose between thumb and forefinger, rubbing... "I must be hungry, I'm getting a damn headache. Say, how about one of those sandwiches?"

"No problem, I'll be right back, don't go away." The copilot unbuckled and rose from his seat disappearing from the cockpit. The flight progressed quickly despite its uneventful nature, and the two men talked about their favorite subjects. The same thing all pilots talk about... planes, girls, cars, more planes... Jack felt much better after eating. He stretched, getting comfortable again, tapping absentmindedly on the glass of one of the gauges. They found themselves flying a wider arc than they had originally anticipated, to be sure they were clear of the moving storm and its effects.

CHAPTER THREE

SAN JUAN, PUERTO RICO: *STAINLESS STEELE*

"Bri, can you check in with San Juan control while I start our descent?"

"You got it." Brian keyed the mic and called the air controller.

After running his fingers through his dark hair, Steele settled in for the task at hand. He eased the throttles back, watching the RPMs drop on the gauges and nosed the B-25 down for its long descent, the engines dropping to a low rumble. Darkness had come early, the storm had seen to that, the sky a deep blue twilight. But there was just enough afterglow to see the island below. The moon was only about half full and not high enough, but every little bit of light helped. It was dark enough to clearly see lights twinkling all across the island but the airport was not discernible yet. The descent was uneventful, local air traffic was light, and the Sweet Susie's crew received an easy, straight-in approach for their glide path.

"We're cleared for final." Brian spoke matter-of-factly. Landings, especially night landings, left no room for anything but strictly business, especially at an unfamiliar airfield.

Jack went down the checklist as the airfield came into view and grew beneath them.

"Here we go... Flaps, one-quarter."

"Roger, flaps one-quarter." As the copilot moved the levers controlling the flaps, the hydraulic pumps hummed.

Jack glanced out over the left wing to watch the flaps extend, "Landing lights, please."

Brian reached up and toggled the switches for the landing lights, "Landing lights on."

"Good..." Jack paused to run his hand through his hair and check their airspeed,"Gear down..."

"Gear down..." the copilot slid the levers and the lock lights on the indicator panel, winked on, as the landing gear dropped down and locked into place with a thump. "Down and locked, Skipper."

Steele adjusted the flaps, "Flaps one-half... OK, let's take her in." He reduced power further and the Susie dropped smoothly and gently, flaring cleanly.

Brian checked with the control tower. "The runway's all yours."

The runway lights shone brightly, leading the B-25 onto the long black ribbon of tarmac... the warbird touched down softly, the tires tamping the ground with a chirp. Jack cut the throttles back to idle and applied the brakes, slowing to a manageable taxiing speed to swing off the runway at the third exit skirt. A small Jeep with a rather large sign and flashing lights joined them, then pulled ahead to lead the plane. The illuminated sign read, FOLLOW ME. The pilots looked at each other and smirked. Proportionately, the vehicle looked ridiculous. "Geez..." laughed Brian, "check out Captain Obvious here."

Jack shook his head, "Wow. Just wow. I mean seriously... what the fuck... The thing looks like a leftover from World War Two..."

"Holy shit..!" snorted Brian. "I wonder if anybody's ever lost him..." Laughing, they executed an exploding fist bump with the appropriate sound effects, obviously tired from the long flight and anxious to get out of the confines of the aircraft to stretch their legs.

Jack retracted the flaps between jokes, as they rolled along behind the lead vehicle and cut off the landing lights. They passed the main concourse, they passed the commercial hangars, they passed the smaller private hangars... "Where the hell is this guy taking us?!"

Brian shook his head and shrugged. As if in answer, the Jeep angled left, toward a row of dilapidated old hangars. "Christ, they're putting us out in the slums."

"Well..." Jack scratched his head, "I don't really care, I just want to eat, clean up and get some sleep. I'm bushed."

"Yeah me too," agreed the copilot.

Fritz was getting impatient, he sat with his head on Jack's lap, staring up with those big brown eyes. He whined softly, wanting attention. The pilot absentmindedly stroked the dog's long snout to appease him and Fritz closed his eyes, remaining quiet. Light spilled out of the open doors of the very last hangar in the row, shafts of light extending across the concrete. As the Jeep got closer to the lit building, it slowed, the sign lights went dark and it peeled off, speeding away.

A flight-line worker with hand lights guided Jack into his rotation in front of the hangar. Jack reached behind him and switched off the air-conditioning unit, sliding open the pilot's vent window, a rush of wind off the port engine flooded the cockpit. It felt so good, Brian reached over and opened his as well. Completing their rotation, the B-25 faced away from the hangar and the line attendant signaled Jack to shut down. The tired pilot held the brakes. "Shut 'em down Bri."

Brian toggled off the ignition switches, and Jack rotated the selectors for the fuel cut-offs and the magnetos. The engines sputtered then went silent as the props spun down to a whirring stop.

Amidst yawns and groans, the two men unbuckled themselves and secured all the systems. The crew groped their way through the darkened aircraft. Feeling for the belly hatch, Jack found the latch handle and opened it, dropping his flight bag to the ground below. Fritz anxiously pushed his way past the two men and dove through the opening quickly disappearing from view. The two fliers dropped through the hatch one at a time, and Brian reached up to close it. "Too bad this thing doesn't have a lock on it, I'd feel better."

Jack shrugged, "It'll be alright, we're not going more than a hundred feet." Stepping out from underneath the plane, Jack stretched his arms toward the star-filled sky... *"Aaarrruugh,"* he growled, releasing the tension from his body. Closing his eyes briefly, he inhaled deeply, breathing in the warm, moist air. The air was sweet and heavy. He stared up into the early evening sky, awed by its starry splendor. "Hmm..." he mused, "clouds are gone."

"Good God, what a dump," grumbled Brian, breaking the silence.

"Huh?" Jack came out of his trance, "Oh, our accommodations... Yeah well, I've seen worse." He snatched his bag up off the concrete and strolled towards the open hangar.

"Where, Beirut?" The copilot glanced at the gaping holes in the roof as he walked behind the pilot. Jack snapped his fingers and the masked Shepherd quietly appeared out of the darkness, startling the mechanic in the dimly lit hangar.

"Sorry pal, he does that to everyone at first." The mechanic stood silently, unmoving, eyeing the pilot. Jack suddenly realized how much shorter than he, the mechanic was. He squinted to see facial features but the dim light defied his efforts. After what seemed a lengthy silence he decided to try again. "You speaka de Englais?" He hoped for English because his Latin vocabulary consisted of fast food menu items.

"Of course I speak English, you ass. And watch who you call *pal,* Mister Steele." The pilot stood wide eyed and a tad stunned as the mechanic

30

removed his ball cap to reveal *he* was actually a *she*. A quite attractive she at that.

"I, uh..." Jack cleared his throat, "ahem, yes, well that is I, um... you, I mean we..." He suddenly realized, he had absolutely no idea what to say. Not accustomed to being caught off guard, his tired mind finally caught up to shut off his runaway mouth.

Cascades of raven-black hair fell out from under the hat, and Jack offhandedly wondered how all that hair could fit under that little cap. A quick glance to his left told him the speechless, open-mouthed copilot, was as surprised as he was. Fritz harrumphed, he wasn't fooled at all. He knew all along and couldn't see how Jack missed such an obvious charade. The dog strolled past the gaze of the female mechanic and away from the trio. "Where does he think *he's* going?" asked the girl, thumbing towards the dog's diminishing shadow.

Brian shrugged, not wanting to be left out, "Wherever he wants... pretty much."

Jack was fighting back the giggles, somewhat unsuccessfully. Regaining his composure and charisma, he got his mouth and brain in sync. "Look, let's start over again. Hi, I'm Jack Steele, pilot extraordinaire. This is my good friend and trusty copilot, Brian Carter. The hairy guy exploring your hangar," he looked above him at the hole in the roof, "such as it is, is my dog Fritz. We are the crew of that fine aircraft out there…" He extended his hand. The girl took his hand, tentatively at first, then shook it in earnest.

"Maria Arroyo, nice to meet you..." she smiled. "I think." Standing this close, Steele could see her very well, even in the poor light. He stared into her dark eyes, still holding her hand. She did not look away. They remained there as if momentarily frozen.

"Ahem." Brian cleared his throat.

The man and woman recoiled, as if burned, suddenly feeling uncomfortable and not wanting to acknowledge what they both knew had just occurred. "Food," said Brian, patiently coaxing the conversation along.

"Ah yeah, we could use a hot meal, a shower and sleep, lots of sleep," said Jack slowly, not taking his eyes off the young lady as she began removing her work coveralls.

"No problem..." She wriggled out of her work suit and revealed a wonderful figure, obvious even under her street clothes. Jack felt mesmerized as he listened to her speak. He found her voice and Latin accent very pleasing. "The showers are that way through the office..." she pointed the way. "While you get cleaned up, I'll go get us all some dinner."

"Sounds like a plan to me," said Brian as he strode off through the office. What there was of it.

Fritz found the cots for the crew of the Sweet Susie. Bored with his exploration, he carefully inspected and chose one to curl up on. He lay quietly, with one eye open, casually watching Jack and Maria discuss available choices for dinner. The dog, sensitive to human emotions, could smell and feel the desire in the air and sleepily wondered what they were waiting for. Not able to resist any longer, the Shepherd dozed off and began to dream. The two people stood face to face without speaking. They had run out of things to say. The unspoken question was whether to make the transition from professional to personal and the only sound louder than their combined heartbeats was the dog's dream muttering. Maria stepped backwards when the pause became intense and uncomfortable. "Um... I guess I, um, I should um..."

"Go get the food?" said Jack, helping her along.

"Yes... yes, get the food..." she stared at him, backing up slowly, "I'll be right back!" She turned and ran from the old hangar.

Jack inhaled deeply, staring at the empty doorway. He picked up his flight bag and headed for the shower, wondering what would happen next and how he would handle it. *Bingo!* said the little voice in his head.

Shut up, he told it.

■ ■ ■

Brian stretched out on his cot, tucking his hands behind his head, "Man, I'm stuffed. That was great, it really hit the spot."

"I'm glad you liked it," said Maria, somewhat preoccupied, although the copilot never noticed. Her mind was on Jack who had been distant all during dinner. Immediately after eating he quietly rose from the table and went outside. From her vantage point, his tall silhouette stood with his shaggy companion, out near the B-25 staring at the sky.

Maria turned out the hangar lights so the copilot could fall asleep and stood silently in the hangar's darkness, near the expansive front doorway. Almost transfixed, she watched the tall American pilot and wondered about his strange magnetism. No man had ever commanded her thoughts or desires like this before. Not sure whether it was envy or jealousy she felt, Maria decided to re-route some of the attention Fritz was getting. She grabbed a folded blanket off the foot of one of the empty cots and strode out of the hangar, the warm air smelling like sweet, freshly mown grass..

Steele could hear the light footsteps approaching from behind but chose not to turn around. He was watching the Shepherd rolling in the grass along the runway, enjoying his comical behavior. Jack could feel the girl's presence at his side, but he neither moved nor spoke. His heart quickened, but he fought to conceal the emotion rushing about inside. *Aw, go on,* goaded the little voice inside him. He ignored it.

Now it was the dog's turn to watch the humans. He righted himself and lay in the grass staring at them.

With the blanket tucked under one arm, Maria stood beside the tall, silent pilot. Her heart hammered as she gazed up at his handsome profile, standing so still he looked like he was made of granite. A gentle breeze rustled his open shirt and Maria wanted to touch him just to reassure herself that he was real. Unable to wait any longer, she reached out and touched his arm. The young woman was almost startled when he turned to meet her gaze. As he stared deep into her eyes, the blanket slipped from her limp hand, landing on the ground with a soft flop. "Do you..." her voice squeaked, so she drew a deep breath and started again, her heart racing. "Ahem... um, do you think I'm pretty... I mean, do you find me attract..." Jack, smiling warmly, placed his fingertips on her lips.

"How old are you?" Jack asked softly.

"Twenty-five," she replied, "why?"

"Well, I'm almost ten years older than you..."

Still holding his arm, Maria smiled sweetly. "So what?"

Jack was playing absentmindedly with the satiny, black curls of hair falling across her shoulder. His eyes flicked back to hers, as he ran his hand through her luxurious hair. Her eyes closed slowly as she lost herself in his touch. "That's all I needed to know," said Steele in a raspy whisper.

He ran his hand up the nape of her neck and buried his fingers in waves of silky, raven hair. The girl, trembling, exhaled softly, as she passed her hands across Jack's bare chest. Drawing her body against his, he closed his hand around the cascade of dark, silken hair. Pulling gently, but firmly, the pilot tilted her head back to view her upturned face, awash with moonlight. Still grasping her hair, Jack ran his lips along Maria's neck, biting softly. She sighed and her knees buckled when he pressed his lips against hers. Holding

33

her body tightly against his, the duo melted together, and the rest of the world ceased to exist.

■ ■ ■

First light turned the inky blackness of the star-speckled sky to deep shades of blue smeared with scattered gray-white clouds. Gentle songs of the first morning birds woke the sleeping Shepherd. Maria's arm was sleepily draped across the Shepherd's shoulder, and he crawled slowly out from underneath, not wanting to wake her. He stretched, glanced at the sleeping couple and strolled off to check his surroundings in the light of day.

When Maria woke, Fritz was nowhere to be seen. She checked her watch and silently chastised herself for sleeping so late although it was only six-thirty. She pulled herself together reluctantly leaving the still sleeping pilot and headed to the shower in the office of the old hangar. Maria passed the copilot as she raced through the hangar. Like Jack, Brian was still sound asleep. Maria wondered if this habit of sleeping late was a guy thing, because she had always been an early riser. Jack awoke when the sun cleared the trees and passed between the old hangars. It was like looking into a spotlight. He ventured a look at his watch and winced painfully. "Damn, seven in the morning!" Steele lay on his back watching the clouds pass slowly overhead, wondering if he could fall back asleep. The beam of sunlight coupled with the grumbling in his stomach told him that this would not be a likely option. Yawning, Jack stretched, pulled himself together, picked up the blanket and headed to the showers with Fritz following close behind.

"Holy cow, you look like shit!" said the ever cheerful copilot as he lay stretched out on the small cot.

"Thanks, but I feel better than I look," mumbled Jack, as he shuffled past, smiling wryly. Steele didn't often allow himself those pleasures because he was not yet comfortable with the idea of someone getting that close to him. He had let the intensity of the moment overtake him because he knew there was no chance of it progressing. Given their separate geographies, Jack reasoned that it would be a safe encounter.

"You didn't..." said the wide-eyed Brian.

"Well, I hadn't planned it, but yeah, we did. And it was *awesome.*"

34

"Oh man..." interrupted Brian as he sat up on the cot, waving his arms, "I can't believe you. You are unbelievable! We're here what, four hours? And you end up..." he was shaking his head in disbelief, "Jiminy Christmas..."

"Jiminy Christmas...?" sputtered Jack, laughing, "Seriously? What the hell is that...? It's not Jiminy Christmas anyway, you freaking tard, it's Jiminy Cricket!"

"Fuck you, you know what I meant..."

Jack shrugged, "OK, so you'd feel better if she was weapons grade ugly, right?"

"Never mind..." Brian flopped back down on the cot. "I wish I knew how you do it," muttered Brian out loud to himself. Fritz made himself comfortable on the empty cot while he waited for Jack to return from his shower.

■ ■ ■

Steele strolled out into the hangar, refreshed, clean and dressed. Khaki uniform shirt, dark blue Levis and boots. The only adornment on Jack's shirt was the silver pilot's wings, pinned above his left pocket. Jack plopped his flight bag on one of the cots, checked his reflection in the office window and headed to the chart table, which someone had thoughtfully loaded with breakfast items. Brian wandered up to the table looking crisp and awake. "Wow, nice spread! Good thing too, cuz I'm starved!"

"Yeah, me too. Say who brought all this stuff anyway?" Jack lifted a jelly sweet roll off the selection and poured himself a glass of milk.

"Maybe your new girlfriend," said Brian, picking up a pastry and pouring himself a cup of coffee. Fritz appeared next to the table as if by magic and Jack slipped him a sizable sweet roll. Brian's eyes widened. "Y'know that overgrown hamster eats better than most people do..."

Jack shrugged, unconcerned. "So what, he earns it." He turned to the dog with a bowl of milk. "Right buddy?" The Shepherd gave no answer other than to happily consume the whole bowl of milk. "And she's not my girlfriend..." added the pilot, while handing the dog another pastry.

"Hi sleepyhead." Jack looked up to see Maria walking through the open door of the hangar from the plane, tool bag in hand. "She's all set, I checked all her fluids and looked her over real good. The fuel truck just left, Susie's tanks are full..."

35

There was a quiet sarcastic voice behind Jack saying something about fluid levels, dipsticks and someone else getting the once over... Jack raised his eyebrows, "Boy, you've been a busy little beaver."

Maria frowned in thought, "Huh?"

Jack wasn't sure which she had heard. He reached to wipe a smudge off her face, "Oh, um, never mind, forget it." He looked past her to the plane, "Hey, who's that?" Brian stepped forward and Maria spun around to follow Jack's gaze. The coverall clad man exiting the open belly hatch, saw he had an audience and began to run towards the departing fuel truck.

"Hey you! What're you doing?" shouted Steele. "Come back here! You don't fuel a plane from inside it..." he growled. Without a word exchanged, Jack and Brian sprinted off in foot pursuit before Maria could react or speak. With his long legs, Jack quickly pulled ahead of Brian. Fritz, eager to participate, passed between the two running pilots and accelerated ahead like they were standing still. The speeding Shepherd was closing the distance to the man in the coveralls with almost alarming speed.

A Jeep suddenly appeared, careening from across the field and slid to a stop, scattering pebbles off the asphalt. As the escaping figure jumped into the Jeep he drew a pistol from the pocket of his coveralls, but the Shepherd, rocketing across the ground, created an extremely difficult target. Popping the clutch as the driver sped away, the man in the coveralls fired, his shot going harmlessly wide and high. Fritz slowed to a trot and looped back, heading to Jack and Brian standing next to the plane.

Winded, Brian stood bent over trying to catch his breath. "What d'ya... think... he was looking for?"

Jack wiped his forehead on his sleeve, "I don't know, but I'm gonna' find out..." The pilot disappeared up into the belly hatch to search the plane. He didn't have to look far. "He found the carbines and the ammo!" he yelled. "Doesn't seem to be anything missing though." Jack fastened the top back onto the crate and re-secured the ammo boxes.

"Why was he looking in the first place?" asked Brian.

Jack jumped down through the open hatch to the tarmac. "Curiosity? I don't know and I don't care. We're not taking any chances, let's get the hell outta' here."

Brian nodded. "Good idea let's get our stuff.

Jack called the dog over to the hatch and boosted him up into the plane. "Fritz, you stay..." he told the dog, who peered down at him from the dark opening. "Watch the plane."

36

Maria met them at the doorway of the hangar, "I've seen him before..."

"Yeah? Who is he?" interrupted Jack.

The group talked as they hustled to gather their gear, "I think... I'm not sure, but I think he's a member of the Secret Police..." Maria looked genuinely afraid. "They pretty much do whatever they want, they're very corrupt. They even deal openly with the drug cartels who move contraband through here."

Brian rolled his eyes and groaned, "Great, we're in the shit now...!" He stuffed his things haphazardly into his bag. "What do you think they want?"

"It doesn't matter want they want," snapped Jack, gathering their charts and flight log, "they're not going to get it. We're outta' here!"

"Take me with you..." said Maria, grabbing Jack's hand.

"What!? Oh, hell no... Look, I don't have time to discuss this, I can't take you with us, end of conversation."

"There's no reason for me to stay, no family, no job after today, and it won't be safe for me here anymore...

"Not safe, why?"

"They'll think I helped you... they know who I am - they'll kill me..."

"Who... why..." Jack rubbed his forehead, this was becoming more complicated by the second.

"The police. Look, just take me with you... *please*..." Her voice was filled with urgency and the sound of sirens in the far distance hastened the situation.

"The police? Oh for the love of G... OK. OK," said Jack, holding up his hands. *"Whatever,* just get your stuff and let's *go!"*

"No one is leaving!" A man in dirty pants and torn shirt emerged from the office holding an old, large caliber revolver, a remnant from another era. He took the trio completely by surprise, a twisted smile on his face.

"Who the hell are you?" growled Jack through clenched teeth.

"*Paulo,*" hissed Maria, "what are you doing here?!" She turned to Jack, "He is an ex-friend of my brother who thinks he loves me. But he is *estupido,* I *HATE* him!" she snarled, her voice filled with venom. "It's because of *him* that my brother is dead."

"But I *do* love you!" The man stepped closer. "And your brother died because of his foolishness - I had nothing to do with it." He stood taller, more erect, "I am saving you from the fate these American pigs will share..." The man's voice was filled with hate and contempt. His wicked smile had

37

turned to a fierce show of teeth resembling a snarl. Stepping closer, he menaced Jack with the revolver.

Jack grit his teeth, "What *next*? We don't have *time* for this bullshit!"

"It was I who reported you to the police," gloated Paulo. "I told them you had drugs on your plane." The wicked smile returned. "They don't like people who don't pay their transport taxes... They will take everything you have and imprison you for life..." He stepped closer still, gloating, self-involved with his impending victory, looking smug. "Maybe they'll even kill you."

"Jiminy Christmas..." whispered Brian.

"Really?" whispered Jack, shooting him a glance, "we're back to that one...?"

"Sorry..." Shrugged the copilot. "That explains our first visitor," he added, changing the subject. "And I'll bet that's him on his way back with friends..."

"Probably..." replied Jack.

"Shut up, *you!*" The man waved the revolver and took another step forward.

Jack's mind was racing, he glanced over at the cot, his 1911 was in the flight bag. *That'll never work.* He began calculating the distance to the man standing before them... Maria spoke and Jack grabbed her sleeve, keeping her from moving forward or getting in the way. He needed to draw the man closer.

"Paulo, how could you do this to me? They will put me in prison too! They might even kill me!" Maria's voice did not waver, but tears of anger rolled down her cheeks.

"NO!" he objected. "They promised me you would not be involved!" Sirens wailing in the distance, grew louder, closer. Brian fidgeted. Jack needed Paulo closer, so he tried baiting him...

"Fucking brilliant Paulo... and you believed them?" He waved his arm dismissively, "Are you that stupid? Of course you are..." he waved again. "You've got to be the biggest *pendejo* on the planet! Have you looked in the mirror lately? Your mother must have fucked the village idiot to produce a person as shit-stupid and monkey ugly as you...."

"Shut up! Shut up! *Shut up!*" Paulo drew closer, his common sense, if there was any to begin with, was gone. There were bits of foam at the corners of his mouth and his eyes were wild. He pulled courage from the impending arrival of the police. The sirens were close, too close. Paulo waved the revolver inches from Jack's face. "I will kill you myself..." he pulled the hammer back with his thumb.

Brian had never seen anyone move so fast in all his life. Jack's reaction was a complete blur feinting right as his left hand, open, swept the gun high and to the left where his hand closed around the cylinder to prevent the gun's function. To his dismay, Paulo never got the hammer all the way back. He struggled to pull the hammer or the trigger, but Jack had total control. The pilot's right fist shot into Paulo's solar plexus with the speed and intensity of a pile driver. Paulo crumpled to his knees, instantly releasing his grip on the gun, his hands clutching his chest in agony. Close to unconsciousness and gasping for air, Paulo's tortured face registered a look of complete and total disbelief... then the lights went out, induced by a brutal strike in the face with the handle of his own gun.

Jack spun on his heel, "Get to the plane! *NOW*!" Pulling his Kimber from his flight bag he slung the holster over his shoulder, sliding extra loaded mags into his pockets. A quick press-check assured him there was a round in the chamber.

"What are you gonna do?" asked Brian, grabbing his bag.

"Give these clowns something to do, while you warm up the plane."

"We're not leaving without you," cried Maria.

"I've got no time to argue. Now get *going*! Brian, you know what to do, she's gotta be ready to take off fast! Here, take my bag..." Brian caught the nylon bag and took off at a dead run with Maria in tow.

Jack ran to the back of the hangar and looked out the rear door, down the airport's gravel access road. What he saw was not reassuring. Several police jeeps loaded with officers were racing up the road to the old hangar. The dust rising from the road prevented Jack from counting the vehicles. He checked over his shoulder to be sure Paulo was still laying on the floor in a crumpled heap.

Brian slid to a stop under the belly of the B-25, almost losing his footing. He threw the bags up into the hatch. Fritz peered down through the opening to see who or what was coming up next. Brian pulled the parking chocks from the landing gear and tossed them clear into the grass, then hoisted himself up into the belly.

Standing at the back door of the old hangar, Jack could easily see the B-25. When he glanced over his shoulder, it was just in time to see Brian disappear into the fuselage. Knowing they were safe, Jack drew the 1911 from its holster, "OK baby, I guess it's just you and me..." Trying to stay concealed, he peered out of the doorway - the lead vehicle so close he could see the faces of the policemen, their white uniform shirts glowing in the sun. "Nice target," he said aloud.

Jack needed to stall for time, no matter what it would take. The vehicles did not look like police cars – more like whatever they had at hand. Captured or arrested was not an option. He was certain these were not real policemen... more likely drug cartel dressed as police. Jack stepped from the doorway in a crouch and dumped two rounds through the grill of the lead vehicle, taking the men dressed as police totally by surprise. The hood of the lead vehicle blew open as the bullets from the .45 ripped through the grill and destroyed the radiator. The startled driver swerved and crashed the steaming jeep into the mesh airport fence, the officers spilling out and scrambling for cover behind the wrecked vehicle.

Jack ducked back inside. Behind him, he heard the B-25's port engine sputter, then roar to life. He ventured a quick glance out of the door. A second jeep roared past the first and turned between the buildings to head for the Sweet Susie. He knew he couldn't allow them to reach the plane. He jumped out of the doorway in a crouch, having to expose himself to get a shot at the jeep as it rounded the corner of the hangar. Slamming his shoulder into the building as he scampered the few feet to the corner he snapped off two shots, the muzzle flame reaching out briefly and the empty shell casings pinging as they dropped to the gravel. The driver died instantly, his head disappearing in a furious splash of red, covering the passenger with bloody gobbets of flesh and bone. The jeep, uncontrolled, careened into the east side of the old hangar, smashing the vehicle and killing the other man, who, thrown from the jeep, bounced off the side of the building like a rag doll. The three men in the back seat survived only by bailing out before the crash. Jack scrambled across the ground on hands and knees to reach the safety of the doorway as the police returned fire from the cover of the first jeep. Bullets spattered and ricocheted off the metal building around him like angry bees. Once inside the doorway, he took a quick account of his body, astounded that he had not been hit. He took another quick peek. Two other jeeps had arrived and slid up abreast with the first near the fence, creating an effective staggered cover for the white-clad police. They fired a volley again and he drew back inside as the bullets clattered like hail against the metal building.

Steele spun around as he heard the B-25's starboard engine roar to life. From their vantage point, the police had a field of fire that extended to the plane... it was a no-man's-land run he was not likely to survive without help. He was going to need a distraction... Paulo stirred on the floor... Jack stared at him for a moment, *hmmm... it might work.* Holstering the Kimber, Jack picked up the man by the shirt, shaking him viciously and dragged him to the doorway. *"Wake up,* Paulo, time for some exercise..."

Paulo came around, vaguely aware of his surroundings. "You might be of some use after all..." Jack snarled, holding him up. Jack used Paulo's gun and fired through the doorway at the police until it was empty, one man tumbling to the ground. He pushed the gun in Paulo's hand and shoved him out into the chaos. *"RUN... RUN!"* Still holding the revolver in his hand, Paulo, confused, stumbled, ran, then stumbled again, waving his arms to surrender. His body twitched, jerked and spun uncontrollably, violently, as the angry police gunned him down without hesitation.

Jack had not stayed to watch the results but was reasonably sure of the outcome. He was running for the huge open doorway at the opposite end of the hangar, taking advantage of the confusion outside. He slid the .45 out of its holster as he ran. The Sweet Susie was rolling slowly... "What the hell is he doing?" hissed Jack through clenched teeth. He was facing the possibility that maybe things looked even more impossible from Brian's vantage point. Jack was almost to the door when two white shirted men, stepped around the corner of the doorway and blocked his escape.

Surprised by their presence, Jack tried to stop and lost his footing on the smooth concrete floor. The officers fired as he slid to the floor, their bullets passing over his head. Jack fired by instinct as he fell. One officer dove head first for cover, the other crumpled in a heap with a gaping hole in his chest, an obscene crimson stain creeping across his white uniform shirt. Steele scrambled behind assorted crates and barrels for cover as automatic gunfire splashed about the inside of the hangar, from both sides. Police had stormed the rear of the hangar. Things were looking grim and Jack decided if he was going to die, he was going to take as many of them with him as he could. He fired between the crates at the men in the rear of the hangar, one man fell to the floor, bleeding profusely. The familiar clack of the slide locking open on an empty mag sounded loud even among the staccato of gunfire. The fire from automatic weapons chewed at the crates around the pilot, showering him with splinters of wood and lead.

Pressed against the wall of the hangar, fairly well protected by the crates and barrels, he popped the empty mag from his pistol and replaced it with another one, tucking the empty in his pocket. He thumbed the slide release,

41

dropping the slide. Time was running out, they would overrun him soon. He peered between the crates towards the front of the hangar and was surprised to see the B-25 was still there, sitting motionless on the runway with the engines running. He could no longer hear the engines over the gunfire. Jack pulled back as gunfire ripped into the crate next to him. He fired blind over the top of the crates in response. *This is not going the way I planned it...*

The cool, almost cold, moisture creeping across the concrete under his left hand interrupted his train of thought. He smelled it. *Paint thinner..?* He turned and read the label on the leaking fifty gallon drum with the skull and crossbones on it: methyl ethyl ketone. *Holy shit, MEK!* A paint thinner yes, but also one of the main ingredients in refining cocaine. And beyond flammable, *explosive* was a much better description. The unmistakable thumping sound of twin .50 caliber machine-gun fire snapped his train of thought. *Jesus Christ! That's all I need!*

Heavy .50 caliber rounds ripped through the hangar, punching holes through the corrugated steel walls like paper. Jack curled himself in a ball on the floor in an attempt to avoid the destruction tearing through the building, praying none of the hot rounds would hit the drum behind him. Lying on the floor, peeking between the shredded crates, he discovered the source. The twin .50 cal. Browning machine-guns in the upper turret on the Sweet Susie was giving the police a glimpse of hell. The white uniformed officers at the mouth of the hangar, lay sprawled on the concrete in pools of blood, their bodies literally cut in half and twisted in grotesque shapes. The wrecked jeep against the building exploded, throwing sheets of corrugated metal into the building as a large section of the wall disappeared. In fear of extermination, the men dressed like police withdrew from the rear of the hangar, dropping their weapons as they ran. They were greedy and corrupt... stupid, not so much. Nothing could override their instinct for survival. They were simply outgunned, not something they were used to. Used to getting what they wanted through intimidation and terrorism, they had no stomach or training for facing military level firepower. The Police Lieutenant had lost about half his men; some real cops and some loaned to him by the local cartel... He would most likely lose his commission, but right now he was more concerned about losing his life. So he ran with his men, what was left of them, and they fled past their vehicles leaving them abandoned. Unfortunately for the Lieutenant, his failure might mean death anyway.

The .50 cal. guns fell silent and Jack extracted himself from his cover, his Kimber still clutched in his hand. He felt drained, shaken. Maria dropped to the runway from the open belly hatch, followed by Fritz. The duo ran toward the hangar, fearing the worst, unable to see Jack in the shadows of the interior. Jack ran into the sunlight, his legs feeling a little like lead. Maria covered her mouth to stifle a cry of glee and Fritz bounded happily to his friend. The pilot dropped to one knee as he shoved the .45 back into its holster. The Shepherd jumped into Jack's outstretched arms almost knocking him to the ground. Maria reached out to him, crying.

"Quickly, they may come back!" she urged. The pilot glanced over his shoulder at the carnage, as Maria helped him to his feet. The exploding jeep had started a fire which was quickly consuming the whole East side of the old hangar fed by the containers and crates inside. An intense fire, so hot, the corrugated steel on the outside of the building began melting, the slag running down into silver-gray pools on the ground.

The leaking drum of Methyl ethyl ketone exploded in an eye-searing fireball, tearing out nearly the entire east wall and half the roof, sending sheets of flames into the air and flaming debris onto the next hangar, a sphere of molten metal spraying out in all directions. The concussion wave sent Jack, Maria and Fritz sprawling onto the asphalt. A dirty black column of dense smoke billowed and rose from the open mouth of the hangar, hot, angry orange flames reaching up towards a perfectly blue sky. The three rose and Maria covered his face with kisses while hustling to the plane. "Hurry sweetheart," she said, urging him along.

Standing below the fuselage, the prop wash felt refreshing and Jack watched Maria boost Fritz through the hatch before climbing up herself. After one last look around, he pulled his weary body up into the plane, helped by the hands reaching down to help guide him up.

"Go! Go! Go! Get us out of here!" Maria reached down and pulled the hatch shut with a metallic clang and latched it tight.

"OK, I'll call for clearance and we're outta here!" replied Brian, releasing the brakes.

"*NO!*" she shouted. "They will try to stall you, or block the runway, just *Go! GO!* Get us up in the air!" Feeling the surge of power as Brian throttled slowly up, she felt a moment of relief.

Brian surveyed the gauges, adjusted the flaps and swung onto the runway, right across the grass from the taxiway, knocking down a runway marker. "Hold on!" he yelled. He cut in front of other planes waiting for takeoff and hammered the throttles wide open, the radio chattering with frantic calls from the tower and startled pilots alike. Brian ignored their calls and turned down the volume. With the engines roaring at full power, the props hungrily devoured the air. Brian eased the yoke back and the B-25 lifted easily off the runway, leaving an airport in complete chaos. Retracting the landing gear and flaps, he kept the warbird at low altitude maintaining full power to get maximum speed. Brian flew her on the deck, just barely above treetop level for almost fifteen minutes, frequently changing headings to avoid tracking or pursuit. Having dutifully filed their flight plans first thing in the morning, Brian chose an alternate flight path not listed on their submission. Instead of flying straight South-Southwest across the Caribbean Sea, to either Maracaibo or Caracas, Brian decided they would fly a half moon, following the British and French islands that created a dotted line from Puerto Rico to the coast of Venezuela. Avoiding cities they logged, he figured they could land and refuel in Bogota, flying on from there.

Jack lay on the floor of the plane across Maria's lap, his eyes closed as she wiped the dirt and blood from his face. Maria wept as she spoke, "I can't tell where all this blood came from."

He opened his eyes and looked into hers, "Don't worry, it's not mine... at least I don't think so." He smiled, and she half giggled, half cried, releasing a mixture of emotions all at once. Jack reached up and touched her face. "I'm OK, really, everything'll be just fine. Enough laying around, I'd better get up to the cockpit and see where we're headed, see what Bri is up to..." He looked down at his torn and soiled shirt, covered with blood and grime. "Dammit, ruined a perfectly good shirt..." He sat up and grimaced, "Aaaauuugh!" Pain in his left side lanced deep down his ribs and took his breath away.

Maria held him. "Oh God, oh God, I knew you were hurt... that *was* your blood!"

Jack held up his hand and Maria stopped ranting. "Just bruised..." he opened his shirt slowly, interesting shades of pink and purple across his ribs. "Bruised I think..." he inhaled slowly, "I hope."

"What do you mean, you hope?" she inquired, confused.

"Bruised, as opposed to broken." Jack said calmly, trying to control his breathing and reduce the pain.

Maria looked a little sheepish. "Oh."

Jack carefully peeled off the torn shirt, wincing. Maria helped him to his feet, handing him a fresh shirt from his bag. After washing with a towel and some cold water from their cooler, he gingerly slid into the clean shirt, leaving it unbuttoned. The ice-water felt good on his tender ribs, making it a little easier to breathe. Maria gingerly pinned his wings above his left pocket and Steele looked down at the young beauty standing before him whose life had been changed so suddenly and completely. What seemed so incredible to him was that she had retained so much composure. *Hmm, a rather unusual and remarkable trait for a woman.* "Can you read a radar unit?"

"Yes... I can fly too," she replied.

"Good..." Jack guided her to the navigator's table and flipped the power on for the unit. "Can you run this one?"

"Yes..." she replied without hesitation, "are we looking for anything special?"

Jack ran his hand through his dark hair. "Any possible pursuit, or any other conflicting flight traffic, because when we come up off the deck, we're going to suddenly pop up on somebody's scope somewhere, and we may have some unwanted company."

"No problem," said Maria smiling sweetly, sliding into the navigator's seat.

Damn, I just love that accent. Of course, the rest of the package is nothing to sneeze at either, said his little voice. This time Jack agreed with the voice. He turned and made his way to the cockpit, Fritz at his heels. The pilot winced and exhaled sharply as he stooped to duck under the avionics console getting into the cockpit. Brian looked back over his shoulder from the captain's seat. "Need your seat, Skipper..?" he unbuckled to vacate the seat. Steele closed his eyes and shook his head, putting his hand on the copilot's shoulder. He eased himself into the copilot seat, gritting his teeth. Glancing at the gauges the pilot drew a long, deep relaxing breath.

Jack belted himself in loosely. "OK, first, let's ease power a bit and open the cowl vents, she's running a tad hot from all this work. Good evasive work, by the way."

Brian nodded as he reduced throttle, "Thanks, did the best I could, did a little sweating too." He adjusted the cowl vents to let more air past the air-cooled cylinders of her radial engines.

Jack smiled. "Yeah, welcome to the club."

"You alright?"

Jack nodded, "Yeah, a little bruised, but I'll live." Steele eyed the gauges as the oil pressure, head and manifold temperature gauges slowly crept down out of the yellow. "OK, now, let's get off the deck and grab some sky, gently though..." Nodding, the copilot eased the yoke back and the B-25 nosed up towards the scattered clouds.

Nobody had ever saved Jack's life before and he wasn't so sure he was comfortable discussing it. He tried to formulate in his mind, how to broach the subject. After several aborted attempts to organize thought and reason, he finally resigned himself to the reality that he would have to just blurt it out. "Listen, um, thanks." Completely uncomfortable, Jack stared at the gauges.

"For what?" Brian wasn't trying to be difficult, he really hadn't a clue as to what the pilot was referring to.

"Um, well, for the heavy artillery support." Not speaking, Brian just shook his head, thoroughly confusing Steele. "What d'you mean no..." he said flatly.

The copilot looked over at Jack. "*Dude*," he whispered, "I couldn't leave the controls..." He adjusted the fuel mixture with one hand. "I just moved the plane..." he thumbed over his shoulder, "where *she* told me to." Brian paused, letting this sink in, watching reality hit home.

"You mean..."

"Yeah..." Brian interrupted, as he eased the yoke forward leveling the plane off at four thousand feet. "She loaded the belts into the guns, figured out how they worked and figured out the turret controls... all on her own. 'Cause I was busy up here."

"Holy shit..." said Jack slowly, his voice trailing off. He felt a sudden chill run up his spine. There was definitely more to this girl than met the eye... a lot more. He wondered if he would ever really know how much... or if he really wanted to know.

Feeling a little like he was caught in someone else's dream, Steele rubbed his face with both hands. He wanted, no, *needed* to think of a new subject. "So where do you have us headed?"

Brian explained the route and the destination of Bogota while Jack pinched his lower lip in thought. "Hmmm..." He pulled their charts out of the pouch, unfolding them across his lap. "A good route basically, but it takes us to a destination too close to our original plans. Bogota is also quite large and will probably be well informed. We need a more back-water place with little connection..." He scanned the chart, "Aaahhh here we go, on the east coast..." he said pointing on the paper, "Georgetown..." He checked it with a protractor and line. "Take a heading of one-seventy-seven..." He glanced at the fuel gauges, and checked his math with a calculator." We should have plenty of fuel to make it, no sweat. Let's go up to about ten-thousand."

"Angels ten. Got it." Brian adjusted course and eased the nose up again. "What next?"

"I'm really not sure, I think we ought to try to get word to Stephen, we definitely need distance between that airport and us... as quickly as possible. We need time to affect damage control... and I'm not really sure how to do that yet. It's a U.S. Territory, so I would expect FBI involvement - maybe CIA since we're outside of the country now..." He pinched the bridge of his nose in thought. "Those weren't cops... at least not most of them. They were cartel."

Brian shot him a glance, "How could you tell?"

"Hard to say... gut feeling maybe, something I saw that I'm not remembering. I don't know for sure... what I *do* know, is that's not how the story will break." Jack slid the charts and protractor back into its pouch. "We'll be gun and drug runners who mercilessly slaughtered an entire platoon of gentle, noble policemen doing their job of protecting the innocent public."

"You're right, that does sound bad..."

"Yeah..." Jack ran his fingers through his hair, deep in thought. His dad was a cop, his uncle was a cop, and he had been a cop. He grew up knowing cops were the good guys. And even when they weren't, as was the case here, killing a cop was close to blasphemy. This didn't sit well with Jack's conscience, even though he knew deep inside, he had done nothing wrong. It was survival mode, plain and simple. Jack looked up and scanned the skies around them after a long stare at the gauges. A long unblinking stare, the kind of wide-eyed blank stare that a man in all-engrossing thought succumbed to. Looking but not seeing. The dry sting in his eyes brought him back to the living.

"Watcha thinking about?" queried the copilot, tapping on the glass of one of the gauges.

"Everything... nothing..." Jack's voice trailed off. He scratched his mustache and ran his fingers through his hair. This statement was not altogether true however, because like most men after experiencing a crisis, Jack was reviewing the events in his mind, over and over again. Like game films in his mind, he hoped to glean another speck of information in order to help solve the predicament they were now in. To his intense dismay, there were no answers there, only more questions. Things like; Paulo had told the police that the plane contained drugs and guns. Of course, there were no drugs, but what about the guns... a good guess? Coincidence? What about the drum of methyl ethyl ketone. He hadn't noticed any painting equipment around the hangar. What was really in those crates? He hadn't time to look.

And why was it so important for Maria to leave with them? He could see no real danger there if she had stayed. There was probably a logical explanation for all of these, but not knowing truly irritated him. Steele wanted to forget about it for a while.

He noted, with a passing interest, that while his ribs had turned an interesting shade of purple they didn't hurt quite as much as they had earlier.

CHAPTER FOUR

WASHINGTON DC: CIA OFFICE

A woman's voice, crisp with professionalism spoke through the intercom, "I'm sorry to bother you sir, but there's a messenger here with an important communiqué for your eyes only." The man behind the large mahogany desk leaned forward from the overstuffed leather chair, put down the official papers he was reading and reached over to the comm-phone on the desk. "Thanks, Maggie, send him in."

The young man in a suit and tie entering the office, sealed manila envelope in hand, was not an ordinary messenger. "This came for you only minutes ago, sir..." he said, handing over the envelope to the man behind the desk. "I got it here as soon as I could..." The young man's voice trailed off, he always felt a little uncomfortable in this office, too close to the top he decided.

"Sit down, Special Agent Cummins," said the man behind the desk with a sweep of his hand. "Coffee?"

The young CIA agent was surprised by the offer but did not refuse. "Why, yes sir, thank you very much." He sat at the table in the center of the room, surveying the trappings of rank. The walls, paneled in mahogany, were covered with souvenirs of foreign wars, medals, decorations and commendations for every conceivable valor. Behind the desk hung two large flags, the Stars and Stripes and the flag of the CIA. A silk banner strung between them read; *John 8:32: "Ye shall know the truth and it shall set you free."*

The man behind the desk spoke into the comm before walking out to the conference table in the middle of the room, "Maggie, coffee for two please." Before he reached the table, Maggie entered with coffee service for two. She poured the fresh, steaming coffee into two white mugs emblazoned with the seal of the President of The United States. "No interruptions, Maggie," said the Director of South American Operations.

"Yes, Mr. Miles," said the girl as she left the office.

Stephen Miles could not bear to review bad news without a good cup of coffee. "OK, let's see what this is all about." The CIA man of twenty odd years tore open the envelope after a sip of smooth Colombian bean. Cup in hand, he read the confidential report. "Holy shit," he grumbled, staring at the paper trying to read between the lines. He took a sip from the cup as he stood. "OK Cummins, you were there when this thing came in, weren't you?" Stephen's back was turned to the agent as he slid the document into the shredder, the pieces of confetti falling into a confidential burn-bag underneath.

"Yes sir, I was."

"What other information came in," said the veteran, sitting back down at the table. "That..." he said, pointing at the document going through the shredder, "was pitifully brief."

The young agent took a sip from his cup. "Yes sir. The details are still coming in..."

Stephen offered a curt nod of encouragement.

"But there wasn't much more than that. At this point, quite a bit is supposition, like our Latin Island operation has been compromised. That the B-25 aircraft owned by Miles Aviation, has disappeared with its cargo and crew..." The young agent had suddenly made the name connection but tried not to hesitate. He sipped briefly from his cup before going on, "Our Latin operative is believed missing too."

Stephen Miles rubbed his face, he hated involving civilians in operations because when things went wrong it always made damage control so much more complicated.

Agent Cummins continued, "There was also some communication traffic about a number of San Juan Police Officers killed - but that is unconfirmed and may be totally unrelated."

Stephen groaned, rubbing his temples, this was getting more complicated by the minute. "*Maggie!*"

Stephen's aide poked her head in the door, "Yes sir?"

"Get Bob Wolf on the phone, tell him I want a plane, not one of mine and not one of the *Company's*. Tell him to rent one, a Lear maybe, something fast, but we need complete anonymity..." he stood up, "and I need it yesterday, got it?"

"Got it," she replied, attempting to leave.

"Oh, and tell Kevin to bring the car around. He and Mr. Cummins here, will be going along."

"Yes sir." She disappeared.

"Cummins, go home and pack. Pack light. Call Maggie, she'll have your directions for the plane... don't be late."

The young man rose, straightening his jacket, "Yes sir."

The Director stood at the window looking out over the city, his back to the agent as he left the office. Stephen Miles had fixed his share of fuck-ups in his career, he'd fix this one too. Dammit, he wanted that plane back. And in one piece. Which means he had to find it before anyone else did, no small task in an area littered with islands. And if Steele hit the South American Continent, shit, he didn't even want to think about that. His only hope was that the kid was a skilled pilot, resourceful too. To find that plane, meant thinking like a civilian. A civilian on the run with police and combat survival experience. An extremely dangerous combination, he decided.

Maggie knocked then entered. "Sir, Kevin is waiting."

Stephen downed his coffee, "Thanks," he muttered, grabbing his jacket and setting the coffee mug on the table. "Call you later." He handed her the sealed burn-bag of shredded documents, "Burn this for me, will you...?"

CHAPTER FIVE

US AIRCRAFT CARRIER, SHENANDOAH: BERMUDA TRIANGLE

The Ensign walked down the seemingly endless corridor, lined with officer's quarters, looking for one in particular. Finding the correct stateroom, he knocked on the open doorway. The occupant was reclining comfortably, fully clothed, on his bunk and looked up from the book he was reading. The lines on his face and the sparkle of silver in his sandy blond hair gained him the nickname *Pappy* by some of the other pilots.

Though he was only forty-two years old, he was still years older than most of the other pilots who were barely in their twenties. He had also flown extensive combat sorties in the Gulf War which made him somewhat of a legend with the newer officers. All in all, the Lieutenant Commander kind of enjoyed the attention because it had never been done with any disrespect intended.

"What can I do for you Ensign?" he asked, with his legendary smile, the crinkles around his blue eyes deepening.

"Sorry to bother you, Pappy, but the Skipper wants you in briefing right away."

Lieutenant Commander Paul Smiley looked at his watch, "What gives? I'm not due to go up for another hour and a half."

The Ensign shrugged, "Beats me, sir, but he said right away."

"OK... Warren too?"

"Yes sir..." replied the junior officer, "do you know where I might find him?"

Smiley swung his feet over the edge of the bunk. "Try the forward lounge; he said something about a football game on TV."

"Thanks, Pappy." The Ensign saluted and disappeared down the hallway, leaving the pilot alone with his thoughts.

Being called to briefing this far in advance of a scheduled patrol launch meant you weren't going out for just a patrol, there was something brewing out there somewhere. Smiley dropped off his bunk to the deck. His five-foot eleven-inch frame was solid and muscular, remaining so due to the rigors of being a fighter jock. A graduate of the Navy's *Top Gun* program, he had long since traversed the stage of being a cocky young hot dog to a cool, calculating, tremendously skilled, fighter pilot.

After donning his flight gear and checking himself in the mirror, he headed off to flight briefing. Lieutenant Commander Smiley met his wingman, Lieutenant JG Mike *Mad Dog* Warren, in the corridor just outside the briefing room. Mike Warren was a wiry kid from Iowa with curly auburn hair. His freckled face made him look much younger than his twenty-five years and his small town, Midwestern upbringing, made him sound as naive as he looked.

Still, despite his sedate childhood, his clear, brown eyes sparkled at the thought of flying just about anything. Mike's enthusiasm was evident in his flying. He had a strong aptitude, and the advanced combat maneuvers Paul had taught him were coming along nicely.

Pappy inspected Mike's flight gear. "Ready?"

"Yep."

"OK... let's go." They entered briefing together.

Smiley was surprised to see eight other pilots already there, each one a combat veteran. In fact, the only one without combat was his wingman Mike Warren. This could be... hmmm, hell, he didn't know what to think. He sat down as they all did, when the Air Boss entered the room.

"OK gentlemen, find a seat and button up your faces..." he waited until everyone was seated and continued, "We have a situation which dictates we must search for, locate and escort a possible hostile aircraft, so listen up. Does everybody know what a World War Two, B-25 Mitchell Bomber, looks like..?" he watched the nodding heads. "OK fine, it seems late last night or early this morning, the details aren't clear on this, an armed B-25 called the Sweet Susie, landed at the San Juan airport and logged some time in at an abandoned hangar. Responding to an anonymous tip, the San Juan Police went out to investigate. They were fired upon and in the ensuing gun battle more than twenty officers were either killed or wounded."

A low chorus of whispers erupted from the pilots. The Commander never looked up from his report, "Shut up ladies and listen... In their escape, they dynamited the hangar, destroying thousands of dollars of equipment being stored there. Not to mention all the criminal laws, they also violated numerous civil air traffic laws, endangering countless lives." He paused before going on. "It is also suspected that they have abducted a local woman. These are dangerous, vicious, people. It is reported that they have a load of drugs and guns in a plane capable of defending itself. Our job is to find it

53

and escort it back to the San Juan airport where there are police and military units waiting for it. These people are desperate, and hostage or no, if you locate them and are fired upon, splash 'em... I don't want anyone returning with holes in their aircraft. Understood?"

"*Aye aye, sir...*" was the somber response that rippled through the group.

"Dismissed..." The pilots rose and were issued their search pattern orders as they exited two by two, heading for the elevator that would carry them to the hangar level, two floors below the flight deck.

Walking through the hangar level, the pilots joked and jousted verbally, exchanging good-natured insults and challenges. Pausing only momentarily to be serious, the aviators wished one another luck before dispersing to do pre-flight inspections of their aircraft.

As Smiley and Warren strolled across the hangar deck, the senior officer pointed out his wingman's plane sitting on the aircraft lift. The engineer standing next to the F-18 waved the two airmen to the lift. The pilots stepped onto the platform and it moved smoothly upwards. "Your bird's already topside Pappy. You guys'll launch first."

Smiley guessed the grizzled engineer's age over fifty. "Chief, what're you still doing way out here?"

The engineer smiled a crooked smile. "Well, I got seven kids, n'it seems like every time I go home, another one pops out! This' the only place I git any peace 'n quiet!" He guffawed at his own joke, slapping the pilot on the shoulder. Smiley laughed along with him. Having come from a small family, the thought of seven kids all in one house seemed simply ludicrous. The Chief climbed onto the tow truck as the lift squeaked to a stop. "Your bird's over there." He said, pointing the way, as he started the motor on the truck. The pilot waved.

Warren waved back as he followed his aircraft. They would be on their own now until they were in the air.

Paul Smiley examined his Hornet inch by inch. He handed the line assistant his helmet to climb the ladder to the cockpit and paused to run his hand gently across the Desert Storm logo just below the cockpit. He was proud of that logo and what it stood for, along with the four kill badges to the right of it.

The line assistant buckled him in and handed the pilot his flight helmet. After switching on all systems, Paul spun up the engines. While they warmed, he proceeded through his lengthy pre-flight checklist. By the time he finished, Mike Warren's Hornet had just left the catapult and Smiley got the nod to roll. He released the brakes, slowly rolling to the catapult under direction of the Line Boss. Smiley closed and latched the canopy, stopping at the Boss' signal.

Several more F-18s sat behind him on the deck, their engines warming, waiting their turn. The catapult linkage connected to the nose wheel of his Hornet, he waited, watching the Line Boss. The Boss was the *Maestro* of the deck. That deck and everything on it belonged to him. Conducting deck traffic like an orchestra, the LB controlled aircraft, deck equipment and men alike. Everyone watched him, a missed cue could spell disaster.

A blast panel rose from the deck behind the plane to protect the fighters waiting next in line. The Boss rotated his hand in the air and Smiley throttled up, the catapult holding his aircraft in place. Exchanging the thumbs up signal with the LB, the pilot's hands left the controls to hold onto the grips on either side of the canopy. The line-controlled F-18 being control sensitive on carrier-launch meant hands-off until the plane was clear of the deck and over the water..

The Boss took a quick look around, saluted the pilot sharply from his crouched position. As his arm dropped, the catapult fired, shooting the Hornet across the deck and out over the ocean. As soon as he was over the water, Smiley took the controls and guided the F-18 into a climbing turn, out of the traffic pattern. He breathed deeply in his mask and grinned; any day flying was the best time of your life. He raised his landing gear. "Blue One to STC, feet wet, proceeding as planned..."

"Roger Blue One," replied the traffic control officer from the carrier, "happy trails."

"Blue One to Blue Two... location?"

"Blue Two, coming around on your port side, Pappy."

Paul Smiley glanced over his left shoulder, "Roger Blue Two... come to a heading of two-four-zero, let's climb to Angels 10."

"Roger Blue One." The two pilots pointed their aircraft on course and before long, began their search. "Why do you suppose they sent the Navy on a mission like this?" Warren asked his senior officer, over a more private air to air channel.

Surveying the sky and glancing at his scope, Pappy shrugged mentally, "I guess there really isn't anyone else."

It was about as good an answer as any. The pilots flew along in virtual silence except for occasional radio traffic and updates to the carrier.

CHAPTER SIX

SWEET SUSIE, SOUTH OF THE BERMUDA TRIANGLE : *HIDE N' SEEK*

Having switched seats, Brian and Jack munched happily on the ham sandwiches Maria had passed into the cockpit, and Fritz watched with interest as they ate. The Shepherd nudged Jack's elbow and he tore off a piece of his sandwich, handing it to the dog.

"How're you doing back there?" Jack called.

"Fine," she replied popping up in between them. "How are your ribs?"

"Colorful..."

"Wow... wook at dat coud formafin!" Brian mumbled, his mouth full of ham sandwich.

Jack looked at his copilot's bulging cheeks instead. "Really?" he said sarcastically, "Tower, message garbled, please repeat..." he chided. "How about you swallow and try that again..."

The copilot smiled sheepishly and Fritz stared intently, hoping some of it would fall on the floor.

■ ■ ■

In the search for the B-25, Blue flight was the first to encounter anything in the sky that day. Mike Warren keyed his mic, "I got a bogie, Pappy... Wait, damn it's gone."

"Where?"

"On the edge of my scope, bearing one-seven-nine." Warren peered out over the port wingtip of his F-18, knowing he wouldn't see it from this distance.

"OK, Mad Dog, let's go check it out. Head up one-seven-nine. Blue One to STC, did you copy?"

"Roger, Blue One. Keep us informed."

The two Navy jets did a wing-over and swung to their new heading, throttling up. "I got my blip back again..." called Mike.

"Yep," replied Commander Smiley, "I got it too. Maintain course and speed." They flew on in formation. The two Hornets quickly closed the gap, approaching the B-25 from behind and above. Ten minutes passed.

■ ■ ■

Maria stuck her head into the cockpit between Jack and Brian. "I've been getting a tremendous amount of interference on the scope and nav systems, but there seems to be a weather front ahea..." It was at that moment she glanced up and gazed through the moisture streaked cockpit windshield. "Saint Mary..." she whispered, "it's even bigger than I thought..." She realized they were headed straight for it, which made a chill run through her body. She rubbed the goose bumps off her arms. "You're not going through that, are you?"

Jack had never been fond of discussing his decisions once he'd made them, especially when he was unsure of the outcome himself. "You've got a *better* idea?"

"Going *around it*, immediately comes to mind!" she said, waving her hand expressively.

Not that he was truly pissed, but his voice and composure turned to a controlled calm, he spoke in a low, controlled voice. "Well... thanks to your fucking buddy Paulo and the keystone cops, we had to make a *hot exit*, not to mention changing routes. We don't have the *fuel* to go around it."

Brian remained silent, he knew better than to intervene. Besides, Jack was right, if not for her, they wouldn't be in this mess... or would they? He decided that might take some deeper and lengthier consideration. Maria returned silently to the navigator's table, tears of frustration burning in her eyes. She hated to cry and fought her emotions. Right then she hated him. She cut herself off in mid thought, wiping the tears from her eyes to focus on the radar screen. At the age of twenty-five, she still hadn't learned to fully control her emotions.

"*JAAACK!*" The scream took him by surprise, a quick glance told him the copilot too. The frantic girl stumbled over the dog as she scrambled back through the cockpit opening. "Jack..." she was breathless and as white as a ghost, "two bogies, moving fast!"

Bogies? The thought that flashed through his mind was that it was a military term... He decided he didn't have time for contemplation right now and put the thought aside. "Where?" he fired at her.

"Directly behind and high, about two thousand feet up, twenty miles out and closing."

"What do we do?" asked Brian, jumping in.

"I don't know..." he turned back to Maria. "How fast?"

She shook her head, "Real fast! About triple our speed!"

"That's around Mach One! Shit, shit, shit!" he said in a growl, pounding his fist on the control yoke. "They gotta' be military, damn!"

"Kinda rules out running huh?"

Jack looked at Brian. "Yeah, I would think so, unless you have a jet engine hidden up your sleeve."

Brian shrugged. "Think they're ours?"

Steele shook his head, "Probably; but it doesn't matter whose they are, it's still bad news for us..."

Maria went back to the scope. She was having a hard time reading the radar because of the distortion on the screen from the storm. "The scope... I can't find them... Wait! There they are. They're about a mile out, they're just pacing us now... damn this interference!" She tried to adjust her avionics. "Sorry, I just lost them again."

"See if you can tell what they are, or who they are." Jack envisioned being shot down without warning, and if that was the case, he preferred to go down fighting, no matter how futile the effort. "OK, don't panic, we still don't know what they want," he said, rubbing his chin in thought. "Maybe they're just curious... I hope."

■ ■ ■

They could see it now, quite clearly in fact. There was no mistaking that twin tail section. They had located the B-25.

"OK, Mad Dog, reduce speed I want to hang back here for a bit."

"Roger, Pappy." Mike eased the throttle back to stay in formation with his wing leader.

Smiley switched frequencies. "Blue One to STC, we have a positive visual contact with the B-25."

"STC... Roger that, Blue One. Good job. Proceed with caution, we will vector additional birds to your location."

"Roger, STC, Blue One out."

The old warbird looked rather majestic, flying through the clouds below. "Damn, Pappy, that thing's in beautiful shape. She looks brand new."

Smiley had noticed that too and for some reason that seemed odd and out of sync with the circumstances. He looked at the mountainous clouds looming in the distance, and the heading they were on. "Mad Dog, we want to corral these folks before we reach that weather front out there."

"Copy that. I'll follow your lead."

"OK kid, hang on my port-stern quarter and keep an eye on that gun turret. If it moves give me a shout, then get the hell outta' the way."

"Got it.... I'm getting some real distortion on my radar. How about you?"

Smiley looked down and the image was so distorted he couldn't read it. "Yeah, mine too. Must be coming from that weather front. Let's round these people up and get the hell outta' here. Follow me in, kid." He proceeded to search for the radio frequency being used by the B-25 as he eased up alongside her.

■ ■ ■

Brian's brow knitted in consternation, "Jack, look at the gauges..." his voice was calm, if not a bit curious.

Jack switched his gaze to the dash to see the gauges doing strange things indeed; their needles bouncing, flat-lining and coming back to life. The closer to the storm front they got, the crazier the electronics and instruments behaved. His eyes widened, "I've got an idea, it just might work too."

Brian had a strange feeling he wasn't going to like this, in fact, he was almost positive.

Fritz distracted the pilot before he could speak, the Shepherd obviously agitated, excited even, standing with his front paws on Jack's thigh to see out the window, fidgeting and whining. The pilot ran his hand across the dog's head, rubbing his ears, trying to keep him calm. The Shepherd, enjoying the attention, remained still. "See? Even he feels it."

Brian, who had been watching the dog, looked past him out over the port wing. "We've got company," he pointed calmly. Jack looked left to see a Navy F-18 Hornet, barely fifty feet off the Sweet Susie's left wingtip. Above and to the left of him was yet another F-18.

"Christ, he's got missiles," muttered Jack. The pilot of the closest F-18 gave a wave, then in sign language conveyed to Jack that he wanted their radio frequency. Jack glanced ahead to the looming storm front, trying to gauge their closing speed. Steele held up fingers for numbers. "I gotta' stall," he told Brian and Maria, who was kneeling next to Fritz. "That front is our only chance."

"I was afraid he was going to say that," groaned Brian.

The fighter pilot found the frequency and amidst the noise and interference, identified himself to the crew of the B-25. "Hello B-25, can you hear me?"

Jack keyed his mic, "Yes I can, what can I do for you, Navy?" Despite his nerves being on edge, his voice was friendly and calm. He glanced at the horizon, they were so close. Stall... *stall*, he thought. His body tingled all over; although quite a unique feeling it was somehow familiar. He tried to put it out of his mind.

"I'm Lieutenant Commander Paul Smiley, United States Navy..." he thumbed toward the other F-18, "that's my wingman, Lieutenant Mike Warren. We are off the aircraft carrier Shenandoah and have orders to escort you back to San Juan airport." The pilot's slow, calm voice, with its hint of southern accent, almost made it an appealing proposition. It was obvious this man was a true professional, completely comfortable and confident. Steele could also see the row of victory badges painted on the fuselage under the cockpit canopy. That was a man who could seriously ruin your day if so inclined. Commander Smiley continued, "I will ask you to totally comply with my instructions, if you attempt to evade or take any hostile action, we *will* shoot you down. Do you understand?"

Jack's mind was racing. "Yes, Commander..." *stall,* he thought. "Commander, I have just one problem..." the three planes entered the fringes of the weather front and visibility was closing in rapidly, "I don't have enough fuel to return there." In reality, this was close to the truth. "I do, however, have enough fuel to reach the coast..."

"Stand by B-25..." There were several tense moments of open static. "Negative, B-25, come to a heading of zero-nine-nine." Smiley seemed totally calm and under control.

Jack smiled to himself, this guy needs to get out of this soup too... probably to call for redirection. Hell, with all this static interference, they could barely communicate plane to plane and they were within spitting distance of each other. He had one trick up his sleeve, and the timing had to be just right. When compared to the Hornets flying off his starboard wingtip, the B-25 was about as maneuverable as a flying grand piano... but there was such a disparity between the flight envelopes of the B-25 and the Hornets that Jack hoped the playing field just might tilt in his favor.

He was trying to see if the F-18s were flying with their flaps deployed... dammit, he couldn't tell through the dwindling visibility. "Please repeat, Commander Smiley, we could not copy." Jack needed just another second or two, their only chance...

"Jack..." Maria grabbed his shoulder, startling him, "the radar screen and nav system just went completely blank..." He shot a glance at the gauges, some were bouncing uncontrollably, others had flat-lined, completely dead. He hoped the systems on the two F-18's were suffering the same problems. "Before they quit, I saw two more bogies coming in..."

▪ ▪ ▪

The Lieutenant Commander tried without success to re-contact the B-25 flying beside him, hell, he could barely reach Warren's aircraft. He was trying to decide what to do, he couldn't even reach the ship for assistance. This was undoubtedly the weirdest weather he had ever seen, and it was quickly getting worse.

"Pappy, can you hear me?"

"Yeah kid, go ahead."

"Pappy, I just lost my radar and all my nav gear, my readouts are scrambled... shit, I can't even tell how much fuel I've got left." Warren's voice was filled with uncertainty, possibly fear.

Hell, losing all your electronics could unnerve even a veteran pilot but Smiley needed his wingman to keep a clear head. "Yeah, me too, but don't worry kid, we'll be alright. Just chill out and hang onto my tail." His voice was calm and stable.

"OK, Pappy." Warren concentrated on keeping visual contact with the tail of Smiley's F-18, gathering mettle from his wing leader's confidence.

▪ ▪ ▪

Jack could still see Smiley's F-18 off their port wing, although a little farther out than before. A strange observation suddenly presented itself. For such a large storm front, there was no wind, none... not only that, but there was no rainfall either... just the moisture held aloft in the clouds. Jack had no time for lengthy consideration, but he decided this was worth a mental note.

"OK, Bri... full flaps on my command, got it?" Brian nodded, still uncertain of what Jack was planning. Shrouds of clouds came and went between the planes and Jack could see the other pilot watching, even attempting sign language. Flying without a physical horizon to see, was extremely disorienting. It was difficult, to say the least, to tell if one was flying level or not. He was relieved to see, out of all the gauges not working, the artificial horizon was still operating, perhaps because it was the original and not electronic.

He eased the throttles back, a little at a time, knowing the Sweet Susie could fly slower than the Hornets... They watched and waited, their hearts pounding... suddenly the whole left wing of the B-25 disappeared in murky veils of moisture, obscuring the Navy jets from view. Jack snatched the throttles back, cutting the power to almost one-third. "Full flaps... *now!*" Brian pulled the handles and the pumps whirred, hydraulically extending the control surfaces. In the span of only a few seconds, they reduced their airspeed by almost a hundred miles per hour, maybe more, without gauges it was all guesswork. But... it worked. Jack saw a quick glimpse of a tail pass by in the murk, at least the shape looked like a tail. It would be impossible to be sure. Hopefully, they would continue on for a while at present course and speed, without discovering the absence of the B-25 in the foul weather. "Retract flaps, we're coming ten degrees to starboard."

Brian shook his head, smiling as he followed the pilot's instructions, "That was really slick, really, but now what?"

"We climb," said Jack, as he pushed the throttles gently forward and nosed the B-25 upward. "Anything on the radar?"

Maria left then returned quickly. "Not only is it blank, but dark too, same with the nav system."

The sky started to lighten and Jack leveled off the plane, not wanting to leave the protection of the clouds. "This is gonna be real seat-of-the-pants flying without gauges or compass. We should be, on a heading of..." His voice stopped abruptly when both engines started to sputter. He shot a look at Brian. "Did you touch anything?"

Brian raised his hands, "No, not a thing, swear to God."

"Shit, *now* what?! This can't be happening! This is all part of someone else's nightmare, they'll wake up and I'll get to go home..." Working while he ranted, nothing seemed to help, fuel mixture, throttle, switching fuel tanks, nothing. If anything, it got worse. With a shudder, the port engine wheezed as the prop windmilled slowly to a stop. He feathered the prop on the stricken engine and added power to the other. Steele ran his fingers through his hair and keyed the mic on his headset, "Pan, Pan, Pan... this is the Sweet

Susie, we have engine failure, losing altitude..." He broadcast their last known coordinates. "Brian, keep calling," Jack busied himself with trying to restart the stalled engine, he was not willing to give up on it.

Steele became aware again of the tingling sensation creeping across his body, it was quite annoying, like pins and needles. Fritz fidgeted incessantly and Jack had to refrain from scolding him. Everyone seemed to be experiencing the same feeling. Jack refused to quit on the port engine, working feverishly to restart the stubborn power plant. He stared at it, out over the left wing, as if by sheer desire or virtue of his will, he could get it to run.

When the sky lightened and the B-25 broke through the wall of clouds, the starboard engine began to vibrate wildly.

"Fuck," growled Jack. He triggered his mic, "*Mayday, Mayday, Mayday,* this is the Sweet Susie. We have total engine failure, we're losing altitude, we're going down..."

"Sweet Jesus..." Brian's voice was low, almost hushed.

Maria's voice quivered, "Madre mia, save us..."

"I know, I know..." growled Jack, "I'm trying..." Maria grabbed his arm. "*NOT NOW!*" exclaimed Jack, shaking his arm free. She grabbed his arm again, this time with the strength of a vice. "I'm kinda busy here..." Jack looked away from the port engine controls and up into Maria's face with surprise. Her face was pale and her eyes wide with fear. He turned and followed her gaze. Letting go of the controls and running his hands through his hair, Jack sat back in his seat, stunned.

Speechless, he covered his mouth with both hands, unable to voice his thoughts. He blinked, wide-eyed and inhaled deeply. When the starboard engine chugged to a stop, the prop windmilling slowly, no one moved or spoke, transfixed by the vision they saw before them. Everything became clear but more complex at the same time; the radar and electronics, the gauges, the engines, even that queer tingling sensation. "What the hell am I looking at...?" he breathed. "Someone please tell me what the fuck that is..."

The sky above them, glowed brilliant blue, crisp and clear. Below them, stretching as far down as the eye could see, was a deep circular valley of clouds. Canyon walls made of moisture reached up from the bottom, so thick, they looked solid. Suspended motionless in the center, fifteen thousand feet off the surface of the ocean, floated an immense, dark, titan on a halo of blue light. Something so incredible, the mind's ability to comprehend was stilted... a ship of massive proportions. At least two miles long and half a mile wide, it lay in hiding, creating its own camouflage.

The technology that had created this monster was not from Earth, that much was abundantly clear. The largest aircraft carrier on the planet looked like a bathtub toy compared to this behemoth.

Bleary-eyed and drowsy, he tried to absorb and comprehend all he was seeing but found it hard to believe something that size could fly, let alone sit suspended in mid-air. Although the ship was long and generally rectangular in shape, it was by no means smooth or even remotely streamlined. The alien ship looked more like a floating city than anything he would have expected. Staggered rows of low profile domes covered almost a quarter of the top of the hull. Farther forward, past the center, was a large dome, glittering in the sun... glass? He couldn't be sure. The gray-black hull made it difficult to see details clearly... or was it his eyes? He sat back and rubbed his eyes.

The B-25, silent and without power, was no longer flying, but yet still continued to move forward. She floated through the air, drawn to the dark shape from deep space, like a moth to a flame. Jack felt at ease now, calm and relaxed. Organized thought was somewhat difficult, it seemed to come in disjointed segments. He looked to the others and found both Maria and Fritz lumped together, asleep on the floor. Brian, like Jack, was having great difficulty keeping his eyes open. Though he felt some distress at being unable to react, there seemed to be no point in resisting the great waves of warm sleepiness that washed over him, urging him to close his eyes. It had been a long time since he'd visited the Dream People...

CHAPTER SEVEN

US AIRCRAFT CARRIER, SHENANDOAH: BERMUDA TRIANGLE

CIA Director of South American Operations, Stephen Miles, stood on the bridge of the U.S. aircraft carrier, Shenandoah. How he got there was unimportant and to the dismay of the ship's skipper, details of why were classified well beyond Top-Secret. The fact was that Stephen had gotten wind of the drama unfolding and finagled a ride in a U.S. military chopper, from San Juan to the carrier Shenandoah.

Steve Richards was the Skipper of the Shenandoah. A lifer, he'd climbed steadily through the ranks since graduating from the Naval Academy in Annapolis, Maryland and passing through OCS Training in Newport, Rhode Island. Now fifty-five and as protective as a mother hen, he had an affinity for the aviators that flew off of his ship. Today had not been one of his better days, but he could ill afford to demonstrate his foul mood to the distinguished visitors, even if they were from the intelligence community. It wasn't that he hated intelligence people, it's just that his experience illustrated, that in many cases, the terms military and intelligence were highly contradictory. He also observed that this was not isolated to the military only.

"Captain Steve Richards, skipper of this boat." The tall, silver-haired man seemed at ease despite all the activity surrounding them. He extended his hand in greeting, "I hope you don't mind meeting up here, but as you can see, we're quite busy today."

"Yes, thank you for seeing us. I'm Stephen Miles, CIA, Director of South American operations, and this is Special Agent Cummins." Everyone shook hands as proper manners dictated.

"So, what can I do for you gentlemen?" The Captain was eager to get these men on their way, so he could get back to the urgent matters at hand.

Stephen spoke calmly and matter-of-factly. "We understand you have a World War II, B-25 Bomber, under surveillance in this area, is this true?"

Captain Richards raised one eyebrow as this happened to be a bit of a sore subject. "Had..."

"Had? What do you mean *had?*" Stephen snapped.

"Had, as in no longer have," said the Captain with some irritation.

"You mean you *lost* it? What happened to it?" Stephen growled, fighting to keep his composure.

The Skipper of the Shenandoah was both annoyed and suspicious. "If we knew, then it wouldn't be lost, would it? Look Mr. Miles, what's *really* going on here? We get a direct request from the DEA office in Washington for assistance in locating and escorting this aircraft back to Puerto Rico. Something about drugs, gun play, dead police officers... and that's fine, we're happy to help. But now, not only is the B-25 missing, but two of my birds as well. *SO*, exactly what is *your* involvement?" He quickly added... "And I don't want to hear need to know either; unless you gentlemen think you can manage to swim back to wherever it is you came from."

"I'm here because that B-25 is ours."

"Oh *really...*"

"It was on a classified assignment. What happened in San Juan and why, is unclear. It'll take some time before we sort that out. But the aircraft definitely needs to be recovered. Bring me up to speed. What kind of progress have you made?"

Captain Richards led the two CIA men to a plotting table which showed flight and search patterns. "We're here," said the Skipper pointing to an icon on the table.

Using the plotting table, he illustrated the chain of events. "Two F-18's, Blue Flight, had a visual on the B-25 about here. It was on a direct heading with this weather system here..." he said, tapping his fingertips on the table. "The F-18's approached and contacted your plane, staying with it. We were monitoring the bird to bird communications and found the closer to the storm they got, the worse their signals got. I've seen a lot of strange weather out here in my time, but nothing like this."

"What do you mean," asked Stephen, scratching his head.

"It was so dense the radar couldn't see into it. It produced some kind of intense interference. We're thinking EM – *electromagnetic*, though I'm not sure how that's possible. The pilots had serious difficulty communicating, both with each other and with us. By their own admission, there was no rain, no wind and no lightning. Just lots of interference. We tried to recall them, but they got so close to the front... well, we lost all contact. Period. All three aircraft went in, *none* came out. We had a second flight of two birds we vectored to join Blue Flight when they first reported contact. As the second flight approached the intercept point, they lost radar and communication started to break up. We recalled them to a safe distance, as they egressed, their electronics returned to normal..."

"What do we do now?" Stephen rubbed his face with both hands.

Richards pointed to the table. "We've got search and recovery birds out, here, here and here. They're flying overlapping patterns. We've even sent two birds through the front on the same heading. The odd thing is that the interference has stopped and communications are completely normal now."

"They wouldn't have shot it down would they?" Stephen was beginning to get increasingly worried, and the headache gripping his temples wasn't helping.

"No, it's not likely, unless they were fired upon. They would need clearance from me to fire upon a civilian aircraft. Besides, that wouldn't account for *my* two missing birds, and anything going down would've left some kind of debris."

"So what you're saying is that you haven't found *anything* yet?"

"That's right, not a thing."

Stephen was trying to wrap his head around the whole situation, "So what the hell happened to them? They can't just disappear into thin air!"

Richards shrugged. "Well, it's a *big* ocean... technically we're not in it, but we are *near* the edge of the Bermuda Triangle," he said offhandedly. "Lots of unexplained stuff happens out here. I don't have to like it, but it *is* a fact."

Stephen Miles never believed in the mysterious stories and was in no mood for levity. There always had to be a logical answer, even if it wasn't immediately apparent. He sat down on a chair at the Con and rubbed his throbbing temples. "Got any coffee?"

CHAPTER EIGHT

SWEET SUSIE, LOCATION UNKNOWN: *DOWN THE RABBIT HOLE*

Jack Steele opened his eyes with a start and smacked his knees sharply on the control yoke. He was greeted by a totally enveloping darkness and slowly came to realize he was still strapped into the pilot's seat of the Sweet Susie. After unbuckling himself, he rubbed his smarting knees.

Fighting the strange disorientation he felt, his mind slowly began to work, and vague recollections of the F-18s came to him. He struggled to remember more, but could get no further than the memory of the failure of the port engine. Jack slid open the vent window and peered into the darkness. The air smelled unusual, but the quiet distant thrumming interrupted his train of thought. Wanting to see into the inky darkness, he flipped on the landing lights but they only produced a weak glow. "Damn..." he turned them off and turned on the interior cockpit lights which weren't much better.

Whatcha doing?" asked the waking copilot, yawning.

"Trying to figure out where the hell we are... any ideas?"

"Not a clue... Wow it's really dark..."

Jack shook his head, "Thank you, Captain Obvious..."

"What's with the lights?"

Jack toggled first the port then the starboard engine starter with no results. "Batteries must be down."

Fritz stretched, dumping Maria on the floor with a thump.

"Ow! Thanks a lot dog..." she mumbled, rubbing her head.

"Mmmmmmnnphhh!" sneezed Fritz, as he shook his coat into place.

"Well, I think Fritz is right, we ought to get out and take a look around, see what's what." Jack worked his way out of the cockpit and to the rear of the plane. He sat on the floor in the near darkness and opened his flight bag. Brian and Maria moved to the back and sat with him, Brian opening a soda from the cooler.

"OK skipper, what do we do first?"

Jack pulled his stainless 1911 from the bag and ejected the empty magazine into his lap. "Not knowing where we're at, I think it's prudent to go fully prepared..." he said, sliding a full mag from the bag into his gun. "Take a carbine and a couple of mags, load 'em up, don't want to go out empty-handed... in fact, give me one too."

Brian crawled past him and opened a crate, pulling out two of the M1 carbines.

"Hey, don't forget me..." urged Maria.

"Are you sure you..." Brian suddenly recalled who had operated the Sweet Susie's gun turret, "yeah, sure." He pulled out a third carbine and canvas belt pouches for the mags. Maria was already searching the ammo boxes for the proper shells. Finding a box, she dragged it back to where Jack was busy reloading the empty magazines for his 1911.

The copilot slid himself beside Jack and handed one of the M1 carbines to Maria, "Here, this one's yours, take good care of it."

"Thanks," she said with a smile, sliding the container of shells in the middle so everyone could reach.

Jack, sitting cross-legged, remained silent as the trio went about the task at hand. Fritz sat on the pilot's seat in the cockpit, looking out through the open vent window into the darkness, trying to identify the strange smells only his sensitive nose could detect. What really bothered the Shepherd was that he couldn't find anything vaguely familiar about this place. Even the sounds were completely alien to him. He grew more and more unsettled, anxious to explore this curious place.

Steele stood, having traded the shoulder rig for the thumb break thigh holster. He belted it around his waist, which put the butt of the 1911 down on his upper thigh. Securing the holster to his lower thigh with an adjustable strap, he tested the height and draw. Satisfied with the results he snapped the holster strap over the gun.

"You about ready there, Wyatt Earp..?" said Maria with some cynicism.

"Oh, you're a real riot, Alice.." he said in his best Ralph Cramden imitation. "A real riot. Keep it up and *bang, zoom... to da' moon*!"

Fritz barked, he had just about enough of this, he wanted out.

"Chill, you overgrown hamster...!" snapped Brian.

"Are you two ready yet?" asked Jack, almost as impatient as the Shepherd.

Maria and Brian stood, carbines in hand. Jack picked up his M1 and a loaded magazine, sliding it into the rifle and pulling back the bolt, chambering a round. "Do it just like that..." he instructed. Jack briefly instructed them on the use of the sights and safety switch. Maria, he thought, grasped it far better than she should have. The trio picked up their mag pouches and headed to the belly hatch. Fritz danced around the exit until Jack made the dog sit quietly.

Laying the M1 down next to the open hatch Jack descended down the ladder. With one hand and foot still on the ladder, he stepped onto the ground below. *"Aaaarrrrggghhh..!"* The shock of static electricity that arced through his body threw him off the ladder and to the ground, numbing his senses. He lay on the ground, stunned senseless.

Maria descended the ladder, "Are you OK? What happened..?"

Steele was still too numb to speak although he tried to warn her before she touched down.

"Aaaaaiiiieeeee..!" Jack saw the blue flash of the shock as it flung her bodily off the ladder with an electric snap, the light momentarily illuminating the fuselage of the Sweet Suzie.

Brian, fearing a catastrophe and getting no response to his inquiries, jumped straight to the ground from the hatchway, carbine in hand. Fritz followed him down, neither being shocked.

"What the *hell* is going on out here..?" Brian, seeing the two people prone but alive and responsive, confused him. Scratching his head, he turned to rest his M1 against the B-25's ladder.

Jack sat up. "*NO..!*" he was a millisecond too late.

"Yyyyeeeeooooowww..!" It sat Brian three feet away, legs splayed. It was obvious the buildup was dwindling, the copilot had not been shocked as severely as Maria or Jack. Fritz, running in circles, got the surprise of his life when his tail touched the ladder. He spun, barking into the darkness, soliciting giggles from the crew.

Jack went cautiously back to the ladder, with a substantial amount of apprehension he put his hand on the rung... nothing happened. With a sigh of relief, he lifted himself inside to retrieve his carbine. When he dropped back to the ground, his crew was waiting.

"What the hell *was* that?"

Jack shook his head, "Some kind of static charge buildup I guess... he touched the ladder again, "the tires isolated the machine; we made the ground connection..."

"Did you notice this?" said the copilot, pointing at the ground, "it's weird, it doesn't look like concrete to me..."

"It's not..." came a voice from the darkness.

The trio spun in unison, carbines leveled, safeties clicking to the off position. Fritz spun, growling, irritated at being surprised. In normal conditions, he could hear or smell someone long before a threat occurred, but this strange place baffled his sense of smell and sound did not seem to carry very far.

"Whoa, take it easy..." said the bodiless voice.

"Step over here... slowly, where we can see you..." said Jack. The three people from the Sweet Susie stood together under her wing in a crouch, fingers poised over the triggers of their .30 cal carbines.

Two men stepped out of the darkness, their hands raised, dressed in flight suits. Jack recognized the Navy flight suits. Lowering his carbine he snapped the safety back on. Maria and Brian did the same. "Commander Smiley, I presume..." said Steele.

"Fancy meeting you here..." said Smiley, putting his hands down, "say, that was some neat maneuver you pulled out there, ditching us like that..."

"Thanks, timing is everything... didn't get us very far though, did it..." It was more of a rhetorical question. "So are we friends or enemies...?"

"Do we have a choice?"

"Sure. You go your way we go ours," said Jack. "Or we work together. As far as I'm concerned, there's no hard feelings here, and besides, there's safety in numbers..."

"Well... you sure don't *sound* like a murdering drug runner," said Paul.

"Drugs..? Funny..." he snorted. "Have a seat..." Jack said, motioning to the ground. "Let me tell you a little story... you'll laugh, you'll cry, you'll be amazed." After everyone introduced themselves, Steele went on to explain what actually happened - from the very beginning.

The conclusion reached and all questions answered, the five people sat in a semicircle in reflective silence. Brian was the first to speak. "Paul, I think you're right, this doesn't feel like concrete, it's too smooth..."

"Like it's not hard enough..." said Mike Warren.

Strange foggy images filled Jack's mind and he changed the subject, "Do you guys have any idea where we're at?"

"None," said Paul shaking his head, Mike was shaking his head too.

"Do you remember landing?"

"No..." said Pappy, scratching his forehead in dismay. "Y'know, that hadn't even occurred to me... till now... How *did* we make it to this landing strip? We were over water, *lots* of water."

"My point exactly..." said Jack, standing up, "none of us can remember anything either. Our landing gear has been deployed, our batteries are near dead..."

"Ours too," added Paul.

"The last thing I remember," said Mike, "was getting lost in that cloud, no navigation, no electronics of any kind..." he paused, staring off into the darkness, deep in thought. "I remember a flame-out... and as I tried to restart it, I closed my eyes to say a little prayer... when I opened them again... I was here."

"Our planes landed themselves," said Jack without emotion, "how is that possible?"

Mike shrugged. "It's the best I can do for now."

"Anything else?" asked Jack.

"Climbing out of my plane and getting the damn shock of my life!" commented Paul.

"Us too," chimed Maria with a grin. "Knocked us on our butts. Jack thinks it was some kind of static charge buildup."

Paul nodded, "That might explain the whacked-out avionics and dead batteries..."

Jack had random images floating through his mind and was finding it difficult to tell which were real and which were manufactured by his imagination. The pieces were disjointed but began falling into place, the puzzle gradually becoming whole. His recollections flooded forth, all the blanks gradually filling in, the pieces fitting together... it still didn't seem real but he knew it was... He stiffened and his eyes widened, watching it play again in his mind.

Brian was the first to notice, "What the hell man, you look like you've seen a ghost!"

Maria grabbed his arm, "What? Jack, what is it?"

Jack spoke slowly, "Think real hard... does anyone remember what was *in* that cloud?"

They stared blankly into the darkness, struggling to remember, laboring to make sense of the bits and pieces. Time passed slowly, one by one, the expression of enlightenment crept over each one of them. They sat speechless, pie eyed, fighting to comprehend what would normally be passed over as a dream.

"We're inside it," said Jack softly.

"Get outta town..." said Mike, standing up.

"Holy shit..." groaned Brian, "I don't want to believe that... I don't want to," his stomach knotted. "It can't be, we can't be there..." he had to work hard to control his breathing.

"Now wait just a minute..." said Pappy, "I've never *disbelieved* in UFOs but this is a little hard to take... there's *got* to be a reasonable explanation... something logical..."

"Who's to say it *isn't* a reasonable explanation, Commander? Just because it's beyond our realm of knowledge or experience doesn't make it illogical." Jack waved his hand, "Do you think the idea of a man on the moon to an early explorer who thought the Earth was flat, would've thought *that* possible..?"

"I get your point Steele, but I'm just not ready to accept that reality yet." Paul Smiley rose casually to his feet.

"OK, Commander, no sweat. You go with that... lemme know when you're ready."

Steele glanced at Maria, who was wide-eyed but quiet, in fact, she looked like she was in shock. He felt the need to inject some levity,"I think we ought to face the fact, boys and girls, that we're not in Kansas anymore..." Even though it seemed everyone else was struggling with it, he seemed to be getting more *at ease* with it, if you could call it that. There was something vaguely familiar about it all. Deja vu perhaps? He couldn't put his finger on it.

Maria stood up and shot him an icy stare, "Is this all a joke to you? We end up who knows where, with who knows what... or who, and you think it's amusing or something?" The rant was semi-coherent but not by much and it looked like there was more to spill out but she stopped, wild-eyed.

"Frankly," shrugged Jack, "I think it's pretty obvious this is an alien ship. You can say it; c'mon, boys and girls, can you say *aliens*?"

"Stop it!" she said poking the pilot in the chest for punctuation. "I didn't spend four years at Harvard and a year in the Academy to end my career as somebody's guinea pig!"

"Why do you instantly assume you would become someone's pet?" frowned Steele. "For God sakes, you think a superior race with the technology to cross the stars would stop on our planet because there's a shortage of suitable pets closer to home? Don't be ridiculous..." His eyes narrowed, "Wait, *Harvard*? As in, Harvard *University?"* You spent four years at Harvard to be an aircraft mechanic..?"

"Um well..."

"Wait a minute, wait just a freaking minute," said Jack waving his hand, "something's not right here. You studied at Harvard and went to an *academy?* What academy would that be..?"

"I didn't say academy..." she said weakly.

"Yes you did," said the men together.

His suspicions peaked, Steele pressed further. "Tell me about this academy. Tell me about four years at Harvard..." His hands on his hips, he towered over her. "So what's the story here? All of a sudden I don't trust you. Why is that?" He backed her up against the B-25's landing gear. In a flash, a landslide of things came into question.

Maria could see Jack would not likely relent and decided that in their present position, telling him the truth had no bearing on the bigger picture. And it was probably the only way she could get the pilot back under control, but she'd have to do it carefully. "I was born in Puerto Rico and my parents..."

Jack was in no mood for a lifetime special, "We haven't all night here, skip to the Harvard part..."

"I'll get to it in a second," she said, pushing him back. "My family moved to California and that's where I grew up. I was a straight-A student and got a scholarship to Harvard. I studied business and communications..."

"Something every good aviation mechanic needs," commented Jack wryly.

"You want to hear this or not...?" Maria didn't wait for an answer. "In my third year, I was approached by corporate recruiters for a company that needed international experts in communication. I began training with them involving intelligence communication as well as working on my studies at Harvard. At the end of my last year, I ended up in Langley to finish my studies there..."

"Langley, as in the FBI?" asked Paul.

"CIA," she corrected. "I didn't know what I had started in my third year at Harvard," she said, rather matter-of-factly. "Had I known what I was getting into, I wouldn't have..."

"CIA..." repeated Brian, automatically.

"Special Agent Maria Arroyo," she mumbled.

"Well whaddya' know..." grumbled Jack, "a spook." His voice was filled with sarcasm as he ran his fingers through his hair in frustration. "That's just great! I knew there was something strange, but I was hoping... aahhh, forget it," he said with a wave of his hand. "I'm not saying another word." Something clicked into place and his brain switched gears, "Wait, Stephen Miles..?"

Maria nodded, "CIA..."

"Son of a bitch," growled Jack, waving his arms in exasperation. "What did you people drag me into? This was some kind of operation wasn't it?" She nodded and shrugged at the same time. "What kind? And just *how long* did he have this planned?" Suddenly everything he'd done for Stephen in the past came into question as clandestine.

"That I don't know. I was just supposed to check the plane," confessed Maria, "and send you on your way."

"Well you did a wonderful job!" snapped Jack. "So did you arrange for that wonderful little sendoff? Or was that what you people lovingly call a little *snafu?* And last night..! *Oooh, last night...*" he groaned, slapping his forehead. "I suppose that was just part of the assignment eh? Anything for the mission, right? Anything for the cause... keep the dupe happy, keep him in the dark..." It might've been a cheap shot but Jack couldn't help himself.

"No it's not like that, you've got it all wrong..." This is not what Maria expected at all, he was furious and it was spiraling out of control. The fiasco in San Juan was a simple fluke of fate. What really hurt was now he thought her feelings for him had simply been part of the job, when the real truth was, she felt something very special for him. "Jack you've got to believe me, last night was very special..."

Steele cut her off with a wave of his hand. "Oh, save it." If there was anything he couldn't stand more than being taken advantage of, it was being lied to, especially when it involved his personal feelings. "Spare me all the bullshit rhetoric you were taught at the academy... cause I don't want to hear it." He turned to walk away and hesitated. "If it wasn't for you, we'd be on our way to Rio... instead of here, wherever here is..." He moved close putting his finger in her face, "Do yourself a favor lady, unless you want your ticket punched, stay out of my way."

She was crying now, she hated to cry. "If it wasn't for me, you'd be *dead,* remember that!"

Jack bared his teeth in an evil snarl, "If it wasn't for *you people* and your stupid *operation,* I'd be home on my beach or driving my Cobra..." It took a moment for that to register, "Holy fuck, my *Cobra,* that *asshole* has my car in his hangar... son of a *bitch!*"

Pappy stepped in between them, before it could come to blows, "Look y'all, I hate to break up this lover's spat, but there are more important things to deal with here!"

"He's right Jack," added Brian.

"You have a *Cobra*?" Mike Warren's eyes widened, "Those are *sweet*! What year?"

"It's a '66, 427 Shelby," he grumbled. "Hey, whose side are you on?" he asked Paul.

Brain sympathized because he was stuck too, but he knew this was getting them nowhere fast. "Give it a rest Jack, let's move on."

"You got any more of these?" said Paul, taping on Jack's carbine. "Because all Mike and I have are these Beretta 9mms," he said, tapping the gun in his shoulder holster.

Steele sighed, "Uh yeah, sure, c'mon up." He motioned to the open belly hatch and paused to shoot a glance full of daggers at Maria. "Bri, stay here, OK? Keep an eye open." The copilot nodded as Jack, Pappy and Mike climbed into the Sweet Susie.

When the men reappeared, Paul and Mike both had their own M1's and loaded mags.

"OK..." said Pappy grinning, "let's go hunt some green, bug-eyed, scum-sucking, space freaks."

"Ahh, a man after my own heart..." said Jack with a smile, "I think we're gonna get along just fine."

"We're missing something important, aren't we?"asked Mike.

"What's that?" said Brian.

"What if they're friendly? I mean, after all, if they didn't like us we'd probably be dead by now, right?"

"If they're this advanced, this thing might be completely automated," said Paul. "We could be the only ones on it..."

Steele shot Paul Smiley a glance, "You're a believer now?"

Paul shrugged, "Undecided. But I'm keeping my options open."

"And maybe," continued Jack, sardonically teasing Maria, "we're their Sunday dinner..." He grinned an evil grin then turned to the others in a more serious fashion. "In either case, we're not getting any closer to an answer standing around. I don't know about you guys, but I'd like to find a way off this tub." He shot one last hateful glance in Maria's direction, "Because I got a personal score to settle back home."

The group decided on a direction and set out. "Hey, where's Fritz? *FRITZ! COME FRITZ!*" Steele suddenly felt a pang of fear. Fear for the life of his closest friend, suddenly realizing, he hadn't seen the dog for almost twenty minutes. "Shit! *FRITZ!*" The worried pilot picked up his pace.

Brian raced forward, grabbed his friend by the arm. "*Easy* Jack, let's not lose our heads here, we can't afford to rush, he could be anywhere, this looks like a pretty big place."

Jack clicked the M1's safety off, "If any harm comes to him I'll..."

"Hey relax, he probably just can't hear you, besides, he can take pretty good care of himself, we'll find him."

Steele clenched his teeth and relocked the carbine's safety, "Yeah well..."

"C'mon let's keep going," urged Brian.

The group continued on, forging through the semidarkness; Jack and Pappy in front, Mike, Maria and Brian, fanned out behind. The soft, distant thrumming of some alien machinery drew closer as they progressed. Only being able to see about twenty feet or so in the poor light, the group moved slowly, cautiously. Soft, muted sounds, their sources hidden by the darkness, drifted through the still air. They had walked quite a distance, two city blocks by Jack's estimation, and yet had seen absolutely nothing.

Nothing except the cruel visual tricks perpetrated upon them by their imaginations. It was curious, that though it was indeed dark, there was some light. Strangely, it seemed to emanate from the ceiling although the ceiling could not be seen and it only glowed above where they stood, not producing enough light to see any great distance.

It came out of the darkness without warning, whizzing across the floor on rubberized treads. It looked about three feet tall and maybe four feet long, basically cubical, with one small arm and a single photoreceptor on a stalk above its body.

"Look out!"

The group scattered, diving out of its way. The speeding automaton passed through their ranks and off into the darkness, mindlessly pursuing its errand, oblivious to their presence.

"What the *hell* was that?"

"Christ, it almost killed us...! Whatever it was."

Jack was crawling on the floor. "It was an automaton..."

"A what?" said Maria, bending closer to see what he was looking at.

"An automaton... y'know, a robot... hey you guys, look at this," the others crowded around him.

"What is it?" asked Mike, getting closer.

"This line, it glowed green when that thing went by, some kind of guidance line or something," explained Jack. They looked at the line in the floor, which basically, looked like an ordinary seam.

"Hmmm..." said Paul thoughtfully, "maybe we should try to follow it, see where it leads."

"Sounds like a plan to me..." Jack stood up, "except, let's not walk the line, if you get my drift, I have no desire to become a hood ornament for the next one that comes by."

The five explorers gathered themselves up, turned and followed the line, heading in the direction the automaton had appeared from. They walked as before, only now, had a direction to follow. From time to time, Steele would call for his missing partner, hoping to find him frolicking irresponsibly like he was known to do. They came to a cross junction of guide lines and stopped to discuss the best route.

Maria heard it first, "*Ssshhh!* I hear something...!" It was coming from behind them, much slower than before. "It's coming back again."

"Shit, let's hitch a ride," commented Mike, "beats walking."

"I don't think it was large enough..."

"This one is! Look!" Pappy pointed to the barely visible form approaching in the darkness. As it approached, it became clear, the unit that had passed them earlier had been sent to retrieve a load. It pushed in front of it a large platform laden with containers of various shapes and sizes. The platform, having no wheels or tracks, was not touching the floor, a blue glow reflecting off the surface underneath. The unit stopped at the group and waited.

"Jack! Look at that, it's not touching the floor!"

Jack dropped to one knee and looked underneath. "Bri's right! Whoa, that's cool... OK," he waved, "let's not look a gift horse in the mouth, everyone jump on." A pang of excitement rolled in his stomach. He was in awe of the technology.

"I hope it can hold us all," remarked Maria as she jumped on.

"If it doesn't, you can get off and wait for us here."

"Funny, Steele, real funny."

The platform dipped under the increased load as each person boarded, but the deft hand of the automaton, quickly compensated for the weight, on the platform's keyboard.

Brian spoke in hushed tones. "Wow, did you see that?"

"Must be some kind of... I don't know... antigravity device..?" Jack wondered, aloud.

Maria snorted. "Somebody's been watching too many Sci-Fi movies..."

"And yet here we are..." remarked Jack, shooting her the evil-eye. "You got a better explanation... Miss; *I Know Everything cause I'm a Harvard graduate?"*

"Well no, but..."

"Hey, do you think he knows we're here?" interrupted Mike.

"I don't know, ask him." said Jack flippantly, not wanting to be interrupted while he was poking fun at Maria.

"OK..." Mike Warren proceeded to address the automaton controlling the platform and was startled, along with everyone else to receive an answer. It spoke in a low voice, remarkably clear and human, but in a tongue foreign to the group. Its photoreceptor glowed brightly in the dark and glanced at each person in turn; leaving no one out, as it conversed, using its single hand for expressive gestures. After a time it fell silent but remained animated, watching the riders and making an occasional short observation.

Robot, platform, riders and cargo, glided smoothly and quietly through the seemingly endless darkness, the only constant noise being the rubberized tracks of the robot rolling against the floor. It was probably a good thing that the containers on which everyone sat were sealed, otherwise their overwhelming curiosity would have forced them to become impolitely nosy.

They all seemed to notice, that wherever it was they were headed, it was getting lighter. Ahead could be seen giant columns and Jack wished the automaton spoke an intelligible language so they could find out where they were headed and if Fritz had been seen. Curiously, the unfamiliar surroundings, however alien, seemed too unreal - like a Hollywood movie set, to provoke any real feelings of fear.

As they neared the columns, it became evident that they weren't really columns after all, but towering stacks of bins and containers. Their mechanical escort spoke, pointing at the aisles as if to explain their significance, oblivious to the fact that his riders hadn't the foggiest idea what he was saying.

Brian whispered to Jack, "What is this thing, a reject from the tour guide factory?"

Jack shushed his copilot. "We don't understand him, but he might understand us. So let's not upset him, shall we?"

Nearing the entrance to the aisles, the robot slowed its platform to better navigate the narrow aisle clearance. It spoke to its riders, waving its arm expressively, which they finally understood to mean; all arms and legs inside. When they complied with this request, the satisfied automaton resumed its previous speed, slowing only at aisle intersections to check for traffic. The light was better here, and they could see the racks of containers, towering to the ceiling far above them. In the limited light, the aisles stretched almost as far as the eye could see, a truly impressive sight. Twice while passing an intersection, they caught a glimpse of other machines, down other aisles, going about their duties.

Coming to another junction, the machine slowed, then turned right down a larger aisle, promptly spilling Maria and Mike Warren onto the floor. Motors whirring to a stop, the machine voiced an apology and waved the lost riders back aboard the platform. Picking their carbines up off the floor, Mike and Maria scrambled back aboard the transport.

Squeaking its rubber treads on the floor, the mechanized driver resumed its task, accelerating smoothly to a speed faster than before, presumably to make up for lost time. In less than a minute, a large octagonal door loomed ahead. The automaton slowed the transport platform to a stop just short of the door. Next to them stood a control pod on a pedestal.

"What now," whispered Paul.

Jack shrugged, "Stay put, can't really do anything else, besides he's done alright for us so far."

The robot reached out with its arm and fingered the keyboard on the control pod. With a loud hiss, the massive door split down the middle and slid open. A whoosh of sweet, fresh air, flooded through to greet them, soliciting oohs and aahs from the riders.

Passing slowly through the doorway, the transport and its riders entered a softly, but well-lit corridor.

Mike Warren leaned forward, "Did you see those doors?" he said in a hushed voice.

Jack adjusted the carbine resting in his lap, "Yeah they're pretty thick, probably like a fire door or something."

Pappy rubbed his forehead, "Fire door? Man, I've seen smaller blast doors in missile silos."

The smooth hallway floor was thoroughly streaked with rubber marks from the caterpillar treads of assorted automatons.

"Think this is a service corridor?"

Jack shook his head, "I don't know, Bri, the whole thing could look like this. We haven't seen anything but robots so far and not even many of them."

"I don't know if I *want* to see anything else," said Maria reverently.

The big door swished closed behind the group. A corridor stretched out on either side of them, but the automaton moved the transport platform straight across into a short hallway with another octagon at the end. This door hissed open automatically. The robot entered without hesitation and the door hissed shut behind them, enclosing them in a room barely large enough to fit the machine and its load. Jack had fully expected the door in front of them to open as well, but since it hadn't, they were trapped.

The room was so small, there was no room to even get off the platform. "I don't have a good feeling about this..." said Brian, his voice uneasy.

Jack didn't like it either, but wasn't about to show his concern. So sarcasm seemed the best answer. "And here we have the voice of the eternal optimist," he said with a wave of his hand.

"Oh that's just great, Jack," said Maria in a snit, "they have us in a potential trap and you're making jokes."

"And now we have the calm voice of reason," remarked Steele. "Just who might *they* be..? *Aliens,*" he whispered.

"*Oooohhhh!*" she growled, her fists clenched. Jack glowered at her, taking some satisfaction in her discomfort. *"STOP IT"* she snapped, "you're driving me *crazy!*"

Pappy had more than he could take, "Both of you stop, or I'll shoot the two of you! Christ, don't you ever give it a rest? You two are worse than a couple of children! What the hell is wrong with you?"

"She started it," joked Steele.

Paul Smiley inhaled deeply and adjusted his composure before continuing. "Now, while you two were practicing your attempts at verbal homicide, you probably failed to notice we are actually on an elevator... going up I believe." He glanced at Brian who confirmed this with a nod. "So let's show some decorum, shall we? I don't want to be standing next to two raving lunatics if perchance, someone happens to greet us at the door."

They sat quietly, if not a bit on edge, waiting for the lift to reach its destination. Progress was slow, presumably because it was a freight elevator and not built for speed. When the lift hummed to a stop at its appointed level, the five riders were united and ready to meet whatever fate had dealt them. Prepared for the worst, they crouched along the walls, facing the door at the front of the elevator, weapons ready for whoever might be on the other side. After a short pause that seemed extensive, the door hissed open automatically to reveal an empty corridor, the group released a collective sigh of relief.

Shooing the people off its transport platform with a lone hand, their mechanical tour guide pointed the way down the corridor, explaining the desired route, and that he needed to leave them to complete his delivery. Neither Jack nor his companions understood more than the fact that they were now on their own.

Standing in the empty corridor, they said goodbye to the helpful automaton, who gave a hearty wave before the door whooshed shut, leaving them feeling lost and alone.

This part of the ship looked much different, the corridors, thickly carpeted, looked warm and livable. Where walls met ceiling and floor, the surfaces curved rather than meeting at right angles. There were no sharp corners at intersecting corridors, walls were heavily padded and they curved around. All doorways were still octagonal, but, were inset almost two feet and luxuriously padded. Colors were in pleasant shades of blue-gray and charcoal. Lighting was good but soft and easy on the eyes.

"Well, this sure looks like it's set up for some kind of habitation, what do you think?" said Pappy shouldering his carbine casually.

"Yep... and five-star accommodations by the looks of it," commented Jack, brushing his hair back one-handed. "Think it could be... maybe, a pleasure liner or something?"

"I never thought I'd say this, but at this point, I wouldn't doubt anything," said Pappy shaking his head.

Brian shrugged, "I stopped thinking an hour ago, I was getting a headache."

They looked at Warren who threw up his free hand, "I'm just along for the ride," he said, smiling weakly. He hugged the carbine with crossed arms, "So, now what?"

"Voices!" whispered Maria.

"We hide!" whispered Steele motioning around the corner.

They waited until the voices disappeared before peeking down the intersecting corridor; it was empty. "We'd better start moving, we're not accomplishing anything this way."

"Exactly what *are* we trying to accomplish, Jack?"

"Well Ms. Arroyo, when I figure it out, I'll let you know. Let's go."

The small group filed down the corridor, in the direction given them by the automaton. Hugging the walls, the explorers would shrink into doorways for cover whenever they heard voices near intersections. They had covered quite a distance, and so far their luck was holding out. They seemed to be on a level primarily made up of sleeping quarters and suites, but that was just a guess. The traffic the companions encountered was fairly light. They were all dying for a peek to see just exactly who or what was roaming the halls, but their need for secrecy was paramount and they dared not risk revealing themselves.

"OK, it's clear, let's go."

The group exited the doorway in single file and raced across the intersecting walkway. Passing several more doorways, they came upon a rather wide but short corridor, richly appointed and decorated. Jack and Pappy ventured a quick look and found a huge door at the end, similar in size to the very first door they had passed through with the robot. The exception was, this one was lavished with intricate designs, gilded in what looked to be gold. They stood wide-eyed, staring at the extravagant show of wealth and design which seemed so inconsistent with what they had observed so far. Momentarily forgetting themselves, Mike, Brian and Maria, also crowded around to gawk at the intricate gold inlay.

The door split down the middle and swooshed open without warning, catching the five gawkers off-guard. They stumbled and fell trying to clear the corner before being seen. "C'mon, c'mon, move it." Steele growled, dragging Maria by the arm and trying not to fall on her.

Loud, intense, rhythmic music, poured through the open doorway, flooding the corridor. Revelers streamed into the hallway, singing and dancing, presumably returning to their rooms, drinks in hand. Their voices preceded them as their mass dispersed and filtered down different corridors, laughing and talking.

"Casino?" asked Pappy in hushed tones, as the five explorers huddled in the recessed doorway.

"Could be. Sounds like a nightclub to me," whispered Jack. It was then he realized several partiers were headed down their corridor. "Shit, shit, shit!"

"What do we do now, genius?" hissed Maria.

Five people tried to force themselves into a corner of the entryway and become invisible, Brian played with the entry's keypad, "Maybe we can get in..." He had always been good with gadgets. "Be patient."

"Patient..? *Patient..?* Are you *nuts..?* they're right on top of us, hurry the hell up!" Maria hissed again.

"Don't rush me..." said Brian coolly, "these things take time." He'd removed the cover and was pursuing a trial and error/educated guess method, of finding the right circuit to open the door.

The alien partiers were so close Jack could swear he smelled the air of alcohol, he switched off the safety on the carbine, not sure whether he would use it or not... "Anytime *now* would be nice Bri..."

"*Wwooooaaaaahhhhh..!*"

Jack, Pappy, Mike, Brian and Maria tumbled simultaneously backwards through the door as it slid open. Sliding closed automatically, it left them laying on top of one another in a semi-darkened room.

"So, how's that for timing?" asked Brian, grinning to himself in the darkness.

"Just fine..." Maria gasped, "now would you mind getting off of me?"

"Sorry."

"I hope this isn't their room..." said Jack, listening at the door on his hands and knees, " Hmmm... well, I guess we're OK for now." Sitting with his back against the door, Jack stretched his legs to relax.

"Were you really gonna' use that thing?" asked Maria, pointing to the M1 in Steele's lap.

"I don't know..." said Jack winking at Paul Smiley, "it depends on how bug-eyed ugly and slimy they were." The two men laughed, primarily to irritate Maria. She sat quietly, sulking.

"We could use some light," said Mike, standing. The room grew perceptibly lighter as he said it. "Wow, did you see that?" They verbally played with the lights, exploring their new discovery. The room was fairly sizable and well laid out. It had all the standard features one might expect of a fine hotel suite on earth, except the architecture was completely foreign in style. Every surface was either padded or curved, and no corners existed anywhere. Coupled with the *shades of gray* color scheme and no windows, the occupant got the feeling of inhabiting a plush cave. All in all, the effect was very pleasing and comfortable.

"Paul, you ready to do some exploring?"

"Sure Jack, what do you have in mind?"

"Well, maybe Brian can get the door to function on command..." Brian nodded, "and we can come and go at will. Y'know, scope things out."

"You want to look for your dog."

"Yeah well, it did cross my mind, but I figure food is important and maybe we can figure out if the natives are friendly or not. In any case, it would be easiest in singles or pairs, because keeping five people from being seen is just too much."

"It would also give some of us a chance to rest while others are out..." explained Maria.

"Right, so it's settled then, Paul and I are going out for a bit, Bri'll rig the door console and you three can catch some shut-eye."

Jack and Pappy decided to leave the carbines behind, feeling they might be a burden to stealth or a hasty retreat if needed. Jack hoped this would not prove to be a mistake.

Brian removed the door's control pad from the interior wall, "Hold on, I'll have this open in a jiffy..." He worked with the circuitry, "Ahh, here's the little rascal..." the door swished open.

The two security operations officers, standing on the other side of the door, were as surprised as the five people standing inside the suite to actually be face to face with someone. Jack moved out of reflex and instinct rather than conscious thought. Feinting to the right and dropping into a combat stance, Steele had drawn the 1911 before the two security people could comprehend the action.

Pappy had no room to move in the doorway and so remained motionless, but Mike Warren had managed to bring the muzzle of his carbine to bear, past his Flight Leader's shoulder. He clicked off the safety and watched one of the ship's security officers shift her eyes to his.

The officers were holding their own weapons but made no attempt to bring them up to action, which was the single reason they remained alive. Jack had thumbed off the safety on the 1911 as he drew and his icy stare told the security officer any hasty movement would mean her death.

Time seemed to be frozen, and for a while, no one moved or spoke.

This gave everyone a moment to take a breath and absorb what they were seeing. The two security ops officers, had seen humans before and knew them to be, what they were; kind and compassionate, but cunning... and fiercely dangerous if challenged. Jack and his group, however, had never seen an outworlder and no amount of Sci-Fi movie-going could have prepared them for this stranger than fiction reality.

Raulya and her companion Myomerr, also a female, were members of a bipedal feline race, from a world known as Ketarus III. Raulya, standing in front of Jack, was an inch short of six feet tall... and the taller of the two Ketarians. Other than their tails and ears, Raulya and Myomerr were very human-like in physical shape, especially since they no longer had full body fur like their ancestors.

Raulya had a thick, golden mane of hair sweeping across her shoulders and down her back. Wild curls hung in her face and fell across her furless chest. Soft wisps of gold and chocolate striped fur stretched from her mane and dissipated at her cheekbones. Her yellow-green eyes gazed back at Jack intently while her little black nose twitched with curiosity. Raulya's tongue darted out to lick her dry lips, lips as human as Jack had ever kissed. Myomerr's mane and sparse fur were charcoal gray with black stripes, her eyes a shiny platinum color. Both Myomerr and Raulya wore a smart light gray uniform made of a clingy material which showed off their sleek, muscular bodies.

No one had moved for nearly half a minute, which can seem like an eternity when standing on the brink of death. Raulya could tell Jack's eyes were no longer seeing her as a target but seeing her as a living, breathing, feeling being. She would not foolishly take this as a weakness but rather a strength of character.

The Ketarian slowly lowered her hand weapon, a small disruptor pistol, and let it drop to the floor. Myomerr, who had been watching out of the corner of her eye, did likewise, with reluctance, but trusted her partner's judgment. They were both relieved to see Jack's finger move away from the trigger of his firearm.

Raulya took a deep breath and then spoke. Steele found the sound of her voice pleasing but, of course, didn't understand the tongue, as was the same with his companions. Raulya watched the humans exchange odd glances and realized they must not be wearing any type of translator.

"Myomerr, do you have an extra disc with you?"

"Yes Raulya, I think so."

"Take it out and give it to me please, but do it very slowly, the weapons they're holding are primitive by our technology but..."

"Yes, I understand," said Myomerr, interrupting. She searched a pouch on her belt and produced a small plastic bag, handing it to Raulya.

"Be very still," she explained to Myomerr, "he must trust me, understand?" Myomerr nodded.

Jack had relaxed his stance but the gun remained fixed on the tall Ketarian, watching her every move.

Raulya dumped the small disc out of the plastic bag into the palm of her hand and held it out for him to see. It was extremely thin and about as big around, as a watch battery. She pointed to the disc, then to her ear, then to his ear. Jack nodded his understanding.

"Be careful, Jack," said Maria, "I don't trust her."

"Relax." Jack knew if anyone was compelled to say anything at that point, it would, of course, have to be Maria.

Raulya moved closer, slowly. She found the Earth man strangely attractive and as she got closer, his scent filled her nose, heightening her feelings. She stared into his eyes, eyes so deep and dark it gave her a chill. Raulya noticed the man had begun to lower his weapon, she took gentle hold of his hand and guided the muzzle of the gun between her breasts, holding it there firmly. She wanted to make him understand, she was to be trusted.

OK, Jack thought, *now what?* In an answer to his unspoken question, Raulya took his face in her hands and turned it gently to the left. Jack could feel her soft, warm breath on his neck and unconsciously closed his eyes.

When she licked behind his right ear, he shivered. Holding his face firmly but without causing discomfort, she pressed the disc against Jack's wet skin. There was a momentary pinch that was forgotten as soon as she spoke softly in his ear, "Can you understand me now?" He stiffened and his eyes grew wide with amazement. "Good, now put your finger on it. That one is not permanent, but it will do for now."

"*Wow...*" he breathed.

"It's a translator disc, you'll all get one. Might we all step into the room? We don't want to alarm any of our guests."

Jack holstered the stainless 1911 and ushered his group into the room, explaining to the rest of the group what had transpired.

Everyone went about introducing themselves. "I don't mean to be rude," said Myomerr, "but this would all be much easier if we got you each a translator, besides, we need to report to the bridge."

"She's right," said Raulya.

Jack, Pappy, Raulya, Mike, Brian and Myomerr walked in a tight group with Maria trailing behind, sulking because she was no longer the sole female. Allowed to keep their side arms, the carbines remained in the suite.

"She doesn't like us, does she?" said Myomerr, motioning towards Maria.

"Let's just say, she prefers to be the center of attention," said Steele with a sly grin.

"She regards you as hers..." said Raulya, more a statement than a question, "she has marked you with her scent."

"Guess I'll have to wash that off..." said Jack raising an eyebrow.

"She clings to the tradition of one mate. You do not...?" Raulya seemed truly confused over human mating practices.

"Let's just say, I choose to remain a free agent."

"Mmmm... good, I will remember that."

The group walked from one interconnecting corridor to the next, until they reached the air tunnel system. It was sort of a subway system, stretching the length of the ship, in the center corridor on every other, of its nine levels. The narrow cars were torpedo shaped and ran in a deep channel suspended on and propelled by a cushion of air. The cars sat two people abreast, five rows to a car. There were two lanes, one traveling to the bow and one to the stern of the ship.

They waited no more than a minute for a bow-bound tunnel car. It hissed to a stop in front of them, summoned by Myomerr on a wall panel in the corridor. They climbed down into the car and after Raulya punched in its destination, it sped away.

Halfway to the bow, the walls and floor disappeared around them. Only the air tunnel tube supported them, the effect quite breathtaking to say the least. Two levels directly above them, another air tunnel tube could be seen. To the left and right stretched about a quarter-mile of open air, surrounded by a glass dome of almost incomprehensible size. Even with the Ecosphere's lights turned down, strange, exotic birds could be seen, flying through the treetops below them. Myomerr pointed out the nine levels of rooms and suites bordering the Ecosphere, as the most expensive on the ship.

Jack looked up through the Ecosphere's dome and saw the endless stars stretching out around them, a chill racing up his back and a pang of excitement gripped his stomach like he had never known before. He took a deep breath and swallowed hard to control the immense thrill welling up inside, "Oh God..." he whispered. Now he understood what the astronauts felt.

The only one who heard him was Raulya, sitting next to him. "I felt the same way my first time..." she said squeezing his hand, "it's spectacular, isn't it?" It was all he could do to nod.

Half a minute after passing out of the sphere and back into the corridor, the air car hissed to a stop near the crew's elevator at the bow of the ship. Trading the air car for the elevator, they rode to the bridge, the only place on the ship with a tenth level.

Pausing in the outer briefing room, Raulya instructed Myomerr to stay with the others while she entered the bridge with Jack. Jack translated to the group before leaving.

Mike Warren looked to his frowning wing leader, You worried, Pappy?"

"No kid, just tired." Paul rubbed his face, stopping in time to catch Myomerr staring at him. She quickly looked away.

"I think she likes you, Pappy," whispered the young pilot.

"It's not polite to whisper kid, besides, she probably hears better than we do." He thought he caught her smiling but couldn't be sure.

Raulya and Jack entered the bridge, the Captain turned to greet them. He appeared almost human with his wizened, lined face, full but trimmed white beard and grandfatherly paunch. What gave him away was probably his webbed fingers and sparkling, sapphire blue eyes.

"Aaah, Raulya, you've brought one of our stowaways..." he gurgled at his personal little joke and extended his hand in greeting, "hello, welcome aboard the *Princess Hedonist.*"

Jack switched hands to hold the translator disc before shaking hands, "Jack Steele..." he shook hands, "thank you."

The Captain pointed at Jack, "You hurt, boy?"

"Oh. No, sir, it's this disc..."

"Raulya! Shame on you! Take these people to the infirmary and get them some regular discs, then feed them and find them some quarters..." He turned to Jack, "I apologize, we don't get many visitors like this. It's late, we'll talk in the morning. Raulya, we shall all meet at the Ecosphere Lounge, on two, for brunch... goodnight Mr. Steele."

"Goodnight, sir."

The group of seven, returned to the air tunnel system via the elevator and took it aft, toward the stern of the ship, to the only infirmary open at this late hour, the one on level nine.

Translator discs were inserted just under the skin, behind the right ear. The medibot did an admirable job, accomplishing the task with no pain and very little discomfort. The only one to put up any fuss, was of course, Maria, complaining about mind control. The others ribbed her about her CIA gibberish and she finally gave in, letting the medibot install the device.

Raulya checked the security log on the ship's computer for any clues to Fritz's whereabouts while Jack and the others were in the infirmary. She also checked the number of accommodations available, finding an ample number of open suites. She returned to the infirmary as Myomerr was leaving with the group.

The two Ketarians stood aside from the others and spoke privately while waiting for the elevator. "So, you want him then?"

Myomerr nodded "I think he's yummy." She looked over at Paul Smiley who was talking with Jack.

"Elevator's here," called Brian.

More tired than hungry, everyone decided to go straight to bed and eat in the morning. On the lift, they decided to split into two groups, Myomerr would show Brian, Mike and Pappy their rooms and Raulya took Maria and Jack. Saying their goodnights, they parted. "That suite you found yourselves in earlier, will be yours," Raulya told Maria, "Jack's is on a different floor." Maria nodded, but she was not keen on the idea of splitting up the group. If she could have had her way, they would all have shared a room.

The elevator stopped at the third level. "Jack, would you mind waiting and holding the elevator? I'll be right back." He shrugged, watching Maria and Raulya disappear down the corridor. The key panel on the room they had broken into, had been replaced and Raulya punched in the entry code. The door swished open. "Goodnight, Maria."

Maria stepped into the doorway. "Yeah..." she cleared her throat, "listen, I saw the way you looked at him earlier, but don't get any ideas, Miss Kitty, because Jack is mine!"

Raulya remained calm, "Oh really? Well, Jack doesn't see it that way..."
"What?!"

Smiling wryly, Raulya gently nudged the stunned Maria back through the doorway, "So, tonight he's mine!" The door swished closed and Raulya entered a security code, locking Maria inside. She could hear Maria screaming profanities and pounding on the door.

Smiling to herself, Raulya returned to the elevator. "Ready?"

"Just waiting for you... where to now?"

"Level nine," she pushed the button.

"I thought those were the crew's quarters?"

"It is. Oh, by the way..." she said, strategically changing the subject, "I've located your animal..."

"Wow, that's *great*! Can we go get him? Is he OK? Where is he?" The elevator door opened and they stepped out on level nine.

"Slow down... he's fine. He's with a crew member and we will get him in the morning, it's too late now, so let's just go to bed."

Steele nodded, he felt better now, like a great weight had been lifted from him. But something she said triggered a thought. "Um, when you said *let's* go to bed, did you mean; let us go to *our* beds, *plural*, or, let us go to *a* bed, *singular*?"

Raulya stopped in mid-stride and turned to him, backing him up against the padded corridor wall. "Do you mean to tell me..." she began seductively, "after all I've done for you, you'd begrudge me some show of gratitude?!"

"I guess a handshake wouldn't do it?"

"I don't think so..." she smiled demurely, her feline fangs showing.

Steele cleared his throat nervously, "Well, what have you got in mind?"

She pressed herself against him, pinning him to the wall and covered his mouth with hers. She kissed him long and hard, grinding her body against his. Finally she released him.

"Whaa..." he blinked hard and inhaled deeply.

"So?!" She stood with her hands on her hips.

"Well I, you, that is, we, I mean I..."

She smiled crookedly, "You mean to tell me, you haven't even *thought* about it?!"

"Well yeah, I mean no, not exactly, but I..."

She pinned him again, this time even longer. While she licked his lips, she asked him again, breathing gently on his face, *"Sssooo?"*

He nodded. His brain felt like jello.

"Good. I knew you'd see it my way." Taking him by the hand, she turned sharply and headed for her quarters. Jack wondered if he was the entertainment... or the main course.

■ ■ ■

Raulya stood in the bathroom, facing the mirror, "Come, take your shower, we don't want to be late to brunch."

Steele opened his eyes in the darkened room and, inhaling deeply, filled his lungs with a sweet, heady perfume, forcing recollections into his foggy mind. He stretched achy arms and legs, casually wondering what was in the incense Raulya burned or the perfume she wore. It seemed to have a very strange physiological effect on him. Hell, *she* had quite an effect on him. He thought that erotic dance she performed for him last night would drive him insane. But no, she had other plans, she wanted to give him a heart attack through sexual exertion. He was glad he stayed fit.

91

Jack sat on the edge of the bed, rubbing the sleep from his eyes, "Sure, I'll be there in a second," he yawned. He looked up and eyed her profile, a silhouette in the light of the bathroom. Christ, what a figure, he thought. He stood and stretched, watching the silhouette primp and apply makeup. "Hmph, women and make-up. Good to see there are some constants," he muttered to himself.

"Did you say something, my sweet?"

Jack cleared his throat and made a mental note about her exceptional hearing, "Ahem, um no, just talking to myself," he said, as he padded past her to the shower.

Smiling, Raulya leaned back as he passed and pinched his bare butt, "Just don't do it in public or you may find yourself in a rubber room somewhere..."

Or another night or two like last night might do it, thought Jack.

Steele stepped out of the shower feeling refreshed and sharply awake. Raulya called him into the other room as he toweled his hair dry. "I had some clean clothes sent up from the commissary for you, I hope you'll like them... boots too."

"What's wrong with my boots?"

"Oh, nothing, it's just that these are meant for the outfit."

Jack held up the pants, "These will never fit, they're much too small."

"They stretch, try them on before you decide."

Jack sat on the bed and dressed. The pants were dark blue, a heavy material like denim, but they stretched remarkably well and fit to every curve of his muscular legs. The boots were black leather and highly polished. They snugged over his pant legs and ended just below his knees. The shirt was a blue-gray, double-breasted button down, with embossed brass buttons. The material was weighty like a dense cotton, but much smoother, almost like satin. It reminded Jack of the shirts worn by Union Cavalry soldiers in the late 1800s. He remembered John Wayne wearing shirts like this.

Looking in the mirror, Jack unbuttoned three buttons on one side and let the flap fold down, smoothing it with his hand. "Hmmm... something's missing... ah!" He went to the bedside and picked up the 1911 and holster, belted it on and returned to the mirror. Strapping the holster to his leg he stood and scrutinized himself in the mirror. The black belt crossed his waist at an angle, holding the holster perfectly at hand height for his right hand.

He turned to Raulya and smiled, "I think you've found me a totally new look."

"Then you like it?! Oh, I'm so glad I think you look absolutely dashing! I got the idea from the Ketarian Royal Air Force, their uniform is similar, only theirs is red with gold braid. Frankly, I thought blue and gray would suit you better."

"Good choice," he snorted, "I'm not a red kinda guy."

"Anyway," she said, "I thought a pilot should look like a pilot. Pilots are greatly respected, no matter where they're from."

"Well yeah I'm a pilot, but I'm a little outta' my element. Not much to fly out here..."

"You'd be surprised," she interrupted, stepping forward. Raulya pinned his flight wings neatly on his new tunic, kissing him on the lips. "There, perfect! Now, let's go we're late!"

CHAPTER NINE

PRINCESS HEDONIST: TOROMEDE SYSTEM

The air car hissed to a stop, just short of entering the Ecosphere. Jack and Raulya stepped out and onto the second level platform. The car sped away and disappeared through the trees and foliage rising from the floor of the forest, one level below. Hand in hand, Jack and Raulya strolled down the short carpeted ramp from the platform to the famous Ecosphere Lounge.

"Well, if it isn't the lost expedition..." Of course, Maria would be the first to open her mouth, thought Jack. He didn't dignify it with a reply. Instead, he greeted everyone at the table, except her, and shook the Captain's hand.

"You look well this morning, Mr. Steele..."

"Thank you Captain. Please, call me Jack if you like."

"Fine, then I must insist we dispense with all these formalities, you must call me Gant, it is short for Gantarro. Now, please, sit, eat, the food here is wonderful."

The table was at the edge of the balcony, overlooking the floor of the Ecosphere. Below them sprawled a small grassy meadow surrounded by trees and dense foliage. Obvious footpaths left the meadow and disappeared into the forest. The sound of a small waterfall could be heard, and the voices of birds of all types abounded. "Quite a sanctuary, is it not?"

Jack swiveled in his seat to face Gant, "Yes, it's beautiful, but how does it survive without sunlight?"

"Mmmm..." Gant paused between bites, "synthetic sunlight, it's quite easy to duplicate." Jack nodded, he knew of grow lights, they were common on Earth, but he never imagined it could be accomplished on this magnitude. "Oh, by the way..." Gant continued, "your friend Fritz is down there somewhere. Playing hide and seek with one of my crew members I suspect. They'll be up when they get a whiff of all this food."

Jack surveyed the various foods on the table that despite their unfamiliar appearance, smelled delicious. His grumbling stomach reminded him to do more than just look and smell. Conversations swirled around the table as they ate, and it was quickly noticed that although the colors varied somewhat, Jack, Brian, Paul and Mike Warren all had the same tailor. It was unanimously decided that not only did they look outstanding, but the clothes were extremely comfortable as well.

"It looks like we've got some kinda' squadron image developing here..." said Mike.

"Some squadron..." snorted Pappy. "Four pilots and nothing even remotely familiar to fly..."

"Oh, I wouldn't say that," interrupted Gant, "I've been thinking, this ship has three shuttles... and only one shuttle pilot. If you would be interested, the simulator could teach you how to fly shuttles, and it's not really all that different from your kind of flying... besides, it would compensate for your food and quarters."

"You mean like a job?" queried Brian.

"You could call it that," said Gantarro, smiling, "but unless we're at a scheduled planet tour-stop, there isn't much to do besides relax and enjoy our hospitality until we hit port. Pretty easy actually."

"Well, we weren't really planning on staying," commented Jack. "We appreciate the offer and at any other time, believe me, I'd take you up on it..." he glanced at Maria and back at Gant, "but we have unfinished business at home. So if you'd just drop us off..."

"Where?" Asked Gant.

"Where we came from, of course," answered Jack.

Gant shook his head, "Impossible."

"What...? Why?"

"Because that was almost a week ago, Jack. We're almost two systems away from Earth already. To return, you would delay our cruise schedule two more weeks, and we're behind as it is..."

"But we just got here yesterday!" protested Jack.

Gant shook his head again. "Five days ago. We didn't know you were here till yesterday when we noticed an overage on our weight. Our guidance system for our shuttles must have drawn in your aircraft before we departed."

"You mean we slept for four days?" asked Paul.

"It appears so," answered Gant.

Jack cleared his throat. "Just how long will it be, before we can return home then?"

Gant rubbed his chin, calculating the equivalent earth time. "Well, considering the cruise line doesn't always run voyages along duplicate routes... and including our return time... hmmm, anywhere from about twelve months to maybe, oh, say four years."

"You're kidding," said Brian, deadpan.

"No," said Gant, sipping his tea.

"Geez... isn't there a faster way?" asked Jack.

"Yeah," added Paul, "I figured maybe a month or so, but one to four years? That's nuts!"

"Look," said Gant, "pilots are hard to come by out here, they make exceptional money, get a tremendous amount of respect, travel whenever and wherever they please and generally lead privileged lives."

"You make it sound so rosy," quipped Pappy.

"I may be exaggerating, but not by much. Besides, I thought Humans were the pioneer type, ready for a challenge, fearless and all that..."

"Well, we are..." said Jack, "but usually by choice."

"Don't be so picky, my friend, an opportunity is an opportunity, no matter what form it comes in. Recognize it for what it is and take advantage of it."

"No offense, Captain, but I guess it doesn't seem like we have much choice, does it?" remarked Jack. "We're pretty much in it for the duration... whatever that happens to be."

"If you're in, I'm in," said Paul, "like you say, it's going to be a while..."

The others concurred. "Sounds like an adventure to me!" said Mike with a grin. Brian glowered at him; he was going to miss at least one whole football season, and a Superbowl to boot.

Gant smiled. "Good, it's settled then, we'll find quarters for each of you. On level three, of course, that's the same as the flight deck. Oh, I just thought of something! Your air ships are probably worth a great deal to a collector, I'll see if I can dig up a reliable dealer for you before we get back to port. That alone could set you all up quite well!"

The four pilots agreed things could be worse and decided to make the best of the situation, after all, this was going to be home for a while. After some thought and contemplation, Steele was beginning to like the idea of selling Stephen's B-25 out from under him and living well off the cash proceeds... It seemed like more than a fair trade for the Shelby Cobra he left sitting in that bastard's hangar. There was a feeling of ironic justice to that.

Notified by a crew member he was needed on the bridge, Gantarro excused himself and departed, leaving the pilots to finish their breakfast and discussion. Fritz, looking freshly groomed, trotted up, tail wagging, tongue lolling, and promptly began to beg for food. Jack frowning, feigned anger,

"Where have you been, mister?!" In turn, Fritz feigned hurt feelings, he lowered his tail and ears, put his face on Jack's lap and blinked his big brown eyes. It was a contest of wills and Jack was losing, he couldn't stare into those beseeching brown orbs and not react. Fritz knew this too, and his tail began to tic slowly from side to side.

The moment Jack's face cracked to a smile Fritz was up in his lap licking his face, tail wagging madly. "OK, OK, I forgive you, you rotten mutt! Now get off me and behave like a gentleman!" Jack slipped Fritz two large pastries and a bowl of milk which were devoured with pleasure.

Raulya and Myomerr went on duty after breakfast, leaving Jack, Brian, Paul, Mike and Fritz to explore the ship, unguided. Maria seemed to have vanished on her own and none of the pilots seemed to have any comment.

■ ■ ■

After shuffling a guest or two, the pilots were assigned four consecutive rooms in a corridor on the third level, overlooking the forest in the Ecosphere. The Ecosphere Lounge, one level, almost directly below, quickly became their favorite place to meet and dine. The four fliers sat at a table in the lounge after inspecting their newly assigned quarters. Jack moved their drinks aside and unfolded a brochure he received from an olive-skinned ship's porter. Spreading it on the table revealed a series of maps for the different levels of the ship.

"Well, looks like we're here..." said Jack pointing to the Ecosphere Lounge on the map.

"What's that? said Mike, pointing at a rather large room toward the bow.

Most of the symbols on the map were self-explanatory, but this one was completely unfamiliar, "Don't know," said Jack pulling on his lower lip. "Looks important though, it's on five levels according to this map." Jack looked through the index that had been printed in English for the new human passengers. "Says here, it's the C.H.A.I.R. room."

"Oh, yeah sure, the chair room, I know what that is..." Brian rolled his eyes and slurped his drink.

"You do? What is it?" asked Warren.

"I was being sarcastic Mike, don't be an idiot, I haven't the foggiest idea..."

"There's a note here, says CHAIR stands for Computerized Holographic Assisted Interactive Room."

"Oh, that's a big help," said Pappy.

Jack shrugged, "So, let's finish our drinks and go explore, that's the best way to find out."

The men up-ended their drinks and stood. "I say, chaps," Jack mused, "shall we walk 'round, or take the rail?" His attempt at an aristocratic English accent was excellent.

"That's a bit of a far plod, old boy, Wot?" Pappy grinned at Jack, pleased at his own attempt. "Time is of the essence, I daresay we should take the rail!"

Jack nodded approvingly, "Well done."

"Then we're off!" Brian suggested.

"Tally-Ho!" added Mike.

Fritz bounced excitedly in circles and bounded off to lead the way to the air tubes.

Startled offworlders stepped away, relinquishing the awaiting air car to the excited Shepherd and his four human companions. Fritz jumped in claiming two seats all to himself as Jack and the others seated themselves, waving to the apprehensive aliens to find seats. None moved, declining his invitations. Shrugging, Pappy punched in the destination and the car sped away, entering the Ecosphere and passing between the trees and foliage. Fritz leaned over the side, tongue hanging, to let the wind whip his face and watch the birds zip past. Jack could see the waterfall cascading into an emerald pool of water on the far side of the forest. Several nude forms frolicked in the spray, but try as he might, Jack could not see more detail through the trees.

Fritz bounded out of the cockpit of the air car as it hissed to a stop and slid on the carpet in front of the CHAIR suites, scattering strolling offworlders.

"Fritz!" Jack snapped, "behave yourself!" the Shepherd shook his hair into place and sat, obediently waiting for Jack. The four pilots climbed out of the car and headed for the entrance to the CHAIR suite with the Shepherd following closely behind.

Jack found it difficult not to stare at some of the more bizarre looking offworlders and voiced this quietly to the others who agreed whole heartedly, laughing. It was quite amazing to see the different shapes, sizes and colors. The four men were quickly becoming good friends, and Jack was enjoying the camaraderie.

The entry to the CHAIR suite slid open, and the pilots strode through the archway, into a hallway lined with art and colorful graphics that oddly enough, resembled movie posters. Fritz wandered down the hall to sniff an unusual piece of sculpture, something that resembled a human but had a technical flair to it. Cautiously, the wary Shepherd walked around it, inspecting it in great detail. Jack watched, unmoving, "You pee on that buddy and I'll smack you!" Brian, Pappy and Mike instantly burst into laughter. Fritz broke his concentration and ambled away sheepishly, watching the statue over his shoulder as if he expected it to move.

Still laughing, the pilots turned their attention back to the posters. Fritz growled a deep-throated snarl and the four men spun, Jack's hand already on the butt of the 1911 at his hip. "I'm terribly sorry if I've startled you," said the moving statue, "I would have greeted you sooner, but I was doing a systems check when you entered."

Jack called Fritz back to his side, who glowered at the figure over his shoulder disapprovingly. "Great way to get shot, pal... say, what are you anyway?" Jack suddenly realized his rudeness. "No offense intended."

"Oh, none taken... my name is CABL 5..." His skin was a pallid gray-white, one eye socket held an infra red photoreceptor and he only had hair on the very top of his head, a wavy shock of gold. In various places, small tubes or strands of wire protruded from his skin only to re-enter somewhere else. His voice sounded metallic and raspy.

"What kind of name is CABL 5?" interrupted Brian.

"Well, it's not a name exactly. It stands for Computer Assisted Biological Lifeform, and I am proud to be your host today and every day, here at CHAIR."

"What does that mean... exactly?" asked Pappy, rubbing his chin.

CABL 5 began to explain the word "host".

"No, no, no," said Pappy, "your name, what you are..."

"*Oh!* Well, I was born a lifeform, and in adulthood, altered by means of electro-micro surgery. Wherein mechanisms, electronics and bio-chips are permanently added to my being, so I may function more efficiently."

"You mean you *elect* to have this done?" Jack felt slightly indignant that an intelligent being would allow this to be done to his or her own healthy body for the simple sake of efficiency.

"I do not know, all memories prior to the bio-work are erased."

"Wow." The pilots exchanged puzzled glances. "Um, look CABL old boy, tell us about CHAIR, OK? What is it?"

CABL 5 took the men into an open CHAIR suite and closed the door. In the small room about nine foot by nine foot, sat a solitary hi-back, padded leather chair with a control panel on a pedestal. The pilots clustered around the chair as CABL 5 switched on the control panel. The room lights dimmed as CABL 5 initialized the panel and turned into a three-dimensional holograph of an eerie, alien landscape. Brian stepped away from the chair and reached forward but touched nothing. CABL 5 explained; "Computerized Holographic Assisted Interactive Room..."

"OK, OK, we get that, and the image is fantastic, granted..." said Brian excitedly, "but what does it *do*?"

CABL 5 motioned to the seat, "If one of you would please be seated..." Mike jumped forward and plopped into the seat. CABL 5 continued. "As you can see, the computer's information is converted into a very realistic, three dimensional world, including the vehicle that you have chosen to use." Jack looked down to see he was standing through the middle of a wing on Mike's aircraft. "Now, it's called interactive because you control the program," he moved the acceleration handle and instructed Mike to use the control stick on the module. The aircraft cruised above the surface of the cratered red planet. The men were extremely impressed and said so. "You can also smell and hear if there is an atmosphere to do so, this is a dead planet, so there is none in the program. You may also change the program, at will," CABL 5 punched some memorized numbers and Warren was flying an intercept fighter into a dense interstellar battle. "There are over a half a million cataloged titles, and I can assist you in any choices, or even help you write a new one." Impressed with his demonstration, the pilots thanked CABL 5 and since it was dinner time, excused themselves, promising to return soon.

Mike was exuberant. "Man! That was *soooo* cool!"

"No doubt!" added Brian, bouncing as he walked.

Jack grinned wildly, "Like the ultimate video game! Can you imagine the fortune you could make with that back on earth!?"

Paul shook his head in disbelief, "Simply amazing..." The four men and Shepherd strode down the corridor headed for the air tubes, acting a little like overgrown juveniles.

"Well, I know where we're gonna' spend our spare time..." said Jack, as he pushed the button on the wall to summon an air car.

"Wanna' come back after we eat?"

"Sure, Mike, don't see why not!"

An air car, partly full, hissed to a stop and they piled in, Fritz lay across Jack and Brian. It was dinner time. The tube system and corridors were busy with passengers headed for restaurants in different sections of the ship.

The pilots disembarked the air car at the exit for the Ecosphere Lounge and strolled down the carpeted ramp. A tall gangly waitress who recognized the pilots met them on the balcony. "Hello, boys, the Captain left a message, he wants you to meet him in the Nova Restaurant on level five." She explained how to get there, they thanked her and departed.

■ ■ ■

The Nova Restaurant was rather elegant, and a formally dressed maitre'd escorted the pilots to the Captain's table. The maitre'd looked disdainfully at Fritz as they made their way through the restaurant, wondering how the patrons of his fine establishment were going to react to such a hairy beast.

Two men were already seated and involved in a cheerful conversation with the Captain. "Aahhh, gentlemen, good of you to come. I took the liberty of ordering for you, I hope you don't mind. You'll find the food here is beyond compare." Handshakes were exchanged across the table as the men found their seats and were introduced to those already present; Professor Walter Edgars and his nephew Derrik Brighton. Professor Edgars, a noted British historian, spent over fourteen years teaching history and anthropology at Cambridge University. His truly human appearance and British identity, gray tweed jacket, pipe, salt and pepper hair and aristocratic accent, revealed nothing of his true off-world origin.

As a historian and anthropologist widely recognized through more galaxies than he could remember, he often spent time on a planet doing research. He found a school of higher learning was often the best place. Determined to track not only the history and ancestry of individual planets, but of entire galaxies, he discovered the migration and colonization of solar systems by early explorers, widespread. In his one hundred ninety-odd years of research, he found reason to believe almost all life in the universe was linked with a common origin. He wanted to find that origin, the place *Universal Historians* referred to as *Base Alpha*. Though it was a hotly disputed theory, more historians believed it than not.

Born to Professor Edgars' late wife's sister, Derrik Brighton was indeed, an earthling. In an attempt to pull himself above his rather dull middle-income upbringing, Derrik joined Great Britain's, Royal Air Force. Standing

101

a slender six-foot even, with ginger hair and trimmed handlebar mustache, Derrik did fairly well with the ladies. He enjoyed the added notoriety and attention that a RAF uniform brought with it and was deeply saddened when discharged after being wounded in combat.

First Lieutenant Derrik Brighton was flying a close ground support mission over the Falkland Islands in a Harrier Jump Jet when it was struck by ground fire. Wounded and with a heavily damaged, smoking aircraft, he refused to abort his mission and completed his run. Determined to return the crippled Harrier back to safety, Brighton was forced to ditch in the ocean, just short of his carrier when the aircraft's leaking fuel tanks ran dry. For his heroism, he was awarded the Distinguished Flying Cross and discharged honorably for medical reasons. Unstimulated and bored as a civilian pilot, Derrik jumped at the chance for the excitement of interstellar travel when his uncle revealed his true identity.

Personally, Derrik was a neat and meticulous person, brought up in the strict *stiff upper lip* style of English tradition. His gray-green eyes were expressive and mischievous. At a late forty-something, his square jaw and chiseled features had lost none of their appeal and, in fact, had probably improved with age. His short wavy ginger hair and handlebar mustache conjured images of the dashing young British pilots of WWII. Blessed with a sense of humor, although dry and occasionally a bit macabre, his personal belief was that life itself was a challenge. Challenges entailed risks and without risks, life would not be worth continuing, as man only endures to conquer more challenges.

Jack, Pappy, Brian and Mike found the Professor fascinating and Derrik very likeable. In the middle of dinner, Maria appeared, drink in hand and plopped into a chair at the table, waving a sloppy hello. All conversation halted.

"You're drunk," said Jack with quiet distaste.

Maria shook her head slowly, "Nnooo noo..."

"Completely snockered, old boy," offered the Professor with a wave of his pipe.

"So-oo I'm a little sstwizzled, showat?" She brushed lightly at some hair hanging in her eyes.

"A little swizzled?" Derrik stroked one end of his long mustache, "Oh I say girl... you're totally stinko!"

"Iamnot," she countered defiantly.

Jack rose from his seat. "If you gentlemen will excuse me, I think I'll escort our little lush to quarters and put her to bed." There was a general wave of acceptance to this idea, as the best solution to preventing an embarrassing public scene.

Derrik rose to his feet as well, stretching his lean, tailored, six-foot frame. "Mind if I tag along? Love to give m'legs a bit of a stretch."

Jack shrugged, "Sure, c'mon." Jack and Derrik lifted Maria from her chair and supported her by her elbows. "We'll be back soon, save us some dessert." Jack called Fritz as he and Derrik guided Maria through the crowded restaurant.

The open corridor was both refreshing and a relief. Jack thought Maria would surely do something unpredictable before they could leave the restaurant, but this was not the case.

Fritz trailed the trio slowly down the hallway, taking time for an occasional short study of a passing offworlder. Although he was becoming more accustomed to their bizarre appearances, there were still many he felt compelled to stare at.

Derrik broke the silence as they walked down the hall, "Uncle tells me, you gents are forming some sort of squadron. Is that true?"

"Well not exactly, I mean there really isn't anything to fly other than the shuttles..." Jack thought a minute, "unless we find a way to acquire our own craft somehow."

Derrik shook his head, "Don't have the foggiest how you could do that... but it seems *you* have an idea."

"Nothing solid yet, but having our own ship seems to be the only way to get back home with any expedience."

"Home? Why would you want to go back? The future and the grand adventure lie out here!" The Englishman made a wide gesture with his arm.

"Well that may be true, but unlike you, the rest of us had no choice in departure... which has a tendency to leave lots of loose ends."

Derrik nodded slowly, "Yes, quite. They can be a beastly nuisance on the conscience"

"I think the biggest thing is, knowing there are people we care about back there, who think we're dead and are mourning us. I want to go back and tell them not to worry, to tell them I'm still alive and love them... maybe to give them the option to leave with us if they want... if that's what *we* decide. We want the *option* to be able to decide for ourselves when and where we come and go."

Derrik nodded his understanding. Jack was talking about the freedom of deciding one's own fate, something man had strived for since the beginning of time. "Listen, Jack old boy, would you consider an addition to your group? I've no real spot yet, and it seems you've the right idea."

They had arrived at Jack's quarters and Jack punched the code in on the door's keypad. The pad beeped merrily at him and the door swished quietly open. Jack scooped Maria up off her feet and carried her through the living area to the bedroom. Fritz followed. Jack nodded towards the bar, "Fix yourself a drink if you like, I'll be out in a minute." Derrik turned and headed towards the bar and Jack entered the bedroom. Maria was already asleep in his arms. He knelt on the bed and laid her gently down, pulling a pillow under her head. Realizing she would probably be uncomfortable, he decided to undress her. Struggling with her limp body, he stripped off her clothes and covered her nude form with the sheets and a blanket.

Jack stared at Maria's sleeping face. How is it, he wondered, that such a beautiful woman, with so innocent a face, could be such a royal pain in the ass? And why was he so attracted to this pain in the ass?

Fritz sat patiently to one side and watched intently, he knew what would come next. Jack turned to Fritz and playfully tousled his head with one hand. "You stay here, kiddo. Keep an eye on her, OK? I promise, I'll bring back some good stuff from the restaurant." The Shepherd nuzzled Jack's hand, then climbed onto the bed. He curled up at Maria's feet and eyed his partner. "Good boy..." said Jack, dimming the lights, "I'll be back later."

Derrik rose from the settee in the living area as Jack emerged from the darkened bedroom. "Will she be alright alone?"

"Sure," said Jack, "she's asleep. Besides, Fritz will keep an eye on her; he's had plenty of practice."

"We're off then?"

"Yep! Let's go get some dessert, before it's all gone!"

"Right!" The young Englishman up-ended his drink and the liquor slid down his throat, emptying the glass.

"Look, Derrik," said Steele, as the two men strolled down the corridor, "if you want to be part of our group it's OK with me, but we're going to do what's best for the group. All for one and one for all... if you know what I mean..."

"Quite."

"Well, if you can live with that, then the more the merrier. I'll talk to the Captain and see if we can get you assigned to shuttle duty too. That'll get you quarters down by us."

"Sounds smashing!" said Derrik. The two pilots shook on it and jogged the rest of the way back to the restaurant.

Dessert was a heavenly fruit and whipped cream conglomerate, laced with liquor and Jack ate more than he should have. Pleasantly stuffed and mildly inebriated, the pilots, Captain and Professor Edgars sat casually around the table exchanging jokes and stories as the restaurant slowly emptied. Jack felt warm and at home. Gantarro, approved the idea of adding Derrik to the list of new shuttle pilots with a grin and a toast.

No longer in duty uniform but casual evening attire, Raulya and Myomerr entered the restaurant and made their way to the table. Raulya sauntered over to Jack and slid into his lap. Myomerr sat in an empty chair next to Pappy and snuggled against him. The heavy scent of exotic perfume surrounded the table and made Jack's head swim. He could feel his pulse quicken and felt a profound sexual urgency. He idly wondered if it had the same effect on anyone else. Raulya nuzzled Steele's ear, sending a chill up his spine. "Miss me?" she purred. He nodded, confused as to what to do next.

Gantarro stood, glass in hand. "Gentlemen, it's late, but before we adjourn, I propose a final toast..." the men rose, glasses poised for the occasion. Gant continued, "I'm sorry ladies, you'll have to wait outside momentarily, this is to be a squadron toast." Some confused glances were exchanged around the table. Raulya and Myomerr thought Gantarro was joking, but he waited patiently, unmoving. Raulya motioned to Myomerr and the two Ketarians walked out of the room, tails flicking in agitation.

Gantarro raised his glass, "To the squadron!" The pilots up-ended their glasses. "OK, now down to the last bit of business. Gentlemen, you must be careful when it comes to Ketarian women..." he seemed to be directing this to Jack and Pappy, "when they take an interest in a man, they have been known, to go to great lengths to secure the affections of that man."

"Like what?" Jack wanted to know.

"That perfume, have you been exposed to it before?" Jack nodded. "Did she burn incense?" Jack nodded again, Gantarro rubbed his forehead. "Both are heavily laced with a potent, synthetic aphrodisiac, highly addictive. It will *permanently* bond you to her, emotionally and physically."

Pappy was wide-eyed. "You're kidding!"

The Captain shook his head. "No, and if I had known yesterday that they were interested in you two, I would have warned you sooner."

Jack was concerned. "How much exposure will cause addiction?"

Gantarro pulled his lower lip, "Two or three times of prolonged exposure during exertion... like dancing... or sex, it depends on an individual's resistance."

Pappy shook his head. "Man, that's scary!"

"Hmmm, yeah, well, no more of that for me!" Jack smoothed his hair.

"Same here," added Pappy.

The group was splitting up as Raulya and Myomerr re-entered the restaurant. The two Ketarians cozied up to Jack and Paul, only to be gently rebutted. "Um, uh, we have to get up early tomorrow, it's been a full day and all..." Pappy was trying to keep his distance from Myomerr and having a difficult time doing it successfully.

Jack put forth a team effort. "Yeah, I'm bushed too... and we start shuttle training tomorrow, need our sleep y'know." He tried not to breathe in the heady perfume.

Raulya eyed Jack suspiciously, "You're not sleeping with that little runt bitch tonight are you?"

"No," Jack lied," what makes you say that?"

Raulya shrugged, her expression became less concerned, "Just haven't seen her around, thought maybe you had her stashed..." Jack shook his head convincingly. "Well, alright I guess we'll catch up with you tomorrow night..." she slid her hand across his groin and he inhaled sharply, wishing he hadn't. His heart pounded and he held his breath as she kissed him goodnight.

The women departed, hand in hand, leaving Paul and Jack to sigh with relief. The other pilots grouped around as they all made their way to the flight crew quarters on level three. Brian looked over his shoulder at the Ketarians disappearing down the hall, "Maybe they'll bond on each other," he whispered. They all laughed so hard they could barely breathe.

They were still breathless with laughter when they climbed out of the air tunnel car at their stop on level three. The pilots gathered in front of their quarters to say their goodnights. "Breakfast?" asked Pappy.

"No thanks, I'm still stuffed!" said Brian, belching for effect, triggering more laughter.

"Scrambled eggs, I could go for some scrambled eggs..." Mike said hungrily.

"Bottomless pit," mumbled Smiley, shaking his head. "Kid eats everything in sight." More laughter. They discussed plans for the following morning and decided on an agreeable time to meet at the Ecosphere Lounge for breakfast. Having done this, they said goodnight and entered their respective quarters.

A thoroughly enthusiastic Fritz met Jack Steele as he entered his quarters, anticipating the goodies promised. Jack shook the bag rustling the contents and Fritz spun excitedly in a circle, wagging his tail, woofing softly. His sensitive nose detected the tantalizing aroma radiating from the bag and he was having a difficult time containing his enthusiasm. Jack knelt on the floor of the semi-darkened living area and tore open the bag, laying it on the carpet like a paper dish. The Shepherd gave his friend a quick loving lick in the face and moved to the food, devouring it with great relish.

Jack rose and stepped over to the small bar retrieving himself some fruit juice from the fountain dispenser. Spotting a vid-screen on the wall which he had never noticed before, he searched for the controls, finding a remote sitting on the arm of the couch. Turning the screen on, he was greeted by a view of the passing stars outside the ship. He decided he liked it and left it on, dropped the remote where he found it and walked away.

Fritz had finished his food and was lying on the floor, eyes closed, licking the remnants of sauce off the paper bag. "Wanna' go for a walk, kiddo?" His trance broken, the Shepherd jumped to his feet. Jack fingered the keypad and Fritz darted through the door before it was even half open.

■ ■ ■

Jack sat on the grass in the meadow of the Ecosphere as Fritz ran from tree to tree. The lights were low and Jack could see the passing stars through the dome, occasionally a bird would flit far above him, but the songbirds were quiet. The pilot laid back on the grass his hands behind his head, waiting for the lanky Shepherd to return. Enjoying the peace and quiet, His eyes closed, he could smell the cut grass, the flowers smelled like lilac... inexplicably there was a breeze and the trees rustled... Suddenly he was eleven-years old again, laying in his yard looking up at the summer stars...

■ ■ ■

107

Passing stars twinkled on the vidscreen as Jack walked barefoot through his living quarters. He carried a glass, half full of a warm liquid as close to ginger ale as he could find, from the bar's soda dispenser. "I don't feel so good..." said Maria as Jack entered the bedroom.

Jack snorted, "I shouldn't wonder, what were you drinking anyway?"

Maria shrugged as she accepted the glass from Jack, "Anything that sounded interesting."

"What was the point of all this, or was there a point... I mean are you just a lush or what?"

"Nooo..." her voice squeaked, tears rolling down her cheeks.

Steele stood up and stripped off his shirt, tossing it on a recliner by the door. "I just hope I didn't get involved with an alcoholic or something..." he stripped off his pants and stood naked at the foot of the bed.

She was crying now and she didn't care, "It's just that you hated me... and you slept with her and, and..." she started to cry, huge, heaving sobs.

"Stop that!" he snapped, "you'll make yourself sick!" It was too late, the heaves were real now, no longer sobs. He scooped her off the bed and whisked her into the bathroom, just in time. Her body rejected the remaining liquor in long wretches into the commode. He held her head and she sobbed in between the heaves. No longer an adult, she was just a helpless little girl.

"I've ruined everything," she sobbed, "you hate me now... you'll never love me again..." she laid her head on her arms, shivering uncontrollably. Jack reached back and turned the shower on warm. Lifting her to her feet, they stepped into the warm jets of water which hit them from three sides. They sat on the smooth floor of the shower, their naked bodies pressed against each other. One arm encircling her, Jack washed Maria's face, hair and body. She stopped shivering and nuzzled his chest. "I love you," she said, "so please don't hate me, I don't think I could bear it."

"I don't hate you..." He kissed her forehead. "Let's go to bed," he said softly.

Fritz was curled up, sleeping on the recliner by the time Jack and Maria climbed under the covers. Maria snuggled her body against Jack, her head on his chest, her arm across his flat stomach.

"I love you..." she whispered.

Jack stroked her damp hair, "Ssshhh," he said quietly, "go to sleep."

▓ ▓ ▓

Jack Steele's sleeping awareness grew to the sound of gently falling rain. He lay motionless on the bed, still shrouded in the gossamer veils of sleep, enjoying the soft, hushing sound. A woman's voice sang quietly somewhere in the distance. He could feel no breeze through the open window, there was no sound of an ever-present surf, and when he inhaled deeply, there was no tangy salt air. He opened his eyes and viewed his surroundings, disappointed to find himself in his stateroom instead of in his bed at home. Maria's naked form appeared in the bathroom doorway, glistening with moisture. Maybe things could be worse, he thought.

Maria sauntered over to the bed and shook her wet hair over Jack's bare chest. He grabbed for her, but she danced away then back again. Jack re-timed his lunge and caught her by her wrist pulling her down on the bed, playfully spanking her bare bottom. She squealed in mock pain and wriggled to get free. A furious tickle fight ensued, encouraged by Fritz who circled the bed, barking. Horseplay quickly lit the fire of passion and somewhere between wrestling and tickling, two naked bodies melted together in physical lust.

■ ■ ■

Sweaty and gratified, Jack and Maria, limbs entwined, lay sedately on the disheveled bed. They listened, without speaking, to the laughing voices passing in the corridor and the sounds of a waking ship, traveling through deep space. Maria looked up from Jack's chest and gazed into his eyes. She wiped the sweat from his forehead and rested her head on his shoulder. "I'm scared," she said into his shoulder, "it's all so strange, so different, y'know?" Her Latin accent was soft, endearing.

"Nothing to be scared of, we'll be alright."

"We? What about Miss..." Jack put his finger over her lips.

"Let's just say *we* and leave it at that. OK?" She nodded and squeezed him tight. The ship's comm unit mounted on the wall behind the bed, buzzed insistently, demanding to be answered. Jack reached over to the night table and flicked a button on the keypad, being careful to leave the vidscreen turned off.

"You coming to breakfast or what?" Jack recognized Pappy's gentle southern accent. "I just love this gadget..." he continued, "how come there's no picture?"

"I've turned it off..." responded Jack.

109

"They must be doin' the horizontal tango..." Jack recognized Brian's voice in the background.

Maria could not resist adding her two cents, "Real classy Brian, guess that's why you get all the girls!"

The comm was overflowing with laughing voices. "Ouch," said Jack quietly. "OK, OK, listen you guys, we'll be down in a few minutes. Try not to let Mike eat them out of food before we get there, OK?" Jack punched the button on the comm's control pad and ended the connection.

"Let's go, kiddo." They slid out of bed and headed for the shower.

■ ■ ■

Pappy sipped his steaming coffee, Brian and Mike were returning from the buffet table, plates brimming with food. Derrik stirred his tea. "All you American chaps eat like that?"

"Mike looked puzzled as he handed one plate to Pappy. "Like what?"

"Like a starving football team..."

Warren grinned. "I'm a growing boy!"

Pappy turned to Brian and changed the swing of the conversation, "I talked to the programming tech in the flight bay this morning, he's got the shuttle training simulator all ready for us." Brian, his mouth full of food, just nodded.

"When are we due down there?" Asked Mike.

"No hurry, whenever we're finished with breakfast I guess."

Derrik frowned into his tea. "Well it's not a Harrier is it. But it'll have to do."

Harrier? thought Paul, *what a tub!* At least when you compare it to the Hornet... But he said nothing, a conversation like that had no profitable outcome. He shot a glance at Mike, to be sure he would say nothing as well. Mike smirked, but caught the meaning and continued eating without saying a word. Fritz raced around the corner and slid to a stop at the table of pilots. Helping himself to a chair he looked around the table smelling the smells.

Derrik took exception to the dog's bold behavior. "Hold on there, what do you think you're doing? Get down, you hairy beast!"

Fritz, sitting in the seat next to Derrik, turned and looked the Englishman in the eye. It was a deep unblinking stare. Without making a sound, he curled his lips, baring his teeth in a sardonic grin. Derrik's eyes widened at the sight, a chill raced up his back.

Brian cleared his throat, "Fritz, cut it out! I wouldn't bother him if I were you, Derrik, he's a grouch till he gets his morning pastry. Right, Fritz?" The dog, his attention now on Brian, snorted in reply. Brian handed him a sweet roll across the table. "Now get off and eat that on the floor." Fritz happily obeyed.

Jack and Maria, all smiles, rounded the corner earlier turned by Fritz. "Morning all!" Called Maria musically. She was wearing the same boots, pants and double-breasted shirt as the rest of the pilots.

"Your great hairy monster was going to eat my face!" said Derrik, pointing at the dog with his spoon.

"You must have pissed him off," said Jack, casually walking to the buffet table.

"I did no such thing," insisted the Englishman.

"Did so," said Mike, "said he couldn't sit at the table with the rest of us..."

"And you called him a hairy beast," said Brian.

"You shouldn't have done that," said Jack from the buffet table, "he's very sensitive."

"But he's a *dog*!" Derrik was thoroughly confused.

"He doesn't know that..." said Jack, returning with his plate, "he thinks he's human."

"Maybe someone should set him straight!" Derrik was incensed.

Jack looked at the amused faces around the table. "Hmmm, well... you could *try*, but I wouldn't recommend it."

"Why not?"

Jack stopped eating for a moment, his fork in mid air, "You really need to *ask*?"

Derrik frowned into his tea and shrugged, "I guess not."

Jack nudged him on the shoulder and laughed, "Lighten up man, give him a sweet roll or a slice of bacon and you'll be friends for life." Hmm, *at least it looks like bacon*, he thought. He decided not to dwell on it - some things were better off left unknown.

Derrik stole some bacon off of Mike's plate and slipped it to the Shepherd under the table. Fritz took it with grateful acceptance.

"Hey!" shouted Mike, "that was mine!"

The Englishman grinned, "Key word *was,* old bean" He slapped Mike on the shoulder and everyone laughed.

Pappy, noticing Maria was wearing the clothes adopted by the pilots, pointed at her with his fork, "You going to be flying with us too?"

She sipped her juice and nodded, "Mmm, well not officially but there's not much else to do so I might as well."

Brian nodded, "Makes sense, more the merrier. Right?" Derrik made a sour face. "What?" said Brian.

Derrik put his hands behind his neck and stretched. "Cockpits really no place for a lady."

Maria fixed him with a deep, steely-eyed stare. "Watch who you're calling a lady!" She snapped. "I can fly as well as anybody!"

"I believe her," whispered Pappy, to no one in particular.

Jack rose from the table, wanting to cut this off before it escalated to a more serious level. "OK, is everybody ready? It's time to get to work and earn our keep." There was a momentary pause, then the sound of chairs sliding on the smooth floor as the group collectively rose from the table.

"JAaaack!" The call sounded almost musical and Steele turned to greet the voice.

Raulya had entered the restaurant from the other end and Maria moved to intercept but Pappy grabbed her by the arm. "Relax," he told her, "he's a big boy, let him handle this his way." Maria stood between Paul and Brian, her arms folded tightly across her chest, her jaw clenched.

Raulya strode boldly up to Jack and put her arms around his neck, "Mmmm, you smell so good this morning..." Jack unclasped her hands and took a step back. He tried not to breathe in the drug laced perfume. She took a step forward and reached out to him. He held her away. She pouted, "What's wrong baby?"

Jack shook his head, "You and me... it's no good..." He pinched the bridge of his nose, he felt a headache coming on. "Look, we're just too different, humans like to fall in love under natural circumstances, we need our freedoms... we don't use drugs..." He thought about that last part for a moment, "Well, some might... but I don't. I never have, never will. I want to make my own choices."

Raulya nodded knowingly, "You love the *little one* then?" She motioned toward Maria.

Jack nodded in return. "You could say that..."

Her feline eyes narrowed, "What does that mean?"

Jack rubbed his chin. "Well it's open for interpretation."

"Well, could we still be friends?"

"Sure," said Jack, "as long as you quit wearing that perfume."

She smiled and held out her hand, "Deal." They shook hands. "One last kiss...?

"Uh..." Jack's eyes shifted uneasily, "probably not a good idea. Quick question... why doesn't it affect you?"

"Generations of exposure and use..." she tossed her long mane. "We're immune."

Jack nodded, "Makes sense I guess... well, listen, we gotta' get going; we have flight training. I'll see you later OK?" Raulya nodded and they parted company.

Steele was relieved Raulya had taken it so well, he wasn't sure what to expect. He returned to the waiting pilots and the group left the restaurant, Fritz leading the way to the air tubes. Maria walked stiffly beside Jack. "*Sooo?*"

Jack looked at her, intentionally playing dumb. "What?"

Maria looked at him sternly, still walking. "*Well?*"

He looked back at her innocently, "Well what?"

Maria stopped in mid stride, Jack stopped too. She threw up her arms in disdain, "What do you mean, *what?*"

Jack knew this was driving her crazy but he couldn't help himself, she just made it too darn easy. They stood there on the air tube platform, the others trying to act nonchalant. Jack shrugged, trying not to smile, "I dunno', what do you mean, what do I mean?"

She stomped her foot, offworlders passing by, stared none too discreetly. "What do you mean, what do I mean? *YOU KNOW* what I mean!" It was beginning to sound like an Abbott and Costello routine. He offhandedly wondered if she knew who they were.

Jack stared blankly at her. "I'm not sure I know what you mean..." he said deadpan.

She lost it. Grabbing him by the shirt she pulled him close, growling. "Sometimes I think I could just *KILL* you... you can be such a *shithead...*" The others had wandered a bit away, unable to control their grins. Maria never noticed.

"Control yourself, woman!" He had a snarky little grin on his face and he knew it.

"*Fuck* control!" she began swearing in Spanglish, which seemed to be easier than remembering it all in English. She tried to shake him by her grip on his shirt with the same effect of someone trying to move a sizable tree. She only succeeded in moving herself.

Jack looked down at her grip on his shirt. "I wouldn't do that if I were you..." His hands were at his sides.

She looked at him defiantly, "*Oh yeah?*" He turned his head to the side and she followed his gaze. Fritz was only a few feet away and was taking more than a passing interest in their conversation. His tail swayed ever so slightly, and he stared at her suspiciously with dark unblinking eyes, ready to intervene. She swallowed hard, almost feeling his eyes drilling into her, trying to read her intentions. "Make him go away," she said softly.

"Nope."

She released her grip slightly, "You're not going to *tell me*, are you?"

"Tell you what?" he said, smiling.

"What happened..."

"When?"

Maria stomped her feet like a child. "You know *what* and you know *when*, you bastard! So quit playing the village idiot, you asshole and tell me what that fuzzy bitch said!"

Jack decided it best to stop playing at this point, "*Geez*, you're so insecure..."

"And you're not helping any!" she snapped.

"Let's just say we agreed handshakes are the limit, OK?"

Maria's demeanor changed, "OK..." She decided she should quit while she was ahead.

■ ■ ■

Mounted on the wall, a lit color schematic illustrated the ship's floor-plan via a touch screen and scrolling directory. The directory displayed the flight director's office, as being at the base of the flight control tower in the flight bay. Brian pointed to an arriving air car, "To the bat car, men!"

The air car covered the mile of corridor to the stern of the ship in about three minutes. The car hissed to a stop and the pilots climbed out in sight of the shuttle boarding gate.

Behind them, the air car rotated lazily on the carpeted turntable and was inserted into the tube on the opposite side of the corridor for a return trip. Hissing as it was released, the empty car accelerated away with a whoosh of air.

The corridor ceiling was higher here, almost two levels tall. Four, wide moving walkways, stretched from where they were standing to the upper level balcony, for boarding and off-loading passengers to the shuttles in the flight bay. The doors to the bay on the balcony were closed. There wouldn't be any planet tours for at least a couple of weeks yet.

The intuitive Shepherd led the pilots between the walkways to the flight bay's crew door, on the main level underneath the balcony. Any one of their private security codes would admit them into the bay. Brian did the honors of working the chirping keypad. The heavy airtight door slid open with a hydraulic hiss, and a wall of warm, stale air greeted them. The pilots recognized the thick smell of lubricants, fuel and electronics, commonly associated with aircraft and other large machinery. They felt immediately at home when they stepped through the doorway and into the thick air of the flight bay.

Jack had no idea which part of the bay they had been in when they first arrived but in contrast, this area was well lit and teeming with life. They headed for the control tower which stood on the other side of the shuttle boarding ramp. The tower looked like a huge pillar stretching from the deck to the ceiling far above, with a glass flying saucer impaled in the middle of it. Jack correctly assumed the glass saucer was flight control.

Off to the right sat a shuttle looking overused and aged, gaping holes where panels ought to be. Contemplating its cause of demise, the pilots paused and gazed at the silent ship like a huge, dead animal. In such disrepair, it was difficult to tell what it really looked like when it was whole.

An automaton whizzed past, pushing an antigravity cargo pad. Close enough to prompt him to step back, Brian wheeled about, "Hey, you overgrown tin can, watch what the hell you're doing!" It did not slow or acknowledge their presence.

"*HEY*!" The voice came from above and the pilots turned to search for its owner. He stood on the walkway that ringed the glass saucer part of the control tower. He leaned over the rail, "Get to that training simulator and quit bothering my work bots!"

He seemed to demand respect and Jack didn't want to start off on the wrong foot. "Yes, sir, where might we find it?"

The man pointed further towards the stern, "Five bays down on your right and hurry up. You're late!"

Paul, Mike and Derrik, saluted out of habit, Jack out of courtesy. Brian and Maria simply followed suit as a matter of decorum. The six pilots turned in unison and trotted towards their destination, Fritz loping along behind, his nose trying to identify the odd scents and new surroundings.

Their flight boots clomping on the steel flight deck the pilots covered the distance to the simulator bay in short time. Halting just outside bay six, they were confronted by a short Saurian with pale gray skin and a furrowed brow. He stood before them, hands on hips, in clean, white work coveralls. Simply put, he did not look happy. "About time!" he barked like a drill sergeant. "Don't stand there like a herd of stupid Bardigs. Get your butts in here and let's get to work." He turned and waddled on his short legs into the bay filled with electronics. The simulator pod stood on an articulated pedestal in the center of the bay, connected by umbilical cords to the Saurian's huge control console.

"Pilots," he harumphed to himself, "pains in the ass... and keep that hairy *thing* out of my bay," he said, pointing to Fritz. Jack thought about responding to this unkind attack but was interrupted by Maria's tug at his elbow. He ordered the Shepherd to remain at the doorway. Obediently the dog obliged, finding himself a comfortable place to sit and watch the traffic go by. The Saurian continued, "My name is Tee and you will address me as such. I am a technician, not an officer, so you will not salute me or call me sir. Understand?" He did not wait for an answer, "Good. Two of you will stay with me the rest will go with CABL 12 here, and he'll show you a shuttle, inside and out."

CABL 12 stepped out of the training simulator, "It's ready now, Tee." CABL 12's voice was raspy and metallic, he looked cold and lifeless, different from CABL 5, yet the same. True, both were CABLs, but 12 lacked the animation the pilots noticed in 5. Derrik and Maria opted to go into the simulator first.

Jack, Brian, Mike and Paul, followed CABL 12 through the flight bay. Ahead of them, Jack could see the noses of several shuttles, sticking out past the end of their bays. He was a little puzzled. "Y'know, the first ship we saw back there..." he thumbed back in the direction of the old shuttle, near the control tower, "seemed a bit smaller..."

CABL 12 nodded mechanically, "Shorter Commander, no engines. We use it for parts." It became clearer to Jack and the others not all CABLs had the same personality either, CABL 5 had been outgoing and friendly, while CABL 12 seemed barely alive.

Mike interrupted Jack's train of thought. "Wow," said Warren, stopping abruptly, "what's that?" The others stopped to follow his gaze into a nearby storage bay. The dimly lit bay, held another training simulator, much smaller than the shuttle simulator they were using. This one was also slimmer, more streamlined. Instead of a side *passenger style* entry, it had a fighter craft type, canopy entry.

"It's not ours, Commander," said CABL 12.

Pappy, accustomed to achieving results through rank, took over the conversation and applied command pressure. "We didn't ask *whose* it was, CABL 12, we asked *what* it was. Answer the question please."

"Yes, Commander. It's an interceptor flight simulator going to a small training outpost in the Ridargos System. It can simulate four different craft and their assorted compatible armament, as well as an unlimited number of combat situations."

"Is it operational?" asked Jack.

"Yes, Commander." The four pilots grinned at each other but the CABL didn't seem to notice. "Shall we continue?" asked CABL 12, coldly.

"By all means," said Jack. They let CABL 12 walk ahead so they could talk with some amount of privacy. "I don't know about you guys, but *that's* what I want to learn how to fly." They all agreed.

"Do ya' think between the six of us, we could figure out how to use the programming console?"

"Sure, Mike," replied Pappy. "All we gotta' do is, while two of us are in the training simulator, the other two watch Tee to see what he does."

Brian shrugged, "It's worth a try..." In an effort to work the bugs out of their plan, they discussed the details in hushed tones as they followed CABL 12.

The shuttle was wide and low, its landing legs were so short, to pass under the craft would require crawling. The nose, although tapered was short and blunt. Cockpit glass, steeply sloped, was large enough for good visibility even on the sides. The long semi-rectangular hull held fifty people comfortably. The engines were fixed to the sides of the hull at the stern of the ship. On the top of each of the two engine nacelles was a gracefully back-swept tail about nine feet tall. The only wings were two, four foot stubs, up near the cockpit, forward of the boarding hatch. Since the shuttle flew mostly by antigravity technology at slower speeds in atmospheric flight, a great amount of wing surface was not needed. The fins and tails were primarily required for stability during forward flight.

All in all, she wasn't a bad ship, a bit utilitarian looking maybe, but not unattractive. Jack noticed some minor differences between some of the other nearby ships but nothing major. CABL 12 explained this was because some of the units could be modified with attachments for military use, others could not. After a thorough look, their questions answered, they returned to the shuttle simulator bay.

Derrik and Maria were stepping out of the simulator when Jack walked into the bay with Paul, Brian and Mike. CABL 12 was instructed by Tee, to take Derrik and Maria to see a shuttle while the others took their turns at the controls of the training unit. Pappy and Mike headed for the hatch of the simulator while Jack and Brian put their plan to work. Jack grabbed Derrik's arm as he passed, "Check out what's in bay eleven, I'll explain later..." he whispered. He let Derrik go.

Jack and Brian watched every move Tee made on the huge control console, and when they got their turn at the simulator, Mike and Pappy took over observation. By the end of their instructions for the day, they felt they knew the console well enough to run it on their own.

Tee stepped out from behind the console to address the six-pilot class, the Saurian's face lined with a perpetual frown. "You will be here on time tomorrow. Your skills are pathetic, and you need practice so bad, you should spend *all* your spare time in this simulator." He turned and plodded away, muttering, "Pilots, hummph, waste of time, pains in the ass..." He turned abruptly and spoke aloud, pointing to Fritz, "And leave that ugly, hairy beast someplace else tomorrow!"

"That does it!" growled Jack. Maria grabbed him with both hands but could not maintain her grip on his arm. He pulled loose with little effort and strode over to the defiant Saurian, snarling like an angry wolf... "*Listen*, you sour, shriveled, little *prick*! I don't know who you think you are, but *we* don't take this kind of shit from *anyone*!" Jack punctuated his point by prodding Tee's chest with his index finger. "You make *nice*, or I'm gonna' tear off your putrid little head and use it for a bowling ball! *Got it?*" The Saurians eyes were wide with surprise. "And one more crack about my friend here..." Jack gestured to Fritz, who was barring Tee's retreat, "and I'll *feed* you to him... understand?" Fritz, watching through sparkling brown eyes, took his cue well. He pinned his ears back and displayed his teeth, adding a little guttural rumble.

Saurians were sarcastic and cocky by nature, which could prove to be unwise in some situations, but they could never be accused of being blatantly stupid. Between this large human, a race he knew to be extremely dangerous, and his subhuman but obviously intelligent companion, Tee suddenly realized it would have been much wiser to hold his tongue. He had no idea what bowling was, but he was sure he wouldn't like it... especially since it entailed the removal of his head. Not wishing to be eaten or torn asunder, his demeanor quickly softened, "I beg your forgiveness, Commander, you are, of course, right. My attitude has been inexcusable; please accept my apology... to all of you."

Jack nodded and motioned to Fritz, who strolled to his side, past Tee. The Saurian turned and hurried out which exaggerated his curious little waddle. No sooner had he cleared the doorway, than the pilots broke into laughter.

"Think he bought it?" said Jack, with a broad grin.

"Hell, I bought it," chuckled Brian.

"You *are* evil," commented Paul.

"Bloody horrible little bastard deserved it," said Derrik with an offhand wave.

"Well, he's not as stupid as he looks," commented Jack, "but he's close."

CHAPTER TEN

PRINCESS HEDONIST: LANTERRA SYSTEM

In an effort to kill time, Jack and Brian started a game of catch with something resembling an orange from the dinner table. *Catch* quickly turned into m*onkey in the middle*, as Fritz raced back and forth, trying to intercept the flying fruit. That game suddenly turned into c*hase,* when Fritz succeeded in a spectacular grab and ran away. All play ended abruptly though, when he *ate* the fruit before he could be caught by his pursuers. Paul looked at his watch, "It's late enough. Let's go."

There were still some lights on in the control tower, but the flight deck was void of its earlier traffic. Feeling a bit like adolescents sneaking into a movie theater, they hustled silently past the tower and the darkened bays, making their way to number eleven. Leaving the overhead lights off, Pappy slid into the seat behind the console. "Looks a bit different than the shuttle's control board, but not much. Who's first?"

"You gonna' be able to run it OK?" asked Jack.

"Sure, no problem, Brian and Mike can help out." They nodded in unison. Pappy powered up the unit, the monitors came on and the board lit up like a Christmas tree.

"OK, guess I'll go first." Jack strolled over to the simulator unit as the canopy opened with the whine of hydraulic motors. He climbed into the cockpit, lowered the canopy and slipped on the communications headset. The others crowded around the monitors to watch Jack's progress. As Jack talked with Pappy over the comm system, they figured out the simulator and its various functions and abilities. It allowed the pilot to fly any one of four specific fighters, each with different characteristics and armament configurations. Jack relied on his eye for lines and chose a ship called a *Vulcan*.

"Looks like a good choice, Jack; according to the stats she carries two Laser Pulse Cannons, two Mercury Gatling Guns and a nice array of missiles. Let's see if we can give you something to shoot at." Pappy fed the mission guidelines into the program, explained the mission to Jack and pushed *execute.*

Sitting in the cockpit of his Vulcan, Jack suddenly found himself awaiting countdown in a launch tube the scenes projected in three dimension on the inside of the training simulator's canopy. He was amazed with the incredible realism of the projections. With the touch of a button, he called up his weapons stores and defense status screens. The defense screen showed the condition of the regenerative power shields, as well as the physical armor of the ship.

"Launch!" The launch tube slid past in a blur, disappearing in the blink of an eye and Jack found himself in the darkness of deep space. A glance over his shoulder and he could see the gargantuan warship he had emerged from. Musical beeping from the targeting computer called his attention to the radar screen. Two red blips were inbound at rapid speed.

Acknowledging the alarm on the threat console, the navigation screen winked out and a line diagram of the target winked on to replace it. One of the blips blinked to inform which target it was identifying. Other targets could be identified by simply touching the threat or targeting keypad. A steady white dot on the radar showed the location of Jack's mother ship. The incoming bandits were medium fighters, fast and heavily armed, their intention; destroy the mother ship. "Two bandits, Vulcan One..." said Pappy, acting as flight control.

"Roger, flight control. I'm on 'em." Jack decided he needed to divide and conquer. The bandits were on a wide arc to approach and attack the mother ship from the rear, "Hmmm, end run, eh? Well, we'll have none of that..." He kicked the nose over and headed straight for the bogies, slamming the throttle handle forward. He thumbed off the safety on the Laser Cannons, they had a longer range.

The fighters came into range and Jack squeezed the trigger. The high-pitched pulse matched the streaks of red racing away from his wings; the sight was mesmerizing. He watched the flashes on their shields and saw the targeting computer register the effect. When the red flashes passed by his own cockpit canopy, Jack stopped being mesmerized and rolled the flight-stick. The Vulcan rolled and he passed the bandits canopy to canopy.

"Shoot them down, Steele, don't ram them!"

"Shut up control, I'm busy!" Successful in getting the bandits to split, Jack cut his power and swung the ship around. Slamming the throttle forward, he squeezed the boost button on the throttle handle, it had the same effect as an afterburner, sending the Vulcan screaming through the simulated void, quickly closing the gap on the second bandit. The first had peeled off out of sight and for now, out of mind. Jack flipped off the safety for the Gatling Guns as he followed the enemy fighter, heading straight for the mother ship. He had to protect it at all costs... in real life it, would be his ticket home. In range now, he could fire but he wanted maximum impact, so he waited... it seemed an eternity.

The bandit opened fire on the mother ship and Jack could wait no longer. He squeezed the trigger. The high pitched pulse of the Vulcan's Laser Cannons, accompanied by the rapid thumping of the Gatling Guns, vibrated through the cockpit. The bandit ship shuddered and bucked as its defense screens flared red, quickly disappearing. It began to trail pieces of debris as its armor plating gave way. Jack realized he had depleted the energy banks for the Vulcan's guns, only after they stopped firing. "Damn!" He chose a missile from stores, not wanting to wait for the weapons generator to restore power to the guns. The bandit boosted away, trailing fuel and oxygen vapor, trying to affect an escape. Powering on only one engine, it had no hope of eluding Jack's Vulcan.

Jack was concentrating so hard, he didn't hear Pappy shouting on the comm about the other Bandit on his tail. The threat light winked on and the lock alarm whistled loudly in the cockpit. Jack could see the missile on his radar scope, closing in. Reflexing, he thumbed the boost and headed for the wounded bandit. Laser fire flashed past his wingtips, Jack held his breath, passing the damaged bandit by only a few yards. He cut his engines completely off and flung the stick to the side. The Vulcan spun flatly around, and Jack saw the bandit disappear in a stunning, yellow flash. *"Yes!"* he shouted, slapping his knee. Jack had passed the bandit so closely that when he cut the Vulcan's engines off, the missile acquired the other craft as its target. "OK," he said, taking a deep breath, "one down, one to go..." He suddenly realized he was sweating and wiped his forehead.

Carried by its momentum, the Vulcan drifted backwards, facing the approaching enemy fighter. Bursting through the cloud of debris like an angry hornet, the bandit savagely attacked Jack's ship, head on. Laser fire, shot past the Vulcan's wings and splashed against its defense shields. Jack calmly thumbed the firing button and released the missile he had readied, without locking it on. Experiencing a substantial decrease in shield protection, Jack decided a hasty exit was more than just a good idea. Simultaneously pulling the flight stick back and slamming the throttle wide open with the boost button depressed the Vulcan vaulted out of the line of fire. He could feel the vibration of the hits against the remaining forward shields which collapsed, leaving the Vulcan's plating exposed.

The bandit never moved to avoid the oncoming missile, he simply never saw it coming and collided with it head on. The detonation took his shields down and spun his ship off course, eliminating his chance for pursuit.

Steele couldn't see the connection between missile and target but saw the detonation flare out the side of his cockpit canopy. He called up another missile from the stores list and rolled the Vulcan to come around. He could see the bandit's profile off to the right and the targeting screen showed a target void of forward shields. He squeezed the boost button and closed in, firing the long-range Laser Cannons. The bandit ship shuddered as the fire from the Vulcan hammered at its exposed plating.

Jack opted for a missile lock but the bandit boosted away just as the targeting computer closed in. For the next two minutes, the two craft spun and rolled in crazy circles, firing and dodging. Jack's shielding had regenerated quickly, the bandit's had not. Obviously some of Jack's shots pierced through the exposed plating and damaged the shield generators. He again switched the Vulcan to full guns, hoping to bring down the bandit's stern shields, since that's all that he could get a good shot at. Since the shield generators were not at full efficiency, this proved easier than he'd expected. The Vulcan's Laser Cannons and Gatling Guns hammered the stern shields into non-existence before the bandit could evade. With all shields down, the bandit made a drastic attempt to run, a fatal error.

Jack's targeting computer finally gave him the lock he was looking for. The missile, released from the Vulcan's wing mount, pursued its target with unerring diligence. The remaining bandit disappeared in a hot yellow flash, chunks and pieces flung out in all directions. A chorus of hoots and hollers filled the earphone of his comm unit.

Jack Steele inhaled deeply, then followed commands from simulated flight control and landed back on the mother ship. As the cockpit canopy opened, he was greeted by the real world, the swirl of air entering the cockpit made him shudder with chill.

"Man, *that* was *intense!*" he stood on the seat in the cockpit and ran a hand through his hair, "it was so real!"

"Not bad," said Pappy, "not bad at all..."

"Not bad?" Jack countered, as he climbed down out of the cockpit, "That was *awesome!*"

"Well, I meant, for your first combat flight, you did pretty good... you smoked two without getting yourself in any real trouble and..."

Jumping to the ground from the last rung on the boarding ladder, his ego a tad bruised, Steele queried sharply, "So you think you could do better?" He knew it was a stupid question the moment he asked it but it was already out there.

"Sure," said Pappy "and so could you. With a little practice. You have great natural dog fighting instincts. A little work and you could be really exceptional." Jack raised one eyebrow.

"This is Lieutenant Commander Paul Smiley," said Mike, jumping in with a grin, slinging one arm over his flight leader's shoulder. "One of the Navy's *finest* Hornet pilots... a *Top Gun* graduate! He turned down an instructor's position to stay shipboard."

Somehow Jack's ego felt less abused, knowing Paul was just being objective, not critical, then a sudden idea hit him, "Say, if you've got the ability to train... why not train us?!"

"Sure, why not?" exclaimed Brian, "that would be a great idea!"

"Let's face it," said Jack, "this shuttle thing is alright for now, but I don't want to do it indefinitely..."

"Besides," interjected Brian, "this would be a blast!"

"I for one, would like to see some of the famous Top Gun tactics," added Derrik. "See how they compare to what I learned in the RAF... it could prove to be rather interesting."

Paul suddenly realized everyone was looking at him, waiting for an answer... smiling faces filled with enthusiastic anticipation. It was a bunch of grown adults caught up with an irresistible new toy. He shrugged, "Oh what the hell. Sure, why not, it'll give us something interesting to do."

"Great!" said Jack, rubbing his hands together, "When do we start?"

Paul shrugged, "Now's as good a time as any. I need everybody to fly at least one mission so I can tell where we're at, ability-wise..." He walked back over to the console and sat down, "So... who's next?"

Taking turns, the pilots flew the simulator into the wee hours of the morning. Paul Smiley found himself surprised time after time at the resourcefulness and tenacity of these untrained pilots in combat. Did they make mistakes? Sure. Did they get shot up? Yes. But he decided there was a good deal of raw talent present, and the possibility of creating a well trained combat squadron was not as far-fetched as he might have anticipated.

Rubbing his eyes, Paul rose from his chair behind the console, "Let's call it a night y'all, I'm burned out."

Jack looked at his watch, "Shit, it is late, isn't it? OK, let's pack it in, kids." The others rose from their various positions of rest, yawning and stretching, as Maria climbed down out of the simulator cockpit. Halfway down the ladder, Jack hefted Maria by the waist and set her gently on the flight deck. "Nice flight," he said quietly.

Maria flew harder than she had ever flown in her life. She was tense and exhausted, definitely in no mood for Steele's strange brand of humor. "Look..." she said pointing her finger in Jack's face. But she had known him long enough to know when he was ribbing her, he'd get that mischievous look in his eyes... and it wasn't there now. "You're serious aren't you?"

Jack nodded loosely, "Yeah, you did good." He put his arm around her shoulder and gave her a squeeze.

"No kidding?"

"No kidding..." he repeated as they walked. "Scout's honor." He held up his hand in a Boy Scout salute.

She smiled weakly, "Liar, you were never a Boy Scout..."

How does everybody know that he wondered, smiling back. "That's beside the point."

Late the next morning, six tired, yawning pilots, wandered into the shuttle simulator bay in silence. They made themselves comfortable and waited for Tee. The Saurian flight instructor never came, he had abandoned his students. Mike rubbed his eyes with the palms of his hands and spoke through a yawn, "Good going, Jack, you probably scared him so bad yesterday, he had a coronary after he left."

Jack smiled mischievously, "Yeah, at this very moment, his body lies face up next to the toilet in his room, blue in the face, his tongue all swollen and purple, hanging out the side of his mouth... and his eyes so bug-eyed they look like two bloodshot golf balls stuck to his face."

Maria made a face of extreme distaste, *"Euuchhh,* that's disgusting!"

"Thank you."

"Actually," mused Derrik, "it would be a bit of an improvement on that little troll."

"You guys are sick..."

"Lighten up Arroyo..." commented Jack, "we're guys, it's what we do."

"Sure," interrupted Paul in a slow southern drawl, "we're just funnin'."

"I think we ought to go eat," said Mike, changing the subject.

"You would," said Maria making another face.

"Well, I think we should go back to bed," yawned Brian.

Jack nodded as he eyed Maria, "that gets my vote." Maria caught the intent of his gaze and turned away to hide her blush. She had to bite her tongue to keep from smiling.

Paul rose from where he had been sitting on the floor and stretched his arms above his head, "Well, y'all can do whatever you like, but I'm going to go eat, *then* I'm going to get some shuteye." The group voted unanimously for that idea and headed for the Ecosphere Lounge.

"Mmm, waffles..." smiled Jack, thinking ahead.

Mike rubbed his hands together, "A nice four-egg omelet and some crispy bacon... Oooh and pancakes or some French toast, maybe some sausage, juice..."

Jack looked sideways at Mike as the group walked down the corridor, "Seriously? Holy crap, do you have a tapeworm or something...?"

Pappy just shook his head and smirked.

CHAPTER ELEVEN

PRINCESS HEDONIST: DEPARTING TRELUS 2, LAN SYSTEM

This was the first full day in about three weeks they'd given themselves off and everyone was thoroughly enjoying themselves.

Jack lay on the blue-green grass of the Ecosphere meadow floor, the picnic lunch Maria had made was resting warmly in his stomach. The wine made his eyelids heavy and he let them close, feeling the artificial sun on his face. Relaxed and at ease, the weight of Maria's head on his chest was somehow comforting.

A few yards away Mike and Brian played catch. Fritz ran back and forth between them trying to intercept the ball, creating an odd version of *monkey in the middle* and Paul and Derrik had wandered off after lunch to see if there were any fish to be had in the pond at the far end of the Ecosphere. Jack could feel Maria's even breathing and opened one eye to watch the gentle rise and fall of her chest. Closing his eye, he sighed quietly, drawing in the warm, sweet, air of the meadow and let his mind drift...

Whether measured by Earth standards or by the similar but elongated ship's version, time passed quickly. In comparison, travel in deep space or the noticeable progress of such, was negligible in perception. This created the illusion of taking forever to go nowhere. According to Jack's log, the group of pilots had been on the ship for well over a month already and had it not been for the rigorous combat flight training they had imposed upon themselves, days would have drifted from one to another without apparent hesitation. Their efforts were not without rewards. With Pappy's expert tutelage, they had become excellent fighter pilots, flying far more hours than would have been possible by conventional aircraft training methods.

Thanks to the amiable assistance of CABL 5 and the use of the CHAIR suites, the pilots were able to practice formation flight and improve their organized flight teamwork. Using computer software copied from the combat flight simulator, CABL 5 linked several suites together to allow the pilots to fly as a unit. Each pilot could see a fully dimensional laser hologram of the other pilot's ships around him. This proved to be a highly effective way of learning and created a tremendous amount of cohesion between the pilots.

Not only did they practice flight combat, Pappy ran them through a series of exercises involving ground and anti-shipping strikes. Jack was amazed at how close the pilots had become, almost like real family. Their affinity for each other was obvious in the way they flew; viciously protecting each other in combat, even when it meant putting themselves at greater risk. Along with the physical application of practice was the studying... of ships and weapons types... provided by research from CABL 5. The technical specifications, uses, advantages and disadvantages, ranges, power, durability and ammunition, when applicable. It was complex but important and useful information.

Though they spent much of their time working on their study and fighter tactics, shuttle practice did not suffer. In fact, a couple days ago, they all did live flights to a beautiful snow planet called Trelus 2 in the Lan System. While the Princess Hedonist did lazy orbits, the shuttles ran for almost forty-eight hours straight, taking sightseers to and from the surface of the sparkling planet.

Working in shifts, the pilots flew over two thousand sightseers to the planet's surface and back. After the last shuttle had finally been recovered and secured by the maintenance crew, Gantarro had called the pilots to the bridge.

"Well..." mused Gantarro, standing with his hands clasped neatly behind him, "gentlemen... and lady," he added, nodding toward Maria, "I want to congratulate you all, on a fine orchestration of flights and a superb effort. Everyone was extremely satisfied." A smile lit up his face as he began to clap, which started a round of applause from the crew on the bridge. The worn pilots smiled weakly and shifted uneasily, unsure what to do with the outward show of attention. Gantarro continued after the applause died down, "You people did in two days, what it normally takes us six or seven to accomplish. If you continue to operate with such efficiency, you may actually get us back on schedule!" The pilots wanted to say something, anything... but no one could think of exactly what.

"I had a feeling you would be good pilots, but then I saw the logs from the training simulator in bay eleven..." He paused briefly and watched the pilots' uneasy glances, "Mmmm, yes," he said, nodding, watching their faces, "I knew, I knew right away... why do you think Tee disappeared? I didn't want him interfering, that's why!" The Captain wore a devilish grin,

"He's an anal retentive, but he really is a good instructor... for beginners though, you were obviously light-years past what he had to offer you. I knew that the moment I saw your logs and tapes..." He slammed his hand down on an instrument console, making everyone on the bridge jump, even the group of pilots. "Dammit, if your records reflect your real abilities in combat, you might be some of the best damn fighter pilots I have ever seen!"

Gantarro took a small engraved steel box handed to him by an Ensign from the bridge crew. "I forwarded your flight files to a close friend of mine in UFW's, *United Federation of Worlds,* Space Academy..." as he held the shining box forward, the top slid open with a hiss to reveal six sets of solid gold wings surrounded by royal blue velvet. The pilots stared in silence at the gleaming wings. "I am honored to have been authorized by the United Federation of Worlds Space Academy, to present you with the *Wings of Honor.*" The presentation was officious, but the Captain could not prevent smiling like a proud father. "Y'know, only Academy graduate *fighter* pilots get *Wings of Honor* and they are the only *gold* wings you will ever see."

Jack had the sneaking suspicion he was wearing one of those struck-dumb kinds of smiles. He looked at his friends, they all had a goofy smile so it must mean he was wearing it too. He hated that. Ah, but what the hell, it was gratifying to have some occasional recognition. He accepted the wings handed to him with a handshake. "Wherever you go, you will be recognized as being part of a very special group," said Gantarro, as he handed the pilots their wings. "And should you choose to remain out here as part of a space faring society, you are offered permanent positions with the United Federation of Worlds with the following ranks," he pulled out a small piece of paper and read from it. "Effective as of today; Paul Smiley - Commander, Jack Steele - Commander, Derrik Brighton - Lieutenant Commander, Mike Warren - Lieutenant, Brian Carter – Lieutenant, Maria Arroyo - Lieutenant JG." The pilots proudly pinned their wings on their tunics as they left the bridge and headed for the Ecosphere Lounge to celebrate.

Gant had explained that the UFW was not only created to improve interplanetary trade but for protection as well. Protection against hostile action from unexplored systems or marauding pirates. The latter were becoming more common and increasingly more successful. The UFW deployed scout patrol craft, cruisers and fighter carriers to create a Network or Net as it was more commonly called. The problem was, the pirates were either finding or creating more holes in the Net than the UFW could cover.

The UFW needed more people, good people, pilots mostly, with combat savvy. The pirates were vicious and ruthless when dealing with the UFW Net and more often than not appeared in numbers sufficient to overwhelm inexperienced UFW forces. Then in true pirate fashion, steal, pillage, or salvage, anything they could get their hands on. They got stronger, the Net got weaker.

The UFW had experienced limited success with ambushes and raids on pirate hot spots. The idea being to keep the raiders off balance, out of the trade routes and away from the Genesis Gates until their bases could be discovered. Though the operations had merit, the UFW had yet to succeed in the capture or destruction of a single pirate stronghold. The UFW was simply spread too thin to effect the needed results.

Jack was not surprised to find pirates often dealt in illicit cargo, after all, greed was a universal motivator, and in any culture, there were plenty of vices to exploit. And with interstellar travel so prevalent, there was an abundance of cultures accessible for the sale of *any* cargo or booty the pirates could obtain.

Steele felt those old familiar *save the world feelings* he got when he joined the Chicago Police Department. The cravings for action, the desire to make a difference, improve his little corner of the world. Some people called men like him *adrenalin junkies*. He wondered how close that was to the real truth.

Compared to most of the planets in the UFW, Earth was considered a savage, warring world, its occupants cunning, ruthless and dangerous. That perception could work to the UFW's advantage if the Federation could be convinced to use Pappy's superior combat tactics. It might be enough to provide them an edge against the pirates and smugglers. With Steele's knowledge of special police tactics, and Maria's covert operations experience, they could help the UFW uncover some of those elusive pirate bases.

His thoughts suddenly turned to home and Earth; family, friends... and unfinished business with Stephen Miles. Mr. Miles... yes, he mustn't forget to settle *that* score. Jack had to go home first, he couldn't forget that. That was to come before all else. It was obvious *life out here* had a lot to offer. It was a new adventure and he was starting to enjoy it. Maybe... just maybe, he... no, they, as a team, could make a difference...

■ ■ ■

"Jack, sweetheart... are you asleep?" Her voice was soft and rich.

Jack opened his eyes to see Maria gazing down at his face. "Hmm," he said yawning, "I guess I was..." He propped himself up on one elbow, "Where's Fritz?"

"He went for a walk with Brian and Mike, they should be back pretty soon." Jack nodded and sat up, amazed at how comfortable the grass was and slightly embarrassed that he had dozed off. Maria stretched and made growling cat noises, making Jack smile. Maria tousled her hair, "Want to go dancing after dinner tonight?"

Jack nodded again, "Sure why not? Sounds good to me." They lay back on the grass and kissed, oblivious to the people animals and aliens around them.

CHAPTER TWELVE

WASHINGTON DC, CIA OFFICE: *ALPHABET SOUP*

Stephen Miles sifted through the piles of reports scattered across his desk. "Dammit Cummins, it's been almost two months and not a sign!" The steady rain pattered across the window of his Washington office. "How does somebody just vanish with a plane like that? And with a plane like that, how could you possibly escape two F-18s? I mean even if they were being flown by two complete morons, there's just no way..." His mind drifted off as he looked out the rain washed window upon a gray and soggy city. Lightning flashed in the distance, momentarily illuminating the silhouette of the Washington monument.

It was a long silence as the two men sat listening to the rain. Bob Cummins shifted uneasily in his seat before he spoke. "The Bureau has been watching Steele's house for some time." The Director's eyes did not leave the window and Cummins continued. "Both his phone and his parent's phone in Chicago have been tapped. I guess the boys are hoping to catch him if he tries to contact his folks. "

Miles continued to stare out the window. "Those Bureau slobs couldn't catch a cold... but keep a team on them in case they get lucky."

Cummins nodded. "Have been, twenty-four hours a day."

"Good..."

The National Security Act of 1947 was very specific about the CIA's endeavors; that they could have no role inside the U.S. Internal operations were to be left to the FBI. There was definitely no love lost between the two agencies and the Bureau had a nasty habit when it found the Agency infringing on its territory; publicity. Public exposure was a royal nightmare. It led to Congressional investigations and hearings, having to answer questions to a bunch of career politicians, whose asses had never left a cushy chair for a serious day's work, judging how he did a very risky and thankless job. Screw that crap. In the end, it remained, Stephen needed to find Steele and the B-25 before the FBI or the military. It would be the only way he could protect him and prevent the operation from being compromised. Jack was a wanted man. Sought by the FBI who were co-operating with the

Puerto Rican government and by the U.S. military, who wanted to know where their F-18s were.

If it came down to it, Stephen hoped he could keep his people protected by the fact that the operation was actually running outside the U.S. If not, what the hell, he wasn't beyond a little dirty pool.

Cummins cleared his throat before he spoke again, he knew this was a sore subject. "Are we going to make new arrangements to send equipment to the team in Sao Palo?"

Stephen leaned back in the leather chair and closed his eyes. "No." He pinched the bridge of his nose, "We lost our window of opportunity on Vasquez, he's already left the country with his shipment."

"Isn't there any way we can intercept him?"

Stephen shook his head, "No, not at this point. Someone tipped him off and we lost contact with our informant in that region a week ago. We have no idea where his port of entry will be. Or even if he's transporting by air or water for that matter."

"You're not thinking Steele tipped him off are you?"

"I thought of it, but no. Besides, it wouldn't explain two missing jet fighters." Stephen Miles had decided that possibility read too much like cheap fiction.

Cummins stared down at his shoes. "How big is the shipment?"

"Two tons."

Bob's eyes shot from the floor to the Director who had resumed staring out the window. "Two tons! Jesus...!" He'd need a calculator to figure out the street value of two tons of cocaine.

"Oh, it's not the cocaine that's bothering me," interrupted Miles, "I'd give that to the DEA boys anyway. I want Vasquez and Restonovich."

"Colonel Restonovich?" Cummins had heard the name a couple of times before, but he had no idea what the man had to do with the Vasquez cartel. "He's Russian military, isn't he?"

His feet up on the desk, Miles rolled his head back and forth on the chair's headrest, popping his neck. He seemed to be transfixed by the rain hitting the office window. "No. Not military... KGB."

Bob's eyes widened, "KGB? I don't understand sir, what would KGB want with a drug dealer? And I thought the KGB was pretty much dismantled, defunct..."

The CIA Director of South American Operations swung his feet off the desk and spun his chair around to look the young agent in the eye. "Don't let all this Glasnost crap fool you, Cummins." He pulled a cigar out of a small mahogany box on the desk and bit the tip off, "The KGB isn't dead, just hiding." He searched for and found his lighter under a pile of reports. "This Glasnost, buddy-buddy bullshit, was a perfect veil for them to slip underground. They're actually more dangerous now than they were before."

"And their connection to Vasquez?"

Stephen puffed on the cigar as he lit it, expelling clouds of foul, gray smoke. "Bankroll a drug dealer. Help him move his shipment. Eliminate him when you know the ropes and take over. It's a perfect opportunity to funnel mass amounts of funds to their cause, *and* aid in the destruction of the fabric that binds our country." Agent Cummins nodded, he was beginning to understand the big picture. "But," continued Stephen, "we need to find that plane and that kid. Anybody else gets him, and they'll blab all over the place. If Restonovich gets wind of it, he'll go completely underground... I'll never get another shot at him."

The Director's aide buzzed him on the intercom. "Yes, Maggie?"

"The field team assigned to the Steeles is reporting in," replied his aide, "it looks like the federal boys are going to make an initial contact. Wilson is still on the line if you want to speak with him."

"Yes!" He picked up on the line that flashed on his phone. "Wilson, what's going on?"

The agent's voice was distant on a secure satellite phone. "We intercepted some comms this morning, sir. The Bureau boys have received orders from their regional; *interview in addition to observation.* And *get them to talk,* was an exact quote."

"Bozos!" growled Miles. "Never know when to keep their noses out of our business... Head them off if you can, let them know in no uncertain terms, their investigation stops now! Quote national security, but no details. Understand?"

"Yes sir. Pressure?"

"Modest. Heavy only if you have to. If they've already made contact, go in and see the Steeles and do damage control. We don't want them warning Jack away, we need to bring him in. I'll be on the next flight out."

"Right, sir." The connection ended and the Director cradled the receiver.

"Cummins," Bob Cummins looked up from his empty coffee cup. "Go pack. Kevin and I will be by to pick you up shortly. We're going to Florida." With a nod, agent Cummins was up and out the door. Stephen Miles rose from his desk, "Maggie! Get Kevin, we're going to Florida!"

"Florida? Can I go too?" she joked, looking at the rain pelting her window.

■ ■ ■

Lynnette Steele stood in the kitchen of her son's home and prepared dinner. As promised she and Kyle had traveled down to see Jack. And as he predicted might be the case, his return was delayed so they called Nina for a key. But he was long overdue and they were both becoming more than a little concerned. There had been no mention of the missing planes on either television or radio so they had no knowledge of any of the bizarre occurrences which had unfolded before their arrival. They enjoyed the weather, the attractions and the beach, basically trying to remain positive about his absence. Calls to his cell phone had garnered no results.

In the interest of keeping busy, Kyle had decided to fix a leaky faucet and went to the hardware store for some parts. Lisa, Jack's younger sister, was walking the family dog on the beach and Nina, who came once a week to tidy up, was in the living room running the vacuum cleaner across the area rug.

Lynnette looked up from the vegetables she was slicing when the doorbell chimed. "Nina, would you get that? My hands are all wet!"

"Sure, Mrs. Steele!" She thumbed off the switch and leaving the machine, headed for the door. Padding barefoot across the rug and the tiled foyer, she opened the door to find two men in dark sunglasses and dark suits waiting patiently. "Can I help you?" She asked.

"Mrs. Steele, please." They knew Mr. Steele had left the house but not for how long. They hoped to play on Mrs. Steele's concern for her son and get her to expose any information she might have knowledge of, before her husband returned.

"And who could I say is calling?"

The taller of the two men stepped forward to look into the house, but Nina moved the door to block his view. He pushed on the door and brushed by her. "FBI," was all he said, as he quickly flashed his ID.

"Hey," she objected, "wait a minute..." but he was already in the house.

The second man followed the first. He looked the girl up and down, "Don't want any trouble, Missy, do we? Is your green card all up to date?"

Nina had an even tan and dark reddish-brown hair, but her only ethnic claim was that she was half Seminole Indian. "I'm a born citizen, you jerk!" she snapped, indignant.

Lynnette Steele turned the corner from the kitchen, holding a towel, drying her hands. "Can I help you gentlemen?"

"FBI, Mrs. Steele," he flashed his ID again, as fast as before. "Need to ask you a few questions."

She stood unmoved. "Hope you don't mind if I get a better look at that..." She pointed to the breast pocket where the ID had gone. The agent drew it out and handed it to her. Lynnette examined the identity badge and returned it. Jack had spent several years on the police department, Kyle had spent over twenty-five. She was not naive and would take no bullying. "OK," she said, handing it back. "Now, apologize to Nina then tell me what you want and why you've been so rude."

The agent apologized, reluctantly. Then they began asking questions. *How does Jack make a living? Where did he go? When did she last see him? When did he call last?* Nina sat quietly on the arm of the couch, but Lynnette would have none of it. "Wait a minute," she said, holding up one hand, "this sounds more like an interrogation than a few questions. Maybe you'd better tell me what this is all about."

"I'm sorry," said the first agent, flatly, "that's classified."

"Well then, I'm sorry," added Lynnette, folding her arms across her chest, "you don't answer mine, I don't answer yours. You know where the door is, " she said motioning toward the door dismissively. "Don't let it hit you in the ass on the way out." The need for more information about Jack was killing her, but she wasn't about to give in.

The commotion outside on the sundeck made everyone in the room turn around. A third agent escorted Jack's younger sister Lisa in through the sliding glass doors gripping her tightly by her elbow. "Caught this one outside spying."

"I live here you moron!" Lisa flailed but the agent gripped her arm like a vice. "Ow! Let go!"

"We don't have any record of her..." one agent said to the other.

When Kyle Steele pulled back into the driveway, there were two new vehicles parked there. He didn't know many of Jack's friends, but he couldn't picture any of them driving long dark anonymous sedans. He parked on the grass next to the garage, out of view from the rest of the house. Having stopped for a few groceries after the hardware store, he hefted a large paper bag under one arm and closed the van door quietly. It made no sound. The freshly mown grass smelled sweet and shooshed softly as he made his way to the open garage door. Once inside the garage, he rummaged silently through the cabinets above Jack's workbench until he found what he was looking for. He set it in the bag on top of the ice cream. Kyle cautiously entered the kitchen through the garage, thankful he'd lubricated the door's hinges earlier that week.

"I don't care if you have a record or not," shouted Lynnette, "she's my daughter!"

Kyle had no idea who these men were. And at this point he was not interested in asking for identification. He ended up behind the agent and Lisa, one arm circling the bag, his free hand resting on top. "Release my daughter," he said calmly, "or you'll pull back a stump." She was released immediately. As the agent turned, Kyle let the bag slide through his grasp and drop to the floor. In his free hand was a Sig Sauer 226, 9mm semi-automatic. When the bag hit the floor, it became an unspoken exclamation point. He aimed over Lisa's shoulder at the man's right eye. "I wouldn't miss at five times this range," Kyle added calmly. Kyle being an expert, meant it would actually be closer to ten.

"FBI," said the man slowly.

"That's nice..." retorted Kyle. He wasn't sure whether to believe them or not yet. "Suppose you back up." Lisa ducked under his line of fire and ran out the sliding glass door to the sundeck.

"We'd really feel more comfortable if you put that away," said the first agent.

"Feel? You're gonna feel a 9mm in your forehead if you don't do what I tell you to do." They made no attempt to resist and retreated towards the front door as he advanced.

"You don't really think you'd get us all if we decided to draw on you. Do you?" The first agent looked blankly at his partner, he couldn't believe he'd said something so stupid.

"Well," said Kyle, sarcastically, "I need what, say two apiece? That's six. If things get a little messy and I have to hurry and need three each, that's nine I've got sixteen. Since you're the asshole with the biggest mouth, I'll make sure you're first..."

"I apologize for my partner's foolish remarks," began the first agent, glaring at the second. "But we are here about your son." He gingerly pulled his ID from his suit pocket, closely watched by the angry father. "It's a matter of extreme importance."

Kyle examined the badge and identification card, "So tell me about my son." He handed it back and dropped his gun hand, tucking the 9mm into his waistband in the small of his back.

"We were hoping you could tell us," said the agent who had grabbed Lisa.

The doorbell chimed and Kyle pointed to the closest agent, "Answer that." The agent opened the door and disappeared like he'd been sucked out. When the second turned to investigate the door swung wide and he was dragged out by his tie. Along with the first, he was escorted down the driveway by well armed Marines in camouflage fatigues.

A well muscled man stepped forward, grabbing the final FBI man by his sleeve, "*You*, out!" He told him, tossing him towards the door. He handed Kyle his ID and tipped his cap to Lynnette and Nina who stood by, their mouths agape. "Special Agent Doug Wilson, Mr. Steele. Central Intelligence Agency. Sorry these clowns had to bother you. It won't happen again." Lisa was escorted up the drive from the street by another agent in fatigues, she entered the house and smiled politely, if not a bit stunned.

"What the hell is going on here?!" Demanded Kyle.

"Maybe we'd better all sit down sir." They gathered in the living room and made themselves comfortable. "First, what I am about to tell you is a matter of national security. I am limited in the details I am allowed to tell you and must ask that what I do divulge does not leave this room." They all agreed.

"Is he working for you?" asked Lisa, rather bluntly.

"In a manner of speaking," began Wilson. "He was delivering a plane for us..."

"Did he know who he was working for?" inquired Kyle.

"That, I don't know," answered the agent.

Lynnette didn't like where this was going, it sounded too past tense. "So where is he now? Why was the FBI here looking for him?"

Agent Wilson decided to answer the question he knew the answer to first. "Well, during the delivery, a situation arose where someone attempted to take the plane away from him by force..."

"Was he hurt?" Interrupted Lisa.

"Not to our knowledge ma'am, there was no indication of that. Anyway, he was forced to defend himself and the plane..."

"And he killed someone in the process..." added Kyle.

Wilson nodded. "Several men."

"That's why the FBI was here!" Lynnette interrupted, excitedly.

"Right." Wilson wanted to tell it and get it over with. "Anyway, he and the plane disappeared somewhere near the northeastern coast of South America in a weather front off the edge of the Bermuda Triangle." He left out many of the sensitive details, especially the missing F-18s, the guns, the dead police, the drugs and the Russians. "The search lasted for almost two weeks, but nothing has been found. Our best information says he had plenty of fuel and likely made landfall." He went on to explain that he had told them all he could and would appreciate their help if Jack should happen to contact them. He assured them, the CIA was only interested in Jack's best interests and could clear up any problems to get him home safely.

"Bullshit," said Kyle, once Wilson had left. "They don't want him back to protect him. They want him back to tie up a loose end." He may not have known all the details, but he knew they wouldn't bother telling the whole truth either. He knew how they operated, *anything* in the name of national security, whatever it takes, whoever it hurts.

"I hope he's OK," mumbled Lisa, tears welling up in her eyes.

"He's fine," stated Lynnette with confidence. "You'll see." She prayed she was right.

CHAPTER THIRTEEN

PRINCESS HEDONIST: DEPARTING, LAN SYSTEM

Carefully smoothing his tunic, Jack stepped out into the corridor with Maria on his arm and was greeted by the rest of the pilots. The group had a big evening planned, dining at the Captain's table in the famous Nova Restaurant then a show and dancing at the Starlight Show Lounge.

After a leisurely day of rest, it was time for a night of fun and frolic. The six pilots, accompanied by the amiable Shepherd who had adopted them all, strolled down the hall in their best dress uniforms. Their uniforms were all the same color now. The double-breasted tunics were a deep royal blue and their pants a charcoal gray with black piping on the leg seam. The pants fit close but comfortable and tucked into shiny, black, knee-high boots. Each pilot had proudly pinned their gold *Wings of Honor* on the left breast of his or her tunic while the right breast had two buttons open with the flap folded down to reveal the silky royal blue lining.

Their spirits high, the group sauntered down the corridor greeting everyone they passed. Even Fritz wore the uniform colors in the form of a two-toned blue bandana tied around his neck.

The pilots were friendly and playful as they made their way to the restaurant. "I say, gents," said Jack in his best British imitation, "don't we look absolutely dashing?"

"Aye," responded Brian in kind, "none better."

"Absolutely smashing!" remarked Derrik. "And I would venture to say," he added with aristocratic flair and a wave of his hand, "no one on this great tin-can enjoys finer companionship than that of our comfy little squadron."

"Well put," said Paul. "Although technically we're a little short for a squadron," he shrugged, "I'm just saying..."

The pilots strolled slowly along the shop-lined Promenade that ringed the Ecosphere on the fifth level and browsed the windows on their way to the restaurant. The shops were filled with strange and unusual gifts and curios from all over the universe. The busy Promenade gave Jack the impression of an old street bazaar teaming with life. Vendors stood in their doorways dressed in colorful clothing and hawked their merchandise to passers-by.

Prospective customers haggled prices with shop owners, and the merchandise was so foreign and interesting it almost compelled one to closer examination.

"Living crystals... living crystals," called the woman from the doorway of her shop. She held one aloft, dangling from a golden chain to sway and sparkle before Maria's dancing eyes. "Not only the most beautiful M'Lady, but also the most unusual... " The woman watched the slivers of reflected light play across Maria's face as she stared in curiosity and wonder. "Very rare," stated the woman after a pause.

Maria impulsively reached out to touch the crystal but it was withdrawn. Fritz sniffed an investigatory nose at an intricate tapestry hanging on a rack nearby, and the woman eyed him speculatively. Jack pretended not to notice. "Let her see it," he said quietly.

The woman had noticed the wings on their tunics and cast her eyes to the floor, "Yes M'Lord." Jack raised one eyebrow in surprise, *kind of drastic,* he thought. But he wasn't sure how to respond to it either, so he decided it was best to just let it go and say nothing.

Jack watched as the woman lowered the glittering, fiery crystal into Maria's upturned palm. Fritz sat and watched with mild disinterest and the other pilots studied paintings from a far away world. To Maria and Jack's amazement the solid crystal began to soften and its polished facets seemed to dissolve. "It's warm!" squealed Maria in amazement. "And look!" Before their eyes, the crystal turned into what appeared to be a limpid pool of clear azure water in the palm of her hand.

"It is very fond of you M'Lady, it does not do that for many..."

Maria's eyes turned to Jack "It's so different, may I have it?" She touched the pool in her palm with the index finger of her other hand and was surprised to see it was more solid than it looked. Jack glanced at the woman in the doorway who was looking thoughtfully at Fritz.

"I will trade the crystal for the furry one." She pointed at Fritz.

"Not likely!" blurted Jack in amusement.

"But this is a Teardrop crystal of Rhomm, very rare!"

Jack shrugged and motioned toward the dog, "He wouldn't like it."

The woman snatched the crystal from Maria's hand, "No furry thing, no Teardrop!"

Maria's face hardened, her dark eyes turned stormy and piercing, causing the vendor woman to step back in fear. Maria turned on her heel, fists clenched and strode purposefully away. "Didn't want it anyway. Right

Fritz?" Fritz stood and shook his head to rearrange his hair, snortled at the woman and her goods and trotted after the angry female pilot.

Jack caught up with Maria a few shops down where they met up with the other pilots. She no longer showed any signs of anger and Jack decided it wise not to pursue the matter further. "Dinner?" It was more a suggestion than a question and was met with a favorable round of approval.

The pilots headed to the restaurant through the Promenade and detached from the bustle of the crowd, chatting amongst themselves. Mike and Brian, oblivious of the dwindling throng around them, walked ahead of the others and discussed flight tactics with their natural good nature, accompanied by the normal animated hand gestures which accompanied such talks. Jack watched with amusement as he exchanged small talk with Derrik and Paul. Maria walked in passive silence, the Shepherd keeping pace at her side, pleased to feel the soft touch of her hand on his head.

"Captain Steele!" The cloaked and hooded figure stood inside a darkened entryway, his face obscured by the shadows. Fritz sensed the dark stranger before he saw him and his skin crawled with a queer sensation which was a sure sign of danger. He walked beside Maria, scanning his surroundings and the beings about him in an uneasy attempt to detect the origin of this assault to his acute senses. It greatly upset the Shepherd when the shadowed figure revealed himself before Fritz could locate his whereabouts. It was but a split second before the protective Shepherd imposed his capable bulk between the hooded owner of the deep voice and his beloved friend, Jack.

Jack turned to meet the shadowed owner of the deep voice despite his use of an improper title and was suddenly aware of the protective dog standing between them. For some inexplicable reason, Jack felt his blood turn cold. He was greatly reassured at the dog's presence but he would have felt less vulnerable had he been wearing his .45 Kimber. *"Commander* Steele," he corrected, "and you?"

"I've been known by many names, but you may call me Voorlak." He stood motionless in the shadows of the recessed entryway.

"I see... and how do you know my name?" With some relief, Jack realized he was now flanked by the other pilots and Fritz still stood in front of him, showing his teeth in a sardonic smile.

"You... all of you, are officers of extremely high-profile. Many know you."

Jack was growing impatient but Paul spoke first, "Yes... well, what can we do for you?"

"I assure you no offense intended to any of you, but my business is with Captain Steele..."

"Commander."

"Yes, of course. Commander. This is a very important matter and I must speak with you... alone."

"What about?"

"Not out here, inside please... and I must insist... alone."

Jack trusted the Shepherd's instincts and his blood ran cold again, neither trusted this being. "The dog stays with me." Jack said curtly. A nod showed the man in agreement. "Look," said Steele turning to the others, "you guys go along, I'll meet you at the restaurant." He read the concern in their faces. "I'll be OK."

"If anything happens," whispered Brian, "he won't see his next birthday."

Jack nodded, "See you all later."

The only light in the room came from the vidscreen on the wall which showed the outside view of passing stars and a nightlight above the suite's wet bar which produced a faint glow.

It took several minutes for Jack's eyes to adjust to the darkness, and he was glad for the presence of the German Shepherd, who would defend him to the death if need be. Jack Steele was not a man easily unnerved, but it was obvious even to this stranger that he was on edge. "Relax, Mr. Steele, no harm will come to you or your friend here." Fritz grumbled softly and Jack thought he saw the man smile but in this light that would be impossible. *Still...*

"Your friend..." he waved a robed arm towards Fritz, "does not like me."

"No I guess not." Jack was anxious to leave and shifted uneasily. As his eyes grew more accustomed to the dim light, he could see the room was much like his own suite.

"Please, sit down Captain..." before Jack could correct him, the man silenced him with an elegant wave of his hand. "Yes I know... *Commander.*" He turned away and eased off his hood. "A drink perhaps?" The old man moved to the bar and poured himself a drink. "An excellent vintage of Ditarian Brandy."

"No thanks."

"Come now, Mr. Steele, surely you don't think I went through all this trouble just to poison you, do you?" The question was not meant to be answered. "Of course not!" he snapped. He handed Jack a crystal snifter half full. "You are parched and tense. Sit, drink and relax. I have much to tell you."

Jack sat and sniffed the liquor pensively. Deciding he wouldn't know poison anyway and throwing caution to the winds, he sipped. It was sweet and heavy, warming him as he swallowed. Jack could see his face now, lined and aged, he studied the face for some time, both men remaining silent. The man, Voorlak, looked very old. "Who, or should I say, what are you?"

"I am by most labels, an *Ancient*... and yes, I am very old. I lost track after two thousand..." he smiled again. "Most stop counting after a thousand but I kept fair records..." he waved a hand expressively, "but then came the *200 Year Pennance Wars* and somewhere during that time, I lost count." Voorlak, lapsing into silence, stared into his brandy, perhaps reflecting upon old memories.

Jack was more relaxed and noticed Fritz reclining sedately, though still alert. "Why do you call me Captain when you know I'm only a Commander?" Straining to see more clearly in the dim light, he watched Voorlak's face.

"Sorry about the light my friend," he seemed to read Jack's mind. "At my age, the eyes become very sensitive, quite a bother really." He sipped his brandy then continued. "Young man, you have a destiny far beyond your wildest comprehension..." Jack watched him with interest but was careful to show no emotion. The old man appreciated his restraint, "You would make an excellent *Ruge* player my friend, you mask your feelings well."

Voorlak stood and moved back to the bar, "You will have your own ship soon. You and you alone will be its commanding officer. Your destiny does not stop there, however, *if* you make the right choices. If not..." he turned to face Jack and shrugged. "Few men have the opportunity to choose between destinies... " he leaned back against the bar, a fresh snifter of brandy in his hand. "You, my boy, stand at the crossroads."

Jack wiped his forehead, he was feeling warm.

"You," continued Voorlak, "can choose to be a man like Herman Shimp, or take a firm hold and step into history like George Washington."

Jack scratched his head, "Who was Herman Shimp?"

The old man shrugged, "A nobody... no one remembers, no one cares."

OK, thought Jack, I walked into that one. He was not surprised that Voorlak knew about Earth history or George Washington. Many offworlders he'd met so far knew segments of Earth's history and found it fascinating. OK, so I'll bite, he thought. "So how do I become like George Washington?"

144

"Well..." said the old man, "let's see... it was quite an amazing chain of events back home, that deposited you and your friends on this ship, was it not?" Jack had to admit that it was. "Are you a positive thinker?"

"Well, I like to think so..."

"Logical?"

"Yes."

"Good! Then you believe everything happens for a very distinct reason?" It was a statement more than a question, and Jack agreed, not completely sure where this was all going. "Right, now then," Voorlak took a deep breath as if all this was requiring a great effort, "since destiny, fate, whatever you wish to call it, has taken such great pains and effort to bring you here, then isn't it logical to say that you must be fairly important to the general scheme of things?" Jack conceded to this also, at least for the sake of argument. "Good, now the crucial part. Then it is being *here* that makes you important!" The old man paused to sip his brandy and let it slide down his throat, warming him. "This means your better choice of destiny must be *out here*. You will choose, Jack, between *Captain* Steele... or our old friend Herman Shimp."

For the first time since he entered this room, Jack smiled. "OK I get the point, but why me?"

"You are a natural leader, my boy. If you lead, your friends will follow, you will never be alone. But make no mistake, Jack, the course of history is rarely an easy one... just ask George Washington." He smiled and took a moment to adjust his cloak as if he was preparing to meet royalty. "I know you better than you think. You would never be satisfied in a life like Herman Shimp... too boring. No excitement, no risks, nothing to strive for, no accomplishments, no goals." He put the empty brandy glass on the bar and moved over to the child-pilot, some thousands of years his junior.

Jack rose from his seat without thinking why and Fritz stood at his side. The pilot stared into the wizened old face and tried to fathom the depths of knowledge that lay behind it, but was able to glean no more than the feeling that he had met this man before, and his words were to be taken as the complete and utter truth. Time would have to bear out the reality of his claims.

The old man bent down and extended his hand to the Shepherd who stared at him with shining black eyes. Fritz leaned into the stranger's hand as it scratched his head and felt no fear or threat. With one last pat, Voorlak straightened up. "He is a remarkable animal... he loves you more than life itself," he shook his head, amazed at the unselfishness. "He would defend you to his death." He could not bring himself to tell the young man that some day this might come to pass. They stood face to face once again and the Ancient pulled the hood over his head in preparation to leave.

"Wait," said Jack reaching out. There were so many questions, but surely he would know that...

The old man placed his hand on the pilot's shoulder. "I'm glad we've had a chance to meet, Jack. I know now, you will make the right decisions. Of that I have no doubts." Jack felt a strange feeling of elation that accompanied the hand touching his shoulder.

"But..." Jack had one last question.

Voorlak squeezed his shoulder. "Ah yes, your mother and father, I feel your concern. Go see them if you must, for you must reconcile your past before you can live your future." He adjusted his garments, pulling them close as if he was bracing for the cold. "Now I must go... sit, finish your brandy." He turned and moved to the wall of the suite that would face the outer skin of the ship.

"Will I see you again?"

"Yes." The Ancient's form seemed to dissolve like a fog as he reached the wall and passed into deep space. "Tell no one of my visit, Captain..." said the fading voice from the darkness. Then Jack was alone, alone except for the Shepherd with the shining eyes, who was sound asleep at his feet.

All in all it was a pretty spectacular departure, as stage exits go. For some strange reason, Jack expected no less, but was still curious enough to walk over and touch the wall through which Voorlak had disappeared. It was of course, solid. Jack sat back down and sipped the Ditarian Brandy, felt its warmth, took a deep breath and reviewed the conversation. So, he would have his own ship to command... *that* stuck in his mind. He'd wanted to ask how soon, when, what kind... but these were just a few of the many questions he had that went unanswered. He somehow lapsed into dreamy thought about home and all the things he missed most. It seemed like an entire lifetime ago.

"Jesus, dinner!" said Jack, jumping to his feet. He had opened his eyes and in a moment of panic, realized he had no idea how much time had expired. It seemed like hours. He had awakened Fritz with a start and the Shepherd stared at him indignantly. Jack put his empty brandy glass on the bar next to the other and headed for the door, the yawning dog at his side. It wasn't until he stepped out into the well-lit corridor that he realized he was

146

not on Promenade 5. He should be facing the open expanse of the upper Ecosphere because Promenade 5 rings it like a giant balcony. All the Promenades do. Instead, he was looking at the opposite wall of a corridor... his corridor! Fritz looked as confused as Jack.

Jack turned around and stared at the door to his own suite. Now he was truly confused! Had he imagined it all? Was it a dream? He rushed back inside and called up the lights. Two empty, but used, brandy glasses sat on the bar. "Whoa," he said to the dog, who stared at him with unblinking eyes. He decided they'd better get up to the restaurant. Maybe somebody else knew what the hell was going on.

Exiting the lift on Promenade 5, Jack and Fritz hustled past the shops, barely casting a glance to their surroundings. Knowing it would prove nothing but wanting to see a familiar face, Jack looked for the woman selling the living crystals. She was not to be seen. Had he imagined that too? When they had left the shops behind, Jack studied the other doors and entryways they passed, they all looked the same. Which one was it? He felt like he was in the Twilight Zone. He shook the feeling off and with the Shepherd at his side headed to the restaurant just ahead, hoping, by some miracle, everything might return to normal or at least have some reasonable explanation.

The Maitre d' smiled politely at Jack as he entered the Nova Restaurant and said nothing about the Shepherd who sauntered in wearing the squadron's colors on a scarf tied around his neck. Jack decided there was more to the shiny gold wings on his chest, than he'd originally expected.

Even in the expansive and crowded restaurant, it didn't take Jack more than a couple of seconds to spot the Captain's table. In fact, it was pretty hard to miss. Four smaller tables had been arranged to form a giant square with the middle open for the food servers. It reminded Jack of a Renaissance painting he once saw, depicting King Arthur's dining hall. The noise and bustle around the table was fairly considerable as the busy waitstaff brought steaming platters of food and the twenty-plus occupants of the table, laughed and joked unabashedly. Food scraps and litter on the floor in the center of the square looked to be remnants of a minor food fight recently subsided.

Jack scanned the faces seated around the table as he approached. Gantarro was there, of course, sitting at what appeared to be the head of the table, his bridge officers sitting on his left and the group of pilots on his right. Jack saw Raulya and Myomerr sitting among the ship's staff, and Derrik's uncle, Professor Edgars near the pilots. In fact, there were only a few people at the table he didn't recognize. Maria was sitting next to Brian and Jack assumed the empty seat between her and Gantarro was his.

"Well, that was fast," said Maria as the pilot took his seat.

"Huh?"

"You missed it `ol boy," sniffed Derrik. "Too bad, a right bit of fun it was, too!"

"Got her good!" offered Gant through a mouthful of food.

Jack looked around puzzled. He knew he must be wearing one of those clueless looks but he couldn't help it. He had no freaking idea what they were talking about...

A waitress, her uniform heavily stained and smeared with food, brought Jack a steaming plate of food and gingerly placed it in front of him. She smiled sheepishly. "I am sorry about your shirt, Commander." She turned and left after clearing some empty platters.

Jack looked down at his shirt then back up. "Huh?" He didn't know how much more of this he could take... Wasn't anyone curious about the mysterious stranger in the hooded cloak? They acted like he'd been at dinner the whole time!

"I only got her with a spoonful..." said Maria.

"Yeah," drawled Paul, pointing to Brian, "but *he* got her with a whole plateful!"

Brian smirked as he bit into a dinner roll, "Couldn't let her get away with dirtying squadron colors..."

"Not without retaliation," added Paul with a mischievous sparkle in his blue eyes.

"This all happened when I left to change my shirt?" guessed Jack.

"That and the inevitable escalation," added Professor Edgars with a wave of his pipe.

"They tried a counter-attack but we had them out-gunned," added Yosha, a tall Alberian woman from the ship's crew, "they surrendered just before your return." The bridge crew chanted a hearty victory cheer.

Jack's mind rolled his meeting with Voorlak like a video playback while he listened to the casual banter and jokes. Maria's voice at his side made him start. "Sorry," she apologized, "why are you so deep in thought?"

Jack shrugged, "No reason." He was just beginning to piece this all together.

"Did the stain come out?"

148

Jack nodded, he felt it best to go with the flow of things until this was all clearer to him.

The pilot was not trying to be rude, but he was only vaguely aware of his companions and the feast of edibles around him. Distracted, he ate half-heartedly even though the food was delicious. In fact, much of it looked and tasted like food from Earth. Then of course, there were the other dishes, the ones he wouldn't touch with a stick. One in particular looked like a bowl full of reddish-brown worms. Jack could swear they were moving. Try as he might, he could not get himself to stay with the conversation at the table. His mind wandered.

Platters arrived full of fresh, hot food and disappeared empty, as did the flasks of wine and brandy. It wasn't until dessert that Jack had assembled a reasonable assimilation of the events that transpired... OK, he argued, maybe it wasn't reasonable, maybe it wasn't even sane, but what the hell, it was the best he could do considering all the unknowns involved.

Steele quickly ruled out that the episode with Voorlak was only a dream. That would be too easy. No, the *Ancient* was real enough. Real enough to pour and drink snifters of brandy, real enough to touch Jack on the shoulder, these things weren't imagined. But anyone who could live thousands of years and could pass through the hull of a ship as easily as walking through a door, was far from an ordinary man. *Was he a ghost? An Angel? God himself? Certainly God would be as old as the cosmos...* The pilot rubbed his temples, this was all a little more than he could wrap his head around.

Jack had convinced himself, more or less, that nothing had really transpired on Promenade 5. As far as he could figure, he went to dinner with everyone else, got spilled on and returned to his suite to change his shirt... and met Voorlak. This is where he had a glitch... not only couldn't he remember sitting down to dinner, but his clothes weren't soiled! Other than that, it made pretty fair sense. OK, admittedly, it was far from a perfect explanation, but no matter how you laid it out, Voorlak went through a lot of trouble to arrange a meeting. Doing so, he demonstrated some pretty amazing abilities. Let's face it, thought Jack, there were easier ways to introduce yourself. He decided the whole thing was done to convince him not only the importance of the message, but of the messenger. And, possibly the origin of the message.

Jack Steele was not an overtly religious man, but he did believe in God. And while he didn't get the impression that Voorlak was God, Jack did not entirely rule out the possibility that the old man could have some fairly

149

direct connections. Jack smiled to himself at a personal joke; *OK, so Moses had his Burning Bush, maybe Jack Steele had his Voorlak.*

"Commander Steele?" Jack turned to see the Maitre d' standing behind him, holding a young girl of about nineteen by the elbow. She was tiny, barely above five feet tall. But it was obvious even in her loose red jumper-dress, that she had a nice figure. Lean and hard, like a skater or gymnast. She had long, wavy, platinum hair that hung almost down to her waist. Some of it fell across her shoulders like rivulets of silvery silk. Fine chiseled features, full round lips and slightly pointed ears gave her a certain Elfin look. But by far her most spectacular feature was her sparkling lavender eyes... smiling eyes.

All in all, thought Jack, quite attractive. He smiled politely,"Yes?"

"This, a-hem... young lady, asked to see the pilot officer with the four-legged furry being. I assumed she was speaking of you and your companion." The girl saw Fritz lying under the pilot's chair and nodded without speaking.

"Thank you." Jack waved the Maitre d' away and without getting up, pulled an empty chair over from the table behind him, "Sit down." The Shepherd slithered out from his spot and sat up to get a better look at the young girl. She pulled back. "Don't worry, he won't hurt you. What can I do for you?" Jack took a long draw on his wine.

"I am Seeta, the daughter of the woman who sells the living crystals on Promenade Five..."

Jack nodded. *So,* he thought, some of what he remembered on the promenade *was* real... *curiouser and curiouser.* "Go on..." he urged.

"Well, there was a woman with you... in uniform?"

"That was me," said Maria over Jack's shoulder.

The girl suddenly realized she had quite a large audience and was self-conscious about her rather ordinary dress.

"And..." prompted Jack.

"And, well... she looked at a Teardrop Crystal of Rhomm." Jack nodded again and the girl pulled a small box from her vest pocket. "My mother would like you to have it." She handed the box to Jack who opened the top revealing the sparkling wonder. When he ran his finger along the cool, two inch crystal shaft, he did not see the girl blanch.

"To what do we owe this sudden generosity?" queried Jack, handing the box to Maria.

The girl explained that her mother had not intended to offend but felt she had. And although rare, the crystal had bonded with Maria upon her first handling of the jewel and no one else could now touch it without fear of ice burn. In fact, she admitted surprise that it had not frozen Jack's fingertip just then, except that the crystal must have felt Maria's close proximity. At any rate, rather than destroy the crystal, because she could no longer sell it, her mother decided to give it as a gift, in an attempt to make amends.

"Why didn't your mother come herself?"

The girl smiled weakly, "She thought I would have a better chance of getting an audience with you."

Maria snickered wickedly, "She was probably right!"

The girl smiled more easily this time and stared into the Shepherd's shining brown eyes. She wanted desperately to make friends with these exciting people and this enchanting animal. She had almost fainted with excitement when her mother had told her they were on the Promenade earlier. Seeta had begged her mother not to discard the crystal. Failing that, Seeta secretly stole the gem out of the refuse decimator before it was destroyed and its particles ejected into space. "I can see why mother wanted him... he is most beautiful!"

"Thank you," said Jack, stroking Fritz's tall ears. "I don't think your mother understood that he's not just a *thing*, or a *belonging* to be sold or traded. He is my *friend*... and that is more valuable than I could ever hope to put into words."

Seeta nodded, "Mmmm, yes, I understand. Unfortunately, my mother is a simple dealer of collectibles. In her eyes, *everything* has a price... it's kind of sad really." Jack found himself agreeing.

Gantarro handed the girl a glass of wine, "You are obviously an intelligent and sensitive lady. We would be honored if you would sit and help us finish all this wonderful food."

"Really?" She had never eaten in this kind of extravagant atmosphere before.

Everyone agreed she should stay. Brian leaned over Maria's shoulder and aided by a little too much liquor, smiled his easy smile and slipped past his shyness. "Listen, Seeta..." She leaned forward and Maria leaned back, feeling like a fence in the way, "Umm..." Brian stumbled but recovered well. "Um, well, you see, we're all going dancing at the Starlight after dinner, would you be *my* guest?"

151

Seeta's head reeled, the personal guest of a *pilot*! And a pilot with *gold wings* on top of it! She almost choked on the words, but Brian would never have noticed, "I'd be delighted!"

Maria traded seats with Seeta and Brian's brain turned to mush. Brian and the young girl chatted comfortably all through dessert, fascinated by each others' eyes. She had never seen hazel eyes before.

As they finished their dessert and waited for their after-dinner drink, a crewman arrived from the bridge with a message for Captain Gantarro. Leaning close, he conveyed the information privately in the Captain's ear. Jack watched with interest, but no one else seemed to notice the transaction. Gant's eyes widened at what Jack imagined to be astounding information, then narrowed, as he nodded his approval of action taken.

The Captain of the Princess Hedonist stood, taking the crewman aside. And, with his arm around the young man's shoulder in a fatherly fashion, spoke quietly to him. The crewman saluted and hustled off. Gant stood motionless and watched him weave his way through the restaurant.

Jack stood, more to stretch his legs than anything else, but he *was* curious. "A problem?"

Gant turned and smiled, he eyes still far away... "No my boy, everything's just fine." The words sounded hollow, an empty deception. Jack did not move away, he felt the man wanted to say more. "We've gotten an automated distress call from a private yacht called the *Eliza Meru*... we've altered our course to intercept her drift."

Drift? thought Jack. His pulse quickened, "Pirates?"

Gant shook his head in distaste, "By the Gods, I hope not, they've never been seen in this sector before. If they are here, they're a long way from any of their normal patterns." He pulled at his chin, "No, I'd have to say this is probably a routine mechanical failure of some kind. In any event, we're required by legal sanctions to assist any call of this nature." He put his hand on Jack's shoulder, "Do me a favor though, stay sober tonight, alright? We might need a shuttle to go out for recovery. Oh, and not a word of this to anyone."

"No problem."

"Good, let's go have some fun!" Gant moved to the head of the table and clapped his hands for attention, "Let's go dancing, people!" Chairs scattered as the group of over twenty rose to their feet amidst hoots and a chorus of applause. Gantarro's mind continued to work on the situation, though he played well at levity. If the pirates were indeed out in this sector, it did not bode well for the UFW. True, he mentally argued, the pirates were becoming more aggressive than ever, but this would be a stretch even for them. He prayed it was just an innocent call for assistance. He tried to put it out of his mind for now; he'd know more in a couple of hours.

The band in the Starlight Lounge played the most intriguing music, compelling one to dance. In a wide variety of styles, they mixed fast and slow dances so couples had a chance to raise their sexual blood pressure with a pounding beat before dancing to a slow, sensual grind. It must work, because the steady flow of groups of singles entering the club was only matched by the volume of outgoing couples. In fact, this was the only thing that kept the club from bursting at the seams. One of the couples ready to join that outward flow was Brian and Seeta. They had not left each others' side since their introduction in the restaurant, and it was not physically possible for them to get any closer without privacy or the removal of clothes.

Jack and Maria were sitting out a dance with scattered remnants of their original dinner group when Brian and Seeta wandered off the dance floor in search of cool refreshment. Their eyes were wide and glassy, their faces shiny with sweat. Seeta clung to Brian's waist and rubbed her face on his arm. "I want to be alone," she reminded him.

Brian shushed her, "I know, I just want to say goodnight to everyone." Retrieving their drinks, they bid everyone farewell and made their way through the crowded nightclub and out the door.

"I say," said Professor Edgars, "quite a short farewell, eh?"

"I daresay," returned Derrik, "I would have done much the same with a lusty lovely like that on my arm."

"A horny little tramp," muttered Maria.

"Oh, and I suppose you're not?" Jack pulled her hair and she almost fell off his lap. "Stop being a snotty little bitch," he scolded.

"If I'm a bitch, you're a dick," she retorted.

Jack rose from his chair, almost dumping Maria on the floor. He caught her by the waist, "Gentlemen," he said, pulling Maria close, "I think it's time I take my drunken Senorita home and remind her of her manners." It seemed beyond a certain volume of alcohol consumption, her behavior changed from amorous to catty. To his dismay he had not yet identified that point of diminished return.

Someone asked Jack how he would punish her. "Spanking, I suppose."

Maria pushed him away, "You and what army?"

153

"Me, myself and I should be enough," said Steele, hoisting her over his shoulder like a sack of potatoes.

"What if she likes it?" someone asked.

"Spank her harder," added Derrik.

"Works for me," said Jack with a grin.

"Captain Gantarro to the bridge, please. Captain Gantarro to the bridge..." the message came over the address system, momentarily interrupting the music.

The Captain rose from his seat at the table, "Jack?"

"I'll be right behind you. I need to deposit this," he patted Maria's bottom, still slung over his shoulder. Gant nodded, turned and left.

Shoot, thought Jack, *I was really looking forward to putting a rosy color on her butt.* Jack made his way onto the dance floor and cut in on Paul who was dancing with Myomerr. He knew if he was going to fly he would need a copilot "You sober?"

"Sure."

"No questions, just meet me on the bridge, ten minutes. OK?"

"You got it."

"Thanks," Jack turned and hustled through the crowd, the protesting Maria bouncing on his shoulder. "C'mon Fritz!" The Shepherd slid through the undulating throng with little apparent effort.

CHAPTER FOURTEEN

PRINCESS HEDONIST: WRECK OF THE ELIZA MERU

Paul Smiley stood in the corridor outside the entrance of the bridge and waited for Jack. He wondered what he was there for and leaned back against the padded corridor wall, arms folded with his eyes closed. The pilot-warrior within him began to speculate about circumstances that would bring him here late at night. If he had been back on his carrier, Shenandoah, he would know what to expect. At the very least, he'd have heard some scuttlebutt, but here... Paul opened his eyes at the swish of the elevator doors. "Hey, Jack. So, what's the story?"

Jack stepped out of the lift alone. "Well, I'm not so sure, it was kinda sketchy, I'll let Gant fill us both in. C'mon, we'd better get in there." About to enter the professional side of the interstellar traveler's world, the two pilots did an unconscious tuck and primp to neaten their already spotless appearance.

Jack touched the numbered keypad and the door slid open with a hiss, admitting them to the bridge. The lights in the command room were muted, almost to the point of being cozy, but it was actually so the bridge crew could read their instruments and see their consoles better. The two pilots stood just inside the entry and waited to be officially noticed and admitted. The room containing the bridge was shaped like a half moon, the entrances from the corridor on the flat side. A domed ceiling met walls without seam, providing the perfect surface for a panoramic vidscreen.

Ceiling and walls, except for the flat side, sparkled with points of light like the planetarium Jack remembered from his childhood. Science and navigation vid-stations lined the curved left and right walls while the ship's communication station occupied a huge console in the center of the *balcony* overlooking the *pit*. The pit and the balcony were not so far away as their names implied. In fact, the pit was only about eighteen inches below the balcony, much like a sunken living room.

The pit was where the actual physical control of the Princess Hedonist took place, three helm stations, a security station, and in the center, the Captain's Command Chair. The CCC, as it was commonly called, held three vid monitors, so at anytime the Captain could view any three vital work stations at a time, checking operations in progress or even intervening if necessary.

The two pilots watched the teamwork on the bridge and admired the efficiency and diligence. They watched the crew, studying their consoles, faces bathed in the multicolored light of the vidscreens, "In range of the visual pick up..."

"Good, on screen," said Gant.

"Yes, sir. Video in four... three, two, one." Where the forward floor length view-screen had previously shown only distant stars and empty space, a small ship wavered into view.

"Focus, please." Gant's voice was almost fatherly.

Jack and Paul stepped forward in a reflex effort to get a better look at the ship which seemed so lost amongst all those stars. One of the crew caught their movement in her peripheral vision and looked up from her work station. "Officers on the bridge," she announced. The two pilots became a momentary center of attention as bridge personnel glanced up from their work.

"Come in, gentlemen," said Gant, "we've just reached visual range." The panoramic screen image became clearer as the crew adjusted focus, and the Princess Hedonist drew closer to the drifting craft. "So far we've had no communications contact with the Eliza Meru. Either they're unable to transmit, or there is no one left to transmit. We'll find out soon enough."

Paul pointed to the screen, "What's that weird glow behind her?"

"Science..." called Gant.

"She's trailing what appears to be a mixture of atmosphere and fuel sir. It's a pretty bad leak."

"Any signs of life?"

"Can't tell at this range sir, but some of her systems are still operating or she would've run out of atmosphere long ago."

"Thank you, Ensign." Gant turned to his own command panel and pushed a comm button, "Tower?" The flight bay's control tower, acknowledged their presence and Gant ordered the work craft readied. He turned back to Jack and Paul, "You two ready for a little flight?"

"Sure."

"Good. We want to check for occupants and after that shut her completely down. Don't waste any time, we don't want to linger in this area. OK?"

"No problem," said Jack.

"Good. The engineers going with you will meet you in the bay. While you suit up they'll brief you on recovery procedure. We'll be watching you from here. Don't use ship-t0-ship communications unless it's really necessary."

Jack and Paul left the bridge and headed for the air tunnel station on the bridge level, knowing it would have the least traffic. They carried with them the uneasy butterflies caused by the unique combination of excitement and the uncertainty of the unknown.

As the air car whistled along, neither man spoke, both lost in their personal thoughts. Even when they passed through the upper reaches of the trees in the Ecosphere, an impressive sight, neither moved or spoke. Jack glanced over at Pappy, his head rested back comfortably on the padded headrest and his eyes were closed. He looked to be totally relaxed. Jack took a deep breath and tried to do the same.

■ ■ ■

The flight bay was a hub of activity. A ten person work craft sat on the loading ramp, its systems already up and running. Mechanics scurried about and technicians made last minute checks of special equipment.

Jack and Paul were ushered to the ready room, fitted with atmosphere suits and given sidearms. On their way down the ramp, Jack looked more closely at the work shuttle. It looked weathered and beaten. "Geez, what a piece of junk!"

Another form in an atmosphere suit, stepped out of the hatchway of the craft, "True, she's not much to look at, but she's got a good heart." He extended his hand, "Trigoss, Chief Engineer... our tech is already aboard." They all shook hands as they stepped through the entry hatch. "This is our spare tractor," said the Engineer as he affectionately patted the inside of the hull. "We had a newer one but no one seems to know what happened to it."

"Mechanical problems?" asked Pappy.

Trigoss shook his head as he closed and sealed the hatch behind them. "No, missing."

"Missing?! How in God's name do you lose a shuttle craft?"

Trigoss was a short, burly figure, with hands like hams. Because of a heavy olive complexion, no hair and a short, flat nose, he somewhat resembled a reptile... sort of. He rubbed a sizable hand across his forehead. "Well, not lost. More probably stolen."

157

Jack was having a difficult time fathoming this and he was hoping he wasn't being dense. "Why, how, would someone steal a shuttle? I mean, what would they do with it? Where could they possibly hide it? This bay is *big*, but there can't be that many places to..."

Trigoss was shaking his head and waving his hand. "No, Commander, not like that. Steal as in starting the engines and leaving in it."

"Oooohhh." Now he did feel dense.

Paul made him feel better. "Well that would be pretty stupid though wouldn't it? Their range is fairly short."

"True," agreed the Engineer, "but there may have been a predestined meeting coordinated. Leave, cruise a short distance, then wait. A little risky but usually successful."

Curiouser and curiouser thought Jack as he climbed into the command seat. Paul drew the copilot's seat. For Jack it was a natural inclination, and if Paul had any objections to it, he kept them to himself. The controls were laid out almost identical to the regular shuttles and neither pilot had any trouble acclimating to the ship.

The tower cleared the little ship for takeoff and Jack taxied it slowly toward the open bay door and the void beyond. At the door, Jack gently tapped the thrust button on the control stick and it sent them slowly out into space. "Gear in?"

"Done," replied Pappy, flipping the switches. Jack throttled up and headed for the drifting Eliza Meru.

■ ■ ■

Trigoss stuck his head into the cockpit, "Circle around her one time, give us a chance to decide the best place to board her. OK?" Both pilots affirmed the request.

The Eliza Meru was at one time a beautiful and graceful ship. Sleek, comfortable and fast for a private ship. She was now twisted, broken, and blackened. "Christ..." murmured Paul, "what happened to her?"

Trigoss stood between the seated pilots, "Doesn't look natural," he said, rubbing his chin. He turned to the rear of the shuttle, "What d'you think Marcus?"

"I've got traces of mercury and argon coming up on the scanner," came the answer.

"Mmmm..." Trigoss nodded thoughtfully.

158

"Holy cow, look at that!" Pappy's eyes widened as the shuttle coasted around the stern of the Eliza Meru.

"Jesus..." added Jack, his voice barely audible. Massive blast holes raked the stern. One of the ship's twin engines no longer existed. The other trailed its vitals and fuel behind it. A twisted hole in the hull just forward of the engines trailed atmosphere vapor.

"Pace her here." Trigoss pointed to the hole forward of the engine section. "And hold us steady above her hull."

"OK... So, what's the mercury and argon mean? And what the hell happened to this ship?" Jack adjusted the throttle to coincide with the Eliza Meru's drift.

"Pirates, probably." Both pilots turned to look Trigoss in the eye, expecting to see some humor there. There was none. "So, we don't want to hang around here too long." He added, turning away, "Marcus, those grapples ready?"

"Aye, Chief."

"Fire away then!" The small shuttle vibrated as the grapple points fired, trailing tether cables. The points pierced the hull of the Eliza Meru around the hole in her hull and opened to hold the cables fast. "OK, Marcus, they've stuck, winch us in." Trigoss was watching from a starboard observation port. The winches hummed as the cables pulled the two ships together, the shuttle's hatch covering the hole in the Eliza Meru.

"OK, boys, we're all the way in. Give us a little reverse thrust, let's stop this drift." Jack applied back-thrust as Paul gathered their gear. Above the top of the crippled hull, Jack could see the Princess Hedonist in the distance, about ten miles out. For some reason, she seemed farther away than that.

The four men donned their helmets and popped the shuttle's hatch. A great *whoosh* and the air disappeared, lost to the starry void through the gap between the ships. The special suits the men wore were not the clumsy, bulky suits worn by Earth's Astronauts. These fit more like a scuba diver's suit, though not quite as tight. The climate and air support equipment was small enough to fit on a utility belt that plugged into the waist of the suit and provided about four hours of life support.

Jack checked his sidearm as he stepped through into the darkened interior of the Eliza Meru. Trigoss touched him on the elbow from behind, "Relax kid, you won't need that. Won't be anything but ghosts here..."

Paul and Jack exchanged glances in the darkness, their faces illuminated by the systems lights in their helmets. Neither said a word. They both had the feeling the Chief Engineer had seen this kind of thing before. The artificial gravity system was still working but just barely, and the men had to carefully negotiate their way through the corridors. Lighting glowed faintly but inconsistently throughout the ship and Paul was glad for the hand-spotlights they carried. Signs of struggle were everywhere. The once gracious interior was strewn with ruined furniture, the walls and ceiling marred with black burns from small arms fire. Since there was no atmosphere, there was no sound and the stillness was eerie and chilling.

The four men split up to inspect the ship, connected only by the comm units in their helmets. Jack's hand itched. He longed for the weight of his . 45, but all he had was the lightweight sidearm issued him in the flight bay. He pulled it from its holster and returned it, his common sense telling him, weapons were unnecessary here. The hair at the back of his neck and his alarm senses made him pull it back out again, it made him feel less naked.

Paul had been in three rooms and found nothing. He was about to head to the bridge where they'd agreed to meet, when he stumbled over something in the hallway, some kind of an animal, a pet most likely, its head and brains blown across the corridor deck and walls. *"Ugh."* He turned away in disgust and continued down the hall. He reported what he saw into the comm unit.

Trigoss' voice came back calm and dry, "Yeah, I got four humanoid casualties over here, probably bodyguards or crew. All done execution style... real thorough too. Be damned if I could even guess what race they used to be."

The last room on Jack's level made him rear back in horror. A woman, probably middle aged and of good physical shape, lay nude, spread eagle and bound to a bed of regal proportions. Her face was frozen in a ghoulish mask of terror and pain. It was obvious she had been raped and tortured.

Cut, lash and burn marks, showed scarlet on her breasts, feet and stomach. Her eyelids had been removed so she could not close them against the horror. Her tongue had been torn out to silence her screams. There was blood everywhere, frozen to the walls and furniture in the cold of zero atmosphere. Even in his years on the Police Department, Jack could not recall anything this horrific. "Oh God..." He clenched his teeth and swallowed hard, forcing the bile back down. He backed out of the room and into the corridor. Leaning against the wall, he turned up the oxygen in his suit and calmed his breathing.

"You OK, Commander?"

Jack turned his head and started, surprised to see Trigoss standing next to him. "I'll be OK." He pointed into the room, "She's been tortured, it's bad." Beads of sweat ran down his forehead and stung his eyes, making him blink.

"Pirates." The Engineer's tone was flat.

"Fucking animals..." Jack's voice was filled with venom. His disgust and aversion was quickly turning to a burning hatred for those responsible for this atrocity.

The bridge was a free-for-all of carnage. The crew was scattered everywhere, slaughtered at their stations, most unarmed. Marcus began unpacking a small satchel on the control console. The satchel contained explosives, detonators and timers. "No one else should ever see this," he said, "let them sleep in peace."

They all agreed and began assembling and installing the charges about the ship. The unspoken additional truth was, they didn't want the pirates using the automated distress equipment as bait either.

■ ■ ■

"Good Lord. What's taking them so long?" Gantarro sat in his command chair on the bridge of the Princess Hedonist, with his elbows on the console and his face in his hands.

"It's been less than an hour sir."

"Dammit, Lieutenant I know *how* long it's been. *I'm* telling you it's *too* long!" The rebuked officer said no more, staring sullenly at his station. "Ensign," said a calmer Gant, "where's our visitor now?"

"Still on the very edge of our sensor grid, sir. Still can't tell what she is yet, she hasn't moved much. Probably a UFW cruiser."

"Never assume, Ensign... gets you in trouble. Let me know if she moves." The mysterious craft appeared shortly after the shuttle reached the drifting yacht and hung on the fringes of the Princess' sensor reaches. Twice it moved restlessly about, but came no closer. Perhaps, not knowing its opponent, feared revealing its identity. Or perhaps its Captain was calculating the best opportunity for assault. Either scenario was as likely as the other, nowadays.

Gantarro stared at the image of the shuttle and Eliza Meru on the view-screen, hoping to see the shuttle break free for its return trip. He knew one thing for sure, if it was taking this long, it must be bad. This made him even more wary of their visitor, more likely its intent was not an honorable one.

Gant seriously wanted to just call the shuttle and tell them to speed it up, but their visitor might hear their transmissions. No, the best course of action was silence. Silence and a deliberately casual and unhurried attitude. This, he hoped, would tell whoever was watching, that the Princess had no fears. Plain and simple... it was a bluff.

"They're pulling out sir."

Gant straightened in his chair, "Who?"

"The work shuttle, it's on its way back."

"Excellent!" Gant slapped his hand on the console. "Navigation, plot the most direct route to get us back on course. Helm, swing our stern to recover that work craft." The bridge became a flurry of activity. "Tower, no radio communications, follow silent signal protocol for approach and landing." Gant watched the little shuttle draw closer on the vidscreen and felt relief. "Where's our visitor?"

"Status unchanged sir."

The Captain rubbed his hands together, "Well, so far, so good."

The Shuttle had detached cleanly from the Eliza Meru and swung away to head for the Princess Hedonist. The return trip took under two minutes. If the crew aboard the work craft noticed the visitor on their sensors, they gave no indication of it, executing a perfect standard approach and landing as instructed by the flight tower. Before the work craft had her systems completely shut down on the ramp, the Princess was under way, leaving the Eliza Meru behind.

Jack, Paul, Trigoss and Marcus, sat in the ready room and stripped off their flight suits in silence. No one even made eye contact. There was nothing that could be said and eye contact could only serve to reaffirm that painful fact. As they rose to leave, Jack decided he could brief Gantarro alone. Besides, he figured he couldn't sleep now anyway. "Look, you guys, uh, go get some rest. I'll take care of this." He turned and strode away from the others, not wanting to discuss it further.

The others watched him go. Trigoss rubbed his chin, "That's one angry young man. Think he'll be OK?"

Paul nodded, "He'll be alright."

"Well... he shouldn't take it so personally, it's not healthy."

"He can't help it, Trigoss, it's in his blood. Once a cop, always a cop. His whole persona revolves around being a good guy in a white hat, and for him, that means being totally intolerant..."

"Well I hope he doesn't let it eat him up."

162

Paul shook his head, "No, I don't think he'd let it go that far, but I'll tell you what, I pity the son-of-a-bitch if Jack ever gets his hands on him."

Trigoss smiled, "I'd like to watch, if he did."

■ ■ ■

The corridors were deserted and quiet. Jack was thankful for the solitude. The ride to the bridge in the air car was relaxing and the cool air rushing by, refreshing. Closing his eyes, he pulled in a cleansing breath and cleared his mind. He would not forget what he saw, but needed to file away the images and anger. When the air car slid to a silent stop near the bridge, a renewed Jack Steele climbed out, calm and collected.

Jack stared at the vidscreen, still locked on the figure of the Eliza Meru. Gantarro watched the somber pilot who seemed to be mesmerized by the image. He looked over-tired. Gant tried to decide whether to send him off to get some rest or prompt him into speaking. It could probably wait until morning but Gant's curiosity got the better of him. "You expecting her to go somewhere?"

Jack looked at his watch and smiled wearily, "Sort of."

"What do you mean?"

"Watch..."

"What will she do?"

"Disappear..." Jack checked his watch again, "about now..." The crew on the bridge of the Princess Hedonist watched as flickers of light raced through the hull of the Eliza Meru and tore her apart in a spectacular final flash. A growing sphere of debris expanded outward to a chorus of oohs and aahs from the crew. Without realizing it, Jack sighed in relief.

Gant wondered how their visitor would react to this. "It must have been pretty bad." It was more a question than a statement.

Jack looked away from the screen. "Disgusting. Trigoss said it must've been pirates. All I can say is, I'd like to meet whomever it was alone in a dark alley sometime."

Gantarro shook his head, "They're getting worse."

"They need to be stopped." Jack's voice was without emotion.

"No argument here, though I must say, it's rare to see this kind of ruthless behavior..."

"Criminals are criminals," said Jack, dryly.

Gant agreed again. It was obvious the young pilot saw some terrible things. His sensibilities would be raw for some time. Discussing it now could only serve to make things worse. Gant put his hand on Jack's shoulder, "Listen, you look beat, go get some rest. We can talk more after brunch." A report would have to be filed but details could wait until morning. He also told him nothing of the ship that had been shadowing them on the fringes of their sensor range. It simply wasn't necessary or productive at this point. "Go ahead son, in fact, I'm going to get some rest too."

Jack left and Gantarro retired to the Captain's ready room, a private office and quarters attached to the bridge. He left strict orders to be notified if their *shadow* made any changes in status. He stretched out on the cushy leather couch and was asleep before Jack had even climbed into a waiting air car down the corridor.

■ ■ ■

Flexing and yawning, Fritz was there to greet Jack when he stepped into his suite. The tired pilot reached down and gave the dog's head a playful tussle, "Hey pal, how's it going?" The Shepherd grumbled through a yawn as Jack wandered through the living room into the bedroom. Maria slept snuggled in a ball, right where he left her in the center of the bed. Jack could see where the dog had curled up on the bed by the woman's feet. "So, you've been keeping her company?" The Shepherd looked at him with sleepy eyes, climbed gently up onto the bed and wagged his tail. Jack said nothing as he sat on the edge of the bed and stripped off his clothes. He was too tired to argue with the animal, who had already made himself more than comfortable. "G'night dog," mumbled Jack, as he slid under the covers behind Maria. He fell into a fitful sleep interrupted by visions of tortured figures. This eventually and thankfully, faded into a deep, dreamless void.

■ ■ ■

"Sir?"

Gantarro opened his sapphire blue eyes and looked up at his first officer. Rubbing his face, he swung his feet off the couch and to the floor. "What is it?" He said, glancing at his watch. Four hours had passed.

"Our shadow, sir, he's dropped completely off the sensor grid. Disappeared about ten minutes ago."

"Hmmm..." This puzzled him. Gant frowned and the furrows on his brow deepened. "What to do next..." There were so many possibilities to consider. "Increase speed... gradually. Maybe we can put some distance between us before he realizes it."

"So you're going under the assumption that it's a pirate?"

"It's a good bet. This is a standard stalking maneuver, it could be nothing... But, if it's planned, I'd rather try evasion now - we have more options." The first officer nodded his understanding and approval of his Captain's wise actions. Gant continued, "Let's see if we can plot a new course, throw these rats off our trail a bit eh?" He rose up off the couch, went to a small plotting table and turned it on. A miniature three dimensional section of universe shimmered into view above the table in the shape of a cube. Stars, planets, moons, and Genesis Gates, all in various colors were shown in relative scale. A pink icon representing the ship, floated among the stars, a pink line showing its present course. The holographic universe, however, had boundaries. These could be altered by changing the chart number the computer was referring to. The two officers studied their present course and using several holographic charts, discussed several alternate routes. It seemed each route had some drawback of one kind or another, but the decision lie in which was the least objectionable and most likely to succeed.

The key to evasion seemed to be the use of one of several Genesis Gates in the area. This kind of detour would get the Princess Hedonist out of the area in a hurry. The drawback was, it would take them several star systems out of their way, and they'd have to take two other Genesis Gates somewhere along the line to get them back on course later. But of course, the possible alternative of being boarded by pirates was much less desirable.

Genesis Gates were a wondrous miracle of space, harnessed by an ingenious method. Once thought to be holes in space, it was actually discovered they were more accurately described as tunnels, linking star systems, galaxies and the whole universes together. Special Gates were designed to mark and stabilize wandering entrances. Once installed, they were numbered for navigation purposes. Some tunnels have more than one destination and passage can be made in either direction. Before entering, programming a ship's navigation computer with the proper gate number will deposit the craft at the desired exit. Travel time can be reduced by months by using a Genesis Gate, versus a standard trade route.

Or as in the case of the Princess Hedonist, lengthened because of a necessary detour. The Genesis Gates' numbers were displayed on the holographic chart and Gantarro chose the one which provided the most difficult pursuit. It had three destinations on the other side. He ordered full speed for its entrance. This would place them at the gate in just over four hours. There was one gate closer but it had only one destination and was too obvious a choice.

Gant lay back on the couch and closed his eyes, "Call me when something happens..." he instructed. Then he fell back asleep. He too saw visions of horror in his dreams, except it was his crew, his passengers, his ship. He tossed and turned, his body attempting to evade the subconscious assault.

CHAPTER FIFTEEN

PRINCESS HEDONIST: *HERE THERE BE MONSTERS*

The Ensign, sitting at the sensor array console, stiffened in his seat, *"SIR!"*

The First Officer sat in the Captain's Command Chair, he looked up from the log notes he was writing, "Yes, Ensign?"

"I've got a *fast mover,* just appeared on the sensor grid. The unknown is approaching from our stern, starboard quarter!"

"Damn! That's where our shadow dropped out of sight!" The officer punched buttons on the Command Chair, calling up the Ensign's sensor display screen on his own video monitor. It was too small to be the same ship that had shadowed them, in fact it was so small in comparison, it could have easily been missed. "Good eyes, Ensign. Projected time of interception?"

"Just over six minutes, sir."

"Damn." With his elbows on the console, the First Officer bowed his head to rest on his folded hands. The Genesis Gate was still over an hour away, and with the Princess' engines running at close to full throttle, the small pursuer was gaining easily. Additional throttle would only run the risk of overheating the engine's forcing cones, it would do little to prolong intercept time. There was nothing he could do. "Security..."

"Yes, sir..."

The first officer lifted his head, "Wake the Captain."

■ ■ ■

Gantarro opened his eyes and raised his head when the security officer touched his shoulder. "What is it, Petty Officer?"

"The First Officer requests your presence on the bridge sir... We've got company," he added.

Gant sat up. "Our shadow's back?"

"No sir. A small, fast ship, on an intercept course. It's overtaking us from the stern."

"How far to the Genesis Gate?"

"Over an hour yet."

Gant nodded as he rubbed the sleep from his eyes. "So... the games begin..."

"Excuse me, sir?"

Gant rose and headed for the door. "Nothing... nothing at all." He knew what came next, the chase, the attempts at evasion. Whoever he was, the other Captain had timed it just right. The Princess was between the two closest gates, about an hour run to either one. Very vulnerable.

The bridge door swished open and Gant stepped onto the bridge from his ready room. The First Officer relinquished the Command Chair. "Helm, full throttle."

The First Officer blanched, "Full, sir?"

"Yep, every bit."

"What about overheating sir?"

"Well, if we make that gate, we have a chance... if not, we're finished. And if we don't go wide open, we'll never make that gate. So... I want every ounce of thrust those drives will produce. Got it?" The bridge became a flurry of activity as Gantarro prepared for the worst.

"Intercept in one minute, thirty seconds."

"Communications, hail that ship. Science, get us an on screen view." The view screen shimmered as the video pickups brought the ship into focus.

"It looks like a fighter craft of some kind, sir."

Gant nodded. "It's an old Warthog. Looks like they're using it as a scout."

"Isn't a Warthog a UFW craft?" asked a young Ensign.

"Yes, but they're outdated, no longer used. Most were junked, some were sold to underdeveloped cultures for defense. So don't expect this one to be friendly. It's probably stolen or war spoils." The pilot of the craft did not acknowledge any attempts at communication. Gant was not surprised. At a distance of only about a quarter mile away, the Warthog fighter shot by the starboard side of the Princess Hedonist like she was standing still.

"Damn that thing's fast!"

Gantarro smiled at the officer's remark. "Son, the Princess doesn't exactly set any speed records... you could pass her with a land speeder," he exaggerated. As the bridge crew watched, the glow of the Warthog's twin engines disappeared as the pilot cut boost and throttle. Doing a wing-over, the fighter went into a tight banking turn and reversed course.

168

"I'm reading an increase in systems power on that ship..." The Science Officer was calm. He studiously watched the readings on his vid-scan console. "He has weapons! He's powering up weapons!"

Gant remained calm, "Easy, Lieutenant. Drop all non-vital ship's systems to half and give me full power to our deflection shields." The rattled officer complied with shaking hands. Gant knew the shields were not meant for combat, but they should have no problem repelling a lone fighter, probably even two fighters. The Warthog flashed by the port side of the Princess feigning an attack run. It did not fire.

The bridge crew nervously watched the fighter on the vidscreen as it passed and cleared the stern of the Princess, repeating its first wing-over maneuver. Banking smoothly, it fell in line behind the Princess Hedonist and matched her pace, neither firing nor attempting to communicate. Gantarro motioned the bridge security officer to his side, "Ensign, wake our pilots. Tell them I need their immediate presence on the bridge." The first officer looked at him with one eyebrow raised. "Don't look at me like I'm nuts, boy... They're from a warring world; they may have an idea or two." He waved the Ensign on his way, "*Go*, and make it fast!" He looked at his chronometer. With luck, it was about fifty minutes travel time to the gate. At this pace maybe they could safely reach the gate before the fighter's mother showed up.

The Science Officer sat bolt upright at his station and swiveled around in his chair, his eyes wide with concern. "Sir, I have three more fast movers inbound... on the edge of the grid about ten minutes out." To the bridge crew, it appeared their luck had run out.

■ ■ ■

Jack was vaguely aware of Maria's singing and the sound of the shower. He consciously listened to the sounds only because he found them pleasant and soothing. Her voice lilted softly in Spanish, and the steady hush of the running water sent waves of warm sleepiness through his mind.

The pilot gently prodded the Shepherd sleeping across his feet when the dog began to snore loudly. Jack stifled a drowsy chuckle when Fritz rolled onto his back and with his feet in the air, continued to snore without interruption.

Jack was almost asleep again when he heard the door chime. He listened carefully, not sure if he had really heard it over the sound of the shower or

169

not. It rang again, repeatedly, urgently. Struggling to free himself from the bed linens and covers, Jack kicked vigorously and dumped Fritz on the floor with a thud. Grabbing a robe to cover his nude form, he headed for the door. "For crying out loud, take it easy will ya'?" He fastened the robe and opened the door.

"Sorry to bother you, sir. The Captain needs you all on the bridge, pronto..."

"What's going on, Ensign?" Jack rubbed his eyes.

"We've got company, sir..."

"Company?"

The Ensign nodded, "Pirates." Jack's eyes widened and the security man flashed a quick salute. "Soon as you can, sir."

Jack found himself saluting an empty doorway and stared blankly into the hallway. "Right away," he mumbled. After a moment, he snapped out of the trance and rushed through the suite. Throwing his robe on the bed, Jack headed for the shower.

Like most women who took their appearance seriously, Maria hated to be rushed, but Jack felt she did an admirable job in expediting her morning routine. While they dressed, Jack filled her in on the facts as he knew them, including a brief account of the visit to the Eliza Meru, minus the ghoulish details, of course. Like most men who looked upon their masculinity with pride, he did an excellent job of being overprotective and withholding his true feelings. But then again, she knew that.

As a personal best for probably both of them, they left their suite, properly showered and dressed, only about ten minutes after the Ensign's visit. Leaving Fritz with the waitress at the Ecosphere Lounge, Jack and Maria headed for the bridge. Joined by the other pilots en-route, they increased their pace. The group could be heard for some distance, their flight boots echoing in the corridors. The talk of pirates had prompted them all to wear their sidearms and passengers stared at the armed officers hustling through the ship. It was not an activity they were used to seeing.

■ ■ ■

The bridge crew, which was normally animated and amiable, sat silently at their stations, eyes glued to the view screen, as if blankly staring and wishing could change what they saw. Only Gant moved when the pilots

170

entered the bridge, turning to greet them. His face was ashen and grim. "In my ready room, please." He pointed the way without his normal joviality.

Jack paused to look at the screen as the pilots made their way across the bridge. The Princess had been forced by the threat of great physical damage to cease all movement, little more than thirty minutes from the safety of the Genesis Gate. With all engines at full stop, she drifted gently in the quiet, starry void, encircled by four out-of-date but very dangerous Warthog fighters. The stubby little fighters were inferior by current standards, but were completely capable of inflicting tremendous damage on the defenseless cruise ship.

Pirates. Jack's stomach tightened and he took a deep breath as he entered Gantarro's ready room. He had a feeling this was going to be a very long day.

Could these be the same savages who committed the atrocities on the Eliza Meru? Jack answered his own question; it was very possible. He had hoped to meet the culprits someday, but he didn't expect it to be so soon. Nor did he expect the sides to be so uneven. *Aint this a bitch*, he thought, *whenever you wish for something and it comes about, it never waits until you're ready.*

Several security people were already there, including Raulya and Myomerr. There weren't enough seats for everyone, so some sat, some stood, but everyone was silent and still.

Gantarro sat on the edge of his desk and cleared his throat uneasily, then spoke softly, "Gentlemen, as you may have noticed, we are in serious trouble. Those are pirate fighter craft out there... I don't know exactly what they want, but I can guess." Despite the cool circulated air, he wiped perspiration from his brow. "Food, fuel, any type of valuable goods or cargo, women and children too..." his voice trailed off. "Jack... Trigoss gave me a full report on the Eliza Meru this morning. If these are the same pirates, either they had some kind of vendetta, or we're dealing with a whole new breed. More ruthless, more vicious, more dangerous than any I've seen before."

A swirl of talk enveloped the room, and everyone seemed to have something to say at the same time. Predictably, it turned competitive and adversarial.

"Great," moaned Brian, "Just fucking wonderful."

Mike stood with his hands on his hips, angry at the general feeling of helplessness. "So what can *we* do? I mean, we don't even have any birds to fly!"

"I say," added Derrik, "I really don't fancy going down without at least giving the bastards a black eye..."

"Well," interrupted Maria, "I suppose we could fly the shuttles if we could find some hardware to put on them..."

"Oh, I say! Steady on, Missy! I mean a jokes a joke, old girl, but you can't seriously consider flying one of those bloody sausages into a swirl... it's simply daft!"

"Quit being a pansy!" Maria lashed.

"A pansy!? You're crackers woman! It would be plain suicide. Maybe you've had a bit too much juice... are you blotto again?" He gripped Jack's shoulder. "I say, Jack, you need to keep this girl off the sauce!"

"I haven't had a drop!"

"Oh, right-o, and I'm Winston Churchill."

Jack couldn't take any more and threw his hands up in the air in a gesture of frustration. *"OK!* That's enough! Everybody just shut the hell up!"

"Thank you," sighed Pappy. He addressed Gant, "Before we know if we have any options or not, we need to know what we're up against. What else is out there besides those fighters? Who are we waiting for?"

Gant wiped his forehead again. "The mother ship. She's a Raider class cruiser. She'll be here in about fifteen minutes."

"How big, size-wise, is she?"

Gant glanced uncertainly at Raulya then back to Paul and shrugged. "Considerably smaller than our physical size, but with enough firepower to blow us into asteroid dust. Why?"

Pappy shook his head. "No reason... yet. The more information the better. Sometimes the most obvious or inane piece of information can be the most important. You can never know too much about your enemy."

"True," agreed Jack. "So, if we're going to survive this, we'd better sit down and talk. Fast. We need to know everything you know about pirate tactics, equipment, habits... Maybe we can find some weakness we can use."

Pappy jumped back in. "I think the first thing we have to acknowledge is that we can't fight them on their terms. We'll lose. We need them to come down to our level somehow, because that will even out the odds a bit."

"Right, exactly. Familiar territory, so to speak."

Paul was speaking from the military level, and Jack was speaking from a law enforcement level, but for some reason, the two facets seemed to go together very well. It also appeared the two men were understanding each others' concepts as they were presented. Something rather important seemed to be formulating in regards to a plan of action and Gantarro could almost see the electricity between the two pilots.

The others remained quiet, watching and listening with intense interest. Gantarro explained that there were many different types of pirates, and there were actually some with ethics and a certain moral code, twisted though it may be. But recently a new breed had been emerging, ruthless and violent, born of necessity to survive the treachery of certain types of smuggling. These had no conscience. The smell of blood and killing of the defenseless held a thrill for them.

Raulya explained that the tactics were as varied as the types of pirates and depended upon the circumstances and equipment at hand. In general, there would be an armed boarding party, whose size was rarely predictable. Their job would be to seize control of the ship, whether it be by force or co-operation, then the officers would board to direct the operations of their salvage and seizure crews. At this point things got completely unpredictable. Sometimes entire ships were confiscated and their crews either executed or sold into slavery. In most cases, they would take what and who they wanted, using shuttles for transports, then depart. Smaller pirate vessels had been known to land in a victim's flight bay, fill their own ship to capacity and then leave.

Myomerr speculated since they were near a Genesis Gate, on a well traveled route, and the Princess had already broadcast a distress call, the pirate Captain would opt for a fast score and be off.

Jack shook his head. "Why? It's just as easy for him to commandeer us and move away from the trade route. He'd have all the time in the world."

"Or take the whole ship," added Paul. "It would make a tremendous mobile base of operations."

"He may not have the manpower," interrupted Gant. "Many pirate crews are understaffed."

"Yeah," said Jack with a smile, "but maybe, like many criminals, he's got an ego. A *big* ego, maybe too big for his own good. I used to see it all the time. They get cocky, think they're invincible. Then they get stupid, make stupid mistakes."

"Geez, that's a lot of maybes," said Maria sarcastically, shaking her head. "I hope you've got something more solid than that."

Paul shushed her with a wave of his hand. "I can see your wheels turning, Jack. What do you have in mind?"

Jack Steele was having a difficult time containing a Cheshire Cat grin, and it showed. The idea had just hit him. It was so obvious he was amazed he hadn't thought of it earlier. As he explained it, it became even clearer. "Look, a criminal uses a weapon not only as a physical but as a psychological means of leverage to accomplish his goal. More often than not, goals revolve around obtaining material objectives. Why? Greed, plain and simple. That is our leverage. To make *him* vulnerable, we need to give him a prize large enough, worth enough, that he has to put down his weapon to pick it up. This is where we'll find out how good our acting abilities are...."

Jack paused to let all this sink in and give him a moment to formulate his conclusion. The room was so quiet, if someone had dropped a pin it would have made a deafening racket. When the door from the bridge swished open, everyone jumped. The Security Warrant Officer stepped halfway through the door. "They're here..."

"Thank you," said Gant, rising. The Warrant Officer left and the door closed again, leaving them in an uneasy silence. Gant stepped over to a small view screen and turned it on. The pirate cruiser was slowing to a stop abreast of the Princess. She was dark and menacing. Though much smaller than the Princess Hedonist, the cruiser bristled with enough firepower to easily destroy the luxury liner. "Oh no..." whispered Gant. While everyone peered at the image, only Raulya and Myomerr seemed to have the same opinion as the Captain of the Princess Hedonist.

"What is it?" asked Brian, who had moved next to Raulya to get a better view.

"It's the Ynosa..."

"You know this ship?" asked Paul.

Myomerr nodded, stroking her whiskers, "She's changed a bit, but yes, we all do. Raulya and I both, served on her. She was a UFW cruiser."

"You mean she's gone renegade?"

"No," said Gant, staring at the screen. "She disappeared in battle over a year ago. All hands were expected lost. Heavily damaged, her communications dead, she drifted out of the battle without power and was never seen again. It was widely thought the Ynosa disintegrated... That's fairly common with her level of damage. Power plants race unrestrained, with no load and no place to dump the overflow of energy, they go into a meltdown. Not a pleasant way to go. We all had friends on her..."

"I'm sorry," said Jack, knowing the words to be inadequate.

Gant shook his head and took a deep breath as if putting away the memories, "No..." he held up a hand in dismissal, "no regrets..." He turned back to the group. "OK, they'll contact us when they're ready. Where were we? Ah yes. Mr Steele, tell us more about the acting abilities we're going to need... and this wonderful prize we're to tempt them with." The Captain's smile had returned. He was feeling devious. Maybe this was a chance to even the score for all those ghosts that walked through his mind.

It was as clear as a bell now, the whole plan. There were lots of variables, of course, not every circumstance could be accounted for. There would be some instances that would require thinking on the run. But, all in all, a very workable plan. Jack was feeling very confident and doing his Cheshire Cat impression again. "OK, so, this is what we need to do..."

■ ■ ■

The pirate Captain's face would be larger-than-life on the bridge's vidscreen, but Jack and the other pilots watched on the small monitor in Gantarro's ready room. With the split screen function, the pilots could see and hear Gant as well as the pirate.

Using a set of small, remote communication headsets, one with the microphone removed, Jack could speak to Gant without the pirate's knowledge. This allowed him to audio-prompt Gant in case something came up that hadn't been discussed, which might in turn, alter the plan. The biggest concern was, of course that the pirates would simply blast holes in the Princess for grins and giggles. For the moment, the vidscreen was focused on the pirate vessel sedately floating in space abreast of the much larger Princess Hedonist.

Gant had returned to the bridge, leaving the pilots and security people to their discussions in his ready room. Unfortunately, there was not much to talk about until they were contacted by the pirates. So they waited. Chatting uneasily, with awkward silences, they stared at the viewer to see if anything changed. Several people jumped when the buzz of the intercom panel interrupted one of those silences. Jack reached over to the desk and pushed the button to answer the call. He could feel his heart thudding in his chest, hoping it was the landing bay crew calling to tell him the preparations he'd ordered were finished. It was and they were.

"Good news?" asked Brian.

Jack smiled as he pushed the button to disconnect the call. "So far, so good."

Paul stood up and stretched. "So what now?"

Jack's smile had not faded and he thumbed at the vidscreen. "We wait for General Custer..." Nervous laughter circulated through the room.

"Check it out," said Mike, who had been examining the pirate vessel on the screen. "It actually has a skull and crossbones on it."

"Get outta' here..."

"No, really, I'm not kidding... look." He tapped his finger on the vidscreen. Everyone moved closer to get a better look and Raulya adjusted the control to enlarge the picture.

"He's right," said Pappy. Jack nodded absentmindedly, staring at the screen and pulled on his lower lip.

"So, what's the big deal?" asked Maria.

"Well it *is* a bit odd..." began Brian.

Jack broke his silence and agreed with Brian, "Damn right it's odd, it's downright strange! We're out in space a zillion miles from home, and there's some guy using an insignia originally used by pirates in Earth's seventeenth century. Christ, I find that pretty incredible! Don't you?"

It was obvious by their expressions that they were beginning to realize how bizarre that really was, but before the discussion could get any further the vidscreen flickered and the ship disappeared. It was replaced by the face of the pirate Captain.

"Look, he's *human!*" A shock of curly reddish-brown hair hung to his shoulders, a thick mustache underlined his strong nose and a well trimmed King Arthur style beard accentuated his jawline. His shifting eyes were dark and flashing. Wearing a loose, white silk shirt with large billowing sleeves with ruffles around the cuffs and down the front, silver buttons holding it closed, a gold medallion handing on a chain around his neck.

The pirate stood with arms crossed and glared confidently, his bejeweled fingers sparkling in the muted light of his command bridge. Raulya adjusted the sound and set the split screen function so they could see Gantarro as well.

"What the hell," groaned Mike, "look at the way this guy's dressed."

"Can't say much for his tailor," added Derrik, tamping a pinch full of tobacco into his pipe.

Jack shook his head in amazement, "He looks like he just walked out of *Pirates of the Caribbean.*"

Raulya shushed them with a wave of her hand, "He's going to speak."

"Good day, Captain. Let me commend you on your intelligent choice of cooperation. Resistance is not only unwise, but very dangerous. Allow me to introduce myself, I am Captain Joshua Kidd." The expression on Gant's face changed noticeably. "Ah, I see my reputation has preceded me. Don't be alarmed Captain," he waved dismissively, "most of the stories you've heard are greatly over exaggerated. Trust me. If you cooperate fully, no harm will come to you, your crew, or your passengers."

"Yeah, sure. And the check's in the mail," mumbled Brian.

"Easy buddy, time to play the game..." Jack had his hand covering the mini-mic on his headset and half turned to Derrik without looking away from the screen, "Is it my imagination or does this guy have an English accent?"

Derrik took a long draw on his pipe and the aromatic smoke curled from his lips. "Sounds more like Scotch or Welsh actually..."

"Hmmm..." Jack stroked his mustache and pulled on his lower lip in contemplation then shook his head. "Nah, couldn't be. It's too far fetched..."

"What is?" asked Pappy.

"I'm just thinking back through my high school history and there seem to be a bunch of parallels here, probably coincidences but..."

"But what?" interrupted Brian. "C'mon, out with it!"

"Well... the insignia on the ship, this guy's name, his accent... there was a pirate in the seventeenth century, Captain William Kidd, died at the turn of the century..."

"Hanged in 1701 I believe," said Derrik.

"Yeah, about then."

"And I do believe he was Scottish," added the British pilot, staring at the glowing embers in his pipe. "Are you thinking this chap is a relative of some sort?"

"It crossed my mind, but even with all the parallels..." Steele had to admit the evidence was so thin it was nearly nonexistent, it was all supposition and conjecture. Simple circumstantial coincidences that were too ridiculous to even consider, like something written into a low budget *B* movie plot. But still, there was something telling him he was on the right track - the little voice in his head and his gut had ganged up on him and were both nudging him in the same direction. He had learned to listen to and trust those lifelong companions.

Maria rose from her seat. "Oh you can't be serious! How would he get out here?"

"Same way we did," snorted Brian. "Ships disappeared at sea all the time. Who's to say what happened to them or where they went?"

Paul wanted to inject some sanity to this discussion. "I think we're reaching a bit here..."

"Maybe Pappy," said Jack, wagging his finger, "maybe not. Point is, he's human. So chances are, he's doing it out of simple greed. That makes it easier on us because we know what to bait him with and what his reactions are more likely to be."

"Well, you're going to get to try out your theory," interrupted Myomerr. "He's sending over a boarding party." The conversation died and all attention turned back to the pirate on the vidscreen. Captain Joshua Kidd was fairly well spoken but terribly long-winded and incredibly pompous. The pilots had allowed their attention to drift, but Myomerr had listened to every word, "Their boarding shuttle will land in our bay in about fifteen minutes. He also asked about the exact dimensions of the landing bay and its doors. Gant promised to cooperate fully."

Paul nodded. "I knew it, he's wants the whole ship..."

"He must have a bigger crew than we thought," added Mike.

"Time out," interrupted Jack with a wave, "let's not jump to conclusions." Captain Kidd signed off and the screen flickered as the picture winked out to be replaced by the view of the pirate cruiser. "And at this point it really doesn't matter. He's a criminal dirtbag who needs to go down. OK, let's get to the landing bay. We've got company coming and we want everything to look nice."

Maria rolled her eyes. "You *are* insane, aren't you?"

"Crazy," he corrected, "not insane. Insane implies I don't have a choice." He winked and everyone laughed as they filed out of the ready room into the corridor.

As the pilots and security people boarded the air cars bound for the flight bay, Gant joined them. He would have to meet the pirate boarding party and guide them to the bridge so they could assume command, or at least, that's what they were to believe.

There were just a little over one hundred security personnel assigned to duty on the Princess Hedonist and Jack could contact them all via his communications headset. Split into groups of ten, he would be able to assign them wherever he needed. All passengers had been confined to quarters and the corridors were deserted.

Jack could feel the butterflies in his stomach as the air cars whistled through the empty corridors towards the flight bay. Taking a deep breath, he closed his mind to the silent torrent of *what ifs* attempting to muddy his decisions. The ride was fairly void of conversation, each person wrestling with their own doubts and fears or perhaps praying to their own God.

The silence in the corridor was almost ominous and it was obvious the group was somewhat unnerved. Fortunately the flight bay was directly opposite and there was too much to do to be preoccupied with plagues of the mind.

The entire body of the security department was waiting when the group arrived from the bridge and questions came from all sides. The pilots left Raulya and Myomerr to deal with their people and moved on to quickly check on other preparations.

The two crates of twenty-four M-1 carbines had been unloaded from the Sweet Susie and lay in a neat row on a tarp stretched across the deck in front of the control tower. The ammunition had been carefully loaded into the mags, several of which lay beside each weapon. Containers of various sizes removed from the storage areas along the Port and Starboard sides of the landing bay were scattered in neat groups and rows around the flight deck. The towering columns of stores appeared completely full and untouched, as all the containers had been drawn from the rear, so their true presence on the flight deck could not be guessed.

From the level of the deck, everything appeared normal. Full storage areas on the outer edges, shuttles and work craft scattered about in various stages of maintenance or repair, tow and transport vehicles moving about and excess storage containers placed in easily accessible places about the deck. Yes, it looked like a completely innocent landing bay... but nothing like its usual neat and tidy appearance.

The reason for the deviously placed clutter was not apparent, until viewed from the upper level of the control tower.

The six pilots stood on the observation deck of the control tower and surveyed the massive flight bay below. At about a half a mile long and a half a mile wide including the storage areas, the bay was just short of seven million square feet. As impressive as its size was, that's not what was holding their attention. It was the curious arrangement of the storage containers that spread out from the base of the control tower and flanked the touchdown pad.

"Check it out," pointed Mike, "it's a maze..."

Paul smiled wickedly as the realization dawned on him, "Not a maze kid, a *gauntlet!* Look, see..." he pointed. "It protects the exits and restricts their use. If you don't know the route, you get cut off..." He turned to Jack, "Very clever, Mr. Steele, so, what's the game plan?"

Jack went on to explain as quickly as possible. Basically, it would be to divide and conquer. Surprise would be their key element to success, although there would be a good deal of play acting and some careful misdirection to boot. The two Navy F-18 Hornets and the Sweet Suzie would be the bait to divert Joshua Kidd's attention. Worth a fortune on the collector's market, they would be very desirable. The catch was, he'd have to get his ship into the bay to load them. Chances were, this was his intention to begin with, but Jack wanted a clincher.

The statistics showed the pirate cruiser would fit in the bay with room to spare, but the door clearance was going to be a tight fit. Jack felt the incentives were enough for the pirate to overlook any possible risks. He hoped he was right.

"Pirate shuttle with boarding party on final approach." The tiny voice spoke into the ear of every crew person wearing a communications headset.

Jack keyed his mic, "Have all the weapons been distributed?"

"Yes, sir..."

"Good. OK, places everybody. It's show time!"

"I say! You weren't thinking of starting without me. Were you?" The pilots turned to meet the voice as Professor Edgars stepped off the lift and onto the observation deck, an M1 carbine cradled casually in his right arm. He looked perfectly at home in the loose fitting, British issue, military fatigues.

Jack raised one eyebrow as Fritz ran to his side. "Professor! What are you doing here?"

"Uncle did a tour of duty in Vietnam in the late sixties," stated Derrik matter-of-factly.

"Leftenant Edgars reporting for duty, sir." He executed a very proper British military salute. "Never could stand to miss a promising scrap," he winked. "Your pooch has been following me since brunch at the Ecosphere so he just came along, naturally."

"Naturally," Steele sighed. "OK, well, I'm not going to turn down any offer - we can use all the help we can get. Professor, stick with Derrik. Let's go, people." They hustled to the lift and began their descent.

CHAPTER SIXTEEN

PRINCESS HEDONIST, LAN SYSTEM: *HIJACKED*

Fritz sat at Jack's side happy to have located him and searched for an approving hand. When the hand stroked his head and scratched behind his ears, he closed his eyes and leaned appreciatively against his friend's right leg. Jack crouched down behind the storage containers at the edge of the touchdown pad as the pirate shuttle settled to the deck. Fritz looked up into the face he knew so well and welcomed the strong arm draped across his shoulders. "You," said Jack, poking the dog playfully on the nose, "gotta do exactly as you're told. OK? No Mr. Mischief stuff, I don't want you getting hurt. Understand?"

He knew there wasn't a better dog anywhere, but wished he could make him understand completely. Jack stared down at the sparkling eyes like polished black Onyx and couldn't help smiling. The dog's tail swayed slowly. "Beep beep." Jack squeezed the dog's nose and watched him make a sneeze face. He snorted instead, wagging his tail, never taking his eyes off the pilot.

Communications were brief as information was exchanged from team to team in an effort to keep abreast of the situation as it developed. Each call chirped before the comm started and chirped again at the end. *"Here they come."* Jack recognized Brian's voice on the comm set and peeked through the space between the containers. He could see the pirates disembarking from the shuttle.

Dressed in mechanic's overalls, Jack and the others could move about in general anonymity, but with over fifty extra people in the bay, all armed, he felt it best to keep everyone in concealment.

Gantarro stood off to one side of the ship with another officer and greeted the pirates warmly. *That's it,* thought Jack, *make them feel at home. No threat, complete cooperation.* Jack's view was partially blocked by the shuttle, but Brian was positioned on the other side. "How many do you count, Bri?"

"Looks like twenty, give or take one or two. All armed too. I don't see their Commander though."

"OK." Jack didn't expect Kidd to be with the boarding party, too risky. Better to find out if the natives are friendly first.

Almost immediately, the pirates spotted the two F-18 Hornets on Brian's side of the bay and wanted to know more. They gestured wildly with excitement and appeared to quiz Gantarro. Several crewmen stayed with the shuttle as sentries, the others moved closer to the Hornets for a closer look.

"Jack, they're asking Gant about the other plane and its crew people."

Steele wondered how they knew there was another plane. The Sweet Susie was on his side of the bay and they couldn't have seen it yet. *And how did they know about the pilots?* "Something's fishy, Bri."

"Maybe it'll be OK. Gantarro told them we stole a shuttle and disappeared about three weeks ago."

"Did they buy it?"

"I'm not sure, but it looks like they did."

■ ■ ■

Several times, Brian and Jack had to order their people to retreat to a more rearward position in order to prevent discovery as the pirates inspected containers and their contents. More than once, discovery was mere inches away... Brian sat curled in a ball, his Colt .45, a semi-auto 1911 style pistol, clutched tightly in his hand. Concealed by a group of storage crates, he fought to control his breathing as a pirate opened the container directly behind him. If he decided to go farther back, Brian was sure he'd be discovered. Guiding his people rearward, the pilot had been cut off by wandering members of the boarding party and now he was trapped. He held the .45 close to his chest with his finger resting along the side of the frame and longed to wipe the sweat from his hands. He dared not put the weapon down, knowing that would be the moment he'd be discovered. Brian caressed the safety with his thumb and wondered how much noise it would make if he released it now.

Bored with the results of his rummaging, the pirate decided to explore further. Secretly stuffing into his tunic the only desirable item he found in the container, he stepped around the stack of crates. The pirate paused only twenty-four inches from Brian's feet and adjusted his tunic as he attempted to decide which stack of crates to pillage next. A half turn to his right and he'd have to be blind not to see the pilot curled on the floor at his feet.

Brian stiffened, his finger moving to the trigger and his thumb resting heavily on the safety release. Beads of sweat rolled down his face and stung his eyes, but he refused to blink. Instead, he angled the barrel of the .45 so the first slug would hit the pirate in the temple. The first indication of discovery, would seal the pirate's fate. Brian held his breath... As the pirate stood, hands on hips and surveyed the landscape of containers, the nervous tension of Brian's thumb, released the .45's safety with a click that sounded deafening to him. A sudden chill raced up his back as he realized the pirate had to have heard the noise...

"Bakir..! Bakir let's go! Kidd wants us on the bridge!"

The pirate shrugged his shoulders heavily and shook his head, "Bakir, Bakir," he mimicked sarcastically. The exasperated pirate sighed and mumbled quietly, "Bakir do this, Bakir do that, the Captain wants this, the Captain wants that... Oh no! Can't disappoint the Captain, by the Gods..." When he turned to depart, he turned away from the exposed pilot.

Unbeknownst to the disgruntled pirate, that simple act saved his life... for now.

Brian took a deep gulp of fresh air and gently clicked the safety back on before dropping the .45 into his lap. He wiped his shaking hands on his coveralls. It took him several moments before he could hear the comm pickup over the pounding in his ears. "You OK Brian?"

"Sure, Skipper, I'm fine," he croaked, as he stared at his still-trembling hands. "Christ that was close."

"Too close... but a good job keeping it together there. Listen, the boarding party is headed to the bridge. It looks like Kidd is moving us off the trade route..."

"That's good, right?"

"Yeah, the First Officer says Kidd's bringing his ship in. The boarding party will take control of the bridge and move us to a meeting spot."

Brian stretched his legs from their cramped position and winced, "You sure that thing will fit in here?"

"God, I sure hope so, it's our best chance." Jack checked over the top of the containers to spy on the pirate sentries near the shuttle. "By all the numbers, it should slide right in."

"Tell me again, what're we gonna' do with it, when we get it in here?"

Jack smiled to himself, "We take his ship."

"Uh huh. That's what I thought you said. Just wanted to make sure I didn't dream it." Brian leaned back against the storage container and wiped the sweat from his eyes. It was time for everyone to take a little breather.

■ ■ ■

"Commander Steele..." the voice was soft on his comm unit, little more than a whisper.

"This is Steele, go ahead."

"First Officer here... We've reached the meeting place. Kidd has recalled his fighters. As soon as they've been recovered, he's planning to board... cruiser and all. He's completely convinced we will offer no resistance."

Jack acknowledged as he watched the pirate sentries through the spaces between the storage containers. They must have already gotten their orders because they were moving their shuttle to the far side of the landing pad to make room for the sizable bulk of the pirate cruiser.

Supervised by the pirates, two of the landing bay work crews were busy moving containers and equipment back for the same reason. *"Stand by to receive pirate cruiser,"* echoed the announcement over the bay's address system. "Entering final approach. Landing Guidance Officer to the tower, please. Landing Observers to the pad."

Jack realized the increasing flurry of activity would hide any excess personnel and their movement. "OK, boys and girls, let's take our places, the real show's about to start." He instructed those with inferior stun weapons to maintain positions up close. Since the stun weapons were small and concealable, many took positions with the crews on the landing pad. Jack, armed with his .45 1911, was concealed on the fringe of the landing pad, while the others who had carbines, took positions further back which offered them a wider field of fire.

■ ■ ■

The nose of the pirate cruiser was visible in the floodlights just outside the bay door. Lights on the ceiling of the bay, once dark, flickered, then shone brightly on the upper hull of the ship, as it was guided expertly in by the Landing Observers and Guidance Officer. Battle scars and repairs, hidden in the darkness of space, now became obvious.

Brian shook his head in amazement, watching the Observers walking around the cruiser to check the clearances. "It's like threading the eye of a needle with a damn camel!"

"You mean, passing a camel through the eye of a needle... don't you?" chuckled Jack.

"Whatever..." muttered Brian.

"Don't you worry about that, sir," said one of the crew on the deck. "We'll get it in here, you just make sure he doesn't get *out*."

Touché, thought Jack. They had a positive mindset and he found that very promising.

As the ship inched its way into the bay, it almost completely filled the doorway. To anyone watching from either side, it would've appeared stuck if not for its forward motion. Only the people in the tower could see the full picture of progress, and thankfully, the Guidance Officer gave a running narrative over the com units. It took nearly thirty minutes to get the entire pirate cruiser into the bay, but it entered without adding so much as a scratch, to its fifteen-hundred foot long hull.

"All personnel, clear the pad, prepare for touchdown." The short announcement sent workers and pirate sentries, scurrying off the pad like frightened mice. And rightly so. Any biological lifeform caught underneath a vessel during the use of its suspension field during landing or liftoff would, in short, be compressed flatter than a pancake.

The pirate cruiser was beautiful, in a brutish sort of way. Jack could see the damage and scars, but could imagine her restored to her former self... fast, lethal, clean, pure. He felt a strange sense of excitement, a mixture of anticipation and a slow build-up of adrenaline as the cruiser settled to the deck.

Her bulk was supported by rows of three-toed landing gear with hydraulic legs the size of tree trunks. Jack correctly guessed the gear was designed to evenly distribute the ship's weight automatically on either rough or smooth terrain. With a hiss like a great sigh of relief, the landing legs accepted her weight and leveled the ship high enough to easily move about underneath her hull with service equipment or vehicles.

Jack was in awe. Forget the fact that the cruiser was sitting in the flight bay of a ship that dwarfed her, she was impressive. About four-hundred feet at her widest, Steele was beginning to wonder if they were in over their heads.

"Christ, Steele," said Mike, interrupting his train of thought. "It's as big as the Shenandoah!"

"Actually," interrupted Paul, "I've never seen our carrier from this point of view, but I think the Shenandoah is a little larger. But not by much..." It was then that a frightening thought hit him. "Christ, Jack, the Shenandoah's crew was over four-thousand... this thing's gotta be able to hold at least two-thousand. Man, I think we're in over our heads."

Even if Jack had his own doubts, he couldn't let others know it, nor could he let them doubt themselves. "No problem, Pappy. Gant told me a full crew doesn't exceed three-hundred..."

"Three-hundred? How could you possibly run a ship that size with only three-hundred people?"

Jack shrugged to himself, "Hell, I don't know where you'd put two-thousand. Gant says a skeleton crew of fifty could run her. He's guessing Kidd's crew is in the neighborhood of about a hundred-fifty."

Paul Smiley leaned back against the interior bulkhead of the Sweet Susie and glanced at Mike who was shaking his head. "Imagine that..." said Paul quietly, "you could run that monster with only fifty people..."

Mike stared at his wing leader in the darkness, trying to see his face in the splinters of light coming from the cockpit perspex. "Maybe someday they won't need crews at all..." Both men fell silent and listened to the muffled sounds outside the airplane. The young pilot switched off the miniature microphone on his com unit. "Pappy..." he whispered.

"Yeah?"

"D'you ever think about death? Y'know, dying I mean?" It was the type of thing most men only spoke of in the protective veils of darkness, granting all men anonymity.

Paul cleared his throat and remembered the air combat over the arid deserts of Kuwait. He remembered the sight of his first Mig kill. The way his Sidewinder chased up its tail and turned it into a fireball, pieces fluttering and spinning slowly to the ground. There had been no chute. "No," he lied. Silence fell once again. An empty, lonely silence.

Maria sat quietly in the upper turret of the Sweet Susie and very diligently, watched the pirate ship. She found if she breathed slowly, she could almost hear the two pilots below her. She strained her ears to hear a sliver of the conversation, desperately wishing to be included. Unfortunately, before she could determine the gist of what they were saying, it grew quiet. *Drat.* It was a feeling greater than just her normal tendency to be nosy, she hated feeling like an outsider. And at that moment, she felt more alone than ever before.

■ ■ ■

Waiting to see what the pirates would do next was like being on pins and needles. Jack relieved the tension by letting his mind wander. Not so far that he was out of touch, but just enough. It wandered home. To a warm, sweet, sun-drenched beach of golden sand, awash with the salty foam of gently rolling turquoise waves... it almost seemed like a place he'd never been, a place he'd only dreamed of...

■ ■ ■

Brian's people were pushed almost as far back as they could go. They watched, weapons ready, as the pirates moved the two Navy F-18s toward the pirate cruiser. The pirates were using automatons like the one the pilots had first encountered, to tow the planes around the flight deck.

Two cargo ramps, one port and one on the starboard side of the cruiser, opened like giant maws to receive goods into its belly. More of the pirate crew disembarked, descending down the loading ramps like worker ants to assist in the theft of the precious booty. A small armed detachment of pirate marines joined the original boarding party to help guard the entrances of the cruiser and maintain control over the flight deck. Though they remained vigilant, it was obvious they did not anticipate any problems. Their demeanor was casual, even jovial with comrades and landing pad crew alike. So far, Jack's plan was proceeding almost exactly as planned.

Jack watched carefully as the pirates cleared the way and rigged up two automatons to tow the Sweet Susie into the pirate ship. He was praying they wouldn't feel the need to look inside the B-25 before moving it. "Pappy, they're hooking you up now." Jack heard the *thump thump* in his earpiece as Paul tapped on his mic to acknowledge. Jack swiveled around to look across under the cruiser. One of the Navy jets had disappeared, the other was at the foot of the starboard ramp. He almost wished they had taken the B-25 in first. This waiting was killing him.

Timing was crucial and time was running short. Pirates were wandering through the rows and stacks of crates to pick and choose their booty... Jack wondered just how long the ambush parties could remain undetected. The B-

25, towed by the automatons and escorted by several pirate workers, rolled towards the port-side ramp of the cruiser. "OK people, get ready, we're gettin' close..."

"Jack, we've got a rather sticky situation developing..." It was Derrik from the roof of the Control Tower.

"Dammit!" Jack wanted to hit something, "What... Where?!"

"Starboard of the tower, they're getting close to a few of our people..."

"Who?"

"I can't tell..."

"Any way to take them down quietly?"

"Sorry, old boy, not a chance."

Jack eyed the Sweet Susie which had just reached the base of the port cargo ramp. "Damn, we just need another minute or two..."

Derrik watched as Professor Edgars adjusted the rear sight on his carbine. "Uncle says he can hit them easily..."

"*No,*" said Jack, "not yet..." He eyed the B-25 which was slowly inching its way up the ramp and the automatons laboring under their heavy tow-load. *Hurry up, you lousy overgrown tin slugs...* He wanted to scream it, but chewed on his lip instead.

"Oh, *man...*" Brian pinched the bridge of his nose.

Part of Jack didn't want to ask but he had to know. "What's going on, Bri?"

"Gant is standing right out here in the middle of the pad with that pompous ass, Kidd. They're going to be right in the middle..."

Jack peered between the crates but could not seem to find them. "Well, let's just hope he's fast on his knees."

■ ■ ■

With heightened feline olfactory senses, Raulya could smell the pirate coming, long before Derrik had spotted him as a threat. But she was trapped. During the last pull-back to avoid the foraging pirates, she had chosen a dead end in the maze of crates and storage containers. Separated from her security comrades, she was on her own. "I want all of you to stay put," she whispered into her mic. "We will not jeopardize our goal for just one person." Clothed only in her security uniform and holding an M1 carbine, it would be obvious what her intent was.

189

She crouched behind her protective cover and watched the burly pirate stroll between the crates and rummage through the containers. He looked big… big and stupid. Her mind raced while she stroked the carbine resting across her thighs. The weapon would be too noisy, she'd have to do him by hand. She was going to need an edge, she'd have to completely surprise him... He was getting close. She quickly pulled off her Comm unit and shoved it between two containers with her carbine...

■ ■ ■

Pangor could hardly believe his luck. The female Ketarian officer was beautiful. Beautiful and unconscious. The pirate stared down at the prone female sprawled at his feet, her tunic laid open to reveal her bare breasts, her uniform pants pulled down to her thighs. It was obvious someone had already had their lustful way with her, but this concerned him not. Women, much less a woman as attractive as this, were more often than not, sold to the highest bidder. And a lowly pirate soldier like Pangor could rarely afford more than the haggard concubines of the various bazaars. He could not resist this delicious opportunity. He glanced cautiously around to be sure he was unobserved. Reassured, he dropped to one knee beside his illicit discovery. He was determined to have her, even if he could not keep her. Pangor laid his laser assault rifle on the deck and slid it carefully out of the way, never taking his eyes off the woman. The lusty soldier rubbed his stubbly beard as he hungrily studied the curvy figure before him.

Letting his desire overtake him, Pangor reached out and stroked the smooth white skin of her stomach as he fumbled clumsily with his own belt. He paused at her breasts and felt her nipples grow firm under his fingers. Losing all restraint, the pirate tore at his clothes as he straddled the woman's body. With the fire of passion burning in his brain, fueled by Raulya's special perfume, Pangor buried his face in her breasts.

Raulya's knee caught Pangor squarely in the groin, toppling him forward. The fire in his brain was replaced by the fire in his loins which raced through his body, crippling his ability to respond. As he cried out, Raulya gripped his head by the hair and brought his throat to her waiting fangs. In a manner more familiar to her ancestors, she instinctively tore the throat out of her enemy.

The taste of fresh blood awoke ancient cravings for battle... the natural animal instincts to hunt and kill. Raulya rolled Pangor's limp body off hers,

190

his life's blood spilling across her face, neck and mane. She pulled up her uniform pants and removing the carbine from its hiding place, never bothered to re-button her tunic.

Alerted by the muffled cry of their crew mate, two more pirates moved to investigate the corner occupied by the Ketarian officer. It was a bad decision. The vision that appeared before them was both horrific and unnerving.

Raulya stepped out from protective cover, her eyes glazed, fangs bared, driven with blood lust. Great crimson stains ran down her bare breasts and matted her golden mane. The two pirates stopped dead in their tracks, transfixed by her appearance. Raulya snarled a long, deep, howling cry, which could be heard throughout the landing bay.

Jack's hair stood up on the back of his neck. *"What the HELL was that?"*

"Raulya," was Brian's simple answer. "The proverbial shit is about to hit the fan in a major way."

Jack glanced up the cruiser's port ramp as the B-25's tail vanished through the cargo door. "It's alright, we're ready! *Go, Go, Go!* Myomerr, take the pirates on the bridge!"

Raulya did not wait for Jack's order, she squeezed the trigger and fire leapt from the muzzle of her carbine. The recoil surprised her but she corrected for the second squeeze. The pirate, still frozen by her horrifying appearance, was knocked backward off his feet. His crew mate, standing beside him, pitched forward, struck between the shoulder blades by a well aimed .30 cal. round from Professor Edgars' M1, shooting from the flight tower's roof.

Several pirates fell before they realized their peril. The flight deck quickly became a dangerous crisscross of fire and return fire as the pirates scrambled to recover from the surprise attack. Quickly realizing they could not advance through the maze of crates and containers, the pirates were forced to take defensive positions, using the docking equipment and the landing gear of their cruiser for protection.

Jack's com-link filled his ear with shouts and cries. He could no longer communicate with his people and it quickly began to show. Most of the ground crews and security people had never seen any kind of combat or conflict and the superior weapons and skill of the pirates would soon panic them into retreat or surrender.

■ ■ ■

Myomerr led her security people onto the bridge of the Princess Hedonist like seasoned storm troopers. The seven pirate guards watching the bridge crew were dead before they hit the floor. Myomerr killed two herself. The first as she entered the door, grabbing his ample hair from behind and pulling so violently, she snapped his neck. The second, with a shot from the hip, with the old Colt .45 she got from Brian. The .45 slug traveled across the bridge and struck the pirate sergeant square between the eyes, splashing his brains across the giant vidscreen in a smeary mess.

Myomerr looked at the pirate corpses scattered about the bridge, "Send out a distress call," she instructed the Princess' helmsman. "And get us back on course. When we leave, seal the doors. Admit no one until you have proper clearance." She admired the .45 in her hand, "I *like* this *WEAPON!*" she snarled. "Let us find *MORE* vermin to kill!"

■ ■ ■

Jack thought he could make out something about the bridge being secured, but he could not be sure. He flinched when the flash of an energy beam destroyed part of a nearby crate. Fritz wanted some action but Jack grabbed him by the collar, "No way buddy-boy..." Peering between the crates, Jack found the source of the assault. Shouldering the storage containers to widen the gap, he took aim and waited... The pirate was good but he exposed himself to get another shot. The two heavy .45 slugs passed through the breastplate of his armor like butter, sending the soldier crashing to the deck. Their armor, designed to shield against energy weapons, offered little protection against the assault of a projectile weapon. The pirates were learning that the hard way.

The deck around the cruiser became a no-man's-land with little hope for survival, should one attempt to cross it. Several soldiers, well armed and heavily armored, raced onto the deck in an attempt to reach and take the tower hoping to gain the high ground. Firing as they ran, their weapons blazed furious flashes of pure, concentrated energy.

Defending fire thickened and cover fire intensified to protect the runners. Two never made it a quarter of the way. The others pushed on, weaving through the fire like they were dodging raindrops. Brian could not believe they were still going... they were almost to the tower...

■ ■ ■

"Are you ready, Uncle?"

Professor Edgars loaded a full magazine into the carbine, realizing it would be a terrible waste of precious ammunition. He nodded. "Together now... ready, set, *GO!"* Derrik and the professor popped up from the protecting rim of the tower's roof, firing at the runners. Empty shell casings showered the roof with hollow pings as the M1s fired .30 cal. rain upon the runners and the deck below. They fell, one by one, their armor perforated like paper.

The air erupted in retaliatory fire, the tower taking the brunt of the assault. Shards of scrap metal and pieces of cast-crete hailed the landing deck like shrapnel.

Through the haze of cordite and seared composites, Brian saw one of the two figures on top of the tower pitch backward by a well placed shot from the pirates. Exposing himself to get a clear view, Brian skillfully manipulated the trigger to nearly replicate full-auto fire, almost literally cutting the culprit in two.

■ ■ ■

"Uncle?!" Derrik knelt down.

"Oh, Bloody Christ, that hurts..." The shot had taken his left arm off just below the shoulder, mid-bicep.

Derrik looked at the charred stump and the blackened carbine still clutched in the professor's right hand. "Oh Lord, Uncle..."

"Guess I've been hit eh?" His breathing was in short gasps. "Ten months in Viet-Nam and not a scratch... Blast the luck."

"Don't leave me, Uncle!" Derrik cradled the professor's head, "Don't you dare!"

"Sooo woozy... Can't seem to... keep..." His eyes closed slowly, like he was falling asleep.

■ ■ ■

Paul, Mike and Maria, using the Sweet Susie like a Trojan Horse, were to gain entry to the cargo bay of the cruiser and prevent any remaining members of the pirate crew from leaving and re-enforcing the soldiers

193

already outside on the landing pad. "Kill 'em, or keep 'em busy," is all Jack had said.

Predictably, as soon as the fighting had started in the Princess' bay, the cargo workers abandoned their chores in the cruiser's bay and attempted to obtain arms to attend the battle. They never made it to the ramps. About a third of them lay dead in their own cargo bay, their bodies ventilated by the .50 cal. guns of the Sweet Susie. The survivors sat quietly on the floor, their empty hands resting in their laps. These men were not soldiers or warriors like others in the crew, they simply worked on a ship that happened to be owned by a pirate. For them, there was no shame in surrender. In fact, it was greatly preferred to death. Maria remained in the upper turret, while Paul and Mike climbed out on the wings of the B-25 to increase their field of vision and prevent a sneak attack. They chambered rounds into their M1s and waited.

"Sounds like murder out there, Pappy..."

Paul nodded solemnly, "Yeah." He was all too aware of the shouts and cries in his headset. Making sense of them was totally impossible. He longed to participate, to contribute what he could, to be able to see with his own eyes what progress, if any, was being made. This sitting was pure anguish.

■ ■ ■

"Pappy!" Mike pointed over the nose of the plane.

Paul spun around as a group of armed pirates poured out of a service lift descending from an upper level. Mike was already firing. Paul dropped to one knee and aimed, dropping the leading soldier with his first shot. The pirates spread out shooting on the run, finding what cover they could to fire from. Hot magenta streaks of energy flashed past, knocking Mike off the port wing. Paul began instinct firing, the empty brass shell casings bouncing across the wing and cascading to the deck below. "You OK, kid?"

"Fine..." Mike gritted his teeth and worked his way to the landing gear, "just fine." Resting his shoulder against the landing gear to steady his carbine, he returned the pirates' fire. "Die, you filthy sons of bitches, *die!*" The pain across his ribs burned like a hot poker. He dared not look at his injury. Instead, he blinked away the tears of pain and concentrated on the anger, the fury which rose within him. The effect of the .30 cal. rounds striking their destinations so fascinated him, Mike almost forgot the agony burning in his side.

194

The intensity and accuracy of the gunfire produced by Mike and Pappy surprised the pirates, who could find no reliable protection through which the M1's rounds could not pass. Completely obscured from sight, pirates were dropping like flies, their lives stolen by weapons they would consider not only ancient but totally inferior, as well.

■ ■ ■

A pirate, the fight brought to him in his own cargo bay, huddled low behind the stacked containers and crates stolen from the Princess Hedonist. "Ragnaar...!" He called.

"Over here, my brother!" came the reply over the din.

Deeter looked to his left and saw an energy weapon firing blindly over the tops of the crates. Ragnaar was not the only one who had adopted this posture. "Ragnaar, what do we do..." He looked at the lifeless bodies of his shipmates laying about him. "These Humans fight without fear, and their weapons... so accurate!"

"True, my brother! They fight like the demons of Hellion possess their very souls!" Ragnaar fired blindly from cover, shredding the starboard wingtip of the Sweet Susie. "I swear I killed the one who fell from the wing, but *still* he fights!" Ragnaar was, although not human, a man. And as men went, he was on the rather large size. Herculean to be a little more precise. And although he had the confidence of a Cerulian Lion, he was not used to seeing someone he thought to be a corpse, up and fighting.

Deeter had no desire to die, but he decided if he was to die, it would not be hiding like a coward in his own ship. "I say we move against them! It is our only chance for victory!"

"I agree. Let us not waste another second on talk!" Ragnaar removed and checked the energy cell which powered his rifle. Finding it low, he tossed it aside and replaced it with a fresh one. "I am ready!" The soldiers passed the word on a rallying advance.

■ ■ ■

Mike leaned against the port landing gear of the B-25 and tried to inhale deeply to ease the pain in his ribs. The searing pain came and went, making him woozy and affecting both his balance and vision. There seemed to be a minor lull, which gave the pilots time for quick introspection.

195

"You OK, kid?"

Mike evened his breathing. "Still here Pappy, think we got `em all?" His voice was pained.

"Don't know, kid. How's your ammo?"

Mike pulled the magazine from his carbine and examined it, "Oh, about twenty rounds or so. How `bout you?"

Paul was checking his own. "That's all you've got? I've got almost two full mags left!" His voice became fatherly, "Look, take it..." he never finished the sentence.

Deeter, Ragnaar and the remaining pirates, executed their plan, storming the B-25 and showering it with bright magenta streaks of energy. Encouraged by the shouts of their crew mates, Maria's prisoners rose and turned toward the plane. Quick on the trigger, the harsh vibrating bark of Maria's twin .50 cal. guns changed their minds.

One arm wrapped around the strut of the landing gear to keep from toppling, Mike fought to focus as he fired, being careful to conserve ammunition. Paul was forced to flatten himself prone against the starboard wing, close to the fuselage to avoid the vicious wave of energy pulses.

Paul fired fiercely at his now limited field of vision. Having lost the advantage of height, he tried to drop to the floor to keep Mike from being overrun but the intensity of the pirate's attack kept him confined. Maria could not help. Her prisoners, prone on the deck, watched and waited for the chance to escape if her gun turret turned away.

Mike heard the familiar *clack* of the bolt locking open on an empty magazine and his stomach fell. He let go of the strut and dropped to the deck. "I'm out, Pappy..."

Paul felt sick inside, his stomach tightening, his hands buzzing with adrenalin, "Hold on, kid." He prepared to drop to the floor to protect his friend and the B-25 shuddered with a hefty boom, violently lurching, pitching to the port side. Paul knew they would try to overrun Mike's undefended position and if he couldn't retrieve his friend quickly, there would be no hope. Paul tried calling his wingman on the com, but there was no answer. He fired rapidly and emptied his magazine, trying to beat the attackers into retreat.

The pirates, their number diminished, but their fervor strong, closed on the plane. Paul rammed his last magazine into the carbine and prepared to fight until his last round. "If they get me, darlin', gun `em all... every single one of 'em..." His southern accent seemed to be stronger under stress.

Maria looked over her shoulder, but of course couldn't see him. She refused to believe it was going to end like this. "OK, Pappy," she replied through clenched teeth. Desperately trying to call Jack on her comm unit rewarded her with nothing but waves of static.

Paul took a deep breath and rolled off the wing. He hit the deck in a crouch and rolled backwards uncontrolled. It saved his life, energy pulses passing wildly around him, the pirates unable to hit him. He scurried to the starboard landing gear amidst a brutal slew of pirate fire and rubbed his swelling left ankle. Mike's motionless form lay almost ten feet from the blackened port landing gear, its shredded tire scattered in pieces and ribbons of rubber around the deck.

The pirates were so close Paul could see their faces. He chose his targets carefully, gritting his teeth to remain calm, wrestling with a fight or flight response that was doing its best to convince him flight was the preferred choice of action. He twice killed pirate soldiers trying to flank him, but as his ammunition dwindled, he realized his luck was going with it... "I'd give my left nut for an M249 right about now," he breathed. "Or a nice big, fat M60..."

Bursts of gunfire erupted behind him, coming from the cargo ramp, and Paul snuggled down beside the wheel of the Sweet Susie's gear. Closing his eyes and taking a deep breath, Paul said a short prayer. "Well, so much for Lady Luck... *lazy bitch.*" Blazing magenta streaks, whizzed by him from behind, striking crates forward of the plane. That was unnerving enough, but it was the war cry, a long, deep, roaring howl, which made his blood run cold. "Christ Almighty! *What the hell is that..?*"

"Just us, Commander..." breathed the husky female voice in Paul's earpiece. It sounded familiar even through the static and disturbance. He couldn't quite discern who it was, but who gave a shit, help was help. Paul shifted his position to venture a quick peek. "Stay where you are Paul, we don't want to hit you," growled another familiar but indiscernible female voice.

Raulya, Myomerr and a contingent of about fifteen of the Princess's security officers, had appeared inside on the loading ramp and raced across the cruiser's cargo deck toward the Sweet Susie, firing as they ran. Some had carbines, some had energy rifles collected from dead pirates. Paul could not remember seeing a sweeter sight, imagining the bugles and cavalry flag fluttering above them as they thundered in on horseback. Shooting from the hip as they ran at close to full stride, Paul was amazed at their remarkable accuracy. He kept his head down just the same.

As they passed through the group of thirty-plus prisoners, several foolishly rose to confront the officers. Snarling, Raulya and Myomerr slashed and hacked with the butts of their weapons, viciously repelling the crewmen without slowing or breaking stride. Excited by the sound of breaking bone and the smell of fresh blood, the two Ketarians howled their savage war cry as they advanced, firing savagely, beating back the pirate soldiers.

Completely unnerved by this sudden, fearless, ruthless, counter attack; the pirates' offensive crumbled. They laid down their weapons and surrendered after losing well over half their men in the bloody failed attack against the Sweet Susie.

■ ■ ■

Ragnaar sat with his back against the storage crates where he had found Deeter lying in a pool of dark crimson. He cradled the lifeless body of his friend in hulking arms, but with a tenderness his generous size didn't belay. He spoke softly to the fallen soldier, "You died well, my brother..." He pinched the bridge of his nose to block the tears he had never shed for other lost comrades. "They must truly be the Demons of Hellion," he continued, "for we have lost..." He considered it briefly, but decided no others could have succeeded in defeating them in this manner. He shook his head, "No, no one else could have done this. I fear for my soul, my friend." The big man was a pirate, but he had not always been so and he was not without beliefs. "As you cross the bridge of Whyte, put in a favorable word for me with the good Lords of Heavenite, eh? I do not wish to pitched into the dark water of Hellion that passes under it."

Pappy, accompanied by Maria, knelt next to his wingman. Together, they grimaced as they looked at the young pilot's charred tunic, fused to the skin all along the right side of his torso. Pappy leaned close to listen for a heartbeat, though he hadn't much hope. Realizing something was jabbing him in the stomach, Paul looked down to see the muzzle of a Beretta 9mm pushing against him. It was firmly held in Mike's right hand, his index finger on the trigger.

"Izat you, Pappy...?" Mike's voice was soft but steady. One eye opened weakly, trying to see through the haze of a mild concussion.

Paul grinned widely. "Yeah, it's me, kid..."

"Me too," added Maria, with tears in her eyes.

"Oh good," Mike's hand dropped to the deck, still holding the Beretta. "Didn't think I could pull the trigger anyway..."

"You did good, kid."

"Really?" Paul nodded. "Thanks." Mike smiled weakly, his speech was slow and a bit slurred. "Could only play possum after that tire went boom. Figured to blow the nuts off the first guy who came to finish me..."

Paul put his hand on Mike's shoulder, "You did just fine. Now shut your yap and relax; the medics are on their way."

Maria's pendant, the Teardrop Crystal of Rhomm, had slipped from the neckline of her tunic and swayed gently above Mike Warren's pained form as she leaned over him. It looked almost fluid, like a fresh drop of rain clinging to the gold chain around her neck. Mike, fixing his eyes on it, had a sudden desire for water. "Christ, I'm thirsty." He swallowed dryly. "Got anything to drink?"

There was, of course, nothing available. And as Paul and Maria looked at each other in silent search of an answer Paul's eyes widened. Maria raised one eyebrow. "What...?"

Paul pointed to the pendant which had begun weeping moisture in slow, steady, sparkling drops. "It's leaking..."

Maria looked. "It's not leaking," she said in astonishment, "it's weeping!"

"Weeping, leaking," said Paul. "What the hell's the difference? It's dribbling all over the place!"

Mike could feel the drops hitting his neck. "Get some in my mouth why doncha..." he mumbled.

Paul was getting impatient, "Where the *HELL* are those medics? The kid's having a hard time breathing..." He unbuttoned his wingman's tunic to make him more comfortable.

Maria touched the wet crystal to her tongue before Paul could object and smacked her lips in contemplation. "That was pretty stupid," said Paul crisply, "What if it's poisonous?"

Maria smiled coyly and making a face, stuck out her tongue. Woman's intuition told her it wasn't, but she wouldn't give him the satisfaction of admitting he could be right. Something told her the crystal was sympathetically reading her needs somehow and was trying to provide for that need, although she had no idea how that could be possible... After all, it was just a crystal. Wasn't it?

199

The crystal's moisture was cool and smooth. It slickly coated Maria's mouth like a light oil, but it had a wondrous sweet-tart flavor that made her mouth water. She smiled at Paul, her mouth tingling from top to bottom. Paul raised one eyebrow, "Well?"

"Yeah," rasped Mike, "well?"

Maria held the crystal over Mike's mouth, "It's safe."

The droplets splashed across Mike's outstretched tongue and Maria wiped the crystal across his lips. "Mmmmmmmm," grinned Mike, closing his eyes. "That's great." Suddenly he inhaled sharply and deeply, his eyes open wide and his body rigid, back arched.

"Jesus!" shouted Paul as he grabbed Mike by the shoulders to hold him down.

"I, I, I don't understand..." stammered Maria, stunned.

But it passed as quickly as it came. The young pilot's body relaxed and his breathing became regular and with greater ease. He closed his eyes and appeared to slip into a comfortable state of sleep.

Paul scratched his head. "What the hell... lemme see that." He touched the crystal and sucked the wetness off his finger. Smacking his lips speculatively, he was pleased by the initial sensations. He was very suddenly aware of a strange sensation sweeping across his body. It took his breath away momentarily, but was pleasing just the same. It wasn't long though, before he realized the ankle he'd injured tumbling off the wing of the B-25, no longer pained him, at least not to the degree that it had previously. Paul wondered if this might have been what Mike felt. It must contain some kind of drug, and since Maria had no injuries, she had not felt the same sensations over her body, just the initial reaction. Paul shook his head, he felt little pain, "Amazing..." It was all he could think of to say.

The messenger trotted to a stop under the wing of the Sweet Susie. "Need to let you know sir," he puffed, "all wounded have to be moved out to the Princess's landing pad near the flight tower."

"Why so far?" asked Paul.

The young messenger shrugged. "Dunno' sir, it's just where they're moving everybody." He turned to leave.

"Hey!" shouted Maria, "why couldn't they tell us that over the com half an hour ago?!"

"Some of the comlinks are damaged," he explained. "About a third of the grid is off line. You must be in a dead spot." He trotted off in the direction he came.

"Shit," muttered Paul, "I can't carry him, my ankle's too weak."

Ragnaar, who had wandered cautiously over, dropped to one knee and gently laid the lifeless body of his best friend in the row with the rest of his fallen comrades, near the port side of the B-25. "I will carry him..." he said over his shoulder, without turning around.

Paul turned and eyed him suspiciously. "How do I know I can trust you?"

Ragnaar rose and unfolded his six and a half foot herculean frame. "The battle is over," he said, gazing at the row of casualties spread before him. He motioned to the bodies with a wave of his hand. "The dead are gone..." he added, turning to meet Paul's gaze, "and it is time to tend to the needs of the living."

"You hurt him and I'll kill you," said Maria, matter-of-factly.

"I don't doubt it," said the pirate casually, meeting her gaze, "but like I said, the battle is over. Besides, I don't kill helpless men."

"That's not what I've heard," growled Maria sarcastically.

Ragnaar ignoring the comment, walked past her over to where Mike lay, and knelt beside him. Placing one hand on Mike's chest and the other on his forehead, Ragnaar closed his eyes. "He is your best friend, no?"

"Yes," confirmed Paul.

"I understand your concern," said the pirate, gently smoothing Mike's hair, "but he has the heart of a Cerulian Lion. He will not die."

"And, just how do you know that?" asked Maria venomously.

Ragnaar smiled. "Because, Miss Arroyo, there are some things I just know..." Without looking up into her stunned face, Ragnaar gently scooped Mike's limp body up off the deck with little apparent effort and cradled him carefully. "Ready, Commander? I believe your friend is in need of some attention."

The men exchanged guarded smiles, it wasn't often Paul saw Maria at a loss for words. He had a feeling Ragnaar knew that too. The odd trio walked toward the ramp in silence, Maria trailing behind and Paul hobbling like mad to keep up with the pirate's long, easy strides.

Ragnaar shook his head, "I'll never understand a race that lets their women fight..." he said quietly, his eyes twinkling with light mischief.

Strangely enough, Paul found the pirate oddly likeable. "Well, it sure wasn't *my* idea..." he countered, smirking.

Ragnaar laughed a laugh befitting his size. "Well," he said after gaining his composure, "you don't appear to be the Demons of Hellion."

Paul looked up at him. "Huh?"

The pirate shook his head, "Oh, nothing, Commander." He smiled to himself about his private joke; he wished Deeter had been there to share it with him.

CHAPTER SEVENTEEN

PRINCESS HEDONIST, LAN SYSTEM: *ADRIFT*

The conflict on the landing pad ended rather suddenly when Gantarro caught Kidd unawares as he tried to escape the crossfire on the pad. With the barrel of a laser shoved in his ear, Kidd had no choice but to order his crew to surrender. Basically, it was an inevitable outcome. But Gant's actions, which he refused to call heroic, prevented an extended conflict which could have easily doubled the number of casualties.

Jack stood at the foot of the steps leading to the control tower, surrounded by wounded from both sides. Medical attendants, both mechanical and biological, attended to those wounded. "Stand still, Commander Steele..." said the medibot in a female voice.

Jack fidgeted as she removed the shards of graphite composite from his forehead and wiped the blood from his face. "Geez, take it easy, will ya? That hurts!"

"It will do more than just hurt if we don't get it all out," she urged. "Be still!" Holding his face firmly by his jaw, her optical pickup zoomed in to inspect the lacerations across his forehead for any remaining debris as she dabbed away the blood. She was a short, boxy, automaton with two arms and five-fingered digital hands, moving on rubber treads and not legs. Her extendable articulated neck supported her shiny oblong head. It contained a single optical sensor with zoom adjustable floodlight and multi-use surgical laser. "You are lucky, Commander, you have a rather hard cranium." She tapped the top of his head with a rubber padded metal digit, "Though I don't doubt you'll have a tremendous headache."

Jack winced as she wrapped his head with a clean dressing, "Y'know, you need to work on your bedside manner..." he grumbled.

The medibot paused, and with a glowing optical sensor, unblinkingly looked him in the eye. She tilted her head in introspection, "But you're not in a bed, Commander." After a moment, she returned her attention to his dressing.

"What I meant was..." he abandoned the thought. "Oh, forget it," he mumbled.

"Hey Jacko..." Derrik, still carrying his M1, strolled up from the tower office.

Jack attempted to turn toward the approaching voice but forgot his head was still anchored by the medibot's grip. "Ow... Hey Derrik. Say, how's the professor doing?"

"Lost his arm, but he'll live."

"Christ," whispered Jack. "Man I'm really sorry, I didn't expect..."

Derrik shook his head. "Forget it," he interrupted, "Uncle has. Call to duty, honor, stiff upper lip... all that rot. As far as he's concerned, we won and that's all that counts."

"Wow..." Jack couldn't help but admire that kind of intense, selfless dedication. "He sure is a tough old bird..."

"Well, it helps to be a bit daft," added Derrik.

Jack smiled weakly, "I suppose."

"So, how's your bean, old boy?"

Jack ran his hand around the newly finished bandage and gingerly touched his wrapped forehead. "I've got a major headache."

"Undoubtedly." Derrik clapped Jack on the shoulder, "But you Yanks have good, hard heads."

Jack smirked, "So I've been told."

■ ■ ■

Brian strolled across the landing pad toward the tower with Fritz at his side after organizing an armed security attachment to guard the swelling number of prisoners. Fritz trotted up to Jack and sat at his side searching for an approving hand. He found it, the pilot rubbing his ears. Jack knelt down and checked the dog again for injury. The crate that had exploded had tossed them both, leaving them momentarily senseless, but it appeared the Shepherd was completely untouched. Jack glanced up as Brian approached. "Have either of you guys seen Pappy's group?"

"No," said Derrik, slinging his carbine over his shoulder by its strap.

"Not yet," said Brian, "Comm links are still down too."

"OK," nodded Jack. "Let's get a messenger up to them, have them bring everybody out here. Get 'em some extra help if they need it. Let's see if we can get this mess all organized."

"No problem, Skipper, it's already been done."

"Super..." Jack rubbed his head, "anybody got an aspirin?"

204

"No," countered Brian, "but I've got another headache for you. Gantarro says Kidd is requesting a meeting with the *commander of our forces.*"

"Aww geez," moaned Jack, "why doesn't he handle it?" Brian shrugged, saying nothing. "OK," conceded Jack, throwing up his hands. "Whatever, just give me a few minutes." Brian agreed and disappeared to find Gant and the pirate Captain. Shedding his bloodied coveralls, Jack Steele adjusted his uniform and smoothed his tunic. His blood had seeped through the coveralls and stained his uniform tunic. "Shit. Well, there goes another good shirt," he muttered to Fritz.

■ ■ ■

The meeting took place on the landing pad away from the wounded and away from the prisoners. They stood in the shadow under the nose of the pirate cruiser; Jack, Derrik, Brian, Gant and the pirate, Kidd. Two armed security people stood off to one side, and Fritz sat at his master's left hand. Gant at his elbow, the pirate Captain stood arrogantly with his arms folded across his chest. He wore a red velvet coat, elaborately decorated with gold braid, resembling something akin to America's Colonial era. It was quite a contrast to his crew's motley attire and a bold statement of his selfish and arrogant nature.

Jack stood casually with his left hand resting on Fritz's head, gently scratching his ears. "What can I do for you, Mr. Kidd?"

"First," said Kidd coolly, "you will show me the respect of my rank you will call me Captain. Second..."

"*First,*" interrupted Steele, smiling wryly, "you are in *no* position to demand anything. *Second*, you pompous windbag, you are the Captain of *nothing*. You're a dirt bag that's going to prison. That ship and everything in it, belongs to me..." He was watching the astonished expression on Kidd's face, but he caught the look of surprise in Gant's eyes as well. He had half expected the man to request fair treatment for his crew or something of that nature. Instead, the pirate aired some ridiculous personal demands. Jack found it easy to detest the man. "Now, sir," continued Steele, forcing professionalism, "if you have a reasonable request, make it. I am willing to listen. Otherwise, stop wasting my time."

Joshua Kidd was indignant. These men were wearing uniforms but nothing civilian or military that he could remotely identify. Yet they had come at him with enough cunning and combat training to lure him in, defeat his crew and capture his ship. He saw no way out and this infuriated him. "Who the *HELLION* are you people?"

"Well, we're from Earth," said Jack, indicating himself, Derrik and Brian.

"I can see that, you nutter, I'm not bloody blind.... so was my great grandfather." The pirate collected himself and adjusted his coat. "I *meant;* who are you, what organization are you with? And by whose *authority* do you hold me and my ship?"

"No organization," said Jack calmly, "just ourselves... with a little help," he added, glancing at Gantarro. "Technically, I guess you could call us mercenaries, bounty hunters..." he shrugged, "take your pick, one label fits as well as another. And as far as our authority, I'm sure there are more than a few agencies happy to pay big bucks for your head. You've been a bad boy, Joshua; murdering people, pirating, who knows what else."

Kidd showed no emotional response and made no attempt to deny any of the allegations. "So," began the pirate arrogantly, his hands on his hips. "You intend to turn us in to the highest bidder... Well if it's *money* you want..."

"No," interrupted Jack, growing more irritated by the minute. "We don't want money, *our* fee is your *ship*. Nothing more."

"My *ship*..?" growled Kidd.

"Don't worry," said Brian coolly, "we'll put it to good use. Besides, you won't need it where you're going."

"It's *MY SHIP*!" insisted the pirate, his face flushing ruddy red.

Fritz was watching the pirate's every move and was the first one to see the flash of silver in his hand, a foolish attempt at revenge. There was no telling where the pirate had kept the derringer-sized laser hidden, or how it had so suddenly appeared with such deft slight of hand. But then again, to Fritz, it didn't matter. A gun was a gun and he would not allow any harm to come to his human. Without hesitation or command, the Shepherd lunged with teeth bared at the pirate's arm. The searing, blue-white laser passed between Jack and Derrik as they jumped apart, more of reflex than anything else. It all occurred in such a blur, no one besides Fritz and Kidd, really knew what happened.

Kidd was on his knees and grasping his throat with both hands, blood running through his fingers and dripping to the deck, his mouth and eyes wide with surprise. Slow to take his eyes away, Jack turned to his left at Brian's insistence. Fritz lay sprawled on the floor, unconscious and Steele dropped to his knees, crawling to his partner, ignoring the wounded pirate. He carefully rolled the limp dog on his side to ease his breathing and was horrified by the sight, cold heat racing up his back, his hands suddenly numb. The laser had struck the right side of the Shepherd's face; skin, bone and brain matter completely fused and charred. "Oh God, oh God no... *MEDIC!!*" Panic stricken, Jack Steele cradled his best friend in his lap while the others stood helplessly by. "Oh *Christ*," he pleaded, "please help him..."

Brian put his hand on Jack's shoulder. "Let him go, Jack," he said quietly, "he's gone now..."

"NO! No, he's not. See? *Look*, he's still breathing, *see*?" The Shepherd breathed steadily, but his body twitched and shuddered, his damaged brain severely short circuited. Brian tried to pull him away but Jack strongly resisted, pulling free. "*NO!*" He objected. He grabbed the medic heading for Joshua Kidd by the leg. *"Fuck HIM!* You get your ass over *HERE!*"

Medical personnel are instructed to always tend to humanoid life first. Animal and other life forms come after. The young tech was only following his training. He pointed to Kidd. "But..."

Jack's helplessness was quickly turning to rage. "*NOW!*" he snarled.

The medic knelt down, putting his field pack beside Jack and the wounded Shepherd. "Don't know what I can do, Commander," he said gently, "he's got quite a bit of damage..." The rage was surging, and Jack Steele was fighting to remain in control.

Suddenly, Jack found he had his .45 in hand. "You do whatever the hell you have to do to keep him alive," he growled, tapping the medic in the chest with the muzzle of the gun. *"Understand?"* The startled young med-tech nodded, opened his emergency surgical kit and instantly went to work. Steele gave the dog one last loving pat and stood up, turning to face Joshua Kidd. "You rotten piece of subhuman filth..." he snarled, blocking another arriving medic. "He won't be needing you..."

"But..." objected the medic.

"Buzz off!" insisted Jack, waving the .45.

Fearfully, the medic backed cautiously away from the pilot with the wild flaming eyes temporarily gripped by insanity. He turned to the group huddled around Fritz and decided to lend a hand there. Whether it was by coincidence or by design, for the moment, the group had abandoned Joshua Kidd.

"Help me," gurgled Kidd, one bloody hand reaching out beseechingly, a growing ruby-red stain ruining his pretty, white ruffled shirt.

"Fuck you, you lousy piece of shit," spat Jack. "There are no words foul enough to describe the depths of worthless human waste that you are..."

Steele thumbed the safety off, "Hear that..? Know what that is..? It's Hell, and it's coming for you..." His voice was cold, deadpan.

"But," pleaded the pirate, blood running between his fingers, "he was only an animal..." There was no humanity in the dark eyes glaring back at him, only blackness. A void without hope, without mercy, vacant of all emotion except hate. He shivered from a wave of cold and realized too late he'd crossed the wrong man. "Oh Lord p-p-please," he stammered, his words and thoughts running together hoping to stave off the inevitable darkness of hell that was rushing forward, propelled by his own stupidity and arrogance. "Just an animal - I'll get you another - I'll give you anything - I can make you rich, yes that's it, rich - *Rich* beyond your *wildest dreams...* "

Having lost control, Steele bared his teeth with seething hatred, *"You are too fucking stupid to live..."* In a flash of electricity, rage overtook him like a tsunami rising up from his core and suddenly engulfing his entire body. Without hesitation, thought or physical connection, the muzzle of the 1911 came up level. Maria screamed as she descended the ramp of the cruiser, but Jack did not hear her, his mind disconnected from his reactions leaving him a bystander, watching it happen. He squeezed the trigger and watched Kidd's head explode, his brains splash across the deck, the empty shell casing tinkling lightly across the deck in slow motion as the near-headless body of the pirate captain limply toppled over. Blood ran freely from the stump of the neck, a growing pool of red breaking away in rivulets running into the seams of the deck. "That was for Fritz," Steele breathed, clicking the safety and holstering the gun. He stared blankly at the odd patterns of gore, the totality of the event unregistered in his mind, void of remorse or other feelings. Numbness faded, the thump of his heartbeat and cloudy hiss of static in his ears slowly turning back into voices like someone surfacing who had been underwater.

Maria touched the pilot on the elbow. "Jack?"

He spun. "Huh?"

"Jack, what happened here?"

"Fritz..." his voice trailed off. It seemed that suddenly his mind shifted back into gear as the rest of his surroundings came rushing back in at him. He spun around. "Where's Fritz?"

They had all been watching, the pirate crew, wounded, medics, his friends. There were quite possibly a hundred witnesses and not one person or being said a word. Brian stepped forward and took his friend by the shoulders. "They took him to the infirmary. So far he's still breathing, but that's about it."

"I want to see him."

"I'll go with you," volunteered Maria.

Jack put one hand on her shoulder and looked into her eyes. The rage was gone now, the tsunami retreating, leaving behind the wreckage and debris of loss, sorrow, grief and despair. "Thanks," he sighed, "but I think I'd rather go alone." He wiped away a tear with the back of his hand and with his head hanging, quietly followed a medibot to the infirmary. The others stood silently and watched him go.

"Alright alright!" yelled Brian, taking charge. "We've got plenty of work to do! Let's not just stand around, let's clean up this mess and get organized!" Once again the landing bay became a flurry of activity.

■ ■ ■

The room was dimly lit and smelled of antiseptic. It took Jack's eyes several moments to adjust to the darkness, so he paused at the doorway before entering staring at the shiny white tile floor of the infirmary. Somehow it was comforting to know, at home or in deep space, some things remained constant. He took a deep calming breath and walked into the room. Fritz lay alone in the room on an infirmary bed, his only companion the lit console of electronics that monitored his life signs and kept him alive. Jack stood at the side of the bed and stared at the hoses, tubes and wires running from the console to his friend. If for only a moment, he contemplated pulling them out and letting the dog slip quietly away with dignity, then admonishing himself for even thinking of it. Pulling a chair over to the side of the bed, Steele sat with his head resting on the edge of the mattress and his hand on the soft fur of Fritz's shoulder. "I'm here buddy..." he whispered. An uneasy sleep overtook him as he felt the gentle rise and fall of the dog's breathing.

Several times throughout the night, medical attendants passed in and out of the room, checking on the dog's status. Except for a slight improvement of his stability, things went unchanged and Jack went undisturbed... until several hours later. "Jack... *Jack!*"

He sat bolt upright and blinked in the darkness. "Huh?"

The hooded figure stood in the darkness on the other side of the bed holding a snifter of brandy. "Are you with me?"

"Voorlak?" He knew it was. It was a question Jack didn't need to ask. "Ditarian Brandy I take it?" He rubbed his eyes.

"Of course."

Jack nodded, "Of course... got any more?" His mouth was dry and he could use the warmth, the room felt cold.

"Wouldn't go anywhere without it," said the Ancient, handing the pilot another snifter from under his long robe.

Jack accepted the snifter and took a slow draw on the thick, sweet liquor. It felt good as it slid down. "Don't suppose you've got anything to eat in there..." he said, pointing at the robe. Voorlak smiled, Jack couldn't see it so much as he could feel it. "No, I suppose not." Stiff and aching, he stood up slowly. "Don't you ever use a door old man?" Jack realized he was probably being a bit irreverent, but he was in no mood for formalities. Besides, he felt he had a kind of strange understanding, a link with the wise man that went beyond the pomp.

"No need," said the Ancient with a casual wave of his hand. "Besides, it's boring... no flair, no style."

It was Jack's turn to smile. "Well, I guess I've got to admire an omnipotent with a concern for style."

"Thank you... really, but I'm not truly omnipotent. At least not yet." Voorlak pulled back the hood of his cloak and sipped his brandy. He stared at the swirling golden liquor and thought. The silence was uneasy, seeming longer than it was and the discussion turned serious, as Jack knew it had to. "I had to come," explained the wise man, "to tell you not to give up on him like you contemplated earlier." He stroked the short fur on Fritz's front foreleg. "He may not consciously be aware of you, but you need to talk to him, touch him, he'll sense you. You need to keep his spirit alive, give him a reason not to give up his soul."

"What good will that do? He'll just be a vegetable, right?" Jack loved his friend with all his heart, but he had no desire to prolong the dog's existence if it held no meaning or quality of life for him.

"You must trust me," said Voorlak, waggling a finger at Jack. "All is not lost, unless he feels alone and gives up." He sounded stern but warm and fatherly at the same time. "Now I don't see you as a quitter; you're not willing to let him go without a fight, are you?" That had never been one of Steele's weaknesses but he was feeling a little helpless. He shook his head no, wondering what he could possibly do to help the canine that had not only saved his life, but had been his twenty-four hour companion for years.

210

"Good," nodded the Ancient. "Now see this..." he moved close to Fritz and while stroking his fur, spoke lovingly to him. The monitoring equipment showed definite and almost immediate changes. "Of course, with your connection to him, you'll probably have better results."

Steele studied the old man for a moment, "You knew this would happen..."

"Yes... I suppose in one form or another, but not exactly when or how. It's not an exact science."

Jack sighed. "You couldn't tell me because you thought it might affect how I handled things? Maybe change my decisions, my destiny?"

"Now who's being omnipotent?" joked the old man, pausing to gaze at the dog. "Actually I don't believe it would not have changed your decisions; you are guided by your heart and conscience. Besides being incredibly imaginative, you have an acute sense of right and wrong which prevents you from being a casual bystander."

Jack thought about that sense of right and wrong and for the first time in several hours, thought about the death of Joshua Kidd... the event replaying in his mind in slow motion; the blood, the splatter, the gore in intense detail. But the gaps were almost more frightening than what he remembered; some of it a blur of color and emotion without definition. He felt an emptiness he couldn't identify mixed with guilt about letting the rage overrun that sense of right and wrong. *Overrun, hell, it got trampled to death.* That brought him down to the same level of principles as Joshua Kidd; he despised himself for that.

"Forget what you are thinking, Jack." Voorlak's voice startled the pilot who had been momentarily lost in the visions.

"But I murdered a man in cold blood..."

The Ancient shook his head, "No... Not a man, something more akin to a rabid animal. And not in cold blood, but in defense of all living things. He was *filled* with evil and you were his polar opposite. As two forces so diametrically opposed, those forces cannot occupy the same space at the same time; the stronger force will win out. The conclusion is always violent as one displaces the other; and the greater the forces, the more violent the conclusion. You were just the instrument of *good* displacing *evil*. It is done and forgotten."

Jack was stunned. "Forgiven... just like that?"

"Just like that," confirmed the old man.

"Can I get that in writing...?"

"Jack? Who're you talking to?" Steele turned to see Maria walk through the open door followed by Brian, Derrik and Paul.

"I..." he turned back but Voorlak was gone, "was um, talking to Fritz." He leaned over and rubbed the dog's frame, "Wasn't I buddy?"

■ ■ ■

Mike Warren and Professor Edgars shared a room in an infirmary facility, several levels below the one in which Fritz lay. After a refreshing shower and a clean uniform, Jack paid a visit to them with the same group that came up to see Fritz. When the group arrived, Mike and the Professor were in the process of playfully harassing a rather attractive, nurse who fought back, deftly fending off the roaming hands. When Jack told the two men to behave themselves and quiet down, the nurse defended her patients, excusing their behavior due to the drugs they'd been treated with. Both men were happily animated and obviously feeling no pain.

The surgeon caught Jack and the others in the hall as they left and explained how Mike and the Professor were doing. It seemed beyond the serious burns, Mike also had three broken ribs and a punctured lung from the fall off the wing of the Sweet Susie. His ribs would knit quickly with the aid of an electronic stimulator which would accelerate the bone healing process. And using a small patch of healthy skin, a sheet of new skin large enough to cover the damaged area could be grown through a cloning-type process which would eliminate the normal massive scarring.

Unlike Mike, the Professor had no hidden injuries. Upon healing, he would receive a permanent, completely functional, five fingered, mechanical hand and arm covered with artificial skin. Unless carefully scrutinized he would appear completely normal. Jack was pleased that two men he called friends would return to good health in relatively short order. But since his thoughts never left Fritz for long, it was difficult for him to feel the happiness or relief he should have felt.

There was much to do after the capture of the pirate cruiser but no matter how long the day, how tired or busy, Jack found the time to see Fritz every day and spend time with him. After a couple of days of stable life signs, the surgeons carefully removed the sections of Fritz's damaged skull and brain tissue. In preparation for what, Jack was unsure, because the surgeons told him little. The only thing he knew was, what they were to attempt was strictly experimental and risky. And like most doctors anywhere, they were careful to not predict the outcome. After the initial surgery, Jack took to sleeping on the same bed as his friend, hoping the companionship would improve the odds of the Shepherd's survival. A week later, Jack entered an empty room and was told Fritz had been placed in a sterile isolation area and could not be visited for some time. Seeing the amazing things accomplished with Mike and the Professor, Jack had no choice but to put his trust in the skill of the doctors. He just wished they'd let him visit his friend.

CHAPTER EIGHTEEN

FREEDOM: *BUBBLEGUM & PAPERCLIPS*

It had been two weeks since the capture of the pirate cruiser, and it was just now beginning to show some resemblance of organization. Jack and Paul stood alone on the bridge and surveyed the system changes. "We've got a long way to go, Jack. These guys beat the piss out of this poor ship, and the repairs they *did* make, must have been done by the Three Stooges."

Jack sank into the command chair. "I can't believe these people were such slobs... I mean the filth, the garbage... like they couldn't be bothered to simply pick up after themselves."

Paul stood with his hands on his hips and shook his head. "It's a wonder this ship could function at all. Half the systems were totally inoperative."

Jack smirked sarcastically, "No wonder they had to send the fighters to chase down the Princess Hedonist. This tub would've had a hard time catching a cold..."

"Now, now," joked Paul, waving his finger at Jack, "that's no way to talk about the *Freedom*."

Steele shook his head, running his fingers through his hair, "I know we all agreed the new name was appropriate, but maybe we should've called this thing *The Money Pit*. It feels like the repairs are going to take *forever.*"

"And it's all ours," nodded Paul with a wave, "at least if we can scrape together enough bubblegum and paperclips to hold it together."

Ragnaar strolled through the open doorway onto the bridge and saluted the two officers. He wore the same uniform as Jack and Paul. "Yes, Lieutenant?" asked Paul.

"Just wanted to let you know, Commander," began the former pirate, "the ship-wide communications net should be finished before the end of the day." Paul nodded his approval; he was getting tired of using messengers for everything.

"What about the automatic door system?" asked Jack.

Ragnaar shook his head. "Still got some bugs left, Captain. Could be another day or two." He rubbed his forehead, "We're not sure if it's hardware or software failures yet."

Jack slouched in his seat and bowed his head. "Good Lord, why was this stuff never corrected before?"

Ragnaar shrugged massive shoulders. "I guess Captain Kidd didn't think it was important enough sir. Besides, he wasn't a man you could say much to either. I saw him kill a man at dinner once, for spilling the Captain's drink."

"You're kidding, right?" asked Paul.

"No, sir."

Jack sat up properly. "Brother, what a psychopath. Well Lieutenant, from now on, there will be no random killing at the dinner table."

Ragnaar smiled crookedly, "The crew will be glad to hear that sir." He saluted and left the bridge.

"I kinda like him," said Jack.

"I knew you would; the whole bunch are good people. Makes you wonder what they were doing with Kidd."

"Shanghaied probably," guessed Jack.

About twenty five crew members had followed Ragnaar's example and volunteered to serve under Jack Steele's leadership. Their services proved extremely valuable, as most were skilled workers and technicians who knew the ship well. They were finally encouraged to work on the equipment they'd been forced to neglect in the past, and they worked in earnest.

Brian, dressed in dirty coveralls and covered in grease, strolled onto the bridge. "Hey! Guess what?" He didn't wait for an answer, "Launch tube two is fixed! It's working like a charm. Wanna' see?"

"Sure," chimed the two men. They needed to go down to the landing bay and check the Warthog fighters anyway.

Walking down the corridor, they passed the ship's servants in the process of cleaning up two years of neglect. The porters, most of them women, spent their years aboard the cruiser as slaves and concubines for the crew. Unpaid, unwashed and malnourished, only the youngest and most attractive, received any care at all. Handed down from the officers to the lower ranks of the crew then discarded like old clothes, their fate was ultimately the same. They all suffered from neglect and ill health. When the ship was captured, they were all released and given their freedom. Paid work with guaranteed care, as porters, maids and cooks, was made available on the ship for any who desired it. It was surprising to see how many of the women returned.

As the men approached a woman scrubbing the wall padding, she paused her chores and greeted them politely. They returned the greeting and walked on. "Y'know," said Jack, after they'd passed, "it's amazing what you can

215

accomplish with a little respect." Most of the corridors had been cleaned and scrubbed to near perfection. The wall padding, which reached from about knee height to about shoulder height, went from shades of dirty gray, back to white, an incredible transformation. Even the carpeting came clean, changing from a muddy gray to a nice, light, blue-gray. Much to everyone's surprise, the ship was actually becoming livable.

As the three men passed through one of the automatic doors which segmented the corridors for safety, the door slid back and forth spasmodically, the system lights lighting simultaneously. "Can't believe these were left inoperable," grumbled Brian. "What an idiot."

The doors were bulkhead reinforced, designed to seal off segments of the corridors in an emergency; atmospheric contamination, fire, a hull breach, even protection against hostile boarding parties. The screen on the system panel next to the door would advise any crew members how severe the hazard was on the other side and how limited the access. Leaving the doors inoperative was inviting disaster.

"Who's working on them?" asked Brian, indicating the epileptic door.

"Can't think of his name," said Paul scratching his head. "Tall, skinny guy, dark skin, glasses..."

Brian nodded, "Yeah, I know who that is. But I can't think of his name either."

They stopped at the elevator and Jack pushed the button. "That's terrible, we've got to get to know these people better." He hated forgetting names. To him, it was like saying that person was not worth remembering.

"Don't worry," said Paul as the trio stepped onto the elevator. "We will. It takes a little time."

The ship was divided into four main levels, the fifth only extended about half the length of the ship at the belly, it was strictly for cargo. The elevator took them from level one, where the bridge was, to level four. Level four held pilot's on-call quarters, flight briefing, ready rooms, flight and landing bay, fighter launch chutes, hangars, and everything else that went along with flight operations, including maintenance and repair.

While not the same size as the mind boggling dimensions of the Princess's bay, the Freedom's bay was sizable at just short of three football fields long and a little over one wide. Bright orange sodium floodlights lit up the common areas of the landing bay, with a greater concentration of white floods and spotlights in the hangars along the outer walls, to illuminate the mechanic's shops and the parked fighters. The only place dimly lit was the prep and launch area which had red lighting to prepare the pilots' eyes for the darkness of space.

After Brian displayed his handy work on the launch systems, the three pilots strolled the empty flight deck and hangars. They stopped in front of a work shuttle and watched the mechanics tinker. "All this room," began Paul, "and all we got is four lousy fighters..." He kicked at a slightly raised rivet on the deck.

"Five," interrupted Brian, pointing at another under a tarp.

"It don't fly," blurted the mechanic, who didn't bother to stop tinkering, his head and arms buried in an open access panel at the front of the shuttle.

"So fix it."

"Piece'a junk," countered the mechanic. "In fact, don't think it ever flew. Use it for parts though."

Jack walked over and lifted the tarp, the fighter was full of blast holes. Its canopy was missing and it sat on an antigravity cargo palette because its landing gear had been torn off. "Whoever used it last, didn't take very good care of it..."

"It used to be Kidd's," said a passing crewman. "He was a lousy pilot." Everyone had a decent chuckle, even the mechanic, who was pretending not to listen. It was obvious Kidd wasn't popular, even with his own crew.

"Captain!"

Jack turned on his heel. "Trigoss! I was just thinking about going to look for you. How's the outer hull coming along?" Using plate steel that had been found in a dark corner of the Freedom's cargo bay, the engineers of the Princess Hedonist had been making structural repairs on the old battle damage of the aging cruiser.

Trigoss waited until he got closer. "Not bad, Jack. Not bad at all. We should have it finished in about a week. And with some material to spare."

"Wow, that's great!" Jack paused, "Uh, look, are you sure Gant doesn't mind you guys giving us all this help? I don't want to get you guys in any hot water."

The burly engineer dismissed the thought with a wave of a ham-sized hand, "Not a bit. In fact, he's kind of tickled. Besides, we're all doing it on our off-duty hours." Trigoss shifted and lowered his voice. "Listen, Jack, I've been thinking. The Princess doesn't really need me. They've got a whole slew of good engineers. I'm usually bored to tears, nothing challenging. Understand..?"

It dawned on Jack that the man was thinking about giving up his position to join the crew of the Freedom. "Wait a minute T, I can't ask you to..."

"Look, Jack," interrupted the engineer putting his hand on the pilot's shoulder, shifting his eyes around. He lowered his voice, "I've got no family ties... I'm bored silly here, and besides I've got the *experience*. You need a good... no, scratch that; you need an *excellent* engineer to hold this tin can together. You find me a decent bone yard and we just might be able to scrounge enough parts to make this wreck worth something."

"What about stability, your pension..."

"I'm double dipping as it is," said Trigoss shrugging his shoulders. "I've been a military brat all my life. I gave them thirty years, then they dumped me for mandatory retirement." He paused as if he was rechecking the dates in his mind. "And, do you know I've been waiting almost ten years to give those lousy pirates the kind of bloody nose you gave them in one damn evening? Hell, Jack, you're a natural. But it won't do any good if your ship disintegrates beneath your feet. Besides," he added, smirking, "I want to be around when you do it again."

"OK, OK," conceded Jack, holding up his hands, "I surrender already, you've got the job. Chief Engineer work for you?"

"Thanks!" With a wave, he bounded off in the direction he came, a bounce in his step.

"Christ," exclaimed Brian, "you'd think you just gave the guy a couple million bucks or something." Jack was speechless and Paul just shook his head.

"Anybody feel like eating? I'm starved!"

The three startled pilots turned around to face the familiar voice and saw Mike striding towards them in full uniform. *"Mike!"* they exclaimed in unison.

"How're you doing?"

"How'ya feeling?"

Mike backed up, his hands in front of him. "Whoa, easy fellas. One at a time... And no hugs if you don't mind. Doc says I can come out and play, but no rough stuff." The four men laughed and it felt good. "Say, where's Derrik? I'm supposed to tell him the Professor gets out tomorrow."

"Does he have his new arm?"

"Not yet, Pappy, they're still building it. He'll get it in a day or so."

The four men chatted comfortably as they strolled across the bay toward the elevator which would take them to the galley, the one place on the ship which had been properly maintained. "I don't get it," queried Mike, "only *four* birds to fly?"

"Yep," nodded Brian, "and one wreck to pull parts from."

"Once upon a time," ventured Paul, "this ship probably held ten to fifteen. Probably different types too."

"Old records," began Jack, "showed it originally held twelve with two shuttles. There were ten active, with two additional in reserve. Look, don't worry about it," he promised. "We'll acquire a few more."

Brian pushed the button for the elevator. "How?"

Jack smirked as they stepped into the lift, "Oh, I've got an idea or two."

Paul groaned, "I don't think I like the sound of that."

Mike rubbed his ribs absentmindedly. "I didn't like the sound of it last time." Their laughter echoed in the elevator car.

■ ■ ■

Lunch was a pretty substantial spread, delicious food and lots of it. Well laid out, it delighted the eyes, the aromas enticed the nose, and the flavors didn't disappoint. Marna, the chef, was a rather small, odd looking woman with shiny gray skin and deep-set glassy eyes. She demanded perfection, controlling the kitchen and dining area like a croupier handling a deck of cards. She watched the food preparers and porters like a hawk. No wine glass went unfilled. No table wanted for anything.

As she explained to Jack, though it was not normally quite this extravagant, the one thing pirates did very well was eat. She had wanted to show the combined appreciation of the female portion of the crew for their freedom, and this was the best way that they could think of to make the new officers and crew feel welcome.

Jack looked around him... there were his people, members of the old pirate crew and members of the Princess's crew that were helping out. All of them chatting amiably and eating happily. But other than the porters, there were no women to be seen, save Maria, Raulya and Myomerr. Jack inquired about this and was told females had never been allowed to dine with the crew they ate what was left, after everyone else was finished.

Jack stood up and raised his glass, ringing it like a bell with a spoon. Everyone stopped eating and the room grew quiet. He saw Ragnaar at the next table watching him closely. "I have been told the Captain used to kill people at dinner." There was silence. "I find that to be a *very rude* habit..."

Light scattered laughter spread through the group. "Well that type of behavior will not be tolerated on this ship!" There was more scattered laughter and applause, but Jack raised his hand to quiet them down. "I have also been told, women were not allowed in the galley until the men are finished eating." He looked around. "What the hell? Seriously? You don't like girls? Whose *dumbass* idea was *that*?" Laughter rolled through the galley, the idea had been Kidd's of course. "Well that stops now, too! And," he added, grinning, "anyone who doesn't like that, I *will* kill... out in the corridor of course, and *after* dinner." The laughter now came easily to them and Jack realized he'd succeeded in breaking the ice, making them all a bit more comfortable.

Minutes later when the women filed in, the atmosphere was light and friendly. The women became at ease when they saw how easily the men made room for them at the crowded tables. They were finally part of the crew.

■ ■ ■

The rest of that week, work on the Freedom went well, she began to take on a new look, inside and out. Pirate insignias were removed from every surface that they appeared. In their place, the silhouette of a gold winged horse against a crimson rising sun. Above each, the name *FREEDOM* in white capital letters.

Jack and the other pilots stood outside the Freedom and stared at the new emblem emblazoned on the hull of their ship. It was then that it gelled, the feeling that it was no longer a concept, an idea or a dream, it was a reality; this was *their* ship, it would take them wherever they decided to go. And soon it would be time to leave. Time to leave behind the place they'd called home for what seemed to be much longer than the few short months they'd actually spent there. But they also realized it *was* time; after all this *is* what they had in mind wasn't it?

The most difficult part would be saying goodbye to all those people who had given and done so much. Jack hoped he had done as much for them as they had for him. He truly did not consider that he had actually done more.

"Well, she's getting there..." Trigoss had strolled up from behind the pilots.

"I keep wondering how we're going to drive something that big," said Maria as she turned to greet the new Chief Engineer.

"Well first, you don't *drive* it, you *navigate* it," pointed out Brian.

"Thank you," dittoed Jack.

Maria sighed, "Well *excuse me*, for being terminologically incorrect!" she waved her arms. "So shoot me!" Miffed, she walked away to survey the work on her own.

Puzzled, Brian looked at the other men. "What'd I say?"

"Forget it," waved Jack.

"That's right, old boy," chimed Derrik. "Don't waste any brain power on it. Won't do you any good if you did. Women are like a Mobius strip, my friend... you never know if you're on the good side or the bad side."

Jack smiled at Derrik's curious philosophy but actually felt a bit guilty. He'd been so all-consumed with the work and progress on the Freedom that he'd been neglecting, even ignoring Maria. He had come to the realization some time ago that Maria was a high maintenance woman, probably due more to her personal insecurities than any other reason. He promised himself he would make an effort to reassure her it wasn't intentional and to spend some time with her very soon.

"Well..." Trigoss interrupted Jack's train of thought, "as I was saying, she's getting there, but we have a few serious problems. And then, of course, a few minor ones."

"Like what?" asked Paul.

Trigoss started walking. "Follow me; we'll walk, we'll talk." They strolled leisurely away from the stern of the ship toward the bow and the loading ramps. "First," he paused, "well, let's just say a ship lives on its ability to generate power. It runs absolutely everything. This particular ship has five main generators and two smaller generators for miscellaneous items. Each genny, has a specific duty, things it supplies with power. If you take a genny away, the others pick up the slack but, of course, they have to work harder."

"So what's your point?" asked Mike.

"Hold on, I'm getting to it." The engineer cleared his throat. "The point is, the ship can safely run on a diminished number of power sources. After that, systems suffer lag time, power losses, even shutdowns."

"So what's the bottom line?" inquired Jack.

"The bottom line is this ship is equipped with five large and two small. Borderline adequate would be three large and two small... you'd have to be very careful in any type of conflict."

Jack was getting concerned. "And we have..?"

"One large and two small," said Trigoss finishing his sentence.

221

"*Whaaat*?!" Jack threw up his hands. "*Holy Shit*, that's it?!"

Mike shook his head. "We're screwed."

"Wait a minute," said Paul, stopping in his tracks. "Then how did this clown, Kidd get away with it?" Everyone else stopped walking, their attention on the engineer.

"Bluffing," answered Trigoss. "The ship will operate. But if you need to use a large system, say shields for instance, you'd have no guns, no launch capabilities, etc."

"Can they be repaired even temporarily?" asked Pappy.

"Nope," countered the engineer, "they're totally hopeless."

The men resumed walking and Jack threw up his hands again. "Well I guess we *really* need to find a bone-yard, and fast."

Mike scratched his head. "A bone-yard? Y'mean like a junkyard?"

"That's right," injected Trigoss.

"Yeah right," said Mike sarcastically. "You mean to tell me we just look in the phone book for a spaceship junkyard..." He added a hillbilly cartoon voice and continued, "Hey `yall, my name is Mel. I got this `53 Desoto spaceship, and I need an alternator, well actually y`see, I need four..." He looked at the others, "Seriously you guys gotta be pulling my leg."

"Nope."

Mike rubbed his forehead, "Now I've heard everything."

"And as long as we're there..." added Trigoss.

Jack shot him a wounded look. "You mean there's more?"

Trigoss nodded, "I'm afraid so." He inhaled deeply. "The engines need parts too..."

Jack held his head as he walked, "I don't think I want to hear this, I know I don't want to hear this." He sighed, "OK, I know I'm gonna hate myself for asking... but what parts do *they* need?"

Like the dutiful Chief Engineer he was, Trigoss continued to explain the needs of the engines. It seemed much of the mechanical problems with the ship could be blamed on the battle it survived before disappearing. But, like the rest of the ship, almost as much could be blamed on neglect.

Much of the plasma fuel feed systems for the Freedom's four low-speed thrust engines sorely needed to be rebuilt. Their valves and flow meters no longer accurately regulated fuel use, and many fuel line connectors leaked. The internal reflectors for the three main ion drive engines needed to be completely realigned and refocused. The outer forcing cones, which adjusted to control the concentration and dispersal of thrust, were badly burnt, were no longer adjusted and needed immediate replacement. The good news was they still ran. The bad news was, not at more than half capacity and not for long.

They all agreed, the first chore at hand upon departing, would be to locate and make all good speed to a place where parts could be found. Jack hoped, that same location would prove an opportunity for additional fighter craft, or at least parts for those he had, as well.

Trigoss had led the men along the length of the ship, up the Freedom's cargo ramp, and wound through the various contents of the bay to the furthest, darkest reaches of its interior. There, in a darkened corner, hidden by tarps, crates and supplies, sat the stolen shuttle of the Princess Hedonist.

"Methinks I smell a rat..." quoted Brian.

Trigoss wiped his hand across the layer of dust on the shuttle's hull, making a clean stripe, "This is the minor problem I spoke of. The men found it early this morning when they were scrounging for materials to finish up the hull."

"Has it been searched?" Jack was concerned about preserving the crime scene, so to speak.

Trigoss wiped the dust onto the leg of his coveralls. "Nope."

Jack, followed by the others, moved around the nose to the access hatch on the other side of the shuttle. "This whole thing is beginning to look like a setup... except it blew up in their face..."

Paul gave him a puzzled look, "I'm not sure I follow you..."

"Too many coincidences, Pappy," answered Jack. "First, this shuttle disappears. Then we answer a distress call, off the main travel route between Genisis Gates..."

"From the Eliza Meru," interrupted Paul.

Jack nodded. "Right. Then about the same time, we acquire a shadow named Kidd. Then, at full sensor range, he's able to tell our ship has no defenses and he only needs to send one fighter to stop our escape. I checked this tub," he indicated the Freedom. "And at that range, that information isn't available. Finally, in Gant's initial conversation with the commander of the boarding party, they inquired about the Earth pilots, and our planes. How could they have known about that? That stuff's been driving me crazy. But this," he pointed at the shuttle, "answers everything! Kidd had an agent posing as a passenger on the Princess Hedonist!"

"But who?" asked Derrik.

Jack, standing at the shuttle's entry hatch, shook his head. He opened the panel covering the keypad. "I don't know. I'm hoping the answer's in here..." The keypad chirped under Jack's fingertips and the door swished open. Since there was no boarding ramp, the men boosted each other up through the shuttle's doorway. "Search everything," he directed.

It was a fifteen seat work shuttle with cargo and luggage space, so the men split up and went to work. It didn't take long. Two pieces of personal luggage were found in the cockpit on the floor in front of the copilot's seat. On the navigation computer, was the course and rendezvous point between the shuttle and the pirate cruiser. "Well," began Jack, "let's see who the proud owner of this luggage might be..." The luggage ended up on the floor in the passenger compartment, surrounded by the six men.

Trigoss knocked off the latch-locks with a heavy spanner wrench and opened the luggage. Kneeling on the floor, the men rummaged through the clothes for a clue of identity. "Whoever he is," said Derrik, holding up a dress shirt, "he's a little fella..."

"He's also Saurian..." added the Chief Engineer, looking at the pattern on the shirt.

"What have we here..?" Jack pulled a leather pouch out of a hidden pocket in the second travel case.

"Open it!" urged the group.

Jack removed the contents and spread them across the mess they'd created looking for clues. Trigoss inspected the various documents, among them, a ledger of some kind. "Hmmm," he reflected, "it's all in Saurian, can't read a word... maybe someone on the Princess can translate for us." He flipped through the pages and a plastic card fell out. He picked it up and scrutinized it, flipping it over. *"Hellion..."* he mumbled, staring blankly at the photo on the other side before handing it to Jack. "It's Tee," added Trigoss, wrinkling his nose. "I never liked that stinking little worm..." The others duplicated his sentiment.

Since he had not been among the prisoners and had not been discovered among the dead, Jack and the others came to the conclusion that, for his efforts, Tee was probably awarded with a shove into an airlock. It was also agreed upon, that a long stroll in space without a suit, had been too good for him.

■ ■ ■

Later that afternoon, in a meeting between Jack Steele and Gantarro, arrangements for the return of the recovered shuttle were finalized, as well as the disposal of Tee's effects. Jack had also prepared a full report for Gant to relay to the Council of the United Federation of Worlds which outlined the new tactic of placing a spy on a ship desired for acquisition. In the search for creative new ways to obtain safe havens, it seemed obvious that large ships like the Princess Hedonist were the newest likely targets by the pirates. They made exceptional places for repair of small to medium ships and would provide a safe, anonymous, facility for crew R&R, or even innocuous transport of large masses of men and supplies.

He also expressed that in the interests of victory, they might want to give the general populations, an incentive to participate in the fight and inevitably have some bearing in the outcome. He explained that rewards, bounties, bounty hunters and privateers, who under the flag of their own world, pillage from the pirates then split the profits with their own governments. This would not only increase the number of ships at the UFW's disposal, but funnel needed funds to the planets that might require added defense support.

He explained, under this principle, he had taken possession of the pirate cruiser, making it his own. And, while his planet was not a member of the UFW or the spacefaring community, he should be considered an ally.

"So, Jack, are you all settled in?" The two men sat in the Captain's ready room, connected to the Freedom's bridge. Jack had wanted to show Gantarro how the ship was coming along.

"Pretty much. Most all the systems are up and running pretty well, a couple of problems, but we're weeding them out."

"Well she looks super. Probably better than when I served on her."

Steele tried not to let his pride get the better of him. "Thanks. Everyone's worked very hard on her. And I want to thank you, for letting your people help us out."

Gant swept the sentiment away with a wave of his hand. "Forget it, most of them came to me and personally insisted on it. Besides, the UFW needs all the help they can get. I'm obliged to make sure if an opportunity arises, that I do what I can to make the best of that opportunity."

A tall, particularly attractive female porter entered with a tray of food from the galley. She had long silken auburn hair and sparkling brown eyes. She strolled gracefully across the room with long, supple legs and set the tray on the table. "Wine?" Her voice was light and musical. Jack nodded and she poured for both men who watched silently. "Will there be anything else, Captain?"

"No. Thank you Alité." She turned and walked out, both men watching her go.

"Y'know, Jack," Gant leaned back in the high back chair and put his feet up on the conference table, "the UFW is liable to claim ownership of the Freedom, being she was theirs to begin with... they lost a lot of good people when the Ynosa disappeared."

Steele, unconcerned, sipped his wine. "I don't know, I think they've got more important things to worry about. Besides," he grinned, "finders keepers..."

Gant dropped his feet off the table and leaned forward, snatching a sandwich off of the platter. "Well," he smiled, "the Council will have their hands full when they deal with you..."

Jack raised one eyebrow, "How so?"

Munching on his sandwich, he waved his free hand. "You have the element of surprise. You aren't orthodox in your approach to things. At least not what they consider orthodox." He smirked, "They'll probably just agree with you. It'll be the path of least resistance."

"See, that's the attitude that's losing their war," commented Jack.

"True, true," agreed Gant, taking a swallow of wine. "They need some fresh approaches, some new ideas. They're too used to playing it safe." He held up Jack's report. "Maybe this will get them thinking."

Jack leaned forward. "I hope so, I really do..." The two men grew quiet, each contemplating their futures and what was in store for them. Secretly, Gant wanted to be back on the bridge of a warship, he missed the military way of life.

The comm on the table buzzed, interrupting the silence. Jack answered it, "Steele..."

"Captain?" said the voice, "Lieutenant JG Raulya and Ensign Myomerr to see you."

"Thank you. Send them in."

The two former security members of the Princess Hedonist entered the ready room from the bridge, dressed in brand new, gray and blue uniforms of the Freedom's crew. They saluted sharply. "Reporting for duty, Captain."

Jack smiled, "Relax, it's just us. So, you two got all your gear stowed? You all settled in?"

Raulya stepped forward and lifted a sandwich off the platter. "We have quarters on the port side, right down the hall from the bridge."

"Real nice too," added Myomerr.

"Good, good." Jack had been surprised when the two Ketarians had expressed an interest in becoming part of his crew, but was pleased to accept them with Gant's blessing. "Listen," he added, "if you two are hungry, Marna can get you something hot to eat in the galley."

"Sounds like an excellent idea," agreed Myomerr.

"Then, get some sleep," added Jack, "we've got a long, busy day tomorrow." It was true. They were scheduled to pull the Freedom out of the Princess's bay, the day after that.

"Raulya looked down at the floor. "What about Fritz?" she asked softly.

Jack looked up and shifted uneasily in his chair. "They won't even let me see him, it's been three weeks..." his voice trailed off as it caught in his throat. It was obvious this was a painful, open, emotional wound. He swallowed hard, "Maybe it's better for him to stay on the Princess where they can care for him..." It was difficult to think it, it was even harder to say it. He took a deep breath to maintain his composure.

Raulya cleared her throat. "Well, I think there was someone waiting on the bridge to discuss that with you."

Jack stood up. "Why didn't somebody say something?!" He hustled to the door and it swished open before he reached it, disappearing into the wall. Gantarro jumped up and followed him out, accompanied by Raulya and Myomerr. Jack ran onto a bridge crowded with crew members. "What the hell is going on here...?" No one spoke as his eyes shifted from face to face, nearly thirty people on the bridge. "Are you all going to stand there grinning at me, or is someone going to tell me what's going on..." his voice dropped off in mid-sentence, as Fritz moved slowly through the crowd which parted silently, shuffling to either side. "OhHhh..." his voice wavered.

The Shepherd looked different, yet the same. Jack was so stunned, he didn't comprehend the changes. Using CABL, *Computer Assisted Biological Lifeform,* technology, the surgeons were able to save the dog's life. The right side of his head, from the bridge of his snout, including the right eye socket, to behind the right ear, to about the middle of the top of his head, was polished stainless steel. This hand-made steel exoskeletal plate, was molded to replace the destroyed part of his skull. His right eye had been replaced with a color, full zoom, optical cell. Shaped the same as his original ear, his new right ear was a mechanically articulated, polished aluminum composite

227

dish, with a digital pickup that tripled his hearing ability. A specialized CABL microcomputer took the place of the damaged right lobe of his brain, which would actually make him smarter as it aged and stored acquired information.

Jack dropped to one knee and opened his arms to greet his friend, tears welling in his eyes against his will. The Shepherd ambled past the people and across the room to the man who willed him to live. Still not completely coordinated, the dog's gait was slow and somewhat mechanical in execution, but his determination paid off when he reached the loving, protective arms that encircled him. Jack buried his face in the long, soft fur of Fritz's neck and cried. "Oh, Christ," he sobbed, "I missed you kiddo... I never thought I'd see you again." Jack raised his head to the sound of steady applause. As he wiped away tears of joy and relief, he realized there wasn't a dry eye on the bridge. The Shepherd stared up at his master with one sparkling eye, as dark as black opal. It twinkled with a spark of familiar mischief. The other eye glowed blue-green and focused mechanically, producing a faint whirr. Fritz saw Jack for the first time in complete living color. They stared at each other nose to nose, as if seeing each other for the very first time, until the dog impulsively licked the man across the face. Jack fell backward and laid on the floor laughing. Fritz stood on his chest and wagged his tail, triggering waves of laughter which rolled across the bridge.

It was a time for celebration. The group filed down the corridors to the galley where more crew waited. Marna, in her effervescent culinary fashion, had created a cake and pastries worthy of presidential consumption. Wine and liquor of all tastes and colors flowed like water. So they had a long day tomorrow, so what? Who cared? So their long day would start a little later than planned, was that any cause for concern? *Not in the least.* There were toasts to be given! They toasted Fritz's recovery, the Professor's new arm, to Jack as a new Captain, the pilots, the crew, the cook. They moved to toasting their home planets, to victory, even the Queen of England was mentioned. And when they ran out of things, they started all over again because they were masters of their own destiny. And a simple hour or two one way or another, wouldn't make a bit of difference in the grand scheme of the things. All was right with their universe.

Well, at least until they all got drunk and fell down.

Sometime in the wee hours of the morning, the celebrating died down and the members of the crew, new and old, dispersed. Trying to find their new quarters in an unfamiliar ship, under the influence of intoxicants and fatigue, proved to be an insurmountable task for some. There were several instances of confused personnel sleeping in the corridors. There were also several more instances, of groups of personnel, in assorted states of dress and undress, sleeping in the same room, even in the same bed. But, the release was good. They had worked hard and it was well deserved.

Jack almost fell over Maria's prone form, sprawled on the corridor floor, as he made his way to his quarters. "What a lush," he chided. "Hey! Are you awake?"

"Mmmphh..." she mumbled, face down on the carpet.

Jack dropped down to one knee and attempted to gather her into his arms. It was about as easy as picking up a bowl full of noodles without the benefit of a bowl. Deciding there was no gentle, delicate way of accomplishing this, especially in his reduced capacity, he heaved her over his shoulder like a sack of potatoes, having to catch himself on the wall of the corridor to keep himself from keeling over. Diligently carrying his load, the inebriated pilot weaved his way down the corridor. He looked down at the German Shepherd at his side, wobbling his way down the hall. "Geez, I'm-I'm-I'm bombed," joked the pilot, "what's your excuse?" He didn't expect an answer of course, he just wanted to talk to the friend he'd so dearly missed.

The dog stared up at Jack as they walked and wagged his tail. There were many things hazy or missing from Fritz's memory, but this man was not one of them. He knew this man was his entire world.

With Maria still slung over his right shoulder, Jack paused at the door to her quarters and punched the buttons on the keypad with his left hand. The door swished aside and disappeared into the wall, swishing closed again after he and Fritz had entered with their cargo. Jack stood motionless in the darkened room, unsure of the furniture arrangement. He addressed the ship itself, "Computer, ambient lighting please." Slowly, the lights came on, producing a soft, comfortable, indirect glow. Not as large as the suites on the Princess Hedonist, the accommodations on the Freedom were quite adequate and more than comfortable. There was no wall, just an archway separating a small salon from the sleeping area. Jack moved over to the bed and dumped Maria bodily onto the mattress, producing an unintelligible mumble.

Fritz sat at the foot of the bed, his chin resting on its corner, and watched Jack struggle with Maria's clothes. The task of removing her uniform, proved to be almost as difficult as picking her up, but with a little perseverance, he succeeded in stripping her naked. He stared at her curvy, cinnamon skinned form, legs and arms akimbo, and wondered how such a desirable woman could be so unappealing. It had been some time since they'd slept together, so many things to keep them busy and apart, so many distractions... Jack had begun feeling the effects. He had hoped tonight they would've had time to spend together, in pursuit of amorous exploration with absolutely nothing between them except their sweat. *Damn,* thought Jack. "Well, maybe tomorrow night," he breathed. With a sigh, he mentally shrugged off the thoughts and rolled the dark-haired beauty on her side, then pulled the covers up over her shoulders. Instinctively, the woman curled into a ball and proceeded to suck her thumb like a small child.

Jack smirked, he couldn't help it. "Goodnight," he said quietly, as he and Fritz headed for the door.

"Grbnitz..." answered Maria.

"Yeah," muttered Jack as he and the dog passed into the corridor, "that's what I said... grbnitz."

The two companions ambled down the silent, half-lit corridor toward the Captain's quarters occupied by Jack. The Shepherd leaned his body into the man as they went, happy to be in his presence. Jack reached down to stroke the dog's ears as they walked and felt the smooth stainless steel plate and the artificial ear. He pulled his hand away as if burned. "Sorry, kiddo," he apologized. "That's going to take a bit of getting used to." He replaced his hand and stroked the dog's muzzle and face.

The problem was, the surgeons could easily produce artificial skin to duplicate any hue, but on ship, fur was a much different matter. It was extremely difficult to produce, much less duplicate in any accuracy with the equipment on board, so they left the technics exposed, hoping that at this point, function was more important than aesthetics.

For Fritz, being alive was everything. The thing that bothered him the most, were the constant holes that appeared in his recollections. To him it seemed like he had lost some kind of instinctive edge, but since he could not clearly remember what that was like, he had no solid grounds for proper comparison. What he did not realize, was that the CABL technology was steadily filling in those blanks and eventually he would regain most of what he had lost. Not only that, but it would make him more intelligent on a level somewhat more Human than dog.

The compartmented doors in the corridors had finally been fixed, the problem mostly being damaged computer components. They opened with a hiss as the two approached, splitting down the center, the halves moving outward to disappear into the walls on either side. After passing, the halves would re-emerge and come together, their edges interlocking.

The Captain's quarters were nearest the bridge and largest of the ship's accommodations, followed by the suite provided for the ship's first officer. Jack had yet to select a first officer and thought about this as he walked past the entrance to the room he knew to be empty. He walked past the door to his own quarters and continued the short distance to the bridge. He stood in the doorway for a moment, surveying the empty work stations, which, in just two days, would be attended twenty-four hours a day. After strolling the *upper deck*, he stepped down the short, wide stairs that ringed the *pit*, the control section of the bridge. Standing in front of the command chair, he surveyed the layout from that vantage point, something he had done dozens of times before. "Whaddya' think, Fritzer?" He looked down at the Shepherd who stared back at him, his tail swaying slowly. "She's all ours y'know... take us anywhere we want to go..." The bridge empty, the ship silent, it was then he began to wonder if he was truly ready for all of this. It felt lonely.

He thought about home for a minute. The void of space felt uncrossable, the distance incomprehensible. He thought about all the people willing to put their faith in him, their lives in his hands. So many questions unanswered, so many variables... the condition of the ship... The accumulative weight of the responsibilities suddenly became painfully obvious. He had tried to avoid thinking about it, but there it was... like a big, fat, towering mountain of dirt – and all you had was a teaspoon to dig your way through it.

"If you sit around all day thinking about something," his father would say, "you'll think of a dozen excuses not to do it. So quit thinking about why it can't be done and just get up off your duff and go do it... *nothing*'s impossible."

Jack battled the doubts and pushed them from his mind. "Thanks, Dad." He turned to leave, "C'mon dog, let's go to bed. I'm bushed."

Unlike the other suites on the Freedom, the Captain's and the first officer's were expansive. They held a salon with a bar in the middle, a bedroom on one side and a small conference room with a computer work station on the other. Jack stood at the bar in muted light and poured himself a glass of something that resembled ginger ale, "Voorlak," he said softly, "where are you when I need you...?"

"Will I do?" asked the soft female voice.

"Huh?" Jack jumped. "Shit," he cursed softly, having spilled some of the drink on the bar. He peered at the figure in the bedroom doorway, but the

231

lighting was so low he could barely see the form. He shot a glance at Fritz who lay calmly on the couch, unaffected. "You're a big help," he whispered to the Shepherd. He left the glass on the bar untouched and moved closer to the bedroom doorway. "Who are you?" He felt stupid having to ask.

"Come over here and find out," cooed the smooth voice. She leaned casually against the doorway, silhouetted against the darkness of the room behind her. She was tall and slender.

Jack toyed with the idea of just turning up the lights but declined the impulse. This was much more interesting. His pulse quickened as he neared the doorway.

"That's it..." she coaxed.

When he got close enough to touch her, she slipped backwards, into the darkness of the room behind her, drawing him into the inky blackness. His senses were alive with electricity, straining to glean a shred of a clue to the mysterious woman's identity. There was a gentle wafting of perfume. *Aahhh,* he thought, it was wonderfully smooth but warm and spicy at the same time. Unfortunately, it was unfamiliar to him.

"Follow my voice," she whispered, "I'm over here..." His heart pounded so hard he thought it would explode, but he moved toward where she directed him. He stiffened when he felt the hands against his chest. "Stop there," she breathed. "Mmmm, a little tense, aren't we?" She began to unbutton his tunic and he reached forward in the darkness to touch her arm. "No," she whispered, putting his hand at his side. "Soon enough..."

"Who are you?" he whispered. It came out more like a croak.

"You'll find out soon enough," she breathed huskily, pulling off his tunic. "I promise you, you won't be disappointed."

"But..."

"Hush!" she scolded, pressing her finger to his lips. She stripped him naked, ran her hands across his body and laid him on the bed where she instructed him to get comfortable. Which he did, piling up the pillows against the headboard and leaning back, pulling the covers to his waist to fight the sudden chill he was experiencing. As he listened in the total darkness, he could hear the *lop, lop, lop,* of something being poured into a glass. "Wine?"

It was the way she said it that caused the tidal wave of instant recognition. *"Alité?"*

"Yes," she acknowledged.

"I..." he realized he had no idea what to say.

232

"Computer, ambient light." The lights came up slowly, illuminating the room in a comfortable glow. Alité stood at the side of the bed, a sheer black veil wrapped around her naked form, holding two glasses of wine. She extended one to Jack, "Disappointed?" she asked softly.

Steele could not take his eyes off her, accepting the glass of wine handed him. He took a sip and attempted to set it on the nightstand behind him. And missed. The glass fell to the floor and bounced on the carpet. He did not notice, nor would he have cared. Taking her hand without speaking he drew her to the bed.

With one knee on the bed, she stopped. "Wait," she said, breathing deeply. Alité placed her glass on the table on her side of the bed and slowly unwrapped the black see-through veil of lace, letting it hang loosely about her shoulders. She was tall, slender and shapely, and Jack was losing his mind. She crawled upon the bed seductively, far more beautiful than Jack could ever have imagined. She pulled his covers off and lay across his legs, reaching up and running her fingernails gently across his bare muscled chest. "I've wanted you," she sighed, "from the minute I first saw you."

"When was that...?" he asked in hushed tones, barely finding his voice.

"The day you took the ship," she replied. She kissed her way up from the flat of his stomach to his lips, so slowly he thought he was going to jump out of his skin. Her long auburn waves of hair danced across his skin setting his nerves on fire. When she reached his lips, he could take no more. He pulled her roughly by the hair and devoured her mouth. She melted into his arms.

When he pulled her away to gaze at her body, glistening with sweat, she stared back at him with sparkling amethyst eyes. Jack's eyes narrowed. "Your eyes... I thought they were brown..."

She smiled and traced his lips with her fingernail. "Brown, green, blue, lavender, they change all the time." Still lying on top of him, she swung her leg over his waist and sat up, straddling him. "But I like your eyes better," she whispered, sliding south.

"Wh, whhyyy izat..?" Jack stuttered, holding her by the waist.

Alité closed her eyes and inhaled sharply, "Ohh... God!" She opened her eyes and looked into his. "Well," she sighed as she rocked back and forth. "I've never seen eyes so black..."

"They're actually br, brownnn..." he managed to counter, gritting his teeth and scrunching his eyes shut.

"Well they're beautiful," she said coolly. "I want to see them. Open your eyes and look at me... or I'll stop."

233

Jack's eyes popped open, "Oh God," he pleaded, "please don't do that!"

They spent the next several hours with nothing between them but their sweat.

■ ■ ■

"Wake up, sleepyhead!"

Steele sat bolt upright in bed, still half asleep, "Huh?" He rubbed his eyes with the palms of his hands.

Alité placed a tray full of fruit and breakfast pastries on the bed in front of Jack. "Do you think, just because you're Captain of this ship, that you can lay around all day doing nothing? Get up, lazybones!"

Jack shot a glance at his watch. "Holy crap! I already missed my morning meeting. We were supposed to look over the navigation system and discuss a possible course for tomorrow." He looked up at Alité, she was in full uniform, and it was obvious she had already reported for duty and returned from the galley. She stole a piece of fruit off the tray and walked into the other room. Jack could hear her at the bar in the salon. "Hey..!" he yelled, "were you late this morning?"

"Just a little," she called back.

"Did Marna give you a hard time?" He picked up a jelly pastry and took a bite. He handed another to the Shepherd who waited patiently at the side of the bed.

"Not really," she answered. "I just told her the Captain summoned me and requested breakfast in his quarters this morning."

Jack grinned, "So you're telling me, you were late for duty, you lied to your superior, and now you openly address your commanding officer in a familiar and un-military fashion?" He took another bite of the delicious pastry.

"Is this better?" Alité appeared in the doorway holding a chilled bottle of Boolorean Champagne, two fluted glasses, and wearing nothing but her sparkling smile. Her eyes, now bright blue, danced. She held the chilled bottle against her body, making her nipples stand on end.

Jack's eyes widened and he swallowed hard, "It works for me!" Alité moved to the bed and eased down beside Jack. She poured, they drank, they ate, they explored. It was the most enjoyable way Jack could think of to spend a morning.

■ ■ ■

They laid side by side, their bodies touching, legs entwined, feeling comfortably worn and warm all over. The tangled bed linens lay askew and partially covered their bodies. After a long silence, Jack cleared his throat. "I guess we'd better get up, or people are likely to put two and two together..."

Alité looked at him. "You are worried about that?"

Jack shrugged, he wasn't sure how he felt about it, but he *was* sure how Maria would feel, and she was not one for tact.

"You are worried about Lieutenant Arroyo, aren't you? Is she your woman?" She looked down at her fingernails. "Do you love her?"

"No." It was the first time Jack had honestly thought about it for a long time. The answer came so quick and easily that he knew it was right. "At one time I think I did. But not anymore."

"Then you should tell her."

Jack thought about that for a moment. "I think she already knows." He got serious and in hushed tones, told Alité the story. How they met, how they ended up on the Princess, and how they decided to take the pirate cruiser. He explained how they drifted apart. Alité listened carefully and agreed. She surmised Maria knew but felt she would deny the reality as long as possible. Jack admitted, that sounded like something Maria would do.

The conversation was interrupted by an incoming call on the ship's commlink. Jack reached over and punched the button on the night table to answer the call. He leaned back against the bed's headboard. "Yes?"

"Hey Jack, Paul here. Listen, I know you're probably involved in something vastly more interesting..." Jack could hear the smile in his voice. "But we've come up with several viable routes and possibilities for parts, we thought you'd like to go over them..."

"Sure, I'll meet you in my ready room, say half an hour?"

"You got it," shot Paul. The commlink beeped once and ended the connection.

Jack stared at the beautiful woman, lying on top of him. She was daydreaming and absentmindedly drew circles in his chest hair with her index finger. When she looked up and caught him staring at her, he smiled. A genuinely warm smile that made a wave of heat flush across her body. Jack peered into her eyes, they were a pale lavender. He brushed a stray lock of silken hair from her face. "Duty calls..."

She kissed his chest and rolled off him. "OK," she said, pouting and mocking disappointment, "if you must."

"I must," he countered, smirking. He got up and strolled to the bathroom. "Listen," he continued as he turned on the shower, "do me a favor; take Fritz down to level three and let him run around the officer's garden for a bit, OK?"

She climbed into the shower with him. "Sure. But then you owe me a favor."

"Like what?"

She soaped his back, "Oh, I'll think of something..."

Jack grinned, "Yeah, I'm sure you will."

CHAPTER NINETEEN

PRINCESS HEDONIST/FREEDOM: DEGOBAH SYSTEM

The bridge was buzzing with crew members working on last minute systems repairs and software testing. Steele hustled through their midst and entered his ready room at the back of the bridge about five minutes late, everyone who was to attend was already there. "Good morning gentlemen!" He looked around but nobody spoke, he was surrounded by seven Cheshire Cat grins. "What..?" He looked down at his uniform for an obvious blemish or a missed button, then it dawned on him. "Alright fine," he shook his head. "Good *afternoon*. Is that better?"

There was a good deal of chuckling and elbowing at Jack's expense, but Brian pulled him aside, "You've got something right here..." he pointed between his teeth and made a sucking sound like he was trying to dislodge a stubborn food particle. Jack didn't realize he was joking and began imitating the routine.

"I don't feel anything," said Jack, picking the invisible blemish with his fingernail.

"Well, it's right there," continued Brian, pointing at his own teeth. "What does it look like to you, Pappy?"

"Gee, I'm not sure..." added Paul, carrying the joke along. He pretended to inspect the spec and imitated Jack by picking his own teeth, making his own sucking noise. Jack was oblivious to the others who were desperately fighting to keep from laughing out loud.

"It sort of looks like..." began Brian.

"Fur pie?" finished Paul. The room exploded with laughter, and Jack tried unsuccessfully to look perturbed.

"Holy crap!" groaned Steele. "I didn't realize we were still in high school... seriously. OK, you guys, you've all had your little laugh. Can we get down to business now?" Jack ran his fingers through his hair.

"First things first, Jacko," called Derrik as it quieted down. "Be a good sport and tell us who the lucky lady was." The other meeting attendees chimed their interest as well.

"Nothing doing," Steele waved dismissively, "you guys keep secrets like a sieve holds water." He hoped he could sit down with Maria and square things with her before she heard it somewhere else first, because he knew this group of gossip mongers couldn't keep it to themselves. "Cmon, let's get down to business here, what are our options?"

The lights were dimmed, and the conference table projected a three dimensional holographic chart above it; star systems, Genesis Gates and trade routes hovering in the electronic haze. Trigoss laid out several route options reaching into the chart and manipulating it by hand, highlighting gates and systems, illuminating the various routes and possible destinations. The mission was to find parts, for free if possible. Trigoss knew the exact location of one such place. It was the closest of the three destinations, unfortunately it was owned by the UFW. Salvaging on the sly would not be a likely prospect and parts would be costly. The second was an independent space salvage yard, but the exact location was unclear. It was in a safer system, but they'd have to cross several sectors heavily occupied and patrolled by pirates. The third was suggested by Ragnaar. Its location was also not exact, and it too required traveling in pirate occupied sectors, but for a multitude of reasons, it seemed to be the lesser of all evils. Ragnaar believed the third facility was owned by the pirates, but didn't feel it was likely to be patrolled or protected, because it was hidden and the pirates preferred stealing new equipment to repairing old. It remained the best chance for obtaining the parts they needed without cost. It was also possible that spare fighters and parts might be kept there.

After a short discussion, a unanimous decision set their course for the third destination. It was also agreed, upon Gantarro's request, that before they departed, the Freedom would fly escort to the Princess Hedonist until they were clear of the present sector. Once clear, the two ships would part company and continue on to their separate destinations.

The door from the bridge swished open at about the same time Jack called for the computer to turn up the lights. Alité strolled through the door with a tray full of sandwiches and beverages. Fritz sauntered in behind her. Her hair was pulled back severely in a tight bun and she looked nothing like the woman Jack had spent the night with. She distributed the drinks in silence but smiled warmly at Jack before leaving, her eyes lingering on him. The men watched her go without a word.

The men thought about their first task and sipped quietly, some taking sandwiches from the platter. Suddenly Brian looked up at Jack and smiled. *"Nooo..."* Everyone turned to look at him.

Mike's eyes went wide, his eyebrows rising, "No what?"

"That was her!" exclaimed Brian. "Did you see the way she looked at him?"

Paul wasn't convinced, "The Ice Princess? Nah, couldn't be..."

"That had to be her!" insisted Brian. Steele tried to look innocent but it wasn't convincing and they weren't buying it. Despite biting the inside of his cheek, he cracked a half smile. Primarily because he couldn't help thinking about last night. "Look at his face," urged Brian, "it's written all over his face!"

"I don't get it," grumbled Mike, "I've been watching her all week, I can't get her to even look at me..."

"Shows she's got good sense," volleyed Jack, still leaving Brian's accusation unconfirmed.

"Ouch!" mumbled Paul sympathetically.

The meeting deteriorated to rolling banter and jokes before Jack was finally able to bring it back to some semblance of order. "We need to talk about crew assignments and placements. First, I think we'll give navigation to Ragnaar. Any objections?" There were none.

Ragnaar bowed. "Thank you, sir, I am honored. I will do my best."

Jack nodded then turned to the Professor. He was the only person in the room, not in uniform. He stood to one side and puffed on his pipe, dressed in a comfortable brown tweed English sport coat. Jack studied him for a moment and tried to remember which hand was real and which was mechanical. "Professor, first I want to thank you for all your assistance on the software for the Freedom..."

Professor Edgars waved his pipe. "Don't mention it, old boy, t'was rather enjoyable."

"Well," continued Jack, "I can't imagine you not being around and I'd like you to stay on with us... as the ship's first officer with the rank of Commander."

His eyes widened, "I say!"

"Look," added Jack, motioning to the others, "we're all pilots. We can do our best for this ship, sitting in the cockpit of a fighter. But we need to know she's in capable hands while we're gone. We need to know we'll have a ship to come back to..." The others all nodded their agreement. "Besides, I can't imagine it'll be boring..."

The Professor tamped the tobacco in his pipe. "Sounds absolutely smashing! And you know me, anything for a bit of adventure... I must say you've taken me a bit by surprise. I was going to ask to tag along, but this is more than a man could hope for. I'd be delighted!" He was welcomed to the crew with a round of handshakes and congratulations.

"How about a toast?"

Thinking of the night before and the all too memorable hangover, Brian rolled his eyes. "Let's not start *that* again." It bought a round of chuckles and light laughter.

"What about ship's security?" asked Paul.

Jack sipped his carbonated fruit juice. "Mmm, Raulya and Myomerr have the clear advantage there, they've served on this ship before. They will share responsibilities of internal security and weapons systems." Ragnaar made a sour face and Jack ignored him. "Well," concluded Jack, "I'll need a list of recommendations for gunnery positions, helmsmen, etc."

"I think I could do most of that," volunteered Ragnaar.

"I can give him a hand," added Trigoss.

"Good. How many people do we have now?" asked Jack.

"Sixty-seven," answered Trigoss. "We might pick up a couple more before we leave tomorrow... adventure seekers." Several of the newest crew members were former passengers on the Princess Hedonist.

"It's far from a full crew," admitted Steele, "but it's a start. I think it would be wise to teach the women some of the other positions." He could see Ragnaar making another face. "I know there are some of us who think women only belong in the kitchen, but the truth is, there might be a time, when an extra hand or two could make all the difference in the world. So do me a favor Ragnaar..."

"Oh please, sir," he said, retreating, "anything but that! Torture me, give me bilge duty, ask me to sacrifice my life... but don't ask me to work with the women!"

Jack was almost in tears trying to hold his laughter. "For crying out loud, relax, Lieutenant! I just want you to pick someone to interview the women and find if any of them already have any talents or experience."

Ragnaar stared at the floor. "Yes, of course."

Laughing, Jack waved it off and dismissed the meeting.

"Oh, one more thing," said Trigoss, as the others filed out. "We managed one more generator."

"That's great! How'd you do it?"

"Well don't thank me yet. It's built from all the parts we could salvage from the burnt units. It only operates at about half capacity, and I'm not sure for how long."

"That's alright," conceded Jack, "every little bit helps."

■ ■ ■

Alone with Fritz in the darkened ready room, Jack Steele stood in front of the conference table and studied the three dimensional holo-chart floating above it, a cluster of systems linked together by their gates. Each point of light represented a star, planet, or Genesis Gate, small identity tags near each marker. He reached in and with a wave of his hand pushed on the chart, zooming out from the system cluster, the individual planets and stars disappearing, becoming entire solar systems. And there were thousands of them. A pale blue cube at one end represented millions of miles of space, their present sector. It was only about an inch square, in a chart over eight feet long. A blue line snaked away, perhaps twelve inches to a pale green cube of the same size, the place where they hoped to get the parts and supplies they needed. From there, a green line departed towards the other end of the table sometimes completely obscured by the lights of alien solar systems, ending in a pale yellow cube almost eight feet away. Fritz was sitting in one of the conference chairs at the far end of the table and Jack moved closer to him and the yellow cube. "Y'know what that is, kiddo? That's snowy mountain peaks, green forests, blue oceans and warm, sunny, golden beaches. That's home, Bunky, that's what that is." The Shepherd wagged his tail. He vaguely remembered running in the water. He wasn't sure, but he thought it might have been fun.

It was difficult even with the chart illustrating it, to comprehend just how far away home really was. But never the less, Jack programmed the table to show the most direct route home at any given time. It seemed to be a good way to keep that fine tenuous thread from breaking and leaving him emotionally adrift and homeless in the starry void.

A general announcement came over the comm, informing all crew members that engineering would begin main engine warmup momentarily and that all unnecessary power consumption must cease until morning after main engine startup. Jack nodded to himself and switched off the holo-chart, watching the thousand-plus points of light dissolve and disappear.

He strolled from the ready room onto the bridge. The operations officers and technicians were busy shutting down the computers, sensors, work stations and anything else that wasn't required. With full generator power, it would not require more than a few short hours for engine warmup, and that was with systems running. But, as it was, the ship would require most of the night to warm up the engine cores. Jack and Fritz left the bridge to head to the officer's garden before retiring for the day as nothing else could be done with all the systems off line. Besides, tomorrow would probably prove to be a full day.

The garden was nowhere near as large as the Ecosphere on the Princess, but it was sizable enough for a fair stroll among the trees and flowers. Jack enjoyed the sweet smell of the air and Fritz seemed to remember about the joys of rolling in the grass. Sitting under a tree, he watched the Shepherd run and frolic, noticing how much more fluidly he moved than just the day before. The dog appeared to be regaining more of his old self back and this made Jack very happy. Fritz found a stick and brought it to Jack, dropping it on his lap. They played fetch for awhile until it became obvious the dog was tiring. "That's enough, dog. Don't want to do too much too fast." Jack stood up and walked towards the garden's port entrance, the German Shepherd trotted at his side, still proudly carrying his stick.

Ragnaar met them at the elevator. Jack and Fritz were going up, the Lieutenant JG was going down. "Here, sir," said the former pirate, "the info you wanted on personnel." He handed Jack a data disk.

Jack took the disc. "Your choices for helm and science stations... are they sound?"

"Yes, sir."

"No favoritism?"

"No, sir. Just the best for the job."

Jack nodded casually, "OK, Lieutenant, thank you. Please inform the first shift you have chosen that they are on duty for start up and pull out tomorrow morning. Work up your recommendations for gunnery positions, we'll review them in the morning."

"Yes, sir." Ragnaar saluted smartly. Instead of taking the elevator, he turned and hustled down the corridor, presumably to notify crew members of their duty status.

■ ■ ■

The lighting in the corridors was muted to save power and the corridor partition doors were fixed open, the system off line for the same reason. The low droning hum of the engine blowers was a new and different sound, a contrast to the silence of the past three and a half weeks.

Jack stepped through the doorway and into his quarters, to discover not one, but two women waiting for him. Maria and Alité. No sooner did he realize this, then he spun on his heel toward the door. *Uh ohh...*

"Freeze!" yelled Maria, jumping to her feet. "Where do you think you're going to, Mister?" Her speech always slipped into Spanglish when she was upset.

"I uhh..." he couldn't think of anything believable, "nowhere," he mumbled. *Dammit.* The dog stood next to him, not quite sure what to do or where to sit.

"I thought we were going to spend the night together. Where did you go?" She stood with her hands on her hips. Alité sat demurely on the sofa, adjusting the slit of her casual evening dress.

"*You,*" said Jack, defensively, "were *unconscious!*"

"So what? You couldn't wake me or wait till morning?"

"*Wake you?* Are you *kidding?*" he snorted, moving to the bar to get something to drink. "I carried you over my shoulder, from the galley to your quarters. I completely undressed you. I even tucked you in. And the only word you said the entire time, was *gribnitz.*"

"Gribnitz? What the hell does that mean?"

Jack leaned back against the bar and shook his head, "Hell if I know." He took a sip of ginger ale. "It came out of your mouth, not mine."

Maria began losing steam. "So why didn't you stay with me?"

"I'm sorry," shrugged Jack, "but I really didn't want to wake up next to... ahhh" he waved dismissively. "I just didn't... It just wasn't an appealing..."

"But we've done it before..."

"I know, I know," he rubbed his forehead. "That's how I knew it might be better... for both of us," he said quietly, staring into his glass.

Maria shifted uneasily motioning towards Alité, "So who's she?"

Alité didn't want any room for misconceptions, "I'm the Captain's personal porter," she said, rising off the couch. "He was here with me last night."

Steele winced. *Oh crap.*

Maria stiffened. "*What*? What the hell is she talking about Jack? Did you *sleep* with her?"

The room suddenly felt warm. "I uuhh..."

"*OH, you did!*" she interrupted, stomping her feet, swearing in Spanish. "I can't *believe* you! How *could* you? Men are such pigs!"

"It wasn't his fault..." started Alité.

"Shut up, *puta!*" spat Maria.

"Whoa, whoa, *whoa!*" yelled Jack, stepping forward with a wave. "That's enough! I think it's your turn to be quiet and listen. You've said enough."

"But..."

"I said *quiet!*" He set his glass on the bar and straightened his tunic, adopting a more professional posture. "Now, *sit* down!" Maria plopped herself onto the couch like an angry child, her arms folded defiantly across her chest. Alité remained standing, looking very elegant, very proper.

"As I was about to say..." began Alité.

"I think you've said enough too," said Steele, sternly. "*Sit down.*" She sat seductively on the other end of the settee and did not bother to close the thigh-high slit of her dress as it fell open. It caught his eye and the pilot momentarily lost his train of thought. "I... ahem, it... um, *look,*" he said to Maria, pulling his thoughts together. "It's been almost four weeks since we've slept together. We haven't talked much, hell, we haven't even seen each other much. We've drifted apart." Maria sat and stared at him with angry child eyes. He rubbed his forehead with his fingertips, hoping to prevent the headache he knew was coming. "I don't know whose fault it is. Yours, mine... it's really not important. The point is, the first night we have to spend together, with any hopes of regaining some of our intimacy, you get so ploughed, you disappear. I found you later, sleeping face down in the corridor absolutely *comatose.*"

"So you're saying this is all my fault then?"

Jack was about to object when Alité took over. "No he's not," she said gently. "But the Lords only know why..." Jack tried to interrupt and she shushed him. "He moved onto the Freedom almost immediately. You waited three weeks. Not only that, you didn't even come to see him in the evenings. He sat here alone most nights studying the ship's systems... or with the engineers reviewing the repairs." She waved her hand toward Fritz, "He had no idea if his wonderful companion would live or die... and through all that, not once did he have any female company... but I could tell he needed it.

And believe me, there are plenty of women on this ship that would have been more than happy to oblige him."

"Huh?" Jack's eyebrows rose, "Really?"

Maria's expression had changed. She listened to Alité but she watched Jack with puppy dog eyes. "How could you tell?" she asked quietly.

"It was obvious," said the porter, standing up. "He was lonely. He had all these responsibilities..." she strolled to the bar and poured herself a drink. "He had all these people to direct, all the things that had to be done to this ship..." She moved next to Jack and slipped her arm around his waist. "And all without showing the terrible pain he was in, losing Fritz and all."

"But Fritz didn't die..." objected Maria, indicating the dog who was sitting quietly, watching the conversation.

"Jack didn't know that," interrupted Alité "I watched it all. And since you didn't, I decided I would do something about it... I simply gave him what he so terribly needed. It seemed obvious he wasn't a priority for you..."

Maria looked through watery eyes. "Why didn't you say something, Jack?"

Alité answered for him, "Because he'll put personal feelings aside to accomplish something. He's dedicated. He doesn't complain. But just because he doesn't *say* anything, doesn't mean he doesn't *need* anything."

Maria rose from the couch and smoothed her uniform. "So I suppose this means it's over then?" She wiped the tears from her face.

Jack pulled away from Alité's grasp and moved over to Maria. He took her face in his hands. "Look, I think we drifted apart long ago, we just couldn't admit it. You are very dear to me and that won't ever change, but let's face it, we're both takers." He moved his hands to her shoulders. "We both need people who have more time to give to us, than we do to them. If for no other reason, than the duties and responsibilities we carry consume so much of our time." It was like walking a thin line through a minefield, one wrong word, and boom! He wanted to carefully traverse the danger without laying blame.

Maria turned away and slipped from his hands. "OK Jack," she sighed, waving her hand casually, "whatever." She moved to the door, not positive if she was more hurt or angry and if it was directed more at him, Alité, or herself.

"Hey," called Jack. Maria turned and paused at the open door. "No more booze for awhile, OK?"

"Sure," she said, in an emotionless, monotone voice. "See ya round the ship, Captain..." She threw him a haphazard salute and stepped through the doorway. The door shushed quietly closed behind her, leaving the room silent.

Jack swallowed dryly. "I need a drink," he croaked. Alité handed him a glass of sparkling juice almost before he finished his thought.

"She'll be alright," soothed Alité, "you'll see..." She ran her fingers through his hair and massaged his aching temples.

"This is *not* the way I wanted it to go," sighed Jack.

"How *did* you want it to go?"

Steele waved his hand in a circle, "You know how it went just now?"

"Yes..."

"Better than that."

CHAPTER TWENTY

FREEDOM: HISTORIC LAUNCH, DEGOBAH SYSTEM

By mid-morning, all that had to be done – all that *could* be done, had been completed, checked and rechecked; history could not be postponed any longer. The very first ship ever to be captured intact, *such as it was,* from the pirates, was ready to be relaunched under a flag allied to the UFW.

Four more people had joined the Freedom's crew that morning; two were former passengers, two were former crew members of the Princess Hedonist. This brought the Freedom's total crew complement to seventy-one. Still well below the standard crew of one-fifty to two-hundred, but as Jack Steele would say; *Every little bit helps.*

The entire crew of the raider-class cruiser, Freedom, stood in single file review outside the port loading ramp. The officers wore the royal blue, double breasted, cavalry style shirts, formfitting, charcoal gray pants, and the polished black, knee high boots. Non officers wore light gray, double breasted cavalry shirts, and the same charcoal pants and black boots. Rank was noted on the collar for officers and on the shirt cuff for non-coms, but only six people wore the coveted pilot's wings on their left breast.

Their brass buttons glittering in the lights of the Princess's landing bay, the small crew was still a dramatic sight. Gantarro, accompanied by Jack, strolled down the line and said goodbye to the former members of his crew he knew as friends and bid the entire group God's speed and protection. As they returned to the beginning of the line, the Captain of the Princess grew more solemn, paused in front of the pilots and faced Jack. His full, trimmed, white beard and sapphire blue eyes made him look a little like Father Christmas. "Captain Steele," he began, "it has come to my attention, that you have no medical staff on your crew. If something happens out there, you'd be in big trouble... any medical assistance, could be days too late. Can't have that. It's not at all acceptable. So..." he continued, grinning, "I'm providing you with both, a medi-bot and a surgically trained CABL."

"Can you do that?"

"I just have, Mr. Steele. And may you never need them." Gant extended his hand.

"Thank you," said Jack, shaking his hand, "you've been a good friend. I hope we'll see you again."

Gantarro smiled politely, "I'm sure we will. Take care, my boy."

Jack stepped aside and his new first officer Professor Edgars, stepped forward, followed by Fritz and the five pilots. They exchanged smiles, handshakes and goodbyes. Jack turned to Ragnarr, "Lieutenant..."

"Yes, sir?"

"Let's round em up and head em out!"

The burly Lieutenant cocked his head. "Sir?"

Steele cracked a crooked smile, "Get the crew aboard and prepare to depart..?"

"Oh yes," the big man nodded, "aye, sir." He turned to the crew and waved them up the ramp. The assigned medi-bot and the specially trained, CABL M7, followed the crew up into the cruiser.

The Professor and pilots, having exhausted their goodbyes, turned and started up the ramp, leaving Jack and Fritz at the foot of the ramp facing Gantarro, who stood on the pad. The old man smiled, and then snapped a sharp salute. Jack stiffened and returned it crisply. When he turned on his heel, he proceeded up the ramp without looking back. Things seemed to have come full circle, and Steele pondered how odd, that every time he departed, someone was saluting him. He hoped the Freedom's maiden flight would be more successful than the Sweet Suzie's.

The Shepherd ran ahead and was at the elevator before Jack reached the entrance to the cargo hold. A technician who doubled as a Gunnery Officer, stood in the hold at the top of the ramp, waiting for his Captain to board. "Thanks, Mister," said Jack, as he passed. "Close her up." The Warrant Officer nodded as he worked the controls to retract the heavy ramp back into the hull. Hydraulic pumps thrummed as the ramp hinged upward to fold itself flush with the hull and seal the cargo opening. Jack glanced back when he heard the hiss of the hydraulics and the squeal of metal on metal, which were the locking rams securing the door. The crewman gave him a thumbs up signal to show the door and hull were sealed tight. Satisfied, Jack gave a wave and stepped into the waiting elevator.

■ ■ ■

It was good to see crew members in the corridors, it made the ship feel alive and vital. Fritz was having to trot to keep up with Jack's long strides,

248

but once he discovered their destiny was the bridge, he galloped off down the hall, happily weaving his way past corridor traffic. It was becoming obvious, the Shepherd was almost back to his full physical abilities already, though some of his personality traits were still absent. *All in good time*, thought Jack.

With the work stations fully manned, the bridge appeared to have undergone a substantial metamorphosis. Used to the quiet, it was almost startling when Jack stepped onto the bridge, but it felt like home just the same. As he walked across the upper level, past the science, communication and sensor stations, Raulya handed him a comm unit. Slightly different than the comms on the Princess, he paused and slid the miniature unit over his left ear and adjusted the wire-boom mic near his mouth. Moving down the steps to the command chair, he shooed Fritz from the seat. "OK, boys and girls, here we go!" He dropped into the command chair and scanned the readouts on his monitors. "Communications, give me an open channel..."

"You have it, sir."

"Thank you." He looked up to the main view screen which showed the flight bay around them, "Hello tower, this is the Freedom, we're ready to shove off."

"Copy, Freedom. Bay doors are open, personnel are clear, flight path is clear... you are free to execute."

"Thank you, tower." Jack sat back in his chair and crossed his legs to feel more comfortable and conceal his anxiousness. He punched a button on his console which would route his communications to engineering. "Are you ready Trigoss?"

"Ready, Captain."

"OK, Chief," continued Jack, "we need power for the antigravity system."

"Gotcha. Rerouting power from the main engine cores, to antigravity... now." The lights on the bridge dimmed momentarily.

"Helmsman," ordered Jack, "take us off the deck."

"Yes, sir." The ship began to vibrate as the Ensign applied power and the ship became weightless, lifting off the deck, "Up and holding, sir." The vibration lessened.

"Good. Lieutenant, retract the landing legs."

Ragnaar nodded, reaching across his console, "Yes sir." The heavy thrum of massive hydraulic pumps drummed from the belly of the ship as they worked to retract the legs designed to support the Freedom's extensive weight. One by one the legs thumped home and locked into place. "Gear up and secure, sir."

"Alright," Steele rubbed his hands together, "now we're cooking. Lieutenant, Ensign, it's up to you, take us out of here."

"Aye, sir," they answered in near unison.

"Try not to scratch the paint job..."

Ragnaar turned from his console, forward of the command chair and looked at Jack over his shoulder. "Not a chance, Captain," he replied with a smile. Steele returned the smile with a knowing nod.

Sitting in his own chair, to the left of Jack's, the Professor eyed his own monitors for trouble. Jack slid out of his position and stood up. Fritz, who had been lying peacefully between them, rose with his human. "Listen, Walt..." It felt strange calling him by his first name but the Professor didn't seem to mind, "I'll be right back, keep an eye on things, OK?"

"Right-o." The Professor didn't look up from his monitors.

Followed by Fritz, Steele moved up the short stairs that ringed the control pit and over to where the pilots stood with Raulya and Myomerr at the weapons console, behind the command chairs. They stood, momentarily silent and watched the landing bay slide slowly backwards on the main screen.

"Pretty freaking amazing," whispered Mike. The others nodded in silent agreement, mesmerized by the scene on the big screen.

Jack broke his attention away from the view screen. "Where's Maria?"

"In her quarters," answered Derrik.

Steele nodded. "Maybe that's for the best right now." The others agreed, knowing what had transpired and her present attitude. "I'm going to call downstairs and have them ready the fighters," continued Jack, "I need you guys to launch as soon as we're clear of the Princess."

"What's up?" queried Brian.

"Nothing yet," said Jack peering at the weapons console, "it's just that we're kinda' vulnerable and I think fighter recons are a good idea. I don't want to get caught with our pants down."

"Good idea," confirmed Paul.

"Thanks, Pappy." Steele checked the big screen then turned back, "Mike, you fly with Pappy. Bri, you fly Derrik's wing. Pappy, you're flight leader, so pick whatever sweep pattern you think is best."

"No problem, Jack." Paul motioned to the others, "Let's go get suited and prepped." The pilots filed out of the bridge and Steele really wanted to be going with them; he wanted to fly something other than a shuttle so bad he could taste it.

But Steele returned to the command chair where he knew he needed to be until the Professor was more familiar with operations. Or they came up with a fifth fighter, *whichever came first.* He plopped himself into the contoured, well padded chair and after a quick glance at the big screen to check their progress, he punched a button on his console, connecting him with the flight bay. "Flight bay..."

"Flight bay, go ahead," came the answer over his comm.

"This is the bridge, arm and prep all fighters for launch." The flight crew acknowledged his order and the computer beeped as the commlink ended. Rotating his chair around, its console and monitors turning with it, he looked at Raulya at the weapons console behind him. "How long will the ship's weapons hold a power charge if they don't fire?"

She glanced down at the console, then back up. "Most will hold a charge in their storage cells for twenty-four to forty-eight hours."

Steele nodded and pulled on his lower lip, deep in thought. Without turning or looking, he addressed his first officer, "Walt, do we have any extra power at all to divert to something else?"

"A little," he answered, checking the status of the generators on his monitor.

"Good..." Steele turned back towards his weapons officer, "Raulya, can you route power to a couple turrets at a time? Charge them up and move on to the next one?"

She was staring down at her console and calling up the arming and powering information. Whole columns of directions outlined the specific sequences. "I'd have to change the prescribed format a bit, but I think I can."

Steele rubbed his hands together. "Good. Do it."

Raulya nodded and began working on the program's format, rearranging it to make it more flexible and allow her the freedom to manipulate the power to individual gun turrets. She paused, "The guns need to be manned..."

"No problem." Jack punched the general-comm button on his chair's console. "All gunnery personnel to your stations. This is just a drill, repeat, this is just a drill. Report when at station." His keypad chirped as he ended the broadcast. When he spun his chair back forward, the view screen showed the Freedom was almost halfway clear of the Princess's bay.

One by one, manned and ready, gunnery teams began reporting in to Raulya. Once all the turret crews had reported in and she had successfully

251

changed the arming and charging program, she addressed all the gunnery personnel at one time, instructing them on the charging protocol. And was careful to make it clear that at no time should they actually arm the weapons in their turrets. Although probably disappointed, all personnel complied and the process proceeded smoothly, though a bit slow.

Unable to start the main engines in the confines of the landing bay, Jack grew concerned about the engine cores cooling before the withdrawal of the Freedom was complete, necessitating more warm up time. He keyed the proper comm button. "Engineering, this is the bridge, how are our core temps holding out?"

"Stand by..." Jack recognized the Chief Engineer's voice and waited through a long pause. "Sorry sir, I was a bit busy."

"Do we have a problem, Chief?"

"No sir, just some adjustments. Our core temperatures are fine, they'll hold for a couple of hours before requiring any additional heat."

"Thanks, Chief. Just checking." Jack sat back in his chair, crossed his legs and relaxed, satisfied that there wasn't much else to do but watch and wait.

■ ■ ■

Paul, Mike, Brian and Derrik, stood in the locker room and donned the flight suits which would protect them in space if ejection from the cockpit became necessary. In appearance, the suit resembled a standard G suit, but that's where the similarity ended. These special survival suits would provide a complete sealed environment with heat and oxygen when the helmet was locked and the suit remained attached to the ejection seat with umbilical cords. The pilot would have several hours of life support in deep space.

The pilots finished putting on their suits and moved through the double doors into the briefing room, carrying their helmets and flight gloves. They sat in the front four seats, glancing around at the twenty empty seats around them. "I say," said Derrik, "it's a mite lonely in here."

Paul shrugged, "Maybe some day it won't be so deserted." He sat in the chair the briefing officer would use, which had a small console and keypad that controlled the flight planning wall chart. Using the keypad, he lowered the lights and called up the chart of the present sector. "We are here." Two ship icons representing the Princess and the Freedom appeared in the center of the chart, prompted by Paul and placed by the computer. "We'll fly in a standard finger four, Derrik and I in front, Brian and Mike as respective wing men." A four craft flight formed ahead of the icons for the larger ships and a red line raced forward, away from the ships. At its furthest point, the two flight groups would split, Paul's winging left, Derrik's winging right. The flight plan formed a diamond, the points facing outwards at the bow, stern, port and starboard.

After momentarily rejoining at the stern point, the groups would split again to create another diamond with points facing out, above, below and again bow and stern, where theoretically if the recons found nothing, they would rejoin and approach the stern of the Freedom for recovery. This, Paul aptly named the Double Diamond Sweep and would become a standard recon used on the Freedom. "Any questions?" asked Paul. There were none. "OK, let's head on out and see how they're coming with those birds." The pilots gathered their gloves and helmets and walked through the blast doors out into the flight bay. Two of the Warthog fighters were completely armed and sitting in the two launch bays with their canopies standing open. The other two were still being armed, but were almost completed. The pilots stood and watched the armorers load the last of the missiles.

The launch assistant, a former pirate, strolled over to greet the pilots, "Any of you gents ready to go?"

"Are we clear yet?" asked Paul.

"Let me check," said the assistant. He keyed the mic on his headset. "Do we have clear launch yet, boss?" He scrunched his face as he listened to the answer on his comm unit. "Not yet," he told the pilot, "but soon."

"We'll wait then," said Paul. The launch assistant nodded and headed back to his station.

■ ■ ■

Able to call up almost any of the ship's systems on his monitors, Professor Edgars was getting an indoctrination of trial by fire. Trying to learn all the different systems while they were *live* and in operation, was stressful and potentially dangerous because his chair's console allowed him access to any one of those systems. But the Professor resisted his professional curiosity and dismissed the urge to experiment. Instead, he concentrated on monitoring the systems he knew best, with only occasional glances at the rest.

Jack knew there was probably something constructive he should be doing, but he had slipped into a daydream. It was about the warm Florida sun, fine white sand, and the feel of the salty surf. Images of his home on the beach, friends, family, a welcome home barbecue... "When are you going to find a nice girl and settle down?" his mother would say. "I would like to see some grandchildren..." She rarely forgot to mention it and sometimes she made it sound like, all it took, was going to the department store to pick them out. "Maybe you're being too picky," she would add. *Darn right*, thought Jack, don't want to end up with a lemon, he'd done that once. One divorce was enough... for any man. He decided no man should be required to give away all his worldly possessions more than once, in any given lifetime. *Starting over from square one was more than enough for this guy.*

"Captain!" Ragnaar's voice snapped him back, "We are clear of the Princess, sir." There was a short round of applause from the bridge staff.

Steele looked up to see the stern of the ship ahead, as the Freedom coasted slowly backwards. He watched as the bay doors began to close. "Thank you, Lieutenant. You and the Ensign did a fine job. Maneuver us on thrust engines, bring us abeam of the Princess."

"Yes, sir." The nose of the cruiser began to swing as the helmsman programmed the controls and the ship vibrated softly as the four thrust engines ignited.

Jack swiveled his chair to face Raulya behind him. "I need that power back for main engine startup..."

"You have it, we're finished."

"Thank you, Lieutenant." He nodded at her, "You may stand down your crews and dismiss them." As he swiveled back around, the communications officer announced an incoming message. "On screen please..."

Gant's grinning face appeared on the screen. "Without a hitch. Nice job, Mr. Steele. Well, you're on your own Freedom. Good luck! We'll send over our nav-course for the remainder of this sector, we appreciate the escort."

"Our pleasure," confirmed Jack. The men signed off and the screen winked out returning to the external view mode. Momentarily abreast, the Princess began to pull away as her main engines lit up. Jack punched his comm button. "Engineering, this is the bridge. We're all set, light em up Chief!"

"Initiating main engine startup," came the reply. The lights dimmed and the ship rumbled like an approaching freight train as each of the three engines roared to life, one at a time. This diminished to a low soft rumble, not unlike distant rolling thunder. "Startup completed, Captain," called

Trigoss. The lights returned to normal - which for the bridge, was muted, to ease the viewing of monitors, control and data consoles and the view screen.

"Good job, Chief." Jack ran his fingers through his hair. "OK helm, let's catch up to the Princess. Mr Ragnaar, plot us a course parallel to hers, but at a distance which will prevent a blind spot in our sensors." Both crewmen acknowledged and set about their tasks. The Princess had become a bright halo in the distance, but they would catch her soon. "Walt, run some of that power to the launch bay, will you please?"

Walt nodded, "Of course."

Jack punched a comm button to the tower. "Flight control, you are clear to launch fighters..."

■ ■ ■

The lights over the prep and launch areas dimmed, then turned red to prepare the pilots for night flying, a perpetual state in deep space.

"Here comes that launch assistant again," mentioned Brian. The pilots turned from their conversation as the gangly young man trotted over from the flight tower.

"The Launch Boss says we're just about clear," relayed the puffing assistant. "You guys should probably get your bones in those sleds and buckle in."

Paul slapped the man on the shoulder, "Thanks, kid." He hefted his helmet under one arm and began sliding on his gloves. Walking backwards, he thumbed over his shoulder at the launch tubes. "Mike and I'll take these, you take the other two." Pappy let the helmet slide out from under his arm and caught it, flipping it over, open side up.

Brian smiled slyly, shaking his head as he pulled on his own gloves. "We'll see you outside!" He picked his own helmet up off the wingtip of the closest fighter where he had set it and walked around to the side of the cockpit, handing it to his mechanic before climbing up the ladder to the open canopy before crawling in.

"Catch, sir!" The mechanic tossed the helmet up into the cockpit before climbing the ladder himself. Brian caught the newly painted globe and brushed invisible dust off the fresh artwork. Each pilot had his own artwork expertly rendered on his helmet, courtesy of a talented deck hand who had practiced and developed his hidden skill. Brian's had the ship's flying

255

Pegasus logo over red and white stripes that wrapped around to the other side, ending with a blue field of white stars.

As the mechanic belted him in and connected his comm link and other leads, the pilot donned his helmet and glanced over at Derrik in the next fighter. He couldn't see Derrik's logo from that angle but he could remember it clearly, a diving falcon clutching a British Union Jack. Derrik glanced up and flashed a thumbs up signal which Brian returned.

The scream of the catapults flinging the first two fighters into space made both men start and look up. After sealing the suits to the pilot's helmets, the equipment crewmen climbed down and removed the ladders. A deck crewman plugged a headset into the nose of Brian's fighter and another did the same for Derrik. "Can you hear me, Lieutenant?" Brian looked down over the side and nodded. "Good," replied the man, "you can speak, I'll hear you. OK, close your canopy and seal it." The pilot slid the handle back and the hydraulics hissed, easing the canopy down, latching and sealing it. The air system came on automatically and Brian could feel the cool air flow into his suit and wash across his face through his open visor. "OK now, flip on only your antigravity system." Brian reached forward and flipped the green and white switch with a click and felt the craft bounce off the deck, the system producing an audible static hum like high voltage wires heard at a distance. "Good, now just follow me... hands on the stick, just point it where you need it to go." The man strolled off towards the launch tubes, tethered to the fighter by the cord from his headphones.

Brian's fighter headed for the left launch tube and Derrik's around the flight tower to the right tube. As Brian neared the catapult, his stomach flip-flopped with anxious butterflies, his mind racing ahead. The deck crewman turned around and walked backwards, guiding the pilot with hand signals into the opening of the launch tube to the recessed catapult. The pilot found he could literally move in any direction on antigravity, including backwards. The man guiding him held up both hands and Brian let go of the stick. "Good. Anti-grav off, Lieutenant."

Brian flipped the system off and the craft settled to the deck with a gentle bump, the static hum disappearing. Brian glanced around for a moment, the darkness of space lay ahead, past a veil of thin blue, which was the stasis field holding the atmosphere in the flight bay. To his right, a heavy steel and formcrete wall. Derrik's fighter would be on the other side of that wall.

Though almost literally side by side, the two launch tubes were separated by a special blast wall nearly eight feet thick. Considering the amount of ordnance and fuel a fighter carried, it was a reasonable and important precaution to prevent a catastrophic launch accident from spreading to the fighter in the next tube.

The magnetic catapult sled rose off the metal launch tube floor, three legs extending upward toward the underbelly of the fighter. The deck crewman ducked underneath and fixed the legs to the grab-slots on the hull, one near the nose and one on either side of the fuselage. "OK," he said, re-emerging to the left, "retract your landing gear." Brian flipped the switch next to the antigravity and the hydraulics hummed, pulling the gear in flush with the skin of the Warthog, green indicators affirming the gear was locked in place leaving the fighter supported by the legs of the catapult sled. "Comm system on, Lieutenant. And switch to fleet channel Delta," instructed the mechanic. Brian activated his communications equipment, switching channels until the Delta sign appeared on the frequency screen immediately hearing the other fighters talking with the tower. He shot a quick thumbs up signal to the crewman.

"OK, Lieutenant, you're all set, so have a good flight!" Disconnecting his headset cord from the nose of the fighter, the deck hand backed out of the catapult bay and using the control panel outside the tube, activated the launch system.

Brian watched as a reinforced steel blast wall rose out of the floor on his left and arched upward to connect with the ceiling of the launch tube. The tube was oval, being widest at the sides, and the wall had just sealed him in, quickening his heart rate. There was a sudden impression of being a live torpedo.

"Flight two," called the tower, "you copy?" Both pilots in the tubes acknowledged. "Good. I know you guys are rookies, but if you follow directions, you'll be just fine. First, never *ever*, arm guns, shields, or ordnance in the tube. Got it?" Both pilots acknowledged.

Brian wondered what kind of window-licker you'd have to be to do something that moronic... And if anyone had ever done it before. Someone really *special* had to have done it, otherwise why would they mention it?

"Navigation on," ordered the tower. "Activate radar, scopes and sensors." As each command was given, it was executed by the pilots and acknowledged. "OK, here we go boys... switch on engine power, but do *not* ignite burners." Brian raised the safety cover for each of the two red switches and flipped them up with a snap. When released, the safeties closed, locking the switches in the on position. A red light glowed above each switch. "Fine. Now, when those red lights turn green, you will be clear to ignite engines." The Launch Boss counted down, "Launching in; five, four, three, two, one..."

The walls of the tube flashed by in a blur. In what seemed to be a nanosecond, he had pierced the blue veil of the stasis field and was cast into the star filled blackness beyond. *"YaaHooooo!"* The engine lights turned from red to green and Brian punched the ignition switches, firing up the Warthog's twin engines as he cleared the tube. "Whoa, *what a rush!"*

"Hey! How about a little radio decorum out there?" joked Steele from the bridge of the Freedom.

"Sorry, Skipper," called his former copilot, "but you've really got to try this. It's freaking awesome!" He rolled the Warthog, started a loop that he turned into a barrel roll and fell in alongside Derrik off his starboard wing.

"Loony Yank," kidded Derrik.

"Aw c'mon," chided Brian, "gimme a break! You guys have done this stuff before... well, sort of... but this is *my* first time!" He looked at the stars all around him, "Christ, this is *beautiful."* The others were more than inclined to agree. To really appreciate its vastness, the beauty had to be seen from outside the ship.

After some general observations and a little horseplay, the flight grouped and settled down for some serious recon work. Leaving the Freedom behind as it continued to gain on the Princess, the fighters flew on, observing radio silence. After about ten minutes they reached the Princess Hedonist, passing over the cruise liner in formation. Rocking their wings in full view of the observation deck and bridge, the running lights of the liner blinked a friendly reply. The fighters continued on at a moderate pace, the Princess Hedonist and Freedom only visible on scanners ten minutes later.

By the time the flight of four fighters had reached their outward bound navigation point, the Freedom had caught up with the Princess and was cruising abreast of her, with about five miles between them. On their navigation computers, the pilots saw the first nav-point turn from pink to blue, indicating they had reached their destination. "See you on the back end," said Paul, breaking radio silence.

"Roger, Pappy," answered Derrik. "Leader two, breaking right." When Derrik's right wing dropped, Brian chopped his power and followed him through the turn letting the other fighter drift across his nose. Brian powered back up and formed on his wing leader's opposite wing. Looking over his right shoulder, he could see Paul's flight as they dwindled to two points of light.

■ ■ ■

"The fighters have reached their outward point, Captain, they're splitting for the return points."

"Thank you, Ensign," said Steele, changing his monitor over to watch the split. At the very forward edge of the Freedom's sensor range, the blip separated to form two smaller blips, traveling on a rearward angle away from each other. At that point, he had a quick understanding of the pattern Pappy had used, the return angle after the split made it obvious. He reached forward and turned the monitor off and got out of the command seat, Fritz rose off the floor next to him. "Looks like you found yourself a new favorite spot, huh?" The Shepherd cocked his head in a most familiar fashion and wagged his tail. "The bridge is yours, Walt. I'm going to get a bite to eat and get some rest." He dropped his comm unit gently on the console, "I'll take over for you later."

"She's in good hands, my boy." Replied the Professor. "Go get some rest, you were up awful early this morning..."

"Thanks" said Jack, yawning. "Call me if you need me."

"Will do."

Jack and Fritz strolled off the bridge and down the hall toward the central elevators. He was thinking how strange it was that the dog was no longer vocal like he used to be, never barking or growling, not making noises of satisfaction or indignation, no whining, no snorting... He wondered if the injury had caused some unseen damage, something the doctors missed. He decided he would speak to CABL M7, maybe have him give Fritz a checkup. They rounded the corner and stopped at the central bank of elevators. Jack pushed the button and waited for the lift. "So what'll it be, Kiddo? Eat first, or a walk first?" The door swished open and Jack stepped in.

"Wok!" barked the dog.

Jack froze mid stride in the elevator's doorway. He wasn't sure if he was more surprised that the dog had finally made vocal noise, or if it was because the vocalization sounded like he had *said* something. Jack smiled, shook his head and finished entering the elevator. Fritz followed him and sat down. "I must really be tired," said Jack, "I'm starting to hear things." He pushed the third button. "I said eat or walk," he mumbled, "and you barked. So it just sounded like you said..."

"Woak," interrupted the dog, improving his annunciation.

The door swished open but Jack didn't move, he stood frozen, staring at the dog who stared back, head cocked to one side, wagging his tail.

"Captain?" Steele just about jumped out of his boots. "Sorry, sir. Are you getting off?" Jack looked at the gray uniformed non-com standing outside of the elevator. He had a heavy electrical tool bag slung over his shoulder. "Are you getting off?" he repeated.

Steele looked at the deck number, at the dog and back at the waiting non-com, "Uh, yeah, sure." He stepped off the lift and past the curious technician.

"You OK, sir?"

"Yes I'm fine," lied Jack. What was he going to say? *I think my dog just talked to me?* Not likely... He waited until the elevator doors closed the crewman inside before he turned to the dog. "Look you, if this is someone's idea of a joke, I'm not laughing..."

"Nyo," said the dog shaking his head.

"No?" Steele ran his fingers through his hair. "You said no?" He looked around, but besides himself and the Shepherd, the corridor was empty. "He said no..." mumbled Jack, sitting down on the floor in front of the dog. "I must be losing my marbles."

"Nyo," countered the dog. He turned and strolled down the corridor.

"Hey!" yelled Steele. "Where are you going?"

"Woak!" answered the Shepherd.

Jack shrugged and got to his feet. "Sure, we'll walk," he muttered. He walked down the hall behind the dog talking to himself. "What the hell, flying saucers exist, aliens are real, there's pirates in space, I know talking cat women, there's even a guy wearing a cloak who drinks brandy and walks through walls... so why not a talking dog?" He followed Fritz into the garden and sat down. "Geez, what a weird freaking universe..."

■ ■ ■

"Hmmm," mused CABL M7, after examining Fritz. "It may not have been expected, but it was surely predictable to a certain extent." He rolled the sleeves of his tunic back down. He was one of only two members of the crew with a green uniform tunic, signifying he was on the ship's medical staff.

"But he *talks!*" insisted Jack, waving his hands expressively. "Dogs aren't supposed to talk... at least not where I come from."

"It's a side effect from the installation of his CABL network. Did the surgeons not explain all the possible side effects?"

"Evidently not," said Jack apprehensively. "Why, what else is there?"

"Sit down, Captain."

Jack was sure he didn't like the sound of that. CABL M7 turned to the dog, "You're all done Fritz, you can go if you wish." The Shepherd nodded and gracefully jumped off of the exam table. "I will send the Captain to the galley when we're done. OK?" Fritz nodded once again and trotted through the sliding infirmary doors. Jack stared in disbelief. "Now," began CABL M7, "there are many possibilities." He leaned back casually against the exam table, arms comfortably folded against his chest. "But the probabilities are more what we're concerned with. First of all, you must stop looking at him as merely a dog. The moment his body adapted to the CABL insertion, he stopped being a dog, he will never be merely a dog again."

He walked over to the small refrigerator used to preserve drugs and specimens. Jack watched him go. He pulled out a jug of ice water and held it up. Jack nodded, his mouth dry. CABL M7 poured two glasses, placed the jug back and returned with the glasses, handing one to Jack.

"There are many different types and sizes of implants. Fritz's is fairly sizable, it will affect everything about him. Mine, for instance, is more specialized. I was already a surgeon when I developed Garginson's Disease, a debilitating illness which attacks the nervous system of my species. It crippled me. The CABL installation cured me. I decided to replace my right eye with this special optical, about a year later because it enhances my microsurgery abilities. No matter how extensive or how small a system, once inserted, it's permanent." He drank some of his water as did Jack.

Jack found it both disturbing and fascinating at the same time. "So what are some of the things I should expect?"

"I'm getting to that," said CABL M7. "A CABL system develops on its own... Learns, if you will, and eventually develops and improves other things. For me, my reflexes doubled in speed, my motor control is beyond my original norm, I'm physically stronger..." He hopped up onto the exam table and crossed his legs, sitting like an Indian. "For Fritz, it will mean a much increased intelligence, the ability to reason, an enhancement of *all* his natural abilities, hearing, smell, intuition, reflexes, speed, agility, even strength. He may even learn to talk..." Jack cracked a smile. "I thought that might amuse you," added CABL M7, grinning. "The more extensive a unit that's installed, the further-reaching its effects on the recipient."

Shaking his head, the new Captain rose from the chair. "Amazing... simply amazing. I wish someone had told me all this earlier though, it would have freaked me out a lot less..."

"Freaked you out?"

"Um, surprised and confused..." explained Jack. CABL M7 nodded his understanding. "Well I better get going, he'll be waiting for me." They shook hands. "Thanks for your time, Doc, I appreciate it."

"It was my pleasure, Captain. One other thing, there's no accurate prediction on how sizable his spoken vocabulary will become, but it will definitely be smaller than his mental vocabulary. Simply because he was not physically designed to speak. This will be frustrating for him at times, so be patient with him."

"I'll do my best, Doc. Thanks again." He turned and walked through the infirmary's sliding double doors into the corridor.

■ ■ ■

"You're not going to believe this Jack," shouted Maria as she ran up towards him in the corridor. "Fritz just came into the galley and ordered a hamburger! I thought I was hearing things, but then he said it again!"

"I know," said Jack wearily.

"You know? That he *talks?"* she squawked, her arms waving in the air. "You have a *talking dog!?"*

Maria fell in alongside Jack as he continued down the hall towards the galley. "Yeah, you could've knocked me down with a feather. Doc says the CABL installation has expanded his intelligence." Jack continued on as they walked, recounting CABL M7's explanation.

"Well how much can he say?" probed Maria.

Jack shrugged, "Who knows? Evidently enough to order lunch!" When they entered the galley, they found Fritz occupying a seat at the head of an empty table. Two hamburger style sandwiches, one half eaten, sat before him on galley plates. He chewed happily and wagged his tail when he saw his human. Sitting down on either side of him, Jack and Maria joined the dog. "You going to eat *both* of those?" asked Jack, pointing. The Shepherd shook his head and nosed the plate with the whole sandwich over to Jack, who felt thoroughly embarrassed about the dog's unselfishness.

"I don't believe this..." muttered Maria.

"Hubugerrr!" barked Fritz, over his shoulder. The porter brought another sandwich on a plate, and Fritz pushed it in front of Maria, not wanting her to feel slighted. He continued to munch on his own as neatly as he could, his eyes shifting back and forth between the two people.

"Jack, I've never had a d-o-g order lunch for me before," whispered Maria.

"Why are you whispering?" he asked, "he hears better than you and me... And stop spelling, he probably spells better than y-o-u." Jack took a bite of his sandwich. "Mmm, it is good," he commented, wiping the meat juice off his chin. "Juicy... try it." Maria gave in and took a bite, nodding her agreement.

"So what do we do now?" asked Maria.

"About what?" responded Jack, swallowing.

"About Fritz. What do we do next? Where do we go from here?"

"I'm not sure," shrugged Jack, "help him if we can, let him develop however he wants to..." Then a sudden idea hit him. "But not before we have a little fun..."

Maria picked at her sandwich. "Fun? Like what?"

"Like watching the look on Brian's face... and Paul's, Mike's, Derrik's... even the Professor." Fritz nodded vigorously and wagged his tail with enthusiasm. Jack smiled at the idea and the dog's understanding of it.

Her eyes sparkled for the first time in weeks. "Oh! That's a super idea! Call them now! Invite them down to eat or something..!"

"Can't," said Jack, his mouth full, "gotta wait till they come back..."

"Come back... From where?" interrupted Maria.

"Patrol," answered Jack.

"Oh. How come I didn't get to go?"

Jack paused to think, holding up one finger to stall, while he swallowed. "Wasn't your shift," he lied. "You'll fly with me once we pass through the Genesis Gate to the next sector." He hoped that would be a sufficient answer. It was and to his relief she offered no complaint.

Jack didn't want her to think he didn't trust her, but he had been concerned that her attitude or frame of mind would affect her performance. But, it seemed that the storm had passed. He decided she would fly his wing, and if everything was acceptable, he would not hesitate to assign her regular patrol duties. "Well I'm done," yawned Steele, pushing the empty plate away, "I'm going to go get some shut eye. You coming, dog?" Fritz hopped off his chair and ambled up next to him as he rose from the table. "You'd better go get some rest too," he told Maria, "you want to be wide awake for patrol."

■ ■ ■

Jack had been asleep for less than an hour when the bridge called his quarters, waking him. He reached over and tapped the comm button on the night table. "Yes?"

"Sorry to disturb you, Jack..."

"No problem, Walt. What's up?"

"We're nearing the Genesis Gate. I've maneuvered astern of the Princess, what else should we do?"

"What's our time to the gate?"

There was a pause while the Professor consulted Ragnaar at the navigation station. "About thirty minutes to entry."

"Are the guys back from patrol yet?" Jack stretched and propped himself up on one elbow.

"Not yet, they're on their return leg from the rearward point."

"OK," yawned Jack, "call `em in. Tell them to come straight back, no detours. We'll relaunch in the next sector. Oh, and find out how long it takes to pass through."

"Right, stand by." Jack could hear the Professor recalling the fighters and requesting travel time from the helm. "OK, the boys are on their way back, and our travel time will be five and a half hours, give or take a few minutes."

"That's fine, Walt. Give me about five, but if you need me, wake me."

"Right-o." The comm beeped as the connection ended. Jack looked down at Fritz who lay curled on the bed near his feet. His optical sensor glowed faintly, but he appeared to be asleep. The young Captain drifted off wondering if the dog could actually see while he was asleep.

■ ■ ■

The two flights of fighters rejoined astern of the Freedom and fell into a finger four formation. But before they could execute a turnabout to begin final approach for recovery, they picked up a blip on the edge of their sensor range. Paul triggered his mic, "Flight leader to base..."

"This is the tower, flight leader, go ahead."

"We've got a bogie out here, tower..." continued Paul, "do we have time to check it out? Please advise..."

"Negative flight leader, begin recovery immediately."

"Roger," answered Pappy. "You heard him boys, loop and roll."

Brian pulled back on his stick and followed Derrik's wingtip through the 180 degree half loop. Once on top, they executed a half roll to right themselves for final approach. Brian throttled back to match his wing leader's speed as Paul and Mike pulled ahead to create a loose diamond formation. Derrik and Brian fell further behind as Paul and Mike began their final approach.

Brian followed the tower's commands as they were given, *gear down, line up on the ship's signal markers, throttle down to one notch before idle, coast and wait.* Paul and Mike disappeared through the giant aft landing bay doors which still looked too small to Brian. Even at his low throttle setting, he was gaining on the cruiser, as it had slowed for recovery procedures.

"Flight one recovered. Flight two, you are clear to land." Brian concentrated on the flashing landing lights that ran down the runway and the instructions from the tower, *engines off, anti-grav on, arm braking jets, arm emergency canopy release.* The controller's voice was calm and even, and his reassuring tone made Brian's first recovery less stressful.

As his fighter passed through the blue veil of the stasis field, the ship's artificial gravity tugged on Brian's fighter, bouncing the landing skids off the deck one time before being countered by his craft's antigravity gear. The solid thump and the shower of sparks skittering across the floor startled him. Embarrassed, he glanced over at Derrik's Warthog off his wingtip but the other pilot hadn't seemed to notice. Firing his braking jets, he slowed and directed by the tower, taxied his fighter off the runway. He coasted on antigravity, maneuvering the craft gently by the stick and followed the mechanic's hand signals to the fighter's parking revetment.

He methodically flipped off the switches for braking jets, emergency canopy release and all his electronic gear before pulling the manual canopy release handle. As the canopy rose slowly with a hiss, he switched off the antigravity and felt the craft settle to the deck with a gentle bump. Unsealing his flight gloves, he pulled them off and reached back to unseal his helmet. Still adjusted to the darkness of space, the bright lights in the parking area made his eyes water. The sound of someone climbing the boarding ladder told him someone was there, but his eyes refused to focus. The extra hands

265

helped unseal and remove the helmet which made the light even worse. Suddenly realizing the pilot's discomfort, the mechanic twisted around on the ladder and shouted at another member of the ground crew, *"HEY YOU!"* he pointed at the man. *"Yeah YOU!* Turn down these lights!" The man jumped at the order from his Crew Chief and the lights dimmed almost instantly. "I'm really sorry, Lieutenant," he said, turning back to Brian. "These new guys..." he explained as he unbuckled the pilot, "some just aren't real swift yet..."

Brian blinked hard and wiped the tears with the back of his hand. "It's OK, Chief. It's better now, thanks."

The mechanic waited on the deck below as Brian descended the ladder from the cockpit. "So how do you like her, Lieutenant?" he asked, patting his hand on the port engine nacelle.

"She handles nice, I like her," commented Brian, stepping to the deck.

The mechanic handed him back his helmet as they turned to walk around the nose. "Yep, she's a good bird," he bragged, running his hand across the hull, "never been whacked. Not even once."

Brian tried to sound reassuring. "Well, I'll do my very best to take good care of her."

The Crew Chief laughed a deep belly laugh and slapped the pilot merrily on the back. "Ah, my boy, that's what they all say..." Brian didn't know whether to feel insulted or not, but he smiled just the same. Maybe he was referring to the landing, thought Brian. Maybe not.

"Ah, now *that* was grand!" exclaimed Derrik, as he strolled over to Brian. "It's good to feel the power again. I almost forgot what it was like," he explained. They headed toward the pilot's ready room, their helmets tucked under their arms. "What'd you think?"

"I had a blast!"

"It *is* fun, *isn't* it?" It was a rhetorical question. "But it can get serious," explained Derrik, "especially if we meet some undesirables out there..."

"Y'know," interrupted Brian, "I'm really not worried about that." He was surprised, but the possibility of that only made it more exciting. "But," he added, deciding to come clean, "I could use some practice on landing."

"Why?"

"Whaddya' mean, why? Didn't you see me touch down? There were sparks everywhere, I bounced pretty hard," said Brian, unzipping his suit as they walked.

"So did I. You landed just fine. The sparks are from the skid plates on the bottom of the landing feet, they're supposed to do that, you wanker..."

Brian smiled sheepishly. "Ah."

Laughing, Derrik slapped Brian in the shoulder with his flight gloves repeatedly. "Wanker, sod, twit..."

Laughing, they entered the ready room through the double doors and sat down with Mike and Paul, who had already shed their flight gear.

CHAPTER TWENTY ONE

FREEDOM, GENESIS GATE - BAHIA SYSTEM: *JOKERS &*
GUNSLINGERS

The comm buzzed once and Jack was awake. "Yes?"

"Walt here, Captain. We're about twenty five minutes from exiting the
Genesis Gate."

"Thanks, Walt, I'll be right up." He jumped out of bed and strolled into the
bathroom, whistling. The constant gentle rumbling of the ship in motion,
made sleep soothing and deep. After a shower and a clean uniform, Jack felt
fresh and energized, excited about the prospect of flying a patrol. He could
imagine seeing the expanse of space through the cockpit perspex,
uninhibited by steel or view screens. The view from the glass of the
observation deck was gratifying, but somehow he couldn't believe it would
compare to the unhindered view from a fighter's cockpit.

Jack checked his watch after he pinned his wings on his tunic. "Are you
ready to go Fritzer?"

"Rrright!" came the gruff reply. He was eager to display his new found
talents.

"Now remember," coached Jack, "no talking until I give you the signal,
OK? " The Shepherd nodded his compliance and the two stepped out into the
corridor and headed for the bridge.

As expected, the pilots were hanging out on the bridge to watch the rather
exceptional spectacle of leaving a Genesis Gate. At a distance, a Gate just
looked like four small points of light in a square with a touch of color in the
middle. Drawing closer, it became obvious the expanse between the markers
was tremendous, and the color was actually a giant, slowly spinning swirl of
brilliant translucent colors. As a ship entered, the swirl enlarged, reaching
out and swallowing the ship into what appeared to be a starless tunnel of
soft, shimmering, silver silk. Entering was beautiful, but exiting was
breathtaking. Surrounded by shimmering silver, the horizon gradually filled
with clouds of undulating, effervescent color. The clouds would grow as the
ship approached, and after a time, it would be totally immersed in the hazy,
wafting colors. Suddenly the colors would intensify, exploding outwards like

a giant Roman candle, spilling the ship back into the star filled blackness. It was better than any Fourth of July fireworks show in the world.

Being a substantial distance behind the Princess Hedonist, the crew of the Freedom had the best possible view. The Gate held itself open as the first ship passed through, showing a stunning array of brilliant colors with an expanse of black, star flecked sky, visible in the middle. Random clouds of color drifted across the opening. Then in an instant, they were out and it was gone.

Jack and Fritz stepped past the mesmerized pilots and down the short steps to the pit and his command chair.

"Never get tired of seeing that..." commented the Professor with a wave of his pipe. "Well, Jack," he added, "time for a dash of sleep. I return the bridge to you, Captain."

"Thank you, my good man," responded Jack, bowing stiffly. They laughed as Walt turned to leave.

"Oh wait! I almost forgot." He turned to Brian who was standing just behind him at Raulya's console with the other pilots. "Remember that joke you used to tell about the dog and the Siamese cat?"

"Yeah..." said Brian, unsure where this was going, "what about it?"

"I don't know why, but it just came to me earlier and it made me think of this other joke..." Fritz jumped up onto Jack's command chair and wagged his tail, paying close attention.

Walt paused on the stairs. "So tell it..." Everyone on the bridge seemed to be listening closely.

"Well," began Jack, "this guy walks into a bar with a dog at his side and they both take a seat at the bar. *Hey!* Says the bartender, *no dogs in my bar.* So the guy says, *but this is the smartest dog in the world!* The bartender says, *oh yeah? Prove it and I'll give you both a free beer!* So the guy asks the dog what's on top of a house and the dog says *roof! So?* Says the bartender. Then the guy asks the dog to describe sandpaper and the dog says *rough! That doesn't prove a thing,* grumbles the bartender..."

"So?" said Paul, impatiently.

"So," continued Jack, "the guy gets the dog to do a bunch of other stuff, none of which impress the bartender. Finally, the guy pulls out a twenty dollar bill and hands it to the dog, telling him to go across the street and get a pack of cigarettes. *He'll have the right brand and the right change,* brags the guy. Twenty minutes goes by and the dog hasn't returned, so the guy and the bartender go outside to see what might have happened. They find the dog

269

in the back seat of the guy's convertible, screwing the local hooker. *What are you doing?* Yells the guy, *you never did that before!* and the dog says..." Jack motioned to Fritz with a sweep of his hand.

"I never had twenty bucks before..." said Fritz, enunciating slowly.

There was a smattering of laughter as everyone looked from Jack to Fritz then again back and forth in obvious confusion. Jack and Maria, who was standing on the other side of Raulya's console, laughed the hardest, but not at the joke. The confused expressions of everyone on the bridge was almost too funny to stand, Jack gripping his sides. Fritz stood on Jack's command chair facing backwards, with his front paws clutching the headrest, tail whipping from side to side. He looked from Jack, to the pilots and back, his tongue lolling casually out the side of his mouth. *This was great fun.*

"How'd you do that Jack?" asked Brian, shifting his eyes from man to dog and back again.

"Yeah," added Mike, "I didn't even see your mouth move!" Jack was in tears and Maria was holding onto the console for support.

"I'm not sure I understand..." said Walt, "did he get the cigarettes or not?" That's when Paul lost it, he had just begun to understand what Jack thought was so funny and the laughter was contagious.

"I say," quipped Derrik "it wasn't that funny..."

"Laf! Laf! Laf!" Barked Fritz as he bounced on the command chair excitedly.

"Good Heavens!" yelled the Professor, laughing, eyes agog.

Jack and Maria were both sitting on the floor, tears streaming down their faces. Brian's eyes were like saucers, "Did *HE* say that?" he asked, pointing at the dog. "Did *YOU* say that fuzzball?"

"Laf! Laf! Laf!" barked the dog again, even louder than before.

"Holy freaking crap! Your dog *talks*...?"* Brian and Mike fell down they were laughing so hard. There wasn't a dry eye or straight face on the bridge. The laughter had spread across the bridge like a tidal wave and like continuing waves of water, spread back and forth as one side or the other slowed to catch their breath.

"What the Hellion is going on over there?!" Jack looked up to see Gantarro's face on the view screen. "I've been trying to reach you!"

Red faced and out of breath, Jack rose from the floor, wiped the tears from his face and tried desperately to compose himself. "I'm sorry, sir," he stifled a chuckle, "we learned last night, Fritz was developing the ability to talk," he glanced at Pappy and began to laugh. "Ahem, so, well we..." he laughed when he looked at Brian gasping for air.

Gantarro found himself laughing as well. Yet he did not know the reason. He glanced at his first officer who chuckled with him, but shrugged. He didn't know why either.

"Anyway," continued Jack, taking a deep breath, "I played a practical joke on my bridge crew, who didn't know of this sudden development. It was quite funny... I guess you had to be here."

"Aaaahh! Well... my congratulations to Mr. Fritz! We just called to wish you luck and thank you for the escort."

"You're welcome, sir," Jack was forcing composure, despite the sounds of controlled humor behind him. "Good luck and God's speed." The screen went blank and the external view returned. The Princess Hedonist turned away on its new heading and began its departure. Jack turned back to the others who had suddenly grown quiet. They were all staring at the screen, watching the image of the cruise liner as it moved away.

"OK, boys and girls..." said Jack, startling half the crew on the bridge, "it looks like we're on our own now..." He reached over to the console on his command chair and turned on the monitors. Fritz, still sitting in the chair, watched intently as Jack's fingers danced across the flat keyboard. The musical beeping made him tilt his head in a curious fashion. Jack found what he was looking for. "Helm, steer a new course, one-five-one, point seven-three-nine, point zero-six-six."

"Yes, sir..." the young bridge officer paused as he entered the course into the computer, "course laid in, Captain."

"Take us there, Ensign. Best speed."

"Yes, sir."

Jack reached over and rubbed Fritz's head. "Off you go, kid, go sit on that one," he pointed at the empty first officer's chair. The dog switched locations and curled up comfortably on Walt's chair, his chin on the console. Jack plopped into the command seat and swiveled around to face the pilots. "Time to go liberate some parts, from our friendly neighborhood pirate supply store..." he wiggled his eyebrows up and down. "Why don't you guys go get some shut eye, I'll call you if anything comes up."

■ ■ ■

It had been over seven hours, and the screens were void of ships, planets or Gates. Jack was bored. Maria was sitting with Myomerr at the weapons console and Raulya was off duty. Jack spun his seat around. "You want to go for a flight?"

Maria sat up straight. "Can we?"

"Sure, why not." Jack called the flight bay and told them to ready two fighters, then he called Trigoss and asked him to come to the bridge. "You don't mind playing skipper for awhile, do you?"

"Certainly not!" he exclaimed, "I'll be right up."

After a brief chat, the two pilots left the command to Trigoss and headed to the flight bay. Fritz stayed on the bridge. "What kind of pattern will we fly?" asked Maria as they walked down the corridor.

"Pappy came up with a thing he called a double diamond, it makes a pretty thorough pattern." Jack went on to describe it in detail.

"That's a four ship pattern though, right? How will we do it with only the two of us?"

"We go deep while we're together, then shallow when we're apart so we're not too far from each other. So instead of a fat, even diamond, we make a long, skinny one." Maria nodded in understanding as she pictured it in her mind.

Jack was cheerful as he picked his helmet off the rack of his locker. Whistling, he rubbed the fingerprints off the fresh artwork on the sides and admired the shine. The logo looked like the Medieval battle shield on his bedroom wall back at home, black shield, fiery-red rising sun with the gold Pegasus silhouette over it, and a gold skull, square and compasses at the bottom tip of the shield. He tossed his flight gloves into his helmet and strode toward the doors to the flight bay.

"Hey! Wait for me!" Maria snatched her helmet off the bench in front of her locker, the cartoon of an angry hornet looking like it was about to fly off of its shiny white surface. She caught Jack as he passed through the doors into the flight bay. "Don't forget *me*," she reminded him.

"I didn't." He smiled then continued to whistle as he walked. The fighters were already sitting in the launch tubes, waiting only for their pilots. "I'll take the other one," he volunteered. She nodded and began sliding her gloves on as she headed for the closest Warthog. Jack used the walkway through the base of the tower to reach the other craft in the far launch tube.

"Hello, Captain, didn't know you'd be flying today..."

"Hi Chief, sure, why not?" He took his gloves but handed the man his helmet. "I'm allowed to have some fun too." With a grin he climbed the ladder to the cockpit. It was snug, comfortable, and it felt like he belonged there.

Setting his helmet on the dash, the Crew Chief went about securing Jack into his seat and connecting his comm and power leads. The Chief's headphones were already plugged into the nose of the fighter so as soon as Jack's gloves and helmet were on, he checked the connections. "Can you hear me, Skipper?" Jack nodded. "OK, sir, you're all set." He began to descend the ladder. "Go ahead, close and latch your canopy, Captain."

Jack followed the Chief's instructions and the tower's pre-flight prompts as the Line Chief sealed the launch tube. Sitting in the darkness, the only light the low glow of his screens and instruments, Steele eyed the blue stasis field wavering down at the end of the launch tube. "Brian's right, I feel like a torpedo..."

"Excuse me, sir?" inquired the tower.

Jack smiled and shook his head, "Nothing." The countdown was far enough warning but the launch still managed to bounce Steele's helmet off his headrest. His fighter flashed through the launch tube, the blue stasis field almost undetectable as the inky blackness of space appeared around him.

Igniting his engines, Steele looked to his left and could see Maria's fighter slightly behind his. "Boy *that* was *fun!* Wanna' go back and do it again?" There was silence. "Arroyo, you OK? Is your comm on?"

"I'm here," she breathed, "I'm just trying to... swallow... my heart. Now I know what a bullet feels like." Steele pondered the abstract idea of making it a thrill ride for an adult amusement park. It was quiet again until she caught her breath. "I never dreamed it would be this beautiful..." her voice trailed off. They both spent the next few moments staring at the stars.

"I always wondered what it would look like from out here," recalled Jack. "Even as a kid I used to think about that."

"I bet you never thought you'd find out first hand."

"No..." He remembered laying in the grass as a boy and staring up into the stars. "But I used to dream about what it would be like if I did."

"So," deduced Maria, "this is sort of a dream come true..."

Jack glanced down at his sensors, there was nothing but their fighters and the Freedom. "Yeah, I guess it is."

"Maybe you were always supposed to end up out here... Y'know what I mean? Like the saying, everything happens for a reason?" She thought for a moment and continued. "You used to dream about it because someday you'd really end up out here... in fact, everything you've done all your life seems to have prepared you for it..."

"Like what?" he interrupted.

"Your police career gave you certain knowledge and skills. You left that to be a pilot... your values, your ideas, your beliefs. They're all needed out here. Then several sets of circumstances all collide and connect to actually bring us together and deliver us all out here. Doesn't that sound like destiny to you?"

Jack admitted it did. But he always believed that a man had more than one destiny and could choose which path he wanted to take. To him this sounded more predestined.

"No," said Maria, "don't you see? This is what you always wanted, ever since you were a little boy. And you did everything you needed. Destiny just provided the right circumstances to complete delivery."

Jack offhandedly wondered if she'd been talking to Voorlak. "When did you think of all this?" He had to admit it though, there *were* too many coincidences to be *just* coincidences.

"Over the last couple of days when I was thinking about you and me and what's happened, or should I say, what's *been* happening..." She went on to explain that she suddenly realized where destiny was taking him. That she was not the right woman, because the right woman would have to be someone who could sit by and wait until he had time to need her. Someone who had the right devotion and patience. "I'm not the right person," she admitted. "Maybe I'm selfish, but I want it when I want it. I don't like to wait, I want first priority."

Jack glanced at his sensors screens and back up. "Well it sure sounds like you thought this out thoroughly..."

"Well, when I have a revelation, I don't fool around!" she boasted.

"Are you OK with it?" They were nearing their break off point.

"Yeah, but I still love you, you jerk."

"Me too... I mean you, not me..."

"Yeah I know what you mean. Listen, I don't know Alité very well," continued Maria, "but she seems real nice, maybe the *right* one. So be nice to her."

Jack cracked half a smile. "Cut it out, will you? You sound like my mother." He looked over at the fighter next to him and could see Maria's silhouette bathed in the glow from the electronics in her cockpit. "We're at point, you ready to go?"

She looked over at him and gave him a thumbs up. "Ready."

He returned the signal. "OK, break." The two fighters split and banked away from each other. Soon they would only be able to see one another on sensors. "Switch to Comm One."

"Roger," came her reply. They had been talking on a short-range, low-power frequency. They would now switch to a long range frequency to keep in touch, though now they would speak only if necessary. This would prevent giving away their location to an enemy.

Jack felt a queer sense of loneliness as he looked at the emptiness around him. Nothing to be seen but the twinkling points of light. Except for the constant rumble of the engines vibrating through the hull and the occasional beep of the sensors as they made their sweeps, it was too quiet for him. He switched off his mic and began to whistle a tune. Then he hummed. Finally he sang. He longed for some familiar rock-n-roll. He was nearing his outward point.

"Bird Two to Leader."

Jack switched his mic back on. "Leader, go ahead."

"I've got some kind of debris floating out here, some large, some small. Please advise."

"Is it ship debris or organic asteroid stuff..."

"I'm on the very edge of it, it's hard to tell from here... ship maybe?"

"Roger. Stand by, hold position." Maria acknowledged the order and pulled the throttle back into the idle position. "Power your shields up," added Jack, in an afterthought. "Leader to tower..."

"Tower, go ahead."

"Wake Commander Smiley and Lieutenant Warren, I need them on stand by." The tower acknowledged. "Leader to bridge, please wake Commander Edgars."

"I'm already here, Jack," responded the Professor.

"Roger." Jack swung the nose of his Warthog fighter to the new course heading he set and pushed the throttle forward until it stopped. "Leader to Bird Two, I'm on my way, full burner." He thumbed the boost button.

"Hurry, Leader, I've got movement out there."

"Hold on, I'm coming! Arm guns, Bird Two." Maria acknowledged. "Leader to Bridge, go to yellow alert!" Jack flipped the switches for his shield generator and heard the whine as it kicked on. He armed guns at the same time. The defense and armament screens winked on.

■ ■ ■

Paul and Mike were heading down to the flight bay when the warning lights in the corridors flashed yellow and the alert horn sounded twice. The two pilots exchanged quick glances and broke into a hurried trot for the ready room. These men were pros at readying for launch, they had plenty of experience and were two of their country's best. In a time any carrier captain would be proud of, Paul and Mike were suited up and heading for the door. Paul snatched up the helmet with the Desert Storm logo on it and Mike grabbed the one with the cartoon of the *Mad Wolf*.

The fighters were already loaded into the launch tubes. "Take that one," Paul pointed at the far tube.

"Right, Pappy!" Mike hefted his helmet under his arm like a football and sprinted off.

Paul reached out and grabbed a passing mechanic. "Ready that shuttle," he commanded, pointing at a small, ten man work craft. "Get it ready to launch and see if you can get some guns on it, we might need it for recovery."

"You got it, Commander!" He ran off in its general direction and grabbed another mechanic on the way.

Paul sprinted to his fighter and went up the ladder one handed, still holding his helmet. "So far you're still on hold, sir," his Chief informed him.

"That's OK, Chief," said Paul, "I got a feeling..." He flipped on his comm unit ahead of schedule. "Tower?"

"Tower, go ahead."

"Find Lieutenant Commander Brighton and Lieutenant Carter. Advise them to prep, there's a shuttle being readied for emergency recovery." The tower acknowledged. He pulled on his gloves and began going through his pre-flight by memory while the Chief strapped him in. "Mike, you ready?"

"Ready, Pappy." Mike pulled the canopy lever and the perspex bubble began to drop, all his systems were on.

Paul glanced at the mechanic as he descended the ladder. "Thanks, Chief." He pulled the canopy lever.

"Good luck!" shouted the Chief as the canopy closed. Pappy waved.

"Tower, we're ready for launch."

276

"Right. Stand by, Leader Two."

■ ■ ■

Ahead, Jack could see the soft glow of Maria's engines on low power as she coasted closer to the field of debris. His scanner picked up intermittent sources of power, but the drifting debris kept interfering with the computer's ability to make an identification. Jack thought he could make out the silhouette of a sizable hull amidst the wreckage. "You get anything yet, Bird Two?"

"Not on the computer, but I've seen them twice... I think." She knew the dot behind her on the scope was Jack approaching. "Glad you're here, I was beginning to get a little lonely."

Jack pulled the throttle all the way back and coasted, firing a short burst on his braking jets. "So what were they?"

"Well it was hard to tell, they were kinda far off..." She could see the other Warthog sliding up even with hers about a hundred yards off her starboard wing. She felt better. "One sort of looked like maybe a shuttle, the other... I don't know." She shook her head, "Like a flattened egg?"

■ ■ ■

"Pass the salt will ya'?" Derrik slid the shaker across the galley table to Brian. "Thanks." He sprinkled it liberally across his hash browns. The galley had a few people in it, but it was not the normal full breakfast crowd.

"What do you suppose we're on yellow for?" wondered Derrik aloud.

"Probably asteroids or something like that," answered Brian, sipping his juice. The announcement of their names over the paging system caught him mid-swallow. "Hey," he said coughing. "That's us!" They jumped up from the table, upsetting glasses and plates of food. "Sorry!" Yelled Brian over his shoulder as the two pilots hustled out. They jogged down the corridor towards the elevators to the flight bay.

"Red Alert! Red Alert! All hands to battle stations! All hands to battle stations!"

The screaming alarm horn sounded red alert as the corridors were bathed in red flashing light. Without hesitation, the two pilots broke out into an all-out run. Brian, a little faster than Derrik, collided twice with other crew members heading for their own battle stations.

277

■ ■ ■

There were four pirate light fighters and an armed shuttle. A split second before they emerged, Jack's computer grabbed recognition and the identity screen flashed a picture of it in red. An enemy. They roughly looked like slightly flattened eggs with forward canted wings, guns were mounted on the wingtips. It was a practiced pirate tactic, to use debris as cover and draw prey into an ambush. The Fallken fighters charged from the field of debris like angry hornets, firing wildly as they advanced.

"Break! Break!" yelled Jack. He slammed the throttle forward and rolled right. Maria rolled left. Jack felt the fighter buck as laser shots hit his shields. "Leader to tower, launch fighters! Launch fighters!"

"We're on our way Leader One!" came the reply.

Jack threw the Warthog into a corkscrew from the roll and tried to lead the last fighter as it passed. He squeezed the trigger and heard the rapid thump-thump-thump of the single Mercury Gatling gun and the high pulsing whistle of the twin Laser cannons. Red and silver streaks raced from the nose of the Warthog but passed behind the speeding Fallken. He'd allowed too short of a lead. The fighter passed untouched. "Shit."

"Jaaaack!" Maria was zig-zagging violently but couldn't shake two of the nimble fighters who had latched onto her tail.

"Hold on!" He thumbed the boost button and looped tightly back the way he came. A pair of crimson streaks flashed close across his bow. He ignored them. "Almost there..." he reassured her. Still a little too far to be accurate, he fired once to get their attention. It struck the first fighter and the two pilots hesitated just long enough... *"Break right!"* They were slow in responding to Maria's evasion and Jack held down the trigger watching the red and silver streaks pound on the rear pirate fighter, decimating its shields and tearing into its plating.

Feeling the kick as a Fallken fired at his tail from point blank range, Jack broke off, easing back on the stick and cutting throttle. The other fighter shot by below him. "Hurry up, Pappy!"

"Right behind you, Jack!" A Warthog screamed by Jack's right wing at full throttle, guns blazing. The Fallken Jack had damaged, disappeared in a hot white flash and a spray of debris flung in all directions. *"Freedom one, Pirates zero!"* claimed Paul, as he winged over and swung right.

278

Jack nosed down and rammed the throttle open in hot pursuit of the pirate who had originally latched onto his tail. He thumbed the boost button but the pirate was still pulling away. "Damn..." Hearing a lock tone, he thumbed off the safety and fired a missile. "Outrun that, shithead..."

"Get this son-of-a-bitch off me!" screamed Maria. She couldn't shake the other fighter.

"Relax," replied Mike, "I'm right here..." He squeezed the trigger, a long, steady burst. "Guns, guns, guns," he announced. The pirate broke off but never finished his turn, Mike had throttled back and turned inside his arc. The Fallken blew in half, spinning slowly outwards. "Gotcha!"

Jack closed on his prey as it wobbled out of control from the missile hit. When it finally stopped rolling, the pirate was facing him; the Fallken, half its shields down, charged, guns firing. Jack throttled back and squeezed the trigger, holding it down. The pirate was unsteady and firing wildly. He only hit Jack's Warthog twice, barely enough to effect its hefty forward shields before his own shields disappeared. Breaking off, the pirate nosed his fighter down to avoid destruction as a stream of charged Mercury balls from Jack's Gatling gun, smashed through his canopy and exploded in his cockpit, blowing holes straight through its belly. Jack did a wing-over and let the Fallken with the crater in its center, drift away. "Scratch one!"

After a deep breath, he saw a flash in the distance, below him and to his left. "Adios, dirtbag!" came Paul's voice over the comm.

Steele had lost track, "Is that all of them?"

"No," answered Maria, "I could use a hand with this shuttle..." She was having a hard time getting a clear shot, the rear gunner taking pot shots at her while she wove back and forth to avoid being hit.

She was all the way on the other side of the debris field and the only one in range of the fleeing pirate. "Back off a bit," coached Paul. "Lay off your guns and let your shields recharge. Hit him with a missile *then* close in and finish him off."

In all the excitement, she was embarrassed to have forgotten the missiles. "Right!" She pulled back hard and reduced power, getting a missile lock a heartbeat later. She thumbed off the safety and fired one, paused, then fired another, jinking to avoid the rear gunner's fire. It was easier from a distance but she didn't have to do it again. Two thirds of the craft disappeared in a double yellow flash. *"Adios, pendejo,"* she sneered. Maria could hear the other pilots cheering her on across the comm as they rounded the debris field.

"Where do you suppose these jokers came from, Pappy?"

"I don't know, Mad Dog. Everybody form up."

"When you get to this side you'll see it," advised Maria. "It's almost at the edge of my sensor range."

"How big?" asked Jack.

"It appears to be about the same size as the Freedom."

When the Warthogs regrouped, the visitor was still there. "Let's see if they want to play," said Paul. He switched to long range frequency as the four fighters coasted wingtip to wingtip toward the distant ship. Paul used his best authoritative voice, "Unidentified ship... this is Squadron Leader Paul Smiley, of the UFW strike-carrier Freedom. What are your intentions? Do you wish to engage?" The ship quickly moved out of their sensor range without replying. "I didn't think so," added Paul.

Steele didn't want to take any chances, "Think we should see if they're really leaving?"

Paul switched back to a local frequency. "I don't expect so. They'll go lick their wounds after a sound beating like that. The Freedom's behind us, outside their sensor range. If I were them, I wouldn't be curious enough to come back and check."

It made sense to Jack. "Then let's go see what they were after."

■ ■ ■

The pilots carefully maneuvered through the drifting debris to its center. It was a large ship but so damaged it was difficult to determine what kind. They could find no markings or identification on it. "Think it's worth doing a walk through?" asked Mike.

Steele looked over at Paul. At about fifty feet away he could see his face clearly through the canopy perspex, illuminated by the soft glow of his instruments. "As long as you're sure they won't be back."

Paul shook his head. "I wouldn't; not if I thought I had to face a carrier. We gave their flight a professionally dealt ass-kicking, they have no reason to doubt our claim."

Jack nodded and smiled. "Pretty slick."

"Hey," called Maria, "my fuel warning light just came on!"

Jack quickly checked his, he was half full. "You must have a leak, we'd better head back." He advised the tower and the four fighters started back to the Freedom in formation. Halfway there, Maria reported a flame-out on her port engine. "Shut it down," advised Jack. She lifted the safety cover and toggled off its power.

With gear down and antigravity on, Maria's starboard engine began to sputter on final approach. "Uh oh..."

"What's uh oh?" asked Jack.

"Bingo fuel," responded Maria, "my tanks just ran dry..."

"That's OK, Lieutenant," said the tower, "you're lined up, just shut it down and coast in." She acknowledged and toggled off the power for the starboard engine, Jack throttling down, cutting off his engines to stay even with her.

As instructed by the tower, Jack applied braking jets as he neared the stern of the Freedom. Maria's fighter passed him by. "Uh oh..."

"Now what?!" shouted Jack.

"No brakes," replied Maria calmly.

The crewman in the flight tower sprang to his feet and slammed his hand down on a large red button on his console, sounding an alarm in the flight bay. "Crash crews! Crash crews!" Huge snag nets stretching across the landing strip dropped from the ceiling of the flight bay, dragging heavily on the deck. "Shut down everything but your antigravity and comm," he told Maria.

Steele was too close to abort his landing and braked hard cutting off his antigravity as Maria's fighter buried itself in the snag nets, tearing off her nose gear, finally coming to rest in the third net. After dropping heavily to the deck with a resounding thud, Jack's fighter slid off the landing strip in a shower of sparks and a squeal of skid plates on metal deck, coming to a stop in the taxiing lane.

Steele yanked the canopy release handle and tore at his harness. He tossed his helmet on the dash, not bothering to shut down all the systems and stood in his seat, pulling all the power and comm leads free. Jumping to the deck, he rolled, bounced to his feet and leaned into a full run towards the netted Warthog. It was a long run, but he got there quickly, the ground crew was still pulling her from the cockpit. Two missiles lay scattered on the deck and one hung in the netting. "Watch those, sir," pointed a crewman. Jack stepped around them.

Paul and Mike braked early on their approach and coasted slowly in for a short, cautious landing. They could see Maria on a stretcher, surrounded by CABL M7, a medic, Jack, Derrik and Brian. But they couldn't tell if she was moving or not. Exchanging glances from their cockpits about fifty feet apart, they too jumped to the deck without waiting for ground personnel or a ladder.

The medic wiped the blood from her forehead while M7 adjusted his sensor pads to monitor her vitals. "How many fingers do you see?" asked Jack holding up three fingers for her to see.

"How many am I *supposed* to see...?" groaned Maria. "Why does my head hurt?" She ran her hand lazily through her hair and touched blood. "Ichh, what's thisss stuffff...?" M7 glanced around and shook his head, making it clear they were not to tell her.

Derrik changed the subject. "That was a spiffy landing, love..."

"What landing?" Her eyes rolled around.

"Time to go..." urged M7, punching the keys on the electric gurney.

Paul and Mike skidded to a stop next to Jack as the medic and M7 trotted off alongside the whirring electric gurney carrying Maria. Paul grabbed Jack's elbow. "Is she OK?" he asked breathlessly.

Steele was watching them go. His arms folded tightly across his chest, he was battling his emotions. He thought about the friend he lost on the police department. "Maybe I shouldn't have taken her out..." He stared at the floor and toyed with the head of a rivet on the deck with the toe of his boot.

"She wouldn't have had it any other way," said Brian. "You couldn't have grounded her if you wanted to..."

Mike nodded, "He's right, she would've never stood for that."

"Stop talking past tense," said Derrik. "She's not bloody dead... she'll be fine!"

A mechanic ran up to Jack and handed him a wireless headset. "It's Commander Edgars, sir."

Jack held the headset to his ear, "What's up, Walt?"

"We're reading several small power sources in that debris out there, Jack..."

"Damn! They're back?"

"No, no, screens are clear. These originated *in* the debris. Maybe you'd like to take another look?"

Jack nodded, "Yeah we've already talked about it. Listen, get a shopping list from M7, if we go aboard, we might see something he needs."

"Right-o." He paused, his voice quieter, "Um, how's Miss Arroyo?"

Steele cleared his throat and blinked hard. "Uh well, um, they took her to the infirmary. We don't know yet."

"I'll ask when I call for that list."

"Thanks, Walt."

Jack turned to the other pilots who stood by. "We need to go out and take another look around, who wants to go?" They all did. "OK, how about this... Mike and Pappy in fighters for cover. And me, Bri and Derrik in the shuttle?" It seemed to be agreeable to all.

A ground crewman walked up to Jack with Maria's helmet in his hand. It had a sizable crack in it. "I don't get it, sir, we just can't figure out what she hit. There's no marks on anything in the cockpit, nothing's broken..." The pilots huddled around and examined it. Someone gave out a low whistle. Jack handed it back to the frowning lineman. "Is she going to be OK, sir?"

Jack smiled at him. He was pleased with the concern. "I hope so."

The Crew Chief for Maria's fighter strolled up. "Well it's fixable, but it'll be a couple of days." Untangled from the nets, the fighter's nose was sitting on an antigravity pad and a group of men began pushing it to its maintenance bay for repairs. The snag nets slowly retracted into open slots in the ceiling. "She took a couple of hits with no shields," the Chief continued. "That caused her fuel leak. Another hit or two and she wouldn't have come back." He scratched the sparse hair on the top of his head. "She's lucky..."

CHAPTER TWENTY TWO

BAHIA SYSTEM, DEBRIS FIELD: *GUNFIGHT AT THE OK CORRAL*

Being that the shuttle was slower than the fighters, Brian had a much easier time winding through the debris than Mike and Paul. Some of the pieces were as small as a bread box, the largest, the size of a good-sized American car. Striking a small piece was of little consequence, hitting something sizable could damage a craft, even with its shields up. "I've got something here to the left," said Derrik who copiloted for Brian.

Sitting behind them at a detailed sensor array panel, Steele examined the oblong shape on his view screen. "Say's here it's an escape pod. Can you get closer?"

"No problem," said Brian. He maneuvered closer. "How's this?"

"Just fine..." Working a set of controls Steele was concentrating on reaching it with an external, mechanically articulated arm. "Gotcha..." he breathed, succeeding in grabbing an anchor ring. Working the controls, he drew it in close to the shuttle's hull and secured it with one of the many grapple claws on the outside of the hull. "Done," he announced.

"There's another one over here," called Mike. Derrik pointed out Mike's position on the scope and Brian swung the nose of the shuttle in his direction. All in all, they recovered four of the pods, three with power, one without. Everyone agreed it would be best to return to the Freedom and deposit the pods before returning to the wreck for a walk-through exploration.

Brian maneuvered the loaded shuttle slowly through the field. With its added girth, Brian was finding it more difficult to navigate. He armed the single Mercury Gatling gun and flipped off the safety. Derrik looked curiously at him. Brian smiled, pulled the trigger and wiggled the nose of the shuttle. The stream of silver balls swept everything from their path, destroying smaller pieces and hurling larger things out of the way.

Derrik smiled in appreciation and nodded. "Good show, mate..."

■ ■ ■

Aware of the life pod recoveries, the Professor had arranged for an armed security team to meet the shuttle as it landed, since the origin and loyalties of the ship and its crew was currently unknown. It was also unknown if the pods contained survivors or not, there was no way to tell until they were opened.

Brian brought the shuttle to a stop in front of the tower and shut down the antigravity system, letting it settle to the deck with a gentle bump. As he busied himself with the task of shutting down all its systems, Steele popped the port hatch and it hissed like a leaking tire before releasing and swinging open, a flood of flight bay air greeting him. He jumped to the deck before the short boarding ramp had dropped all the way down.

Leading the security team, Raulya greeted him on the deck, "Hi Jack," she said quietly, taking him off to one side. "I talked to CABLE M7 while we were waiting for you..."

"Yeah?" Steele moved closer. "How is she?"

"She's got a concussion and some swelling, but he said she'd be OK in about a week." Raulya adjusted her tunic absentmindedly. "He said she's grounded for about a month though..."

Jack sighed a deep relaxing breath, "Who cares, as long as she's going to be OK." His stomach had been in knots since M7 and the medic took her away. Brian and Derrik stepped out of the shuttle and over to where Jack and Raulya stood. "Raulya talked to the Doc," he volunteered, "Maria's going to be alright, but she's grounded for a while."

They both expressed a similar sigh of relief. "Mind if I pop up to see her?" inquired Derrik.

"Nah, go ahead," waved Jack. "We got this covered." He glanced at the mechanics who were working on releasing the escape hatches on two of the pods. "Tell her we'll be up a little later." Derrik nodded and trotted off.

One of the pods was sweating condensation profusely, creating a puddle of water underneath. "That doesn't look good," commented Jack.

"It's not," offered a mechanic. Jack could see M7 and the medic standing behind the security team. They were leaning casually against the gurney, talking quietly. Jack turned back when he heard the hiss of the hatch, first for one, then the other of the two pods. There was a cold rush of air out of the first, as the door squeaked open, the hinges frozen with ice. Two frozen figures covered in frost, one man, one woman, sat huddled together, wrapped in blankets. The mechanic shook his head in sorrow, "Total system failure..." Ironically, the second life pod which was functioning perfectly, was empty.

Everyone moved around to the other side of the shuttle, to open the last two life pods. Again, the doors hissed as the seals were broken. A man stood in the doorway of the first, wrapped in a blanket. He shielded his eyes with his hand from the lights in the landing bay. "Where am I?"

"Safe," said Raulya, taking his hand. "You're on the cruiser Freedom."

"What is your alliance?" he inquired as he stepped to the deck.

"Independently owned, we ally with the UFW." He nodded and looked relieved. M7 and the medic assisted him to the gurney. As he lay down, the blanket parted and revealed a tattered uniform tunic and a bent pair of wings. Raulya noticed but said nothing.

"What of Dakkah... Mozzy..." The medic hushed him and administered a sedative.

The last pod held a prone occupant cocooned in blankets. Raulya and M7 entered to see if he was alive. His eyes opened slowly and did not blink. "Let's get him outside," said M7. He was carefully moved out and placed on a second gurney. With the assistance of security, M7 and the medic moved the two survivors to the infirmary.

Jack grabbed a line Chief. "What about the other two?" He was referring to the unfortunate couple who had frozen to death.

"Well," he thought for a moment. "We'll probably just seal the pod... permanently," he added, "then eject it with the others."

Jack nodded. "OK, but wait until after dinner to eject it. I'll see if we can find out who they are, and we'll say a few words first."

The mechanic had no idea what Jack meant by a *few words,* but it didn't make any difference to him. "Sure, Captain, whatever you want."

The pilots agreed to eat dinner and visit the infirmary before taking a third trip to the wreck. Ground crews ejected the empty life pods and busied themselves doing prep and maintenance on the ships that would be going back out. The pilots went to dinner. "I'm going to the bridge to see the Professor first," said Steele, "I'll meet you guys in the galley."

■ ■ ■

"Listen Jack, I know you want to check out that wreck, see if there's anything on it we can use, Lord knows we need everything... but I think we should move on."

Jack sat in his command chair and scratched Fritz's head. "What's on your mind Walt?"

"I just get the very distinct feeling that our *friends* will be back. And very possibly with some assistance." He could see the doubt in Jack's face. "Let me show you why," he continued, rotating a monitor on his console toward Jack. "We're here..." he pointed. "Here's the gate we're heading to, it's about three hours off. According to the logs on your fighters, that pirate cruiser went this way..." He drew a line on the screen with his finger, to another gate. "Towards this gate, less than an hour away from his last position."

"OK," said Jack thoughtfully, "what does that mean to us?"

"That gate..." Walt hesitated, "goes to heavily patrolled pirate territory." He held up his hand before Jack could interrupt. "And I did a bit of digging on that wreck out there. It looked familiar, but I wasn't sure, I mean with all that damage..."

"What did you come up with Walt?" interrupted Steele, growing a bit impatient, his stomach growling.

"I believe that's a Royal Velorian freighter."

Jack shrugged, "OK..." The name meant nothing to him.

"I only know, because I saw one when I visited Rathskell Spindle Spaceport, in..."

Steele raised one eyebrow, "Get to the point, Walt."

"Oh yes. Well... Royal Velorean freighters are very fast. Owned by the royal family of Veloria, they are usually reserved for cargo of extreme importance. Sometimes diplomats, but usually rare goods, even military equipment. We are like the proverbial lion who has stolen the prize from the jackals. They will return with the pack."

Jack sat perfectly still for a moment, staring at nothing. The Professor's concerns were well founded, but he just couldn't pass up a peek. It was like finding yourself in the ladies locker room and not sneaking a look into the showers. Half the thrill was getting away with it. Jack snatched the wireless comm headset off his console and jumped up. "Keep an eye on things, Walt." He trotted towards the door followed by Fritz. "Leave us on yellow alert..." he passed into the corridor.

■ ■ ■

"Pilots to the infirmary, pilots to the infirmary." The pilots stopped eating when the page called and looked up, expecting more. "That's Jack," said Brian.

"Wonder what's up," said Paul, rising from the galley table. Brian rose, sandwich in hand. He picked up another, wrapped it in a napkin one handed and carried it with the first.

"Still hungry?" asked Mike.

Brian shook his head. "Jack didn't eat yet..."

The three pilots hustled down the hall, still eating what they could carry from the galley.

Jack and Raulya were waiting outside the infirmary door when Mike, Paul and Brian arrived. Derrik was inside, still visiting with Maria.

Jack gratefully accepted the wrapped sandwich from Brian. "Thanks, Bri, I'm really starving."

"So what's up?" asked Paul.

"A bunch of stuff. First, Raulya thinks these guys are pilots. And quite possibly military pilots..."

"Anybody talk to them yet?" asked Paul.

"Not yet," answered Raulya. "M7 was giving them an exam and some tests. He's just finished."

Alité emerged from the infirmary doorway. She had bought Derrik and Maria dinner from the galley and was heading back to get food for the two survivors as M7 had asked. "Ensign Arroyo is asking for you, Captain." She was always conscious of proper protocol when others were present.

"Thank you Alité" replied Jack. He continued briefing the others as Alité headed down the hall. "Anyway, the Professor did some records checking and thinks that junk out there used to be a Royal Velorian freighter..."

Alité stopped dead in her tracks. She whirled around. "Did you say a *Royal Velorian freighter?"*

Jack was puzzled and a bit annoyed at another interruption. "Yes..." She left the galley cart in the middle of the corridor and dashed back through the confused pilots into the infirmary. After an odd moment of exchanging blank glances, the pilots filed in after her. Alité had pulled the curtain back that separated the two halves of the room.

"Princess?!" The pilot sat up in his hospital bed.

Alité's eyes were wide like saucers. "Walrick..? And LaNareef! My Lord! I had no idea!" She stood between the two beds.

"Alité?!" LaNareef opened his eyes and tried to get up. "We thought you were dead..."

"Lay down you fool!" she scolded. "You're not well enough!" Raulya, Jack, Paul, Mike and Brian, stood in a group behind her. Maria and Derrik watched from the other side of the room.

LaNareef lay back down and took her hand when she offered it, kissing it gently. He smoothed his silver blond hair and looked upon her with devotion, his gray eyes sparkling. "It is good to see you again. Your father will be delighted when you return."

Walrick leaned over and reached for her other hand. She gave it and he pressed it to his face. "Home has not been the same since you left."

"How are Dakkah and Mozzy?" she asked. Neither man answered. "Do things go well?" she insisted.

"No..." answered LaNareef. "The war goes poorly. The pirates intercept even our fastest transports. We have great difficulty getting supplies to the Navy." He'd succeeded in changing the subject, though temporarily.

"So, will neither of you tell me of my brother and sister?"

Jack had moved closer and stood directly behind Alité. Both pilots saw the gold wings and the Captain's insignia. They each in turn looked him in the eye, then cast their eyes down in silence. Then he knew. Jack put his arms around her from behind, pulling her close against him. She turned to look over her shoulder but he held her tight. "I'm sorry..." he whispered softly. Jack had a flood of questions, but now was not the time.

She had let go of Walrick and LaNareef and reached back behind her to touch Jack's face. She clutched his hair and pulled his face against her neck. *"Nnooo..."* she cried, *"nooo, please..."*

"I'm sorry," he whispered. Her knees went weak but he held her up, one arm around her waist the other around her shoulders. He half turned her and lifted her up, carrying her to the bed next to Maria. He laid her on the bed and she sobbed into the pillow as he pulled the covers over her. Jack clicked on the mic on his headset as he walked back over to Walrick and LaNareef. "How do we look, Walt?"

"Everything's clear so far," came the Professor's reply.

"Thanks Walt." He turned off his mic and faced the two Velorian pilots. "Gentlemen, I'm assuming since we both share the pirates as enemies that we fight on the same side. With that in mind, we need to know what's on your ship. What were those pirates after?" The Velorians shifted uneasily. "C'mon guys," prodded Steele, "would you rather the pirates got it?"

"Military stores, supplies," answered LaNareef reluctantly. He stared down at the bed linens.

"What kind?" If it was ground equipment, Jack decided he would just destroy it to keep it out of pirate hands.

"Tell him." Alité swung her legs off the bed and sat up. "This ship needs equipment. *Tell him.*"

Walrick looked at his hands then at Jack. As a Velorian Navy pilot, he was sworn to protect the secrecy of their operations, but he could see no benefit in that now. "Lancia fighters, a couple of Zulu gunships, missiles, parts, tools, food..."

"Nice..." Steele fought the urge to celebrate though it felt like a win for the Freedom, it wasn't a win for the Velorians and that put him in a sensitive position. "OK," he interrupted. "This is what Walt was afraid of... the pirates know what's on that ship. They'll be back and they won't be alone. We've got to hustle." He clicked on his mic and called Walt on the bridge and Trigoss in engineering so they could listen to the briefing. "Pappy, you, Mike and Derrik launch, pronto. Go to the far side of the debris field and sit on its edge. You'll be hidden to their sensors just like they were to ours. Watch for company, but whatever you do, don't get in over your head. Stall em' and pull back. Go now." Derrik kissed Maria goodbye and the three pilots hustled out and down the corridor. "Walt, the first sign of anything, go to red alert. Trigoss, you're flying the shuttle, take a few good men and your tools. Swipe anything you need, but set demolition charges behind you. Three hours. Whatever we can't take, we burn. Bri and I will get as many craft back to the Freedom as we can."

"Let me go too." Walrick swung his legs off the edge and got out of bed. "I'm OK, I can fly. Please, I want to help..."

"Me too..." chimed LaNareef as he struggled to get up.

"No," ordered M7, "you're not well enough." He turned to Jack, "Walrick can go if he wants, he's fine. LaNareef needs rest."

"Thanks," smiled Jack. He extended his hand to Walrick. "Glad to have you." Walrick's grip was firm. "Trigoss, see you in the flight bay." He switched off his mic and kissed Alité. "Keep an eye on Maria for us, OK?"

"OK," she sniffed, "be careful."

He stepped away and touched her face, staring into her eyes. Without a word, he turned, dashing out the door and down the corridor. "I will!" he called. Fritz stayed at her side.

"Princess..."

"Yes, LaNareef?" She answered him without turning around, staring at the empty doorway.

"He seems like a fine man... do you love him?" He could not bring himself to look at her.

"With every molecule of my mind and body," she breathed. She turned to face the man who had promised to marry her when they were only five years old. "Now tell me, old friend, how did my brother and sister die?"

LaNareef looked up at her and shivered.

■ ■ ■

By the time Jack, Brian and Walrick reached the flight bay, the Warthogs were gone and Trigoss had the shuttle warmed up and ready to go.

"Hold on!" Jack turned and ran over to examine the outside of the failed pod that had been moved to the side of the flight line. Followed closely by Brian, Jack grabbed one of the mechanics and pulled him close. "See any reason for this thing to have failed..?"

The mechanic shook his head. "Uh, no, sir... there's no damage to the outside that I can see. Sometimes they get hit with something, damage the systems, but this one's totally intact..." He shrugged, "it might have been faulty off the manufacturing line..."

"Really?"

The mechanic shrugged again. "Well, I've never *heard* of it happening, they're supposed to be pretty bulletproof - but nothing's impossible..."

Brian leaned in, "What're you thinking, Jack?"

"I don't know Bri, something just doesn't seem right." He turned back to the mechanic. "Can these things be tampered with..?"

"Sure, any system can be altered - but why would someone do that to a life pod though?"

Jack shook his head, "I don't know... yet." He turned to head to the waiting shuttle and stopped in his tracks, turning back to the mechanic. "Test it, disassemble it... see if you can find out why it failed..."

"Yes, sir..." he scratched his head, "but I'll need help..."

"Then get help," called Jack as he headed off to the waiting shuttle, Brian in full stride behind him. There were five other crewmen with Trigoss as the two pilots hustled up the boarding ramp.. "Shove off," called Jack as he sealed the door.

"OK, hold on, boys." Trigoss eased the shuttle off the deck and accelerated smoothly, clearing the bay door at almost twice the normal launch speed. *"Nnyyerrooommm!"* roared Trigoss making engine noises. "Flew shuttles and airbuses," he called over his shoulder, "for three years before I started on the Princess Hedonist."

Jack was gripping the armrest like he had claws, "Uh huh..." he grunted, trying to be nonchalant.

Weaving expertly through the floating wreckage, Trigoss brought the shuttle to a stop at the stern of the Velorian freighter. Arming the Gatling gun, he thumbed off the safety and aimed at the outer edges of the door. He squeezed the trigger, a stream of cryogenically frozen, charged mercury rounds reaching out. Without any shields to protect it, Trigoss succeeded in blowing the loading bay door off its tracks in less than a minute without damaging anything in the bay. Using the mechanical arms and crabbing the shuttle sideways, the shuttle crew was able to pull the door free and casting it adrift, completely cleared the entry to the bay.

Trigoss engaged the engines and idled carefully forward through the doorway into the darkened cargo bay. Flipping the switches for the shuttle's floodlights, the beams reached into the bay's darkness casting long shadows. Jack was watching over the engineer's shoulder. "Holy shit..." he breathed in astonishment. "Wall to wall fighters..." He pointed to a row of four burly, brutish-looking assault craft. "What are those?"

"Those are the Zulu gunships," answered Walrick. Brian whistled low and quiet. "You said it," added the Velorian. "They are some of the most devastating birds in the air. The only drawback is, they require a four man crew for battle."

"Set us down, Chief," said Jack. "Let's get this show on the road."

"Right." Trigoss maneuvered the shuttle, again crabbing it sideways to allow room to get the fighters off the deck and out of the bay. The shuttle touched down with a thump. Donning their helmets, the men helped each other seal their suits. After they closed their visors and flipped on their personal life support systems, they checked for leaks. Finding none, Jack released the shuttle door with a hiss of outward rushing air.

"Walrick, which ones have fuel?"

"They all have plenty to get back to your cruiser, Captain."

"OK, let's go!" Steele turned to Trigoss as he disappeared in the darkness, his hand-light shining ahead of him. "See if you can find parts for these birds, will you?" The engineer waved and kept going. One of the crewmen stayed with the pilots to help them board and take off in the darkness.

The Lancia fighters were fast looking, graceful craft, smaller and lighter than the Warthogs. Steele admired the lines as he climbed into the cockpit, illuminating the dash with his hand-light and searched for the systems switches. "Ah," he mumbled, flipping the master switch the panels coming to life. "OK... let's see now..." he commented, surveying the dash and electronics layout. Going through the pre-flight in his head, he activated the switches as he went along. Engines warming, all systems running including atmosphere, he pulled the canopy lever and it dropped silently in the zero atmosphere of the bay. Once sealed in and the cockpit pressurized, the visor in his helmet opened automatically. Jack connected his comm and power leads.. "Bri, Walrick, you guys ready?"

"Ready." Brian switched on his Lancia's antigravity system, Jack and Walrick doing the same. Guiding the three Lancia fighters with hand-lights, a ground crewman coached each of them in a 180 degree turn and headed them single file toward the star filled sky. Flipping on their landing lights, the three pilots taxied their Lancias past the shuttle and coasted out into space. Switching off their antigravity and retracting landing gear they ignited their engines.

Jack looked over the armament screen, four Pulse Laser cannons, two on each wing, and a Mercury Gatling gun in the nose. Plus seven hard points for missiles or accessories. He was pleased and impressed. "How's it looking out there, Pappy?"

"So far, so good, Skipper. You on your way back?"

"Yep. And thanks to Walrick, we're moving three at a time."

"Cool... how many are in there anyway?"

"Believe it or not, more than we can carry," boasted Brian.

"*Wow!* What a break, huh?" Paul slapped his knee in jubilation. "Are they nice?"

"Real nice..." Jack inhaled the sweet smell of a new machine. It was crisp like a new car. "Fresh off the dealership's lot..." he joked.

"Brand new huh?" Mike rubbed his gloved hands together. "Man, I can't wait to fly one of those babies."

The Lancias rounded the stern of the Freedom and simultaneously fired their braking jets. "Gear down," said Jack, "engines off, anti-grav on... OK tower, line us up, we're coming in hot, we got a schedule to keep."

The landing lights flashed on and the tower lined up their V formation. The Lancias came in fast and braked hard, bouncing solidly on the deck. The pilots popped their canopies early as they slowed to a reasonable taxiing speed, swinging off the runway. Unbuckling as they taxied, the three pilots shut their systems down before they had completely stopped. The Lancias slid momentarily on their skid plates and the pilots jumped to the deck without ladders. "Let's go!" exclaimed Jack. They sprinted to a waiting shuttle and closed the hatch. "Go ahead, Ensign," prompted Jack.

Myomerr glanced over her shoulder. "Yes, sir." The shuttle lifted off and accelerated from the flight bay.

■ ■ ■

The cargo bay of the Velorian freighter was fairly well lit when Jack, Brian and Walrick returned. Myomerr maneuvered around and slid up in front of the first shuttle and killed the systems. Closing their visors, they exited the work craft. Myomerr opened the cargo door for loading, then headed for the loaded craft to fly it back to the Freedom. The three men headed for more Lancias.

Two crewmen were loading the last parcels of cargo off an antigravity pallet into the stern of the first workcraft. "It's all ready, Ensign," commented one of the mechanics. Myomerr checked the cargo and its stability before she readied the shuttle for takeoff. Finding everything acceptable, she lifted off shortly after the Lancias.

The landing on the Freedom was a carbon copy of the one before it with the exception of the loaded shuttle taxiing in afterward. Knowing they could not return to the Velorian freighter until this shuttle had been emptied, the three pilots dismounted their Lancias at a leisurely pace.

Empty antigravity palettes were lined up behind the shuttle as deck crew hustled to unload the cargo. Jack, Brian and Walrick, walked to, and stood outside the shuttle, waiting for the crews to finish unloading. Jack had given some thought to lending a hand, but it was obvious the crews had a rhythm and he didn't want to interfere with their performance.

"*All hands to battle stations! All hands to battle stations!*" Suddenly, lights everywhere flashed red and the alarm klaxons sounded throughout the ship.

Jack grabbed a headset off a passing lineman, palming the earpiece against his ear. "This is the Captain, what's happening, bridge?"

"A signal from Commander Smiley," said Walt, "hold on I'll route him to you..."

"We got company, Jack..." Paul's transmission was full of static.

"How many?"

"Three," came the answer, "looks like small, medium and large, on the edge of our grid."

"Fighters?"

"You wish," replied Paul. "The small one looks to be about the size of the Freedom..."

"OK," called Jack, "stay put for now, I'll get back to you." He saw the last loaded palette leaving the back of the shuttle. Tossing the headset back to the lineman, Jack turned to the pilots. "Let's go, everybody in..."

"Where are we going in this thing?" demanded Walrick.

"To help our people finish over there," yelled Brian. "Now, *get in!*"

Jack and Brian took the cockpit seats, Myomerr and Walrick sat behind them. "Ready?" Jack was already powering up. The shuttle whistled through the bay and out the door. "Tower..."

"Go ahead Captain."

"Ready three of the Lancias, I want them fueled, armed and ready to launch when we return." The tower acknowledged. "Bridge..."

"Yes, Captain..."

"Walt, make sure all the gun batteries are fully charged. Plot a course straight away from the freighter which keeps *it* directly between us and the pirates."

"That will deviate us from the gate we're headed to, Jack."

"That's OK, Walt, I have an idea." Jack jinked hard as he entered the field of debris. "Trigoss, you almost ready to go?"

"Almost... I had one of the boys warm up three more craft for you, they're ready to go."

"I don't know if we have time for that Chief." Jack swung hard to avoid a hefty piece of scrap. The bay door yawned close ahead.

"It'd be a shame to leave them behind..."

Jack could see them all at the stern of the shuttle in the bay, loading cargo as fast as they could. It was almost full. He passed through the doorway and braked hard, setting the craft down next to the first. Jack left the systems on. Walrick was at the door, he pulled on the release handle. "Wait!" Brian yanked his arm away. "Put your visor down, turn on your suit..."

"Sorry..." Walrick felt foolish, his zeal had gotten the better of him.

"Warthog Leader to Shuttle Two..."

Jack stayed to answer Paul while Brian and the Velorian pilot exited the craft to help Trigoss finish up. "Go ahead, Pappy."

"They're getting kinda' close Jack. You mind telling me what you got in mind?"

"Do you think," Steele's mind was racing, "you could make them think there is more of you than there really is? Like spreading out and maybe popping in and out of the field?"

If Paul hadn't had his helmet on he would've liked to scratch his head. "You're kidding right?" Jack admitted he wasn't. "Well, maybe... I don't know," shrugged Paul. "Sounds kinda' lame, but we'll try it."

"Thanks." Jack wanted to avoid an engagement. Three to one was lousy odds, not to mention being severely short on crew and ship readiness. He dropped to the deck from the shuttle to see Trigoss and the ground crew, now loading *it*. "What are you doing?! We need to get out of here! Let's go!"

"Just another minute, Captain," said Trigoss, we're almost done. You go, we'll be alright."

Jack just then realized Brian and Walrick were nowhere to be seen. "Where'd they go?" He looked around frantically.

The engineer thumbed over his shoulder. "Took two Lancias and headed back, you should too..." He never stopped loading the shuttle. "Go on, get out of here. Myomerr's got the other one, I'll get this one." Jack looked up as the loaded shuttle lifted off the deck, Myomerr waved through the cockpit perspex before rotating towards the bay door.

Jack looked around at the fighters. "Which one?"

"That one..." Trigoss pointed at a Zulu gunship. "These two wouldn't start," he motioned toward the next two Lancias in line. "So we warmed up that one. Get going Captain."

Steele trotted across the bay to the boarding ladder hanging from the belly of the gunship. "Hurry up, Chief," he urged before ascending the ladder. The Engineer watched the ladder retract as he loaded the shuttle.

The Zulu had a two man cockpit but one man could fly it without any assistance. The second officer acted as an offensive weapons officer, and other two crewmen operated the defensive gun turrets. One turret was on the bottom at the stern of the ship, the other on the top of the hull, forward of the center.

Jack glanced around at the panels, all the systems were on and the engine burners warmed up. He flipped on the antigravity and started his taxi glide as he secured his harness. He steered clear of the parked Lancias and, pushing the stick forward, accelerated past the shuttle and toward the open bay door. Once outside, he retracted the gear, fired the four engines and headed toward the Freedom. As he cleared the debris field, he saw two fighters emerge from under the nose of the Freedom.

"Warthog Leader, this is Flight Two, vector us to your locale." Jack recognized Brian's voice.

"Roger, Flight Two, here are the co-ordinates..." Paul read off the numbers. "Where's Leader One?"

"He'll be along shortly," answered Brian.

The three ships had advanced about halfway into Paul's sensor screen and stopped. He contemplated contact to see if he could determine what their alliance might be. His identification screen gave him a technical two-view line picture, but it was in white which meant the computer received ambiguous information about the target's identity. He decided to wait.

Jack rounded the stern of the Freedom, lowered his gear and fired braking jets. "On my final approach, tower..." The tower cleared his approach.

"This is Shuttle Two," called Trigoss. "We're clear of the freighter and on our way back." The tower acknowledged the transmission.

"Well done, Chief," injected Jack, "did you remember to leave behind our party favors...?"

"That is affirmative..."

"Excellent. Hustle up, Shuttle Two, it's starting to warm up out here..." He passed through the stasis field, braked early and bounced hard on the deck. He quickly adjusted the pressure up on the antigravity, he'd forgotten this was a much heavier ship than the others.

"Warthog Leader to tower, one of these ships is a light carrier. It has just launched! Please advise!"

Jack tore at his harness and flipped off the Zulu's antigravity. He was out of his seat before it had stopped sliding on the deck. Popping the belly hatch, he slid down the ladder holding its sides and dropped to the deck. A crewman struggled to keep pace with the pilot's long legs as he ran towards the Lancia waiting on the port launch tube. "Tell him to engage!" shouted Jack as they ran. "Hit and run! We need time to recover the shuttle and take up the new heading!" The lineman repeated the orders into his headset as they ran, falling behind the faster pilot.

■ ■ ■

"Roger, Freedom." Pappy did a wing over and broke toward the enemy formation. "Let's go, boys. Time to mix it up." he throttled up to half, waiting for the others to group up. "Derrik, you're Leader Two, keep the fighters busy."

"Right-o."

"Mad Dog," continued Paul, "you're with me. We're going straight through to that carrier and ruin their day." Mike gave his wing leader a vigorous thumbs up.

Eight Fallken fighters spread out in a line abreast. Derrik sent the two Lancias wide, he stayed in the center. Paul and Mike, some distance behind him, were ready to take advantage of any hole in the line and dash for the carrier.

Derrik nosed up, rolled and increasing throttle, came down on the Fallkens from above. "Tally-Ho, boys! Give em' hell!" Brian and Walrick swung inwards and screamed in from the flanks, firing their laser cannons at range. Derrik switched to full guns and waited for the distance to close for his Gatling gun. He lead the first Fallken perfectly and hammered it soundly. It rolled to one side to evade, its shields utterly decimated.

Brian had hit the fighter on his end with four laser cannons. While not as powerful as the Gatling, they had twice the range. So by the time the Fallken was in range of Brian's Gatling gun, its shields were gone. The pirate turned his fighter away from Brian, offering an irresistible shot. Brian squeezed the trigger and watched the strikes walk down the side of the Fallken's hull. Tiny flashes of flame appeared, then disappeared, unable to burn on in space. Brian released the trigger only when he realized the guns had exhausted their charge. He winged off, disappointed to not see the pirate fighter die. It was only momentary. There was a brief flicker of light below him, and a lone Fallken wing sailed past. "Hasta la vista, dude..." He throttled up and headed back toward the melee.

Derrik had put some serious damage to his first strike-victim but couldn't seem to get behind him long enough to finish him off. He kept having to shake off other fighters. "I say, *die you filthy little rodent!*" He squeezed off a brief shot as the pirate zigzagged his damaged fighter.

Changing tactics, he backed off to get a missile lock. The sudden vibration coming from his stern told him he had other problems. He twisted around in his seat to see two Fallkens scissoring behind him. Laser streaks flashed by his cockpit. "Oh bloody hell!" He glanced down at his defense screen, his stern shield was gone. The computer toned, indicating a lock and he thumbed off a missile. At almost the same time, the Warthog bucked hard. Warning bells rang and he fought the stick as the Warthog spun flatly sideways. He thumbed the boost button and the instant thrust snapped him back into straight flight, blowing the forcing cone out of his damaged port engine. The middle of his engine glowed red hot as ruptured fuel lines sprayed fuel over the outside of the thrust burners.

Walrick was just behind the pirates on Derrik's tail but he couldn't get there fast enough. His heart sank as he saw the damaged Warthog spin away. He picked a fighter and locked on. Clearing the safety, he fired two missiles and broke off, winging after the second one. If Derrik was still alive, Walrick knew he needed to keep the pirates away. He chased down the second fighter and destroyed it with a long burst from all guns. The pirate made no attempt to evade, he foolishly tried to outrun the faster Lancia.

As Jack emerged from the Freedom's launch tube, he flew straight into the guns of an approaching Fallken. "*SHIT!*" He squeezed the trigger out of reflex and yanked back hard on the stick. His guns did nothing, he hadn't had a chance to arm them yet. But he felt the impact of the pirates lasers on his own shields. He thumbed the boost and reached for the gun switches.

The pirate didn't follow, instead he broke off and attacked the Freedom. Gun batteries opened up on him, drawing from their charges. Once empty, they would not be able to recharge, as all power would be dedicated to the ship's defensive shields.

Jack winged over, guns armed, pursuing the pirate low over the surface of the Freedom's hull. "Warthog One to Freedom, looks like they're launching a second wave..."

"Damn! Bridge, this is the Captain, take up the new course heading and shove off. Now!" Jack powered back and jinked to line up his guns. He squeezed the trigger and watched the Fallken disintegrate, its shields already damaged by the Freedom's gunners. "Clear!" He pulled back on the stick and looped back, heading toward the far side of the debris field. Jack looked at his watch, there wasn't much time left. He shoved the throttle open and fired boost.

Paul and Mike could see the first two Fallkens emerge from the center launch tubes on the pirate carrier as the cruiser and destroyer moved forward to protect it. Paul and Mike jinked and weaved their Warthogs through the increasing veil of laser fire. "I have lock, I have lock..."

"Then let `em go!" shouted Paul. Mike was slightly ahead of him. Paul watched as Mike fired missile after missile, with only a slight pause in between. Paul had lock now and was waiting his turn. "Inbound! Inbound! Break! Break!" The threat lamp was lit, the alarm whistling as the computer tracked two missiles on the screen. Pappy rolled left and Mike broke right, with only one of his own missiles remaining on each wingtip.

The in-bounds passed between, one going straight the other arcing to follow Paul's fighter. Paul boosted, cut a ninety degree turn and facing the carrier again, cut power. The inbound arced wide, searching for his exhaust heat. Paul got lock tone again and fired missiles at the carrier, four in all, before the advancing destroyer forced him to break off. When he boosted to evade, the inbound recognized his fighters profile and resumed pursuit. He jinked to avoid laser fire, but the missile detonated on the edge of his shields sending his fighter tumbling end over end. He wrestled control back somewhere between the carrier and destroyer. The defensive fire was thick enough to walk on and Paul's shields were almost non-existent. He flipped off power to his guns, hoping it would help his shield generator restore protection. He thumbed boost and held it down, ducking his head out of reflex. The Warthog bucked and rocked, he held the boost.

Mike was in a roll when the two Fallkens latched onto his tail. He'd shake one, only to regain the other. He looked for Pappy but couldn't see him anywhere. "This is Mad Dog, a little help out here..?"

"Cut power Mike, break right!" Mike did as he was told and the two pirates shot by him on his left, closely followed by a blurred Lancia, guns blazing. The rearmost Fallken blew in half, its wings spinning outwards. Another Lancia screamed by and peeled off to pursue the first pirate, out of Mike's line of sight. He swung his Warthog around just in time to see Paul's four missiles hit the front of the carrier, just as two more pirate fighters emerged from the launch tubes.

The first volley of missiles had dropped the carriers forward shields. The second, detonated against exposed plating and the open launch tubes, destroying the unprotected fighters being launched. Brilliant flashes, one after another in rapid succession, danced across the front of the carrier. The newly-launched Fallkens, consumed in the explosions, added their own fury to the force. Giant fireballs jumped from three of the four launch tubes. The carrier's nose was left a mass of burnt, twisted metal.

Secondary explosions ripped through the ship's forward torpedo bays, belching short-lived balls of flame into space. Steele was out of range of the destroyer's guns and throttled back, looking over his shoulder at the carrier. "Leader One to all birds... back to base." Jack searched the space behind him for Warthogs but could only see one. The destroyer was still firing at something between it and the carrier... "All Freedom's fighters back to base..." urged Jack, looking at his watch. They were running out of time. A heartbeat later, a blackened Warthog under full boost emerged from between the two ships. It made a straight-line, all-out run, for the safety of distance.

"Mayday! Mayday! This is Pappy, I'm in trouble. Mayday! Mayday!"

Jack made a tight right hand bank, shouting, "Cover fire! Cover fire!" Jack locked onto the destroyer and thumbed two missiles. Mike looped back hard and, sighting upside down on the destroyer, fired his last two missiles. Dense laser fire reached out toward the two pilots who had turned back to protect their friend. "Break! Break!" They swung outwards, away from each other. Heavy streaks of red and green passed between them.

"Mayday! Mayday! I can't hold her together..."

"Eject, Pappy! Eject!" shouted Jack. He searched the sky to his right to pinpoint Paul's craft. "Where is he?" asked Mike.

Jack was about to answer when a brilliant flash made him jump in his seat. A small sphere of debris expanded silently outwards. Jack suddenly felt drained, he let his body go limp, letting the Lancia fly itself. No one spoke for some time. "Pappy..." muttered Mike. Jack's eyes burned.

The other fighters had vectored to the retreating Freedom as ordered, only Mike and Jack remained. The carrier motionless, the destroyer damaged enough to deter pursuit, only the cruiser remained untouched. But its Captain had chosen to remain with the carrier.

"I'm on bingo fuel, Skipper," mumbled Mike.

They had won the fight, but Jack felt like he had lost something greater... a part of himself. "We'd better head back," said Jack quietly.

"Shuttle One to Leader One..."

"This is Leader One," answered Jack lethargically, edging the throttle forward.

"We're picking up a beacon off your starboard bow."

Jack throttled back and glanced down at his scope. There was a green blip with a blinking green ring around it, signifying a distress beacon. He looked up. It was right about where Paul's fighter disappeared. "I see it too..."

"Roger," answered the shuttle. "Then we're moving in, to intercept and recover."

Jack saw a green blip appear as the shuttle emerged from the edge of the debris field surrounding the Velorian freighter. "How long have you been out here, shuttle?"

"Just got here," lied the pilot.

"Uh, huh," agreed Jack, unconvinced. Jack turned to Mike, he could see him across the forty or fifty feet of space between their cockpits. "Head back Mike, I'll hang with the shuttle."

Jack could see Mike shaking his head. "No way," he objected. "If that's Pappy out there, I'm staying."

Jack was worried Mike would run out of fuel. "Boogie Lieutenant, that's an *order.*"

"Yes, *sir*!" The reply was curt, if not downright contemptible. Jack ignored it. He knew how Mike felt. In fact, he was cutting it pretty slim too. He watched the Warthog accelerate away and swung the Lancia's nose toward the emergency beacon.

CHAPTER TWENTY THREE

BAHIA, TWO SECTORS FROM DEBRIS FIELD: *RESCUE & RECOVERY*

Derrik glanced over his left shoulder through the cockpit perspex at his port engine. The forcing cone gone, large sections of plating and cowling missing, it drooled long strings and gobbets of gooey foam. It was messy, but he was still alive. Had he shut down the engine *before* blowing the canister of fire foam, the back feed of fuel would have pulled the burner flame into the fuel tank. Instead, it pulled in the thick, gooey substance, sealing the fuel line.

Funny, he thought, that was the same side that his Harrier got hit on in the Falklands. Though this time, he had not been injured. He offered a private thanks to whichever God might be listening.

Derrik refocused his attention on the Freedom's bay as he neared its stern. The Freedom had slowed to recover fighters, but she had put a good distance between her and the pirates. Derrik flipped the switches for gear and antigravity. He was surprised when the indicators showed both systems operative and responsive. Even the braking jets were still working properly, prompting a sigh of relief. The runway lights winked into existence, clearing his final approach. Two nets hung before the tower in case he developed problems... he hoped he wouldn't need them. Walrick, who had escorted him back, had landed first.

The damaged Warthog passed through the stasis field and touched down nicely, splashing huge blobs of gooey foam all over the deck. He keyed his mic, "Sorry about the mess, tower. Had a bit of a row with the neighbors." Firing braking jets, more foam slopped and gushed, making a gooey trail down the runway. As he taxied toward the Warthog's parking revetment, he popped the canopy and pulled off his helmet, laying it in his lap. The rush of air felt more than just good. "Ahh, home sweet home..."

■ ■ ■

Professor Edgars was afraid if he went too much further, the fighters would run out of fuel before they reached the Freedom. "All stop, helm."

"Yes, sir."

"Tower, how many craft are unaccounted for yet?"

After a quick count, the tower replied. "Well, sir, Lieutenant Carter is on final approach, so that leaves two Warthogs, one Lancia and shuttle number one."

"What the hell is a shuttle doing out there? Who took it out?"

"Ensigns Myomerr and Arroyo," replied the tower.

Walt slammed his hand down on the console. "Arroyo's supposed to be in sick bay, dammit!" He rubbed his forehead. "Tower, prep two Lancias and put them in the tubes. Tell Walrick and Carter they're on standby, those stragglers might need some protection." The tower acknowledged. "Helm," he continued, "bring us around, then full stop. Raulya, drop shields. Transfer power and recharge all guns."

Brian touched down and a lineman directed him to taxi directly to a prep skirt in front of the tower. After a quick inspection and finding no damage, a ground crew swarmed around the Lancia and began to refuel and rearm it. Brian laid his helmet on the dash as a Crew Chief climbed the ladder. "What's going on Chief?" The pilot pulled off his gloves.

"You're on standby," he began, "until the others return." He started unbuckling Brian's harness.

"Should I stay in the cockpit?"

"Nah. Just don't wander off, Lieutenant."

As soon as it was finished, Brian's Lancia was moved back into the launch tube.

Mike was so low on fuel when he landed, that when he fired braking jets as he entered the bay, they fizzled out mid-burst. He quickly flipped off the antigravity and the Warthog dropped to the deck with a thud, screeching down the runway on its skid plates. It came to a stop with its nose, just inches from the safety nets before the tower. Mike pulled the lever, popping the canopy, "Man, what a landing," he announced. "Am I fucking good, or what?!" The lineman, climbing the boarding ladder, pointed out the burn marks and blast holes in the Warthog's left wing without saying a word. Mike's eyes widened, then narrowed. "I said I was good," his voice took a more humble tone, "not perfect." He sat quietly and let the crewman unbuckle his harness, standing on the seat and stretching after he was finished. "Boy, almost three hours in that cockpit..." He dropped his helmet over the side to the crewman on the deck.

Derrik and Brian approached from the pilot's ready-lounge at the base of the tower on the other side of the grab net. "Where's Paul? What happened out there?" called Derrik.

Mike had turned around to descend the ladder. "Haven't you heard from them yet?" He asked, looking over his shoulder.

"We're on radio silence," said Brian, clinging to the grab net. The two pilots looked like people watching a softball game through a mesh fence.

"Damn..." said Mike, stepping to the deck. He walked to the net shaking his head, "I'm not sure exactly what happened, we got separated." Brian and Derrik pulled up on the net lifting the bottom edge off the deck and Mike ducked underneath to their side. "We split to evade some inbound stuff," he began, walking with them back to the lounge. "The next thing I know, I got two bandits on my tail and I can't shake 'em. All of a sudden, two of those new birds," he points to a Lancia, "come out of nowhere..."

Brian was nodding, "That was me and Jack..."

Derrik was nodding too. "Don't feel bad, same thing happened to me." He pointed to his Warthog sitting in its revetment. "That's mine."

Mike made a face like he'd swallowed bad medicine. "What's all that white shit?"

"Fire foam."

"Geez, what a mess," sympathized Mike. "So," he said, changing the subject, "did you get him?" He was looking at Brian.

"Yeah, sort of. I had to chase him clear round the other side of that floating junkyard out there. I took his shields down, so he tries to shake me by taking a left into the debris... *smack!*" Brian clapped his hands together, "He crashes right into a huge piece of scrap." He shook his head, "End of story, film at eleven."

They entered the lounge and threw themselves on the loungers, stretching out. No one spoke for awhile. "Do you think he made it?" asked Derrik. It was a disjointed question but they all knew he was talking about Pappy.

Mike shook his head slowly, he had been trying not to think about it. "I don't know... I hope so." He fidgeted. "There *was* a beacon."

"That's a good sign," said Brian. "Right?" He looked at Derrik.

"Could have been automatic..."

"Maybe..."

"Think so?"

It grew quiet again. Until the announcement from the tower, "Craft on final approach, recovery crews stand by." The three pilots jumped to their feet and ran for the door and didn't stop until they reached the net. Mike's Warthog had been moved and the runway was clear. They waited. "Well?" said Brian. "Where are they..?"

Barely visible outside the bay, a Lancia suddenly popped into view as it slowly passed through the blue veil of the stasis field. The fighter moved lethargically as it touched down, moving down the runway as if it was in slow motion. "What's he doing?" asked Mike. No one had a clue. The canopy popped open and rose quietly as the fighter neared the safety net and swung off, taxiing to the skirt where the Lancia coasted to a stop of its own volition. The three pilots exchanged confused glances as Steele descended the ladder from his cockpit. *Where was the shuttle?*

With a loud whoosh, the shuttle passed through the stasis field at a speed more normal to landing spacecraft. It braked hard and touched down halfway to the tower, coasting to the net before stopping. Jack trotted to its side entrance and waited for the hatch to open.

"Is Pappy OK?!" shouted Mike. Jack cupped his hand around his ear to show he couldn't hear Mike, who was becoming visibly more anxious. The three pilots lifted up on the net and scooted underneath as the shuttle's hatch and ramp opened. "I *said*," yelled Mike, trotting over to where Jack stood, "is Pappy alright?" Jack looked sullen or tired, Mike couldn't tell which.

"I'm fine kid..." Paul stood in the shuttle's doorway, grinning from ear to ear, his helmet dangling from his left hand. He strolled casually down the ramp.

Mike met him halfway and grabbed him by the shoulders. "Man, am I glad to see *you!* I thought you were a gonner..."

"So did I. In fact, I almost was..."

Jack clapped him on the shoulder as he reached the bottom of the ramp. There was a round of handshaking and backslapping as the five pilots released the tension of uncertainty and gave private thanks for getting their friends back in one piece.

"What about me?" Maria descended the ramp, her arm linked with Myomerr's arm for support. Paul turned around and, with arms opened wide, hugged them both. "*Why* did you wait so long to eject?"

"Well," said Paul stepping back. He suddenly had a full audience. "I couldn't punch out too close, I would've been toast. I had to wait till I got clear. I figured if I timed it right, they'd think I went up with my bird and wouldn't come looking for me. I had to hope y'all would find me first." He hugged Maria and kissed Myomerr full on the lips. "Good eyes kids."

"*You!*" said Jack, pointing at Maria, "should be in bed."

"I can fly, I just can't stand. Besides, I couldn't let her go out alone, you need at least two for recoveries." She wiped the sweat off her forehead. "If we hadn't been out there, Paul would still be out there." She pointed at Myomerr, "We were the only two who were *free* to go... everyone else was at battle stations."

Jack smiled and scooped her up because she was beginning to wobble. "Well you did a fine job. Now it's back to bed with you." The group moved off the runway together and headed for the ready room to remove their flight suits. "Chief!" shouted Jack, still carrying Maria.

The mechanic stopped his work on the shuttle. "Yeah?"

"Close up the bay and the tubes. Call a stand down, we're done for the day."

"What about that cruiser out there?" asked Derrik.

Paul shook his head. "Gone."

"Where'd it go?"

"To that big cruiser Heaven in the sky," he said, waving his arms expansively, his helmet still in his left hand.

Mike's eyes narrowed, "Huh?"

They all started walking again. "Wait'll I tell you this," joked Paul, "this is gonna' kill you..."

■ ■ ■

Paul kept them in suspense until they had all cleaned up. Jack had checked in with the bridge and now they were all seated together on the floor of Maria's suite. LaNareef, feeling stronger now, was there with Walrick. Alité was there with Jack, Myomerr with Paul, Seeta with Brian and Mike was with a cute little porter named Tilee. Jack was surprised, he had no idea Mike was seeing someone. Food and wine had been provided by Marna's culinary wizardry.

Maria was tucked comfortably in bed. She lay on her side, facing the group and absentmindedly played with Derrik's hair, who was sitting on the floor with his back against the side of her bed. The rest of the group, mostly boy-girl couples, sat on the sofa or gathered around the coffee table where the platters of food sat and chatted as they ate. For some of them, it was the first decent meal they had eaten in ten hours. Jack stared into Alité's eyes as they ate, they were pale lavender now. Every time he looked at her, she seemed to get more beautiful, more alluring. She was wearing a sheer white leotard with a matching knee length bloused gown that was both low cut and slit up the sides. He couldn't take his eyes off her, he wished they were alone.

"Alright," said Brian, after sipping his wine, "tell us your story..."

Paul held up one hand. "OK, OK." With his other hand he poured wine for Myomerr. He picked up his wine and watched the burgundy liquid swirl around. "Once upon a time..."

"C'mon!" interrupted Mike, "quit goofing around..." Tilee pulled on his arm to let him know he was embarrassing her.

Failing at begging, Fritz took advantage of the various distractions and stole food off the table. Seeta tweaked his nose in reprisal and shooed him away with his prize.

Paul got serious. "Alright." It took him a second to decide where to start. "Well, we did some pretty serious damage to that carrier, pretty much tore the bow off of her and crippled her launch capabilities. We took the fight out of her but good. But in the exchange that caused that damage she got a couple missiles out." He adjusted the way he was sitting and leaned forward. "I get hit by one of those inbounds from that carrier and it tosses me, end over end. By the time I get it back under control, I'm somewhere between that destroyer and carrier getting the shit kicked outta' my bird. My shields are gone, so I cut off my guns to keep them from pulling power, and I make a bee-line for the first empty patch of sky I see." He takes a sip of wine. "Well, these guys are throwing everything they got at me and my bird is flopping around like a kite in a hurricane. I'm getting the hell beat outta' me cause I'm slamming all over the place..." He pulled the collar of his shirt aside to show the purple bruises over his shoulder from the harness straps.

"Those are worse than mine," commented Derrik.

"Hurt like a bitch," added Paul. "So anyway, every warning light in the cockpit is screaming at me; no shields, inbound alert, flame-out, fire, hull breach... and probably a few I didn't notice. I wait as long as I can... hoping I'm clear... and I punch out." He sipped his wine, "Just in time too. She blows, right *under* me..." He held out one hand, "I know what all the scientists say, there's no sound in space... bull*shit!* Cause I *swear* I could hear it! Well, I must have blacked out for a minute from the concussion, cause when I woke, I could see the shuttle coming - I hadn't seen it before that. But then I see the cruiser is coming too! I was betting that Captain was good and mad by now... he *wanted* us. *Bad.* Then, I see *this* lunatic," he pointed to Jack. "He comes screaming in, guns going like crazy, flinging missiles everywhere... He buzzes around that cruiser like a pissed off hornet! Probably drives the Captain nuts. Well it works, cause for some reason he forgets us and decides to chase Jack..."

"Because he was calling him names on an open channel..." added Maria.

Brian looked at Jack. "You called him *names*..? Like what?"

Jack shrugged. "I don't really remember that," he smirked, handing an after dinner pastry to Fritz who was quietly nudging his elbow. "Whatever came to mind... I guess."

"Dickbreath," said Maria laughing, "asshole, chicken-shit..."

"What's chicken-shit?" whispered Alité.

Jack almost snorted a mouthful of wine through his nose. "I'll tell you later," he promised.

"So anyway," continued Paul, "Jack heads for the freighter, and the cruiser follows and launches two fighters. The girls pick me up and we head out for the Freedom. Jack suckers the fighters *and* the cruiser into the debris. They can't even touch him, he's all *over* the place. The fighters are shooting at him, the cruiser's shooting at him, not a scratch. The cruiser blows up one of their own fighters, the other crashes into something in the debris field. Jack takes off. So the cruiser plows through the debris and stops next to the freighter and just sits there..."

Mike was dying in suspense. *"So what happened to it?"*

Jack pointed to his watch. "Three hours..." There were a lot of confused looks. "Remember what I told Trigoss? What we can't take, *burn!* The Chief stuck one of the charges between the engine cores. When it went off, it must've opened the cores and it went up like a nuke. That cruiser wasn't more than fifteen-hundred feet away." Jack waved, "Bye, bye cruiser."

"I was worried," said Paul, "I didn't know what he was doing. I thought if that cruiser finds the Freedom, we could be in deep trouble. Because I *knew* the Freedom couldn't outrun, or outgun it."

"It turned out to be a lot bigger than we thought too," commented Mike.

"I thought he was nuts," announced Maria. "I thought, no way is he coming back. No way could he survive attacking that thing alone..."

"But he slid through it like he was covered in Teflon or something," reflected Paul.

Brian thought about the airport in Puerto Rico and raised an eyebrow. "I've seen that before..."

"Stainless Steele," said Mike.

"Huh?"

"Your new call name," continued Mike. "All fighter jocks get one, yours is going to be *Stainless Steele.*"

"Is that what I am? A fighter jock?"

"You are now... *Stainless*." Paul smirked crookedly.

"It kinda' does have a nice ring to it, doesn't it?"

"What about me?" asked Brian.

"Gunner," said Derrik without hesitation. "Did you know, all they had to do when he came in was to refuel his bird and refill the Mercury pods for his Gatling? He got two bloody kills without lighting one damn missile!"

Brian shrugged sheepishly. "I kinda forgot I had them..."

"Sounds like it fits to me," said Paul chuckling.

"OK, Gunner it is," accepted Brian.

"How about me?" asked Maria.

"Lifeguard," said Jack. He'd already thought about it.

"Oh I like that a lot," interrupted Paul. "That's perfect," he winked at Jack.

Maria snuggled down and yawned. "I like it too." The door chime rang and the person closest was Walrick who reached up and palmed the control on the wall opening the door allowing Trigoss to walk in. The Engineer handed Jack a printout of everything they had recovered from the Velorian freighter. His other hand was concealed behind him.

"What else you got, Chief?"

"That other little thing you asked me to take care of Captain." The helmet was in plain sight to everyone behind him but not to Maria.

"Perfect timing, go ahead and give it to her, Chief." Trigoss stepped around the couples on the floor and handed Maria the new helmet.

"That's from all of us," said Jack. "You broke your other one." The brand new helmet had the same determined little hornet on it, except he was wearing a lifeguard shirt and a pith helmet. In the front, side by side on the forehead, was a miniature life-ring and a miniature skull and crossbones.

"Oh I love it! But what are these?" She pointed to the little emblems.

"You downed one pirate and you saved one life," said Trigoss, matter-of-factly. "They'll all have little pirates," he whispered loudly. "But you and Myomerr will be the only ones with life-rings..." he beamed like a proud father.

"I'd like you to consider being our permanent recovery and rescue pilot," suggested Jack. "Myomerr would be your second officer. You don't have to answer now, just think about it. OK?"

"Does that mean no more patrols?"

"Not necessarily."

"OK, then I'll think about it."

"Good," yawned Steele. "Well people, I don't know about you, but it's been a long day, and I'm bushed. I think we ought to call it quits and go to bed." They all agreed, most of them had been yawning all through dinner. Saying their goodnights, the weary pilots rose from their various places on the floor, several assisted by their dates.

Jack lifted a half bottle of wine and two glasses off the table as he and Alité prepared to leave. "Something for later," he whispered.

LaNareef looked painfully at Alité as Walrick helped him to his feet. He ached more of heartbreak than physical pain. In his heart, he knew she was a Princess and though a decorated officer, he was only a commoner. And because he was a realistic man, he also knew nothing could ever come of his childhood promise to marry her. But that had never seemed to interfere with their twenty-five year friendship. In that twenty-five years, he had become her best friend and self-appointed protector. And although he respected Steele's rank, LaNareef found it extremely distasteful that Alité should want to throw her affections at a man who was so obviously a rogue, not to mention being a commoner of another world. To him it was clear, her capture and the time she spent with the pirates had severely corrupted her Royal morals. The only thing unclear was what he was going to do about it.

Alité caught his look and shook her head, making it clear he was to say nothing of his objections in Jack's presence. She had guessed correctly that Jack did not suspect she was a real Princess, and she wanted to be able tell him in her own time and in her own way. A careless slip like Walrick's in the infirmary could ruin everything.

Jack sent Alité and Fritz ahead and detoured to the bridge to check on things before retiring for the night. "How're you holding out, Walt?"

Professor Edgars stretched in the reclined command chair. "Just fine, my boy, just fine. I took a couple of cat naps and things are real quiet. We enter Gate 24-024 in about an hour." He called up some information on his navigation screen, "Passage is a little over seven hours, so we probably won't see another ship for the next eight hours. Go get some sleep," he whispered, "you look like hell."

"Think I will. Thanks, Walt. Call me if you need me." He started up the stairs and stopped next to Raulya. "May I borrow your comm for a moment?" He realized there was one thing more he should do.

Puzzled, she pulled off her comm and handed it to him. "Thanks," he replied. Steele palmed the earpiece to his ear and adjusted the mic, turning it on. "Attention all personnel, this is the Captain... we did what many might think was fairly impossible today. We severely damaged a light carrier, damaged a destroyer and destroyed a cruiser. All this from an impaired ship with an understaffed crew. While we *were* blessed by God and fate today, we must not overlook the performance of this ship and the exemplary efforts of its crew. You all did a wonderful job, and I thank you all. Goodnight." He handed the comm back to Raulya and the bridge crew applauded.

It was sad, thought Jack, as he walked the short distance to his quarters, that such a good group of people should have had to serve under a man such as Kidd. He wondered why one of Kidd's own people hadn't killed him in his sleep. Surely, most of them despised him. OK, granted, half the survivors of the ship's pirate crew, were as crooked as he was... That's why they ended up prisoners of the UFW patrol vessel that answered the Princess Hedonist's distress call. But the rest of these people were dedicated and hard working. He wondered how many other pirate vessels were run just like this one had been, how many good people had been caught up in the clutches of men like Kidd. It *was* nice to know, however, reflected Jack, that at least humans had not invented deceit and treachery, nor did they curb the market in it. What did bother him was that they spent so much time trying to perfect it.

CHAPTER TWENTY FOUR

FREEDOM, DEPARTING BAHIA SYSTEM: *HEAD OVER HEELS*

All thought escaped Jack Steele when he entered his suite. Alité stood near the bar in a long, flowing white gown of the sheerest material he'd ever seen. He froze in the doorway and swallowed hard when she turned silently away. The gown was mostly backless to the waist, and the wispy material fluttering in the breeze of her movement revealed side slits from her ankles to the top of her thighs. "Wine?" she asked, turning back. She extended a glass toward him but did not move.

"YoOu..." his voice cracked and he cleared his throat, "always seem to be asking me that..." He stepped forward and the door swished closed behind him, plunging the room into semidarkness. He stepped forward, hand outstretched, and she slid the glass into his hand. "Thanks..."

"You're welcome," she breathed. "It is my pleasure to serve you."

"Stop that," he scolded mildly. "You're not a slave or a servant. I want you to be here, because you *want* to be here. Not because you think you *have* to..."

"Oh, but I am, I do" she corrected. "No one could make me give my love if I didn't want to... not even Kidd." She looked down at her glass then back up at Jack. "He used to try though."

"Did he punish you?" Jack was almost sorry he asked, the second it came out of his mouth. He could imagine Kidd's cruelty, and he didn't think he could bear to hear what she might have been forced to endure.

"Sometimes. But not much." She didn't want to say more.

Jack could see this was an uncomfortable topic. "So," he smiled, changing the subject, "how do I get you to give *me* your love?"

Alité grabbed the folded-down flap on his tunic and pulled him closer. "You're doing just fine," she cooed. "Now if I could just get you to loosen up a bit. Quit being so proper..." She unbuttoned his tunic with one hand and put her glass on the bar with the other. "Quit being such a gentleman, I won't break." Jack raised an eyebrow. "I am yours," she continued, "I want you to do what you're thinking, let loose, take me..." Jack grabbed her by the hair

313

and pulled her face to his. "Yesss..." she hissed. He pressed his lips against hers and backed her against the bar.

She let him kiss her for awhile, then fought him back. He glared at her and she could see the smoldering want, in his eyes. She held him at bay, with one hand on his bare chest, the other gripping his hair, holding back his head. She felt his chest muscles ripple under her fingers. "If you want me," she whispered, "you'll have to take me."

Dropping to one knee, he dragged her down on top of him. Toppling to the floor, they rolled and he pinned her to the carpet. "You are mine..." he growled, holding down her hands.

"Never..." she teased.

"Yes," he countered, easing his body down onto hers.

"Yesss," she breathed.

Jack Steele had always been fascinated by the human body's capacity for sensations, and he always knew the mind could manipulate those sensations either heightening or reducing their intensity. He always felt he had a rather good grasp on how to use them to his best advantage, until now.

In Alité's world, much like Earth, its people placed a great deal of effort and value on giving and receiving personal pleasure. The biggest difference being, their elevated use of the mind and its psychologies to effect, expand and intensify. He knew for some time he'd been falling in love with her, but this sealed it, wrapped it, and tied it with a bow.

She was the first woman Jack had been with in a long time who gave as much as, or more than, she got in return, physically, emotionally and intellectually. He hadn't thought he'd ever get *those* feelings again... He simply didn't allow a woman that close. Maybe it was because he wasn't naive enough anymore, to fall for the unrealistic fantasy expectations of what love should be. Maybe it was because once burned, twice shy. At any rate, keeping a safe distance from the flame seemed a wise way to provide insulation against injury.

But she had found the chink in his armor, she had gotten under his skin. She knew how to treat him, what to say, when to say it, how he felt, how to reach him and how to get him closer. He had forgotten how good the warmth of that flame could feel. And after feeling it again, he wondered how he'd gotten along without it.

There was no getting around it, no sense in denying it, he was in it up to his neck. He was in love with her. And frankly, it scared the shit out of him.

He rolled on his side and stared at her profile in the darkness... she was quite possibly the most beautiful creature he'd ever seen. He slid his arm under the covers and across her stomach, drawing himself closer to her. She uttered a soft little moan and rolled on her side with her back toward him.

Even in her sleep Alité felt him there, his thoughts, his being, his soul. Or as they called it on her planet, his *Rae*. She snuggled back until her body touched his, fitting together like two spoons in a silverware tray. With one arm under her neck, his other draped over her body and across her breasts, she felt comforted by Jack's warmth. Alité became more lucid as her breathing gently rubbed her right nipple on the palm of his hand. As she awakened, growing more conscious, she could feel the contemplation in his Rae, it was like a disturbance in its completeness. He must have sensed she was awakening and lightly kissed her shoulder and neck. She inhaled deeply and smelled the sweet musk of their combined bodies. "What's wrong sweetheart?" she whispered.

Jack had not realized he'd wakened her. "Nothing," he replied softly, "go back to sleep, I didn't mean to wake you."

"You didn't," she replied. "Why are you awake? Can't you sleep?" She felt him shrug. "Tell me..." she urged, "what are you thinking about?"

"I don't know, nothing I guess." He was feeling a bit vulnerable, exposed, like she knew what he was thinking. "Just thinking..."

Alité reached back and ran her hand up his thigh, pulling him against her. "Tell me..." she whispered, "it'll make you feel better."

"I, well... ahem," he had to clear his throat. He wanted to say something, tell her what he was feeling, but he just couldn't form the words or put them in a coherent sentence. It seemed like his thoughts ran around in his head, like a circus gone mad. "I um... lo..." He stopped himself.

Alité could feel his inner conflict and it worried her. She turned over in his arms and touched his face. "It's OK... just tell me."

He wanted to tell her, he *needed* to tell her. But his brain said no and his heart said yes. So he wrestled with it.

She could feel the waves of emotion; then it grew calmer, more whole.

When Steele pulled away, he touched his hand to Alité's face and brushed the hair from her eyes. "I..." he swallowed hard, "I..." he didn't expect it to be so difficult.

"Go on..." she murmured.

"Christ," he breathed, "I love you..." There, he'd said it. Fine. It was out. And he'd never meant it more. He felt a wave of relief.

315

Alité shivered as the thrill raced up her spine. "And I love you," she sighed, "with all my heart... more than life itself."

Jack wanted to jump out of bed and scream at the top of his lungs. But he pulled her close and hugged her instead. He didn't want to let her go. There was just one little thing that nagged at him... "What about LaNareef?"

Alité realized at that point, Jack was far more perceptive than he let on. "What about him?"

"I don't know," said Jack, rolling on his back and drawing her on top. "I just get the feeling like there's something more, like you were more than acquaintances or something. He's not too fond of me, I can tell that, for sure." She attempted to speak but Jack continued. "Like he calls you Princess..." He looked up at her, "That's a kind of endearment, a familiar you use when you're real close with someone." He decided to take a stab in the dark. "Do you still love him?"

Alité giggled. "Yes, but not in the way you think. We could never..." Her voice trailed off. She wasn't sure what affect it would have to tell him about her lineage, her capture...

"Why not?" interrupted Jack. Alité didn't want to lie, and she realized she had to tell him sooner or later... it seemed it would have to be now. "So you love him like a brother then?" asked Jack, pressing on.

"Well yes, I guess you could look at it like that." She noticed another disturbance in his Rae, but it was so fast it escaped before she got a good feel for it. What she *could* feel though, was his heart pounding against her chest as she lay on top of him. She decided she would tell him now and settle his mind, get the matter out of the way. "I..."

Steele cut her off with a kiss, his heart pounding like a drum. She mistook it for arousal and began to slide her body sensuously down his torso. He grabbed her and pulled her face back to his. "I love you..."

"I love you too..." she cooed.

"I want you to be my wife." Even as he said it, he thought maybe he shouldn't have. But he wanted to say it before he lost his nerve. The little voice in his head was absolutely screaming... *Nooooooo!*

"What?" Alité sat bolt upright on his stomach, the blanket sliding off her shoulders.

He couldn't believe he said it the first time, he didn't want to have to repeat it. "I love you... very much," he said, slowly, deliberately, "and I'm asking you to be my wife." *Nooooooo...* screamed the little voice. *Shut the fuck up*, he told it. He could feel the rush of heat rising across his face.

Alité leaned forward, putting her hands on his chest and held herself at arm's length. "Wait, there is something you don't know, something I need to tell you..."

"You're married?"

"No, of course not!"

"You're engaged?"

"No..."

"You're promised to someone..? Dating..? Good friends..?"

"No, no, no..." she slapped his chest, giggling.

"Are you saying no?"

"*NO I'M NOT*! Not exactly," she added quietly.

"Then *what*?"

"Shut up and I'll tell you!" She held her hand over his mouth and he mumbled through her fingers. She needed to tell things to Jack, to explain her parentage and her capture. "Are you done?" she asked. He nodded. "Good. Now, the reason I could never get involved with LaNareef, even though we've been friends for over twenty years, is, I am Royalty and he is not."

Jack's eyes widened. "Mmmphfy?"

She stared at him, her hand still on his mouth. "Yes, *Royalty,*" she confirmed. "I was captured by Kidd over a year ago when he attacked the ship I was on. Just like that freighter we saw. And..." she inhaled deeply, approaching the hard part. "I spent over a year as a servant, a slave..." her voice dwindled to a whisper. "I did many things I'm not very proud of. And I'm not so sure you would be asking me this if you knew..."

She could see the questions in his eyes. She shook her head and swallowed hard. "No, no... In that whole time, he never touched me once... but he never hesitated to torment me." She cleared her throat, "He had a tremendous ego and wanted me to throw myself at him. Since I wouldn't, he took great pleasure in my humility. He couldn't kill me. After all, a dead Princess isn't worth a Trillian penny in ransom..."

"Pfingpss?" She squeezed her hand over Jack's mouth.

"Yes, Princess. *Hush*... let me finish before I lose my nerve." The memories flooded forth in detail, forcing her to remember things she had not wanted to tell. But Steele had broached a subject she had up until now, only dreamed of. And she felt he had a right to know what he was getting into.

She took a deep breath. "Sometimes Kidd would not let me eat for several days. Then he'd force me to watch while he ate a feast, taunting me with the food and making me beg on my knees for scraps. He would strip me naked and force me to eat what he'd given me off a dish on the floor like an animal." Her eyes burned, she blinked hard. "To punish me for improperly thanking him, he would rape or have sex with one of other girls and make me watch. Then I'd be locked in my quarters. No one would be allowed to touch or speak to me, sometimes for days or weeks."

"Pfingpss?"

"Yes," she sighed, *"Princess.* A real Princess... can we get past that? Are you listening?" He nodded.

Despite her efforts, the pain and anger began to show. "I'd cry in frustration... Seeing it, smelling it, hearing it. Eventually even *wanting* it. Something, *anything.* The touch of a hand, a voice... So, one night, one of the other girls snuck in... against the threat of death, and made love to me."

As much as Alité didn't want to tell it all, afraid of what Jack might think of her, it poured out. "After that," she continued, "the girls would take turns and secretly visit me when they could."

Alité sighed heavily, her heart aching. "I was so desperate once, I raped a new girl. I still can't believe I did it, I'm so ashamed. I felt terrible then too, because Kidd had succeeded in making me as bad as him. I felt so bad I wanted to die, but she forgave me." Alité stopped to rub her eyes and wipe the tears that had escaped down her cheeks. "We became good friends... and lovers," she added, after a pause.

Steele could see and feel her pain, gently pulling her hands back to his mouth and kissed her fingertips. "What happened to her?"

Alité smiled but there were tears in her eyes. "She's gone, dead. Kidd killed her... caught her sneaking from my room one night..." She hung her head, and tears hit Jack's chest. Raising her head sharply, she tossed her hair back. "That son-of-a-bitch had her... right on the floor in the corridor, then gave her to the crew. Almost everyone on the crew had her that night." Tears of anger streamed down Alité's face. "I could hear her screams coming from the galley, all the way down the corridor into my room. She had never had a man before. She was a virgin." Alité shook her head and sobbed, "She was dead by morning." Shuddering, she sat upright, covered her face with her hands and cried. "I thought I was next..."

"And you were a virgin too..." guessed Jack, gently running his hands up her arms. His gut ached for the pain she endured.

Alité nodded as she slid her hands down her face and peered over her fingertips. "Until you." She cracked a little smile behind her hands.

"I was your first?" He stared into her eyes. She nodded again. Due to this revelation, the conversation took a sudden left turn. "How could you have remained a virgin for so long?" Alité was almost his age and he couldn't imagine being a virgin at twenty, much less thirty.

"It was my duty. A Princess is supposed to keep herself pure until marriage. At all costs," she explained. "But I failed. I had coupled with women and released my sex drive. So technically, I was no longer a pure virgin." She went on to explain that while her society did not frown upon same-gender relationships, it was not acceptable behavior for a Princess and violated her guidelines of conduct. She would probably have to forfeit all claims to her title and rights of succession. Especially since she'd slept with Jack.

"Then why did you do it?" he wondered aloud, feeling a bit guilty.

She folded her arms demurely across her breasts. "I couldn't help myself... you were so handsome, so compassionate to us... even before I really knew you, I would have done anything you asked of me."

"Really?" Jack was both surprised and flattered. "And now...?"

Alité shivered as she took a deep breath, gathered her composure and looked into his eyes. She felt the ache in her heart and knew she should face the fact that in his eyes he probably saw her the way she saw herself; soiled and unwashed. The Velorian Princess decided to be blunt. "I am a Princess, most likely without a crown. I have no honor, I have no purity. All I have, is my being, my life. But I would forfeit that too if you asked me."

"I don't want you to forfeit anything." Jack grabbed her firmly by the arms, "You love me, right?"

She sobbed, exposed, unable to cover her face with her hands and hide her shame, "With every fiber of my being," she whispered.

"There is no other?"

She shook her head violently, "No! I *swear*..."

"Then be my wife."

"You could still want me, after all I've told you?"

Unintentionally, Jack shook her by the arms. "Of course I can!"

"But," she objected, "what about..."

He cut her off, knowing what she was going to say. "Your crown doesn't matter to me... only your happiness matters to me. You will be *my* Princess... You will be my *Queen*! As for the rest of it... well, you have more honor, more compassion, more integrity in your little finger, than most people have in their entire body." He touched the center of her chest with the palm of his hand. "That's here, in your heart. *No one*, can take that from you..." He eased her body down against his and pulled the covers over them. She was shivering. "Tell me you will be my wife..." he whispered. The little voice in his head had nothing to say this time.

"For ever and ever," she breathed. They clung tightly to each other in the darkness and slid back into sleep.

CHAPTER TWENTY FIVE

FREEDOM, CALO ALTO SYSTEM: *DESTINATION UNKNOWN*

Jack opened his eyes when the comm on the headboard chimed. As he lay waking, it chimed again, reminding him it was unanswered. He reached back over his head and felt for the button. He found it. "Yes?" whispered Steele.

"Ensign Quixetta here, sir. You're needed on the bridge, Captain."

"OK. What do we have, Ensign?"

"Chief Engineer needs to see you, sir, it seems we're having some mechanical problems."

"Right. I'm on my way. Follow any recommendations he gives you, until I get there."

"Yes, sir." The comm beeped as the connection terminated.

Jack looked down at Alité who was curled up against him, sound asleep, the blanket pulled up to her ear. "Fritz," he snapped his fingers, "come..." The sleepy Shepherd slid off the sofa in the other room and plodded through the suite into the bedroom. He stopped at the foot of the bed and shook himself to settle his coat. Jack could see the green glow of the dog's electronic eye in the darkness and called him up onto the bed to lie next to Alité. The Shepherd stretched out on top of the blanket, then curled up comfortably next to Jack's betrothed. "Thank's, buddy..." he stroked the dog's head and watched the glowing green iris dim as Fritz went back to sleep.

After dressing, Jack knelt on the bed and kissed the top of Alité's head as he tucked the blanket in around her. Her hair was soft and sweet with perfume. He drew it into his lungs, wanting to carry it with him the whole day. Jack didn't want to leave, but he was glad Fritz was there to keep her company so she wouldn't wake alone. He grabbed a quick glass of juice from the bar in his suite and headed to the bridge.

"Sir..? Captain, sir..!" A young mechanic trotted up the corridor toward Jack, an electronic notepad tucked under his arm like a football.

Jack stopped, turned and waited for him. "Yes?"

"ABS Vestemore, sir... from the flight bay?" He saluted, "You asked me to go over the life pod and see if we could find any reason for it to fail, remember?" Jack returned his salute and looked him over - the young mechanic cleaned up well, he almost didn't recognize him.

Jack nodded, "Of course, what did you find?"

The mechanic pulled the electronic notepad out from under his arm and turned on the screen, moving closer to Jack and beside him so they could view it simultaneously. "You were right to be suspicious, Captain, the pod had definitely been sabotaged..."

"You found proof...?"

"Yes, sir..." He pulled up a video on the screen. "We found this as we dismantled the pod..." The video showed blackened scorch marks, small but definitely visible.

"Tell me what are we looking at, Vestemore..."

The ABS freeze-framed the video. "The scorching had trace nitrates, so they used a small amount of explosive, and this is an area of the pod that is not checked during scheduled inspections – so there's no telling how long it was in there." He advanced the video until there was a wider view and stopped it again. "The area is a tunnel for all the power leads from the battery compartment at the bottom, past the atmosphere system, up to the computer and controls above. It's actually a pretty simple system and pretty well protected... All the critical areas are armored from damage occurring *outside* the pod..."

"So they just took out all the power connections..."

"Pretty much. A few lines survived, but I think they were for the distress beacon - all the computer cables were shredded." He paused as he pulled up another screen with a few photos. "It would be pretty easy to rig something that small, probably used a little G force meter for a trigger." He held up 2 fingers together so they were touching. "The whole thing wouldn'tve been any bigger than this. The pod was live and functioning until it launched, then the G forces of the launch triggered the device and that was it."

"They probably wouldn't have even heard it during the pod launch..." said Jack, thinking out loud.

"Probably not. And it was most likely pretty quick. Fifteen, maybe twenty minutes tops. No oxygen, no heat - they would just fall asleep."

"Have you discussed this with anyone else...?" Jack tapped the screen.

"No, sir, er, well, the other mechanic that helped me disassemble it knows... ABS Toncaresh. I needed his help, he knew these type of pods better than I did."

"Can he be trusted *not* to discuss it with anyone other than you or me?"

322

"Yes, sir."

Jack nodded, "Good, let's keep it that way. This information doesn't go beyond the three of us..."

■ ■ ■

Steele shook Trigoss' hand. "Morning, Chief, I hear we have a problem. What's up?" Trigoss gave a puzzled frown and looked up at the ceiling. "No, Chief," said Jack laughing, "I mean, what seems to be happening?"

"Oh," said the Chief Engineer reflexively. Another human saying that meant nothing like it sounded. He harumphed. "Captain, we've had to shut down engine number two. It got far too hot and the connecting rings failed which creates pressure leakage among other problems. The worst being, a possible reactor leak."

"Any danger?"

"Nah," he countered with a dismissive wave, "we caught it soon enough."

"How'd it happen?"

Trigoss turned and moved to the engineering station on the bridge and called up some information. "We're simply pushing them too hard." He pointed at the screen. "I had helm drop us down to half power..." Jack groaned. Trigoss pointed back at the screen. "Had to. If the calculations are correct, we would have lost number one next. They just can't take the pressure, Jack. Now I got a good bit of parts from that freighter, but I haven't had time to do any work yet. And if we push the other cores too hard, there won't be anything left of them to rebuild."

Jack nodded. "Understood. You did the right thing, of course." He turned to the helm, "How long at present course and speed, Ensign?"

"A little over forty-three hours to planned destination sir; from there it's search and guesswork."

"It's double our planned time," acknowledged Trigoss, "but it's the only way without blowing the ass-end off the ship."

"I know, Chief." Jack put his hand on Trigoss' shoulder. "It just leaves us kind of vulnerable."

"Can I make a suggestion, sir?"

Jack turned to Raulya at the weapons console. "By all means..."

"Round the clock, constant roaming fighter patrols. It'll be tiring, but it would be the best way to protect ourselves."

Jack nodded. "I was thinking the same thing. And let's set up a regular schedule for keeping the ship's gun-pods at full charge."

Raulya nodded. "I've already laid one out."

"Good. Well, let's get to work." He picked his comm unit up off his console and slid it on. When he glanced at the communications console, he saw a face he didn't recognize. "Hello..."

The young woman in the gray tunic rose and stood at attention. "Petty Officer Stacell, sir."

"Good morning, Petty Officer Stacell... Is that your first or last name?" He was only curious.

The young woman's eyes shifted nervously, "I only have... one name. Sir..."

Jack was getting used to that, it was fairly common. "Oh, OK. Well, relax Stacell, I'm not going to bite your head off..."

"Thank you, sir." She seemed a bit more at ease, but her eyes never left him. Maybe just in case he changed his mind.

Jack smiled. If he said boo, she'd probably jump right out of her uniform. "Stacell..." he kept his voice soft, "please locate and inform all pilots to come to my ready room for a briefing." He turned back to the bridge crew. "I'll be in my ready room if anyone needs me..." Except for Professor Edgars, most of the faces had changed to a fresh crew. "Walt, get lost." Smiling, Jack thumbed towards the door to the corridor. "Get some rest and don't come back till I call you."

"Right you are..." The Professor started out the door and paused.

"I'll send up some breakfast," he called. Jack nodded and Walt disappeared out the door, it closed almost silently behind him.

■ ■ ■

The comm chimed and Derrik rolled over and palmed the button on the nightstand. "Yes?" He said sleepily.

"Sorry," said the voice on the other end, "I'm looking for Lieutenant Arroyo, who's this?"

"Lieutenant Commander Brighton..."

"Terribly sorry, I must have gotten your suite by mistake..."

"No, wait." He reached over and shook Maria by the shoulder. "Wake up, love..." he whispered.

■ ■ ■

"Lieutenant Warren here, go ahead." Mike and Tilee were already dressed and getting ready to go to breakfast when the comm chimed.

"Your presence is required in the Captain's ready room for flight briefing, sir."

"OK, thank you, Stacell..."

"By the way, sir, you wouldn't know where I might locate Commander Smiley, would you? I can't seem to find him."

Mike glanced at Tilee and rubbed his chin. "Try Ensign Myomerr's quarters..."

"Thank you sir," came the voice over the comm. Petty Officer Stacell was beginning to wonder if anybody was where they were supposed to be this morning.

The comm beeped off. "I guess I'll meet you for breakfast after the meeting," said Mike. Tilee nodded. She was shy and didn't talk much, but Mike didn't mind, she was adorable and sweet. He kissed her and headed for the bridge.

■ ■ ■

Jack was sitting at the head of the briefing table in the semidarkness studying the plotted route on the holo-chart when Brian strolled in. "Whatcha' doing, Skipper?"

"Just checking our progress."

"Oh," nodded Brian. "Want to go to breakfast?"

"Not till after..."

"Excuse me, Captain," Petty Officer Stacell entered behind Brian, "I can't seem to find Lieutenant Carter..." She glanced at Brian and saw the rank on his collar. "Is that you?" Brian grinned and nodded. "Oh." Stacell walked from the room shaking her head. "Never mind."

"Thank you Stacell," called Jack as the door swished closed. He smiled at Brian. "Seems she's had a tough morning already..."

"Mine was pretty good," beamed Brian.

"Mine too," reflected Jack. "And you'll be the first to know..." he took a deep breath, "Alité and I are getting married."

It took Brian a moment to recover from that *finger in the light socket* look. "*Really*? No kidding?"

325

"No kidding..."

Brian jumped forward and thrust out his hand and Jack shook it. "Well shit! Congratulations, buddy, that's *awesome!*" He stopped for a moment. "Wait, you don't *have to,* do you...?"

"No," chuckled Jack.

"Then it's *awesome!*" Brian sat down in the chair next to Jack. "But I thought after your last fiasco, you'd sworn off it for good."

Steele shook his head slowly, "So did I. But I guess things change, I changed... or my feelings about it..."

"What changes?" The two men turned as Maria and Derrik entered the room.

"People do," said Brian jumping from his seat. "Jack's getting married!"

It happened so fast, Jack couldn't stop him. The little voice in his head was screaming in slow motion *Nnnnooooo...* A little *late* he told it. He wanted to tell Maria alone, explain things...

But Maria beamed. "Married? *You?* That's *wonderful!*"

Jack's little voice only had one word, *Huh?* That was not the response he was expecting from her at all.

"Who's gettin' married?" asked Mike as he entered the room behind the others.

"Jacko is," volunteered Derrik.

"To the Ice Princess? No kidding... *Wow!*" Mike looked stunned.

"Hey, hey, *hey*!" countered Jack, rising from his seat in mock anger. "Watch how you talk about the woman I intend to marry... I might shoot you at the dinner table." There was a short round of laughter as Paul entered, followed by Walrick and LaNareef.

"What's going on?"

Mike spun around. "Hey, Pappy! Jack and Alité are getting married!"

OK, thought Jack, *I've totally lost control of this, it's getting way out of hand...* Perhaps this wasn't the best venue for this... *or maybe I should've added, please don't say anything in front of the Velorians!*

Paul expressed surprise, Walrick expressed friendly indifference and LaNareef expressed horror and rage. *"How dare you!"* he screamed, lunging forward.

Jack dropped the charging Velorian to his knees with a stiff-arm to the chest. "Get a grip," growled Jack sarcastically.

"She is..." LaNareef gasped, trying to get his breath back. "She is Royalty! A Princess!"

326

"I am fully aware of that... You do realize, *she* has some say in this, right?"

LaNareef was clutching the ache in his chest and breathing hard. "She will lose her crown if she marries outside the Royal Circle. I cannot allow you to do this..."

"*You* cannot allow?" Jack chortled defiantly, his hands on his hips. "Just who the hell do you think you are? The *marriage police*? I can't believe you have the balls to stand on the bridge of *my* ship and insult me... I think you'd better do a reality check, pal, because you're not at home anymore." The others stood about in silence as Jack continued. "Alité will *always* be a Princess. The difference is, *here*, she has the freedom and safety to do what she wants. So find solace in her happiness because she *is* happy. And if that proves difficult, just remember who saved your sorry butt from the pirates." Jack pointed his finger at the kneeling pilot. "Because if you give me a hard time about this, or cause Alité grief, *any grief*, you'll find yourself on the wrong side of an airlock. Is that clear?"

Walrick stepped forward and clamped his hand over LaNareef's mouth from behind. "He understands completely," said Walrick. "And if he doesn't," he squeezed his hand tighter, "I'll *explain* it to him again."

Jack stared at the two as if he was trying to make up his mind about something. "Fine. Then it's forgotten." He turned away. "We have some ship's business to discuss, take a seat." He turned back.

"You mean she's *really* a Princess?" asked Mike, grabbing a seat.

Jack smiled and pulled up his chair. "Yeah, pretty amazing, eh?"

"Does that make you a Prince?" whispered Brian.

"I don't think so," chuckled Jack. He glanced at LaNareef who stared silently at the surface of the table, sullen and gray-cast. *They're losing the war,* thought Jack, *and all this idiot can think of is, who's supposed to marry whom... like they did such a great job of protecting her in the first place.* Maybe space wasn't so different from Earth after all; you can't fix stupid. Steele realized for the first time, he hadn't thought of that emerald and sapphire planet as home. Merely a place. He guessed Voorlak would have something insightful to say about that.

■ ■ ■

The briefing went as planned and a strategy for constant fighter patrols was hammered out. The patrols would run until repairs to the Freedom's power plants could be effected, which was not likely to be until they reached the space station at Blackmount. There they would use the station's indoor facilities to install any parts they might acquire along the way.

Halfway through the meeting Trigoss rang in on the intercom. "Sorry to bother you Captain... remember that generator we built before we left?"

"Yeah, what about it?" answered Jack.

"Well it just quit, for good. The armatures just melted down. We're back to one large and two small."

Jack closed his eyes and pinched the bridge if his nose. "Dammit." Everyone else in the room sat in silence.

"The good news," continued the Engineer, "is that I managed to pull an undamaged large off the freighter before we had to run..."

"That's great!" interrupted Jack. "Y'know, you could've *led-off* with that tidbit of information…"

"But, I can't install it without shutting most of the systems off for at least several hours."

Jack sighed, "Yeah, well that figures. Alright, how about this Chief, pull the old one now. Mount the new one in its place and get it ready to hook it up? We'll shut down and you can do the installation hookup in the salvage yard..."

"We *can* prep the new one, but we can't touch the old one since she's wired in... We're liable to damage computer systems without shutting them down first."

Jack groaned, "But we can do this in the salvage yard, right...?"

"Before we go to Blackmount Station..? Yeah, sure we can. But we'll be awful vulnerable out there..."

There was a lot of space between them and UFW Blackmount in the Feerocobi System, four or five systems to Jack's recollection. And from where they were, that was the closest location. He was pretty sure doing repairs at a protected facility, with proper equipment, was ultimately the way to go but that was a long time to be running underpowered, under-shielded and under-gunned while your ship was undermanned. He hoped the salvage yard would be a quiet out-of-the-way place where they could find some parts and make a few critically needed repairs. If they could find salvage that they could use for more extensive repairs at Blackmount, that would be a bonus. "Well," Jack paused, "I don't expect there to be too much traffic out there, but we'll pack the pilots a lunch, put out every bird we can, charge the ship's gun pods, then, go dark and play possum."

"Play possum..?"

"Never mind, I'll explain that later."

"OK. In the meantime, we need to cut down on some of the systems so we don't overtax these gennys."

"If it's necessary..."

"It is," confirmed Trigoss. The comm beeped as the conversation ended.

Jack set his elbows on the table and his face in his hands. "Holy crap, what next..?" He mumbled. It was a rhetorical question.

The comm-link chimed again. "Captain, we have two ships at full sensor range."

"How big are they, Mr Ragnaar?" The pilots rose from the table in unison.

"Not very big, sir, but fast." Until the Freedom could acquire more parts for its aging and damaged sensor array, clear identification of ships was impossible beyond one third of its normal range.

Jack looked up at the pilots, stalling them with a wave of his hand. "Any guess Lieutenant?"

"They're using a standard UFW patrol sweep, and they're too small to be destroyers... The pirates rarely use anything smaller than that. I'd say UFW interceptor ships. Crew of about thirty."

"Thank you, Lieutenant, maintain course." Jack ended the connection and turned to the pilots. "Paul, Mike, you two are the welcoming committee. Take Lancias and get going." They turned and left. "Derrik, Bri, you sit on standby. Lancias. Mister LaNareef, are you ready to fly?"

"Yes, sir," he nodded.

"Fine. You and Walrick are ship's cover. You'll launch last in Warthogs." They also turned and left.

"Hey! What about me?" complained Maria.

Jack stood, shaking his head. "How soon we forget." He tapped his head. "You are grounded until the Doc clears you for flight. I want to keep your brains in your head where they belong. You're no good to me if your gray matter comes running out of your ears."

"Aw c'mon..."

"OK, you want to be useful? Tell you what. Go down to the flight bay and have one of the techs hook that Zulu up to a simulator. Find out everything you can about it. How it handles, range, arms, you name it."

Maria screwed her face into one of distaste but decided it was better than sitting around. "Alright."

"But if anyone catches you near a live ship," added Jack, "*zoom*!" He swept his hand. "Back to the infirmary where the Doc can keep an eye on you. And that's *after* I put you over my knee and take away your wings."

Maria smiled as she turned for the door. "Yeah?" she said playfully. "You and what army?" She strolled out without looking back, the door swishing closed behind her, leaving Jack alone.

■ ■ ■

Jack sat in the command chair watching the view screen and could feel the bridge vibrate as Paul and Mike's Lancias launched through the tubes. Then he saw the flares of light as they ignited their engines, appearing from under the nose of the Freedom. "Freedom, this is Pappy. Flight One is clear."

Steele acknowledged him. Scant moments later, the flight tower notified the bridge, Flight Two was ready, and Flight Three was standing by. It seemed to him the flight crews were getting faster at prep and launch.

It wasn't more than a couple of minutes before Paul and Mike were able to see the ships on their Lancia's sensors. "Flight One to Bridge, you can stand down Flights Two and Three. We have confirmation, two UFW interceptor patrol vessels."

"Roger Flight One. Is that Visual?"

"Negative, sensor only. We'll be in visual range in approximately five minutes."

"Understood. Continue standard patrol after visual contact," advised Jack. He decided to keep the other flights on standby until after Paul's visual confirmation of identification. The next five minutes passed slowly, Steele eying the chronometer on one of his command screens.

"Flight One, identity confirmed. Forwarding data, proceeding on patrol route."

Jack acknowledged and called a stand down for the other flights. A short time later, the Commander of one of the patrol vessels hailed the Freedom as the two vessels slowed and staggered their formation in a defensive tactic. "Hello, Commander," began Jack politely. He stood between the helmsman and Ragnaar at the navigation station. "What can I do for you?" The face of the UFW officer appeared on the view screen, he did not look trusting. His skin was blanched and drawn in a perpetual scowl.

"Identify yourself," he said bluntly.

"His shields are up..." whispered Raulya.

Jack moved his hand behind his back to indicate he'd heard her. He hoped Paul and Mike hadn't gone too far. "I'm Captain Jack Steele. This is the cruiser Freedom, Raider Class. Our home world is Earth and we are allied with the UFW."

"Stand by." The screen went blank while the Commander consulted with his crew and the other patrol ship. The screen winked back on. "We can find no records on your ship. And as far as your origin, the Terran System has no space travel capabilities to my knowledge."

"We do now," countered Jack.

"What is your mission, your purpose..." inquired the patrol vessel Commander.

"Right now," began Jack, "we are heading for parts and repair, then home."

"You're headed the wrong way my friend." The Commander sneered like he'd caught Jack in a lie. "Beyond us is pirate territory." The three ships came to a stop, facing off miles apart. "So why don't you tell me what you're *really* doing out here? And why is your ship so well armed?"

Steele snorted at the absurdity of the question. "Well gee, I heard there were pirates out here..." he countered sarcastically. "As I said before, this is a Raider Class cruiser, the guns kinda come standard on this model..." Steele could see where this was going and motioned behind his back to cut communications. Petty Officer Stacell caught the signal and ended the connection. "Thank you, Stacell." He turned to Raulya. "Call the tower..."

"You can't launch," she interrupted, "he'll read the power surges of the launch equipment on his sensors. He could gun us to pieces before I could bring up our shields."

"I know..." he snapped. "Have Brian, Derrik, LaNareef and Walrick, taxi and launch out the bay door, engines off. Have them wait there." He turned back to Stacell, "OK." The screen winked back on. "I'm sorry, Captain. Where were we?"

"You were about to tell me, you are a pirate heading for pirate territory in a pirated ship." His sneer was back. "And that you surrender so I don't have to blow you out of existence."

"He's powering up weapons," whispered Raulya. Jack acknowledged again with a discreet hand movement.

Jack shook his head. "Untrue, Commander, untrue. We took this vessel *from* the pirates who took it from *you* the UFW. This vessel was originally

331

the Ynosa and we simply stole it from the thieves. So, by the interspace law of *finders keepers* we have confiscated it for ourselves."

"Finders keepers..?" The puzzled Commander glanced off screen for an explanation from his crew. There was none.

"Right," confirmed Jack, "while aboard the Princess Hedonist. In fact, if you contact Captain Gantarro, he can confirm this..."

"Did you say the Princess Hedonist?"

"Yes. Why? Do you know Gantarro?" Ragnaar reached back and tapped Jack on the leg, out of view of the other Captain. He pointed to his sensor screen. Jack could casually glance at it without being noticed. It showed the second patrol vessel swinging wide in an attack posture.

"Mr. Steele, the Princess Hedonist was attacked and disappeared about two days ago. Its fate is unknown." Jack could feel the heat rise in his face as he hazarded a quick glance in Raulya's direction. Her eyes were wide with astonishment. "About the same time, a Royal Velorian freighter was attacked and destroyed back in the direction you're coming from. There was quite a battle. The freighter must have done well. But by the time our cruisers got there, it was over. Only a crippled pirate carrier was left." Jack was still in shock about the Princess Hedonist and did not answer. "I'll just bet if I searched your vessel, I'd find either equipment or prisoners from one of those ships, wouldn't I?"

"Whoa, hold on a minute!" exclaimed Jack. "You got some good facts there, but they're in the wrong order! Not to mention missing a few vital pieces..."

"That's not really my problem," claimed the other, with a face somewhere between a sneer and a scowl. "I have a man in space from a world which hasn't the technology, in a ship that is not his own, knowledge of a ship that has since disappeared, and coming from where another has been destroyed. Now I see no signs of physical damage, but my sensors tell me your ship is operating well below its standards... did we over exert ourselves in combat? Blow a few systems?" He shook his head, "No Captain, I think I have plenty..."

Jack kept telling himself this man was just doing his job. "Look, Captain, I can appreciate how all these circumstances coincide, and that's just what they are, coincidental... But we can clear all this up if you'll contact the UFW Directorate on Tanzia. That's where our wings and ranks were issued from..."

"Do you think I would really waste their time on the word of a pirate? Do you think me a fool?"

Well yeah, thought Jack, *actually moron might be more accurate.*

The Commander waved his hand to dismiss the thought. "No, Mr. Steele, we will wait here. The cruisers I summoned will be here shortly, and their Marines will board and take over your ship. Your pirating career is over."

Jack was seriously beginning to lose his patience. This man had appointed himself both judge and jury, convicted him and was about to pass sentence. "Look, Commander..."

"Mr. Steele..."

Jack noticed the man no longer addressed him as Captain.

"I hope you won't do anything foolish, because I will not hesitate to destroy you. We would prefer you and your crew alive, so we might interrogate you." He grinned wickedly. "Besides, it would look better on the citation I will receive for this..." His grin faded. "But I must warn you, ANY actions on your part, we will consider hostile." He frowned again and the screen winked off abruptly.

"We're on the *same side, you ass*!" Growled Jack at the blank screen. "What a moron." Stepping over to his command chair, Jack keyed the comm to engineering. "Trigoss, I'm gonna' need every bit of speed you can muster in a couple of minutes."

"I'll give you what I got..." came the answer.

"No more mister nice guy," growled Jack, "I'm not playing their stupid game, they want to fuck around? Fine! Let's see if they can play with the *big dogs!* Tower, silent signal protocol. Alert Flights Two and Three, they will split and attack on the outer flanks on my order." The tower acknowledged. Neither Paul nor Mike was visible on any of the sensors, but Jack had to believe they were not far off and had somehow found an obvious place to hide. "Raulya, shields up on my command, not before, OK?"

"But, sir..."

Jack held up his hand to cut her off. "They're gonna' have plenty to think about. Hitting us is going to be the least of their concerns." He palmed the red button on his console and the alarm klaxons blared their *Red Alert* warning. Jack was betting a multitude of instant actions at once would confuse the crews in the patrol ships, stalling their reactions long enough to gain the upper hand. He didn't want to have to destroy them, just run them off or damage them enough to be able to affect an escape. He wasn't about to delude himself or the crew, that surrender was a viable or safe solution.

"Forward guns manned, Captain," reported Raulya.

Jack nodded and thumbed the mic on his headset. "All flights *TALLY HO*!" Four white trails arced around the rear of the Freedom and headed for the flanks of the patrol vessels. Jack spun on his heel. "Shields up Raulya!" He switched the comm channel. "Trigoss, full reverse, *now!* All guns, *fire at will!* Make em count!"

The patrol vessels crabbed sideways to divide the Freedom's firepower and move to her more vulnerable flanks. But they didn't count on Mike and Paul, who after passing earlier, had come around and coasted up behind them, engines off. Masked by the energy wakes of the patrol ships, the two fighters went undetected.

Extremely maneuverable, the UFW patrol vessels attempted to circle around the lethargic cruiser like a boxer looking for an opening. Had it not been for the fighters, it would have been a short match. Determined and unwilling to back off, the Commanders of the UFW ships took their licks and hung in there. Their heavy guns took a quick toll on the inadequate shields of the Freedom and kept the fighters maneuvering defensively.

"Forward shields at sixty-five percent," shouted Raulya. The ship shuddered under another blow. "Port mid shields down to fifty-five percent and port quarter to thirty-five percent!"

Jack keyed his mic. "All ahead *FULL* Chief!" The ship lurched a moment later as the main thrust burners ignited.

"Sir!" Shouted Stacell, "I just intercepted a message. There are two UFW Liberator-Class cruisers on their way. They're about thirty minutes out!"

Jack wondered if it could get any worse. The Freedom took another blow along the bow and shuddered. "Forward shields sixty percent and holding, port stern down to fifteen percent!" The patrol craft crossing the Freedom's bow, disappeared in giant chunks as the Freedom's port, main gun battery blew huge holes in its hull. Constant hammering from the fighters had depleted its shields. A quick cheer rolled across the bridge. "Most forward gun batteries have exhausted their energy pods," reported Raulya.

Harassed, damaged, and low on shields, the remaining UFW vessel fired as it retreated, trying to outrun the fighters and reach the safety of the approaching cruisers. The stern shields flared and the Freedom shook hard. Then shook again. "Hull breach! Hull breach!" Alarms *whooped* throughout the ship and the Freedom's speed began to dwindle.

"Son-of-a-bitch," snarled Jack. He keyed his comm mic on the fighter's frequency. "Don't let that bastard get away, Pappy!"

"Not a chance," came the answer. A moment later the remaining ship split in half, spreading debris and spilling its crew into space.

The Freedom had dropped to about one quarter speed. "Trigoss, what's happening back there? What's going on?"

The reply was laced with static and background noise. "Not now, Jack, we're kinda busy..." the connection fading away.

"Commander Edgars to the bridge," paged Jack. "Raulya, shields down, recharge all guns. I'm going down to engineering to see if I can help. Mr. Ragnaar, you know where we're going, point us there. I'll see what I can do about more speed." Still wearing his comm, Jack left the bridge and hustled down the corridor.

■ ■ ■

The pilots had no problem catching up with the Freedom and could have easily found it without their sensors. Once they were in clear visual range they were stunned by what they saw. "Holy shit..." muttered Mike.

"My God..." added Brian.

Paul reached through his open visor with a gloved hand and wiped the sweat from his brow. "Son-of-a-bitch," he whispered. At least one third of the Freedom's port engine was missing. Forward of that was a gaping hole in the hull of the ship, twisted and jagged, exposing deck two or three. Maybe both. The remains of the port engine trailed anonymous vapors, assorted bits of debris and giant gobbets of fire foam. The wound in the hull bled streams of atmosphere vapor leaking from damaged safety doors.

Derrik shook his head. "Bloody horrible little bastards. Look what they've done to our pretty ship."

Walrick and LaNareef said nothing.

"We'd better get back and see if we can lend a hand," volunteered Brian.

"Good idea," began Paul, "besides, we might be having more company. We need to restock and refuel these birds." The pilots called for and received clearance to land, strung out in three pairs.

As they neared the stern in formation, Mike spotted a strange glow ahead and to the right of the Freedom. "Hey, Pappy, what the hell is that?"

Paul looked to the Lancia on his left and followed Mike's point to the distant glow, which could only be described as being on the horizon. The pale blue and purple haze glowed and pulsated, seeming to undulate like waves of water. "Don't know kid, maybe we should take a look... Flight

Leader to tower, Flight One is breaking final approach, Two and Three will recover..."

"Negative, Leader," replied flight control, "Recover as planned."

Paul shrugged to himself, "Roger, tower."

"Commander?!" LaNareef's voice sounded strained.

"Go ahead," coaxed Paul.

"I have two large ships appearing on the rearward edge of my sensor range..."

■ ■ ■

Steele jogged down the corridor towards the stern on deck two, slowing as the smoke grew thicker. Despite his caution, he stumbled and fell across someone laying on the floor. He crawled over on his hands and knees to the prone form and dragged him to clearer air. The crewman was blackened by smoke and unrecognizable. Jack rose and opened an emergency panel on the wall, extracting an air bottle. He slid the plastic mask over the man's face and opened the valve. After two gulps of air, his eyes popped open and he sat upright, gasping. "Easy," said Jack, holding him by the shoulders. "Breathe easy. You'll be alright..." He slid the man against the wall and pulled another bottle down for himself, "Stay here, someone will come for you." He turned away and fingered the mic on his comm, "Fire control teams to port engineering, deck two! Medical team, deck two!" He slid on his own mask, slung the bottle over his shoulder by its strap and turned on the valve as he crawled into the biting smoke on his hands and knees.

Blinded by the smoke, his sensitive nose scorched by the heat and acrid smoke, Fritz had to feel his way backwards down the corridor while dragging his burden. Blood ran from the swollen lining of his nose, but the dog refused to release his grip and take even one breath through his mouth. After weaving his way through the port engine room, he proceeded backwards down the corridor in search of assistance, using his tail as a guide.

Unable to even see his hand in front of his face, Steele advanced on hands and knees with his eyes closed, tears streaming down his cheeks from the stinging smoke. He rammed something soft with his right shoulder, toppling himself over. Whatever, or whomever it was, grunted. He righted himself and reached out, searching, finding thick fur and a tail. "Fritz?" The Shepherd snorted in response, blood spraying from his nose, choking,

336

refusing to relinquish his grasp. Jack felt forward and realized the dog was dragging a crewman and grabbed the collar of the uniform tunic, pulling, sliding the limp form across the carpet. "Let go," urged Jack, "I've got him." Fritz growled, refusing. Together they dragged the unconscious crewman to clearer air where Jack had previously left the other man. The air bottle remained but the crewman was gone, presumably moved to the infirmary. As soon as they reached the clearer air, Fritz dropped to the floor, exhausted, still gripping the man's arm in his mouth. Jack instantly understood why Fritz refused to let go of the crewman; his arm was missing below the elbow and the Shepherd was trying to keep him from bleeding to death.

Steele pulled off his air bottle and laid it on the floor. "It's OK, Fritz, let him go..." Jack slid off the dog's squadron scarf and wrapped it around the man's arm, tying it off above the dog's grip. Fritz unmouthed the crewman and exhausted, rolled on his side hacking up blood and the blackness he'd been breathing. Jack turned on the air valve and moved the bottle in front of Fritz's muzzle who drew it in open-mouthed. Taking the abandoned bottle, Jack placed the face piece over the mouth of the wounded crewman, then tightened the scarf around his arm like a tourniquet.

"Bridge, this is Steele, get some more people down here on deck two... we need some help!"

"Right you are, Jack," replied the Professor. He issued a page over the comm system. *"How bad is it?"* asked Walt after the page.

"I did't find any fire, but the smoke is pretty thick. Can you find the Doc? I've got a guy missing an arm down here; I've tourniqueted his arm but I can't leave him." The Professor acknowledged and signed off. Steele cradled the injured man in his lap and held the tourniquet tight. Fritz was breathing easier and he could see again. "Good job, Fritz," commented Jack, "you probably saved his life." He wanted to reach out and touch the dog, but his arms were full. Fritz wagged his tail, slowly thumping it on the floor.

Steele jumped when Trigoss suddenly appeared through the smoke. "Well it's finally out..." his uniform was scorched and charred, he didn't even have an oxygen bottle. "Hate that taste." He spat on the floor.

"What was burning?" asked Jack.

Trigoss coughed once and spat again. "Tyrillium bulkhead..." The sound of many running feet echoing down the smoky corridor, interrupted their conversation.

Several crewmen wearing complete breathing gear ran past, disappearing into the acrid clouds. Paul, Mike and Brian, tromped to a stop, still in flight gear. "You OK?" asked Brian.

"I'm alright. Help me get this guy to the infirmary, I don't know where the Doc is..." Jack started to rise.

"He's coming," said Paul, thumbing over his shoulder, "we just passed him. It looks bad from outside, Jack. How bad is it really?" Paul didn't frown much, but this was an exception.

"Bad," answered Trigoss. "We're down to one engine."

"Damn..." Paul rubbed his chin. "Y'know we're leaking all sorts of stuff too..."

The Chief Engineer nodded and spat. "Fuel, atmosphere mostly. Got several doors leading to the damaged area that buckled. They're leaking. We can seal them though."

"That's the least of our problems," added Mike, "we've got more company coming..."

"What?" Steele sat rigid as CABL M7 bought the gurney to a stop next to him. "Who? Where?" They all helped lift the unconscious crewman onto the gurney.

"They're coming from behind us," answered Brian, fastening a strap on the gurney. "They're big *and* fast."

Jack handed M7 control of the tourniquet, "How long do we have?"

Paul shrugged. "At this speed? Maybe twenty minutes."

Jack turned to Trigoss, "Chief, we need that other engine."

Trigoss made a face and shook his head. "If it was run-able, which it's *not*, and we directed *all* the ship's power to warming the burners, it would take at least two hours before I could ignite it..."

"Geez, isn't there any way to do a cold start?"

"Well, yes, but in its present condition," Trigoss indicated the mess behind them, "the best it will do is make it look like this one."

"There's *no* chance of success?"

"None. Think of something else..."

"Maybe we should get ready to launch," suggested Brian.

"Bridge to Captain Steele..."

"Now what?" Steele clicked on his mic, "Steele, go ahead."

"Jacko," started the professor, "we've got on*e hell* of an ether storm brewing out here... quite colorful actually..."

"A *what?!*" exclaimed Jack, cutting him off.

338

"An electrical ether storm, sir," explained Ragnaar over the comm.

Jack looked at Trigoss, "A storm? In space?"

The Engineer nodded, "Pretty common."

"I think we're out of ruddy luck, Jack. Those cruisers are coming up fast, and this front is too big to go round..."

"Go straight through it," whispered Trigoss. Jack looked at him sideways. The Chief Engineer nodded confidently, and his hand sliced through the air in front of them. "Right through the middle."

"Head straight for it, Walt," advised Jack. Not so sure himself.

"Right. Consider it done..." The comm connection ended.

Trigoss proceeded to explain his idea. "Sensors are pretty much useless in plasma and ether storms. And visibility is close to nil but..."

"So we'll be navigating blind," interrupted Jack.

"More or less," continued the Chief. "But the cruisers won't be able to see either. The trick is to plan out your course changes before you get to the storm. Once inside you execute maneuvers at set times. The cruisers will try one of two tactics, either they'll try to track you, which is next to impossible, or try a standard search pattern."

"Won't they be able to follow all that debris we're trailing?" asked Paul.

"Nah," claimed the engineer, waving his hand, "the storm'll sweep it all away."

"Well, the problem is gonna' be beating them to the storm," commented Jack. He turned to Trigoss, "Think we can push number three a little more?"

"I'll try..." The engineer turned and headed back into the dwindling smoke. "But don't expect too much..."

Jack, Paul, Brian and Mike, strode up the corridor towards the bridge. "Will Fritz be OK?" asked Brian after some silence.

Jack nodded, "Doc says it's smoke inhalation and nasal swelling from the irritation. A few hours of medicated oxygen treatment and he'll feel much better. He might keep him overnight for observation."

Paul smirked, "Saving a guy's life by holding his arm just right to keep him from bleeding to death and dragging him two hundred feet to safety while blinded by smoke..." He suddenly realized he was thinking out loud and stopped.

"Freakin' dog deserves a medal," concluded Mike, finishing Paul's sentence.

"It *was* pretty incredible, wasn't it?" agreed Steele.

The ship shuddered, the men missing their footing on the moving floor and bouncing against the padded corridor walls. "What the *hell* was that?" shouted Paul, bracing himself.

"I don't know," said Jack, breaking into a cautious run. The Red Alert klaxons sounded as another shudder shook the floor beneath their feet and Mike hit the floor. The others ran on as Mike scrambled to his feet, eerie red light bathing the corridors.

"What the hell is going on?" screamed Jack, as he burst onto the bridge followed by the three pilots.

"They're firing at us long-range," explained the Professor.

"You mean they're in range already?" Jack plopped into his command chair and switched on the console.

"Not quite," continued Walt, "they're trying to convince us to surrender. They'll be in range in thirty seconds."

"You're kidding..."

"No. These are a brand new class of UFW cruisers..."

Jack didn't listen to the rest. "Trigoss," he shouted into the comm, "can we get any more?"

"We're at top, Jack. In fact, she's starting to heat up already... ten minutes, fifteen tops, then we're *dead in the water*, as you would say."

"Keep it going," instructed Jack. He turned off the comm. "How long to the storm front, Lieutenant?"

"Eight to ten minutes, sir," replied Ragnaar. "The front surges, so the time is variable."

"We're in their range in five seconds..." announced Walt.

"Helm, evasive action!" Jack knew it would be useless to return fire, the Freedom's guns had only about half the range.

"Jack!" shouted Paul, "let us launch!"

"*NO!*" He swiveled his chair. "Lieutenant, cut power to all non essential systems, that includes all gun pods," the ship shuddered as the first in-range volley from the cruisers, missed. "Route all extra power to stern shields," he continued. Raulya nodded and went to work, her fingers dancing across her console as fast as she could.

"I know what you're trying to do, Jack," shouted Paul from the upper level behind him, "but it aint gonna' work this time..." The pilot was remembering the maneuver Jack used in the B-25 when he entered the cloud bank over the Bermuda Triangle back at home. "Let us go," he urged, "we can slow them down!"

Jack ignored him. "Helm, nose down!" Quixetta keyed in the command and the coming volley passed close over the Freedom. "Level off."

"Incoming message, sir..."

"On screen, Stacell." The face of a determined young Captain appeared on the main screen.

"I am Captain Kelarez of the UFW cruiser, Archer. You are commanded to surrender."

"I'm sorry," apologized Steele, "I can't do that..."

"Word is," interrupted Kelarez, "you're a dangerous man, Captain. But surely you must realize," he continued, "your ship is in no condition to outrun either of our ships. The Archer and the Bowman were specially built for pursuit. And you surely couldn't hope to outfight us. So do us all a favor and surrender."

As long as he's talking, thought Jack, he's not shooting. "Sir," he began, "I am Captain Jack Steele of the cruiser Freedom. Earth is our home planet and we are allied with the UFW."

"Your ship does not meet any recent profiles on current ships operating in UFW space," said Kelarez.

"We defeated a raiding party of pirates and confiscated this ship for our own use. Our rank was issued us by the UFW directorate, so it's all very official."

"I'm sure it is..." injected Kelarez politely.

"But you folks don't seem to want to be bothered with those kinds of details," commented Jack. "We have been attacked not only by pirates, but by UFW vessels as well." Jack folded his Arms across his chest. "So tell me, Captain, why should I choose to trust you? Does the UFW treat all their new allies like this?"

Captain Kelarez pondered this for a moment before he spoke, his handsome face bent in a frown. "I am truly sorry your travels have been troublesome. But I am afraid it will get worse before it gets better. I am a Captain, not an Admiral. And as such, I must follow orders. They are, to capture your ship and crew, then provide escort back to the UFW facilities on Phi Lanka, where this would all be investigated and hopefully straightened out..."

"There is a federation prison there..." whispered Ragnaar.

"Barring that," continued Kelarez. "I would be required to destroy your ship and crew. Frankly, I would like to avoid that unpleasantness. I would

341

prefer to escort you. Especially if this all turns out to be just a complicated screw-up of some kind."

Jack glanced at the plotting screen on his console's monitor. The cruisers had slowed but were gaining with ease, the Freedom was still four minutes to the storm front.

"This escort you speak of..."

"Marines," interrupted Kelarez with patience, "would take over all operations of your ship. You and your crew would be confined to quarters."

Prisoners on our own ship, how nice. "Well," Steele said thoughtfully, "just how far is this Phi Lanka?"

Ragnaar turned around and scowled at his Captain, thinking him serious. The others were none so sure either. Only Paul, Mike and Brian knew what he was up to.

"Phi Lanka is only about two weeks away," replied Kelarez.

"Here it comes," whispered Paul to Mike.

"Well there is a problem," explained Jack, "we seem to be having some propulsion problems. It would require total shutdown for a day or so, to sufficiently make repairs to complete the trip..."

Captain Kelarez raised one eyebrow, his patience running short. "We would have to bring your crew aboard then, and leave your ship here. Or destroy it." He added.

"Oh I couldn't do that..." bemoaned Jack. "They *love* this ship... isn't there some other way? Couldn't you tow it with a tractor beam or something?" He glanced down at the plotting monitor and back up.

Paul, Mike and Brian, exchanged silent glances.

Kelarez frowned, "A tractor beam? What kind of foolishness is this? I think you've been stalling and playing me for a fool, Captain. I am not. Do not mistake my kindness for weakness... I have run out of patience, and you have run out of time. Surrender or die, choose now."

Steele pursed his lips, "Stand by, let me consult my bridge officers." He turned his back on the screen, "Audio off, Ms. Stacell."

With his back to the screen, Jack addressed the crew on a ship-wide comm. "We are faced with a dilemma, people. To surrender or not to surrender is the question, and I don't feel I can rightfully answer for all of us." He took a deep breath, "I don't want anyone to think of the word coward... as far as I'm concerned, no one on this ship could remotely fit that description. But if there is even one person that thinks we should surrender, speak now... and that will be the course we will take..."

342

There was absolute silence, save for the hiss of the open comm channel. He waited. But the silence *was* his answer.

Steele motioned to Stacell and the comm was replaced by videocom audio as he turned back toward the screen. "Captain Kelarez, on my planet during World War Two, General Anthony McAuliffe had a reply for a similar situation as this... *NUTS!"*

Kelarez raised an eyebrow, "Excuse me?"

Jack smiled, "As Winston Churchill once put it, ...*we shall defend our island whatever the cost may be. We shall fight on the beaches, we shall fight on the landing grounds, we shall fight in the fields and streets, we shall fight in the hills, we shall never surrender...* Well, sir, this is *our* island and we will not surrender..."

"He's nuts..." whispered Paul.

"It's a practiced talent," commented Brian.

"Have it your way, Captain!" shouted Kelarez, red-faced. The screen went blank.

"Hard to port!" snapped Jack, straightening up. The horizon swung producing a blur of colors. The storm front so large now, it seemed endless to the left, right, above and below. The Freedom shuddered and lurched, the fire from the cruisers closer than before.

"They're being careful to stay out of our range, Jack."

"I know, Walt. Helm, hard starboard..." As the bow began to swing back, the ship bounced forward, shaking her hard enough to make people hold on to anything solid. Jack sat back down.

"Direct hit," announced Raulya. "No damage, stern shields down to sixty percent."

"A couple more of those and we're done for." said Walt, rather matter-of-factly.

"Helm, nose down!" The bow of the Freedom pitched forward. "Get those shields back up, Lieutenant." Jack knew she didn't need to be told, but it felt better to say it. The ship wavered as another volley of fire passed over the Freedom and glanced against the stern shields.

"Sixty-percent and holding..."

The Archer and the Bowman had taken up stern flanking positions to limit the Freedom's evasive maneuvers. It would only be a few moments until their gunners were able to predict their target's next move.

"Engineering to bridge, she's in the red now, I don't know how much longer she'll hold out..."

343

"Just a few more minutes, Chief, she's just got to hold..."

"I'm doing all I can, Jack, she just doesn't *have* any more."

"Hold on, Chief, just hold on!" The laser fire came in bursts now, bracketing above and below the Freedom's hull, as the helmsman did his best to be unpredictable. Laboring, she began to slow as her remaining engine began to overheat beyond its capacity to operate. She bucked hard under a direct hit, then another.

"StErn shields fifteen-percent..." Raulya's voice cracked, she preferred hand-to-hand combat.

The front moved faster toward them than they did to it. They were so close, Steele felt like he could reach out and touch it. "Just a little farther, baby..." he whispered. The deck shook hard under his seat, and the ship lurched sideways under a secondary explosion.

"Stern shields down!" yelled Raulya.

"We're still under power though," stated the Professor.

Jack punched the comm button. "What was that, Chief?"

"The rest of Number One just took a direct. It's completely gone. You got five minutes left on Number Three... tops." The connection beeped off.

"We're in! We're in!"

Jack looked up from his console as the nose penetrated the forward veils of the storm. "Quixetta, hard to port and nose down on my command." He was attempting to time it just right. "Stern turrets, are you still at stations?" He received confirmation that they were. "Evacuate. All but one; I need a volunteer as a spotter. We needed someone to tell us when we are completely enveloped, otherwise this might not work..."

"They're closing in." announced Raulya. "They don't want to lose us."

"Don't recharge," advised Jack, "but let the main turrets fire when they're in range." She nodded and relayed the message to the gunners.

"I've got ten-percent back on stern shields."

"Good." Jack rubbed his hands together nervously, "We just might make it yet."

"Fire!" Raulya commanded. The bridge crew could hear the distinct *zzwuump, zzwuump* of the main gun batteries on either side of the hull as they returned fire, vibrating the floor.

"Captain!" Startled, Steele looked up from his plot screen showing the fading positions of the three ships. Emerging from the squall line of the storm, was the bow of a carrier, so close, Jack figured he could heave a stone

as far. "It's UFW!" shouted Ragnaar. The logo on the hull nearly filled the screen.

"Hard to starboard!" ordered Jack, bringing the ships to pass port-to-port.

"Their weapons are on line..." breathed Raulya. "Their shields are up!"

"Bloody hell, we're sunk..." muttered the Professor.

Paul, Mike and Brian, stood open-mouthed, speechless at its size and bulk, the hull literally bristling with guns.

"How did they know?" asked Ensign Quixetta.

"They didn't..." To Jack, it was more a gut feeling than really knowing. "Stacell, open a channel, *quick!*" A moment later the face of a grizzled old officer, appeared on the screen, the picture broken and distorted from the storm's interference. Jack couldn't see the Vice Admiral's rank pips.

"This is the Conquest, what can I do for you, Captain?"

"Pirates!" shouted Jack, feigning terror. Actually he was closer to desperation, but it made for great inspiration. "Right behind us... Help us! Please, we're heavily damaged..."

"Easy, Captain, what are their coordinates?" Jack read off the coordinates for the two cruisers, and the Vice Admiral could hear the *zzwuump, zzwuump* of the Freedom's gun batteries in the background. "What kind of ship are you?"

Jack wanted to avoid that question. "Hurry, *please*," he pleaded, "our shields are down. One more hit and we're done for..!"

The Vice Admiral paused for a moment, trying to see Jack's face on his own screen through the distortion. He made his decision. He half turned toward his crew, "Battle stations" he said casually. The screen went blank.

"Cease fire!" instructed Jack. "Helm, swing to port and cross behind the carrier as we pass. Then straight again. We'll keep her between us and the cruisers." Steele took a deep breath as the carrier's guns flashed, throwing green and red streaks past the Freedom, making the nebulous clouds of ether flare and glow around them. "Sorry Kelarez," he said under his breath, "maybe some other time." He blinked hard and looked up but there was nothing left to see on his monitor. The storm obscured all. "Helm, drop to half power."

"Sir?" Ensign Quixetta turned in his seat. "We're adrift, I just lost all power."

"Shit." Jack fingered the comm button, "Chief?"

"Sorry Captain," came the reply, *"that's all she had left, she's done..."*

345

"Dammit. Alright, Quixetta, power up the thrusters, we need to put some distance between us." Steele hoped there would be enough confusion between the carrier and the cruisers that it would allow the Freedom to slip away before they could regroup and set up a search pattern. He watched the Ensign make the course adjustments and start the thrusters, but in the drifting, swirling clouds, the ship's movement was undetectable.

Static lightning flashed through the murk, and Jack turned his attention back to the comm. "Chief, you've got your work cut out for you. Use whatever parts you've got and see if you can bring one of those engines up. In about ten to twelve hours, we'll shut down and drift until we can get that other generator on line too. We might as well use this storm as cover..."

"Right." Trigoss paused. "Y'know I could really use some help down here, some good, strong backs."

"You got it, Chief." Jack keyed off. He stood up and ran his fingers through his hair as the tension begin to ebb. He took a deep cleansing breath. Thanks to God and a well placed storm, he'd managed it again.

Lightning flashed again and Steele narrowed his eyes at the momentary shapes in the swirling mass. Then nothing. He sighed and rubbed his eyes; he should let everyone stand down. Ragnaar had said these storms could last for hours. Even days. "Raula, let's relieve all..."

There was another flash of colored lightning and a jolt that sent him sprawling onto the floor of the command pit. "Stern shields are down!" he could hear Raulya saying. Her voice sounded hollow, underwater, distorted.

"Thrusters off line..." said another voice. Jack struggled to his knees, his world a wash of red. Holding the back of Ragnaar's seat he tried to regain his footing against the moving deck, but the peal of the bell in his head matched the pain above his left eye, where the skin puckered and the blood ran freely. The clamor that surged threatened to drown him, the world dissolving into a dull, fuzzy grayness.

CHAPTER TWENTY SIX

UFW LIBERATOR CLASS CRUISER, ARCHER: CALO ALTO SYSTEM

"Captain, we've struck something!"

Kelarez raised an eyebrow. "Really?" He waved his hand angrily, "How about telling me something *useful*... like a *damage report!*"

"Starboard engine nacelle heavily damaged," stated the engineer, saving the navigator from further rebuff. "That engine is off line."

"Get it back," growled Kelarez.

"Sorry, Captain," continued his First Engineer, "nothing we can do out here, it'll have to wait till we get back to base. It's external damage and it appears the hydrogen scoops are crushed and inoperable."

The UFW Commander slid back in his chair and silently cursed the Vice Admiral in the UFW carrier for ordering his ship into the storm. "First he shoots at us then he sends us into this mess... Take us out of this soup, Mr. Hanett."

"Yes, Sir!" The Ensign was as glad as anyone to be leaving the storm.

There was no way of telling what it was that they'd struck. The carrier, debris, Steele's ship... And at this point, what did it matter? Kelarez knew of only one instance of a ship being successfully tracked through an ether storm like this. The UFW destroyer had emerged in pirate territory, chasing his pirate quarry straight into a pirate fleet. The destroyer and its crew narrowly escaped, only by going back the way it came... into the storm.

The images of that armada flashed through Kelarez's mind. *Almost lost my ass on that one,* he reflected.

"Get your cruisers back in there, Captain! Find that bastard!" The Vice Admiral's lined face scowled at Kelarez from the view screen. "Nobody plays me for a fool!"

Of course not, you fat moron, thought Kelarez. "I'm sorry, sir, but between the damage you inflicted on us and damage from the collision, we must return to base for repairs." His voice was even and respectful, but his eyes spoke volumes of animosity for the man. The Vice Admiral was not a field commander, just a desk potato looking for a field service bar and a promotion before retirement. Vince Kelarez turned to his communications officer. "Ms. Notsobe, send a message to the Bowman, fall in, we're returning to base."

"You are a coward, Kelarek," spat the Vice Admiral, "I will see you court-martialed! I'll have your pips in my hand! I'll see that you lose your command!" He paused his tirade and turned away. "Tell the Bowman to get back here! Where's it going?!"

"Vice Admiral," interrupted Kelarez, "the Bowman is under my command and will only follow my orders. So I suggest if you want Steele's ship you'd better go in and get it yourself." He adjusted his tunic. "And if you're going to court-martial me, you'd better get my name right. It's *KELAREZ*, not Kelarek." He turned to his comm officer and drew a line across his throat with his thumb. She ended the videocom connection. "Navigation," he said, turning back. "Plot a course for Yarwa Station. Helm, take us there." Kelarez took a deep breath and relaxed as the Bowman pulled into cruising formation. The Captain was not a coward, not by a long shot. He just knew that sometimes discretion was the better part of valor.

"Think he'll catch Steele?" asked the navigator as they watched the carrier disappear back into the iridescent swirls of the ether storm.

"No," said Kelarez, "the Vice Admiral couldn't hope to catch a cold, standing naked on an ice planet in the middle of winter. Besides, Steele has too much luck." *He's good too,* he thought.

The Ensign nodded thoughtfully... "Do you think the Vice Admiral will really court-martial you?"

Kelarez ran his fingers across the row of gold pips on his collar. "I'm sure he'll try, but after we tell the brass at Phi Lanka he fired at his own cruisers, I think he'll cease to be a problem." Vince Kelarez had an exemplary and decorated field career. There were many benefits to this, primarily the honor of credibility that rose above mere rank.

He headed for his ready room to study his charts. *Good luck, Captain Steele,* he thought, *I look forward to meeting you again. Maybe someday we'll get a chance to tip a glass and toast to our health.* Kelarez couldn't help but admire the admittedly odd but tenacious Earth man.

After setting the program, Vince Kelarez sat back and put his feet up. He knew this might take awhile and closed his eyes. The holo-chart flickered on and began to search the vast stores of its memory to find in the great expanses of the universe, a quiet sector of space containing a small, little traveled planet... called Earth.

■ ■ ■

The first thing Steele noticed was the dull pain above his left eye that seemed to reach deep into his skull. Trying to open his eyes made it sharper, so he stopped. Wherever he was, it was warm, dark and very very quiet. He tried to think back, but that produced throbbing agony that made his head swim. As he lay there he slowly became aware of weight upon his body and the sound of steady breathing. He tried to reach out with his left hand and found that it was immobile. But his right hand was free... It felt as if it were made of lead, but at least it moved.

Steele dragged his arm up and touched the body that lay across his. "Fritz?" The weight shifted as the dog moved forward to nuzzle and lick his chin. Jack also found he could now move his left arm. "Hey, buddy..." He rubbed the Shepherd's coat, "Where are we...?"

"You're in sick bay," came a voice from across the room.

"Zat you, Doc?" Jack's speech was slow and slurred.

"No. Name's Lil Toncaresh. I'm an ABS, *Able Bodied Spaceman*. You can call me Lefty."

"Lefty?"

"Yeah," continued Toncaresh with a sigh, "lost my right arm in an explosion in Engine Room One, a few days ago. Doc tells me that animal with you saved my life. Wish I knew how to tell him, thanks."

"You just did," said Jack. "He udernerstan... unnerstanns... *understands*..." His mind unfocused and his tongue slow, he stumbled over his words. Jack felt guilty about the man's injuries and wondered if all the decisions he'd made lately had been good ones. "Sorry about your arm..."

The ABS shrugged. "It's OK. Doc says he'll fit me for a replacement in a few days. I'll be good as new. Hell, Commander Edgars has one and you can't even tell..." Toncaresh shifted in his bed. "How's your head..." he realized he didn't know the name of the man with the dog. "What *is* your name anyway?"

"This is Fritzzz..." He patted the dog. "I'm Jack. Jack Sssteele. And my head hurts like the blazes."

"Steele? As in *Captain* Steele?"

"That would be the one... but call me Jack. OK?"

"Uh... yeah, sure," he stammered. "Geez, sir, I mean Jack. We were all pulling for you..."

349

"Who all?"

"All of us here in sickbay," answered Toncaresh. "There's about ten of us here. We were worried. You've been out cold since you came in."

"Howww long have I been here?"

"This is the sixth day," said another voice.

"Six days..?" Jack tried to sit up but pain lanced through his brain in a sizzling white hot flash.

"His eyes!" said the second voice.

"Lay down, sir! *Lay down!*" urged Toncaresh.

Jack dropped back down to the pillow in agony. "Jesus!" he groaned. He brought his hands over his eyes to keep his head from exploding and felt the wires and IV lines emerging from under the bandages across his face. It took him several moments to recover, catch his breath and clear the pain. Then a chill raced up his back. "Who said eyes? What about my eyes? Oh God... am I blind?"

"No. No, not completely," said the second voice. "At least I don't think so..."

"We were awake when they bought you in," said Toncaresh. "The Doc said something about a fractured skull and your left eye..."

Jack ran his fingertips gingerly across the bandages producing a spike of pain where his left eye should be. "Oh God," he whispered. His left eye was gone, the tubes and lines seemed to run into the empty socket. "What happened?" he mumbled.

"We got rammed," said a third voice. "That's how most of us ended up here. Bounced around. You know."

"I am *so* sorry..." The bandage became wet around his right eye.

"For what?" asked the second voice. "It wasn't your fault. Besides, most are just bumps and bruises. Most people went right back to duty."

"Doc only lost two..." said the third.

"Shut up, you dope!" Hissed the second.

"Who?" shot Jack.

"Try to get some sleep, sir."

"God damn it, Toncaresh! Who?"

"ABS Mystic..." He paused.

"*And?!*"

"*Please,* sir..." pleaded the ABS.

"Who else, dammit!"

"Chief Engineer Trigoss..."

350

For a moment, there was silence. Steele's stomach knotted. "Aw damn...
Trigoss..." it was barely a whisper. "Damn. Damn, damn, damn..." He took a
deep breath to choke back a sob and swallowed hard. "What happened?"

Toncaresh's voice was deadpan. He liked the Captain and didn't want to
see him put himself through this. "The collision ruptured the interlink
connectors and started a fuel leak on two of the thrust engines. There was a
fire. Mystic was trapped and the Chief went in to get him. He didn't even
hesitate. They never came out..."

The three crewmen lay awake in their beds and listened to their Captain
cry himself to sleep grieving for the loss of a crew member - a friend. In a
moment of unspoken communication, they realized how much this man
cared and agreed never to reveal to anyone, what some might perceive to be
a moment of weakness. But they would never forget the compassion he
displayed.

CHAPTER TWENTY SEVEN

EARTH, CHICAGO ILLINOIS: *OH WHAT A TANGLED WEB WE WEAVE*

Lynnette Steele sat bolt upright in bed and stared wide-eyed into the darkness, cold with sweat. Sliding out from under the covers, she padded across the bedroom carpet, her flannel nightgown clinging damply and causing her a chill. She found comfort in the heavy robe she retrieved from the back of the bedroom door. Wrapping it tightly around her, she made her way through the darkened house, the only light coming through the dining room window from the streetlight outside. She stopped on her way back from the kitchen, brandy glass in hand and stared at the falling snow. The quiet Chicago side street was covered in a thick blanket of pure white. Clean and pristine, it sparkled in the light of the streetlights. She wondered if it was snowing where he was and tried not to think of his name because she knew it would make her cry. She shivered as a blast of wind whipped the snow against the windowpane, then sipped the brandy, letting it warm her, numb her, so she could sleep.

She was still there when Kyle found her. He put his arms around her, embracing her from behind and watched the swirling snow for a moment in silence. "Another nightmare?"

She sipped her brandy. "Uh huh."

He kissed the top of her head. "Are you alright?"

She patted his hand and nodded. "He's alive you know..."

"I know." Kyle learned long ago to trust her intuitions about certain things, but he also knew the realities and the inherent dangers involved in clandestine operations. He wanted to believe Jack was still alive, but he had serious doubts. Lynnette began having nightmares about a month ago, when more details of Jack's disappearance came to light via an old friend of Kyle's who was still in the FBI.

■ ■ ■

"He's in it way over his head, Kyle," said Cooper. "I'm sure he had no idea, they were just using him as a delivery boy. The CIA set up some convoluted, semi-legal operation, but it had some terrible snags which doomed it from the start. The whole thing was the brain child of some CIA big shot named Stephen Miles who cooked up this scheme to catch a Russian named Colonel Restonovich," explained Cooper. "He's KGB, supposedly backing someone in the Vasquez drug cartel somewhere in the Sao Palo area. "

"But the CIA is supposed to be limited to actions outside of the U.S. and its territories..."

"True," agreed Cooper, "but the principal was a Russian KGB agent, and Vasquez was a Brazilian national operating out of Sao Palo, Brazil. He was often in Puerto Rico and that's where things crossed the line, but they can rationalize that they were tracking a foreign national - the higher-ups will look the other way. We're supposed to share information across agency lines - but that rarely happens. Everybody's competing for budgetary allowances - the most successful agency gets the lion's share of the pot - nobody *wants* to share."

"What about the B-25?"asked Kyle, unmoved.

"Yes, well, Miles' personal pet project..." Cooper answered. "Evidently, it inspired an idea for disguising a large number of operatives in the same place at the same time. A movie set. The whole thing was a cover. But, of course, Restonovich and the Vasquez people already knew that."

"How?" wondered Kyle.

"Simple. A double agent. Miles routed all the planes through Puerto Rico where he had an agent posing as a mechanic. She would inspect and fuel the planes, make sure everything was ok. Well I don't know how the CIA got her, but she was a Soviet first and foremost. She's actually Cuban, posing as Puerto Rican. She's also Restonovich's niece. He lived and got married in Cuba during the missile crisis in the early sixties."

"Jesus..." sighed Kyle.

"Right," Cooper agreed, "double Jesus... Unofficially, her hand had been promised to Marcus Vasquez to solidify the deal between the Soviets and the cartel. She disappeared the same day as Jack, and Marcus was hopping mad. We only knew about her because Puerto Rico is basically American soil. Our fifty-first state, if you will, and we have agents there. The DEA was tracking Vasquez and as a co-op, asked us to watch a few players for them. Marianna was one of them." He took a moment to light a cigarette, then continued.

"Somehow, information about Jack's cargo leaked out, and someone on the island decided they wanted it. Or maybe it was the plane they wanted, doesn't really matter at this point. But it happened so fast our people couldn't do anything about it. And nobody's talking after the fact."

Cooper took a long drag on the cigarette and watched the smoke rise for a moment. "Your kid held a good account of himself though. As far as we can tell, he got out without a scratch. Final score, Kid: 12, Bad Guys: Zip. Hell of a kid, Kyle... hell of a kid." He paused, thinking.

Kyle studied him for a moment. "What happened then?"

Cooper shrugged as he stubbed out the cigarette in an ashtray. "It gets iffy here. They headed south, probably to avoid air traffic and were sighted over open water heading south somewhere along the British Virgin Islands by a couple of F-18s on patrol from the Shenandoah. The B-25 was visually confirmed, so we know the Hornets were up close, but communications between the carrier and the planes were problematic. Maybe storm interference. The three planes entered the weather front together... None came out. Or at least none were *seen* to come out."

Kyle threw up his hands. "So they wrote it off as UFOs? The Bermuda Triangle? Ghosts, gremlins? What..?"

Cooper shook his head. "The Navy doesn't take the loss of two multimillion dollar aircraft lightly. There's got to be an explanation, we just don't know what it is yet. Nobody's stopped looking... that's the dangerous part. Jack's officially cleared of the incident at the airport, I've seen to that. But Vasquez wants his bride back, the Soviets want their agent and Restonovich wants his niece. All *one in the same,* of course, but still, it's a lot of people looking. Not to mention the Navy and the CIA. Any one of these groups might kill him for any number of reasons."

Kyle had his hands steepled and was supporting his chin on his fingertips. "What are his chances if he's still alive?"

"Hard to say," said Cooper lighting another cigarette.

"Try," said Kyle.

"Honestly," said Cooper, inhaling on the cigarette, "there are so many variables it's impossible to tell. And that kid of yours is the biggest wild card in the deck. He's resourceful, and it appears... very lucky." The conversation turned to a series of situational comparisons. A myriad of *ifs* and *what if*s. The bottom line was the odds could swing wildly in any number of directions, but the safest place was with the FBI. Or so that's what they'd have the Steeles believe. Kyle wasn't sure if Jack wasn't better off staying invisible somewhere.

That's when the nightmares started, about a month ago. Lynnette hadn't said one word through the whole conversation. Sitting quietly, sipping her coffee, she watched with detachment as the two men discussed her only son's fate.

■ ■ ■

Shortly after that, the dreams and visions. He was far away. *Very far,* farther than he'd ever been. But he was alive, she knew that. Then the never ending darkness. At first she thought this meant death. But no, there were other things, wondrous things. Now there was distress. He was in trouble. And pain, that was the latest one. Blinding pain.

Lynnette took a deep breath and finished the brandy as she watched the wind swirl the snow around the cars parked at the curb. Neither she nor Kyle took notice of the dark blue sedan sitting down the street with its motor running, the only vehicle for blocks without a blanket of snow covering it. It, or the gray one, which was always around somewhere.

"Let's go back to bed," said Kyle. She nodded. He decided then, they'd go to Florida and spend the rest of the winter at Jack's. Maybe she'll feel better there, he thought. The winter had come early and the cold weather was already wearing on them both.

CHAPTER TWENTY EIGHT

FREEDOM: TULOCHAH SYSTEM, GEO ZEE - PIRATE SALVAGE
YARD

Steele drifted in and out, one day running into the next, inseparable and imperceptible in their passing except for the lessening of pain in his skull. Sometimes he would wake to feel a hand holding his, sometimes to voices, speaking softly. He came to the realization his bunk mates were disappearing one by one. But almost always, Fritz was there.

Alité sat in a chair at the side of the bed, her head resting on the edge of the mattress, her eyes closed. One hand held Jack's, their fingers intertwined, her other rested on Fritz's shoulder as he slept on the bed alongside his human.

She was awake the instant his hand squeezed hers, watching his face. The bandages, tubes, wires, all were gone now. All that remained was the surgical patch over his left eye socket. He would be in pain when he woke; the doctor had ended his medications. She moved her chair closer and hovered over him, squeezing his hand and kissing his arm. "C'mon, Jack, c'mon. Come back. We're waiting, we need you..."

"Sssshhh..." he whispered, "my head hurts."

"Oooh!" She squealed and jumped out of her chair. She leaned over and kissed his face over and over. Fritz was licking his chin.

He opened his eye and tried to focus in the dim light. "Where are we?"

"In our quarters," she replied. "CABL M7 thought you'd be more comfortable here. Besides, he needed the room."

"He likes it better when you call him Doc," mumbled Jack. "Why does he need more room?"

"For the refugees..."

"Refugees? *What* refugees? How long have I been here?"

"Look," she began, "I'm doing this badly. Let me start over..." She went on to explain that after the collision, the Freedom was adrift for almost a week, carried by the currents of the ether storm. After about a week the engineers were able to make sufficient enough repairs to restart two of the thrust engines.

Jack turned to look at her. "I guess I made a pretty good mess of things, haven't I?"

"Don't be silly," she scolded gently, "you did what you had to do to keep us all safe. If we would have surrendered, over half the crew could have been imprisoned. They knew that. The ones who used to be pirates would likely have faced life in a work prison... maybe even execution. You saved them and they know it. They speak of you in hushed tones, whispers. They almost worship you. You risked your life for them, they don't look at it the other way around. No one else has ever done that for them. No one else has ever cared..."

"But so many hurt..." He thought of Trigoss and swallowed hard.

"We lost two people... and saved a hundred..."

"The refugees?"

"Yes, you saved them too, without even knowing you did. If we had simply surrendered they would have starved to death, trapped here on a derelict ship with failing systems..."

"How did we find them...?"

"All of our sensors were useless in the storm, so when we got the engines started, we just went the direction we were pointed in. No destination, just go. When the storm cleared, we were here."

"Where's here?"

"The salvage depot you were looking for, of course." She kissed his hand.

"Of course," he mumbled, his mind reeling.

"We've been here since, making repairs."

"And the people?"

"We found them on one of the ships while we were looking for parts. Thirty seven of them, all good people. They've been stranded here for several months, but they're *ours* now." She smiled like they were her own children. "You would be so *proud* of the crew... *your* crew. They've worked so hard. I think they're trying to repay you. I just can't believe they're almost finished..."

Jack was puzzled. "Finished... With what?"

"The ship, sweetheart." She touched his face.

She must be talking about *some other ship*, thought Jack. He couldn't believe there was enough of the Freedom left to work on. "*Our* ship?"

"Yes. This ship, *your* ship."

"Good Lord, how long have I been here... A year?" He realized he'd asked that before but couldn't remember if there had been an answer.

"Well you've been here in our quarters about four days," she paused, "but it's been over four weeks since the collision."

"Collision... oh yeah..." he remembered it vaguely, or was it that he remembered being told about it... it was hard to separate the two. "Wait, did you say four weeks?"

She nodded, "More. Doc had to induce you into a coma for your own good..."

"Geez," he groaned, "all I did was fall down... I think."

Alité smiled, "Walt said you were thrown over ten feet. M7, er, Doc, said he was surprised your neck wasn't broken. When you landed, a broken piece of the console went through your eye and into your brain. You would have died if Ragnaar hadn't carried you straight into surgery. I heard he told Doc if he let you die, his life wasn't worth a plugged Ulurian nickel."

Jack smiled for the first time. "The Lieutenant has such a way with words..." As he stared at Alité's face and thanked whatever God was responsible for her presence, she held his hand to her lips and he saw the gold band on the ring finger of his own left hand. "What's that?" He asked trying to focus on it fully.

She lowered her eyes pensively, "I... I was so afraid you wouldn't come back to me... and I didn't think I could bear to live without at least a part of you." She sniffed. "So I took your name..." She held up her left hand to display her own ring. "You aren't angry, are you?"

"We're married...?" She nodded silently and Jack smiled, he felt warm all over. "How could I be angry with the most precious, beautiful creature in the known universe..." She held his hand against the smooth skin of her cheek and he could feel her blush. He smiled again, her eyes staring down into his, a warm amber, swimming with swirls of liquid chocolate. Mesmerizing.

"Besides," she cooed, "our baby needed a *sir* name."

"Baby?"

■ ■ ■

"Flight One to bridge..."

"This is Walt, go ahead Pappy."

"We've got company..."

"The UFW carrier again?"

"Negative. Definitely pirate. Looks like a cross between a destroyer and a small cruiser. There's another smaller ship with it."

358

"Right. Go to blackout status." He thumbed the comm button to address the Freedom's crew, ship-wide. *"This is an alert, all crew to battle stations. All systems to blackout status."* He repeated the announcement.

"Flight leader to all flights, blackout status, we've got company!"

The depot was nothing more than a vast field of ships, most of them wrecks, held by a harmonic-pulse stasis field around an automated central generator plant. The Freedom had found it by luck in an asteroid belt orbiting a planet called Geo Zee. The depot was easily two hundred miles across in any direction, being shaped as a sphere. When the Freedom had maneuvered in and shut down her engines, the depot's automatic system locked on and held them in place. There were ships of almost every shape, size, type and origin. Some were nothing more than hollow skeletons looking like a zebra carcass after the jackals and vultures had picked it clean. But there were just as many that were fairly intact with full bellies, ripe for the picking... it was these that the Freedom needed to salvage parts, supplies and equipment from.

All around the perimeter of the depot, the Freedom's fighters maneuvered into the shadows of the larger vessels and shutting down their systems, clung to the darkened hulks like a flea to a dog. Only their comm units would stay on, the pilots would breathe and be warmed by the two hour reserve of the ejection chairs their flight suits were tethered to.

The Freedom herself appeared to be a hulk, showing no signs of life. Her crew would breathe bottled air if needed, when the static supply ran low. This was the third time in as many weeks this exercise had to be used. The first two times to remain undetected by the UFW carrier which seemed to be so bent on their capture. Now from a pirate patrol. *Playing possum* as Pappy called it, would continue in strict radio silence until an all clear could be called.

Paul had latched his Lancia onto a derelict ore freighter of enormous proportions. He eyed the two ships approaching through his cockpit perspex, coming right at him. Even though he knew he was literally invisible to them, he felt uncomfortably exposed. The pirate cruiser slowed as they approached, but the smaller of the two, which Paul's computer had identified as a small, fast, armed supply vessel, continued its egress. The cruiser slowed to a stop just short of the depot perimeter, but Paul experienced a chill as he realized the supply ship intended to enter the depot, presumably to scrounge for parts. He held his breath and watched as the ship passed close enough for him to see the lights of the bridge.

Brian was on the opposite side of the depot two hundred miles from Paul and had a different view. He could not see the pirates, but he could see something else, and he could tell no one... the UFW carrier was *back*.

■ ■ ■

The lights flickered and went dim, staying at half power. "What's going on?" asked Jack.

"We must be going to battery backup," answered Alité.

Jack propped himself up on one elbow. "But why?"

"That pesky carrier keeps looking for us, he must be back again. But it's alright, we're safe. The Commander puts us on complete blackout status and that stupid carrier just wanders by. Paul calls it *playing possum*."

Jack smiled and nodded. "Of course he does."

■ ■ ■

"Starboard turret five to bridge."

"Bridge," answered Walt.

"Pirate supply vessel is visible about twelve miles off starboard stern quarter. It appears to be shutting down."

Walt Edgars sat back in his chair after acknowledging the gunner's report. "That's just bloody wonderful," he said to no one in particular. "Just how long do they intend to stay?" The same gunner called back some moments later to inform the bridge the vessel had just launched what appeared to be two shuttles. Commander Edgars was not pleased.

■ ■ ■

Brian watched in absolute horror as the carrier slowed and began to launch fighters outside the edge of the depot. He was too far to actually see the fighters clearly, but he could easily see the bright flares of light as each ignited its engines upon clearing the tubes. He was half tempted to switch on his computer to find out what type of fighters they were, but he knew this would broadcast his presence. He counted the flares as they appeared, ten fighters in all, grouped in two formations of five each. He lost them as they turned towards him, their engine flares no longer visible. What should he do? He fidgeted nervously and craning his neck, searched the darkened hulls around him. Can anyone else see them? He wondered if his hiding place was dark enough to hide him from the close scrutiny of a fighter. Then suddenly they were there, entering the depot... ten top-of-the-line Vulcan fighters.

Paul was twisted as far around in his seat as humanly possible, looking to see where the pirate's supply ship had gone to when he spied the shuttles gliding across the depot. To him it looked like they were angled toward the Freedom. "Oh for the love of God," he whispered to himself, "don't do that, *pleeease*." Then he looked around but could see none of his flight members. *Just everybody stay put...* he thought.

■ ■ ■

The gunners relayed through the Freedom's intership comm, the shuttles' movements. "Starboard turret five, they're passing right underneath me now. They're armored shuttles, good size, probably a 30 man shuttle at least."

"Port turret four, I see them now. They're really giving us the once over."

"Port five, looks like they're trying to find a place to board..."

■ ■ ■

The chills gave Brian the shakes as his body filled with adrenaline. He felt as obvious as an eleventh hour pimple - the one a teenager gets in the middle of the forehead an hour before a big date. The closest UFW fighter was only about a hundred meters away, close enough for Brian to see the figure of its pilot bathed in the glow of his electronics. Brian Carter forced his head back against the headrest and fought to control his breathing and the nervous energy which demanded to be let loose. The Vulcans slowly passed the Lancia, invisible in the shadows of the ruined tanker.

■ ■ ■

"Conquest Control to Flight Leader, progress report."

The flight leader of the Vulcans thumbed his comm button, "Flight Leader to Conquest," he hissed, "why don't you just take out an ad in the interstellar news and tell *every*one where we're at?" He released the comm button and shook his head. *What an ass* he thought. The Vice Admiral would surely get them all killed eventually. They had been out to this location five times this month without seeing a damn thing. The Vice Admiral was so obsessed with finding this rogue cruiser, he was taking risks and making mistakes that went beyond simple stupidity.

They were in pirate territory, alone, and navigated about recklessly and predictably, inviting a pirate task force ambush. He put it out of his mind and turned his attention back to the matter at hand; sneaking up on that cruiser... Hopefully it would be the right one and they could soon go back to regular duty.

■ ■ ■

Paul wiped the beads of sweat from his forehead as he watched the pirate cruiser angle towards him and the depot. He had lost the shuttles as they disappeared behind the Freedom, he hoped the pirate cruiser wasn't thinking of joining them. Then a sudden rush of fear swept him when fighters emerged from under the nose of the cruiser. "Oh God, we're in it now..." He flipped the safety covers off the engine igniters and locked them in the on position. He would do a cold start. He wondered just how fast he could get all his systems running, detach from the freighter, and get his shields up. More fighters emerged. Paul rolled his head around to loosen the muscles of his neck and held his thumb poised above the comm button. *OK boys...* he thought.

■ ■ ■

"Bridge to all stations... status, can anyone see what they're doing?"

"This is port turret three, they're not doing much of anything, sir. They stopped next to us and it looks like they've shut down."

The Professor sat back in his command chair and rubbed his chin. "I don't get it. Do you, Lieutenant?"

Ragnaar turned in his seat. "They could be waiting to ambush someone, sir..."

"Starboard turret six to bridge, *fighters!*" She was watching through hand viewers. "Coming in hot from the stern... Two flights of five!" She added, after counting. "They're headed right for us!"

"Bridge to all stations," announced Walt, "stand by to power up on my command..." He turned to Raulya, "Full shields too, my dear."

"Sir..!" Ragnaar's voice snapped the Commander around. "Sir, we have six more fighters, coming in from ahead!"

Walt rose from his seat. "All stations..."

"WAIT!" Everyone turned to the voice. Jack Steele stood in the doorway of the bridge, dressed in uniform and warmed by a flight jacket draped across his shoulders. Alité stood under one arm, keeping him steady on his feet. "If they were a threat to us," he continued, "they would have already hit us by now. Wait it out..." They watched in silence as the two flights of UFW Vulcans screamed over the top of the Freedom's hull then angled off to engage the approaching pirate fighters.

"How could you have been so sure?" asked Walt.

Jack shrugged weakly, "I wasn't - not a hundred percent anyway." He eased to the floor with Alité's help. "Whew... that was a long walk, I need a rest."

■ ■ ■

Paul took a deep breath and tried to swallow his heart when he saw the Vulcans. He was relieved and concerned at the same time if that was possible. It meant the Freedom hadn't been spotted, but for how long? He would just have to wait and see.

Fighters from both sides raced back and forth through the depot, zig-zagging around the wrecks held in stasis, the dogfight raging in tight swirls and running pursuits. Pirate after pirate fell to the guns of the UFW Vulcans. One hot pirate pilot managed to escape destruction by weaving his Falken fighter through the exposed engine supports of a rusting tanker. The pursuing Vulcan pilot wasn't lucky enough to make it through, his only legacy a blackened smear on the tanker's hull, pranged engine supports and some twisted, floating debris.

The pirate fighters were no match for the UFW Vulcans and even after launching additional fighters, could do little more than play hide and seek in a game of tag that encompassed the entire depot. Seeing the difficult position of his fighters and their dwindling number, the Captain of the pirate cruiser chose to withdraw and abandon his charge, the supply ship. Maybe he was actually hoping to draw off the carrier and let the smaller ship escape. In either case, the result was the carrier discarded its position of anonymity and took chase.

The Flight Leader of the UFW Vulcans caught the departure of his carrier on his sensor scope and broke off pursuit on a sure kill allowing the pirate pilot to escape death. "Leader to all Conquest birds, disengage! Repeat, disengage!" He wrenched the stick to avoid the hull of a darkened cruiser and did not notice the two shuttles hiding in its shadows.

"The Brass Clown has moved base," announced the flight leader, annoyed. "Repeat, base is *mobile!* Form on me!" He knew all flight communications were recorded, but at this point, he did not care. Nine of the ten original Vulcans broke free of the depot and resumed formation to pursue their carrier, which was dogging the pirate cruiser at full speed. The carrier had quite a lead on the fighters and wasn't slowing. The Flight Leader edged his throttle further. "Dammit! Why doesn't he just launch more fighters?" The Vulcan flight would be low on fuel when they overtook the Conquest and would be unable to land at that speed. The Flight Leader decided he would slow it down with laser fire if necessary. Then he would have a personal little chat with the Vice Admiral.

Shortly after leaving the depot, one of the Vulcan pilots began experiencing mechanical difficulties due to battle damage; his flight leader directed him back to the depot. He felt he would be safer hiding there than drifting out in the open and promised the young Ensign they would be back for him promptly. The flight leader didn't know it then, but they would not be returning for his younger brother.

As soon as the Vulcans had cleared the depot, the pirate shuttles returned to the supply ship with haste. As did the three remaining pirate fighters, landing carefully in the crowded little landing bay. The Captain of the supply vessel decided there was nothing here worth his ship or his life and made a rather reckless departure, obviously unnerved at the thought of having a UFW carrier returning to clean up any survivors. The pirates had lost nine fighters, the UFW lost one with one damaged.

■ ■ ■

From his fighter's position perched atop the bridge of a derelict destroyer, Lt. Commander Derrik Brighton had a pretty good view of most of the altercation. He watched over his shoulder through his canopy as the engine flare of the supply ship became a small white dot in the distance. *"We're all clear gents,"* he called over the fighter's comm channel. The Freedom's fighters began checking in one by one from all over the salvage yard. He flipped the switch for his antigravity and it bounced his Lancia off the derelict's surface. He flipped it back off and pulled in his landing gear, initiating his systems and lighting his engines.

"Bridge to all flights..." the tired voice made its way to the ears of all the pilots scattered around the salvage yard. "Nice job keeping it all together kids... C'mon home everybody, dinner's on the table."

Brian knew that voice. *"Skipper?"*

"Yeah, Bri, it's me."

Brian popped off the tanker hull and accelerated away with a snap roll. *"Yes!"*

"Mad Dog to Freedom, I have a single small inbound," Mike had just detached from the wreck of a rusting salvage carrier when his sensors' view cleared the bow. "Looks like a damaged Vulcan and it appears he's got no power. No engines."

"Copy, Mad Dog," replied Jack. "Keep him in view, we'll send out a shuttle for recovery." Pappy stayed with Mike and the rest of the fighters returned to the Freedom, passing an outgoing shuttle.

■ ■ ■

Ensign Duncan Taylor was a promising young UFW fighter pilot with three kills to his credit, but the fact that his beloved Vulcan was smoking like a chimney was not a reassuring sign and the likely prospect of having to eject was not an appetizing thought either. Life support in the fighter would run on batteries and continue from twenty four to thirty six hours. If he had to leave the cockpit... two, three hours tops. He tried to decide which was worse, the incessant smoke pouring from the electronics consoles or the fact he no longer controlled the craft. He had vented the cockpit and discharged the extinguisher canister but the smoke persisted. The only thing left was to open the canopy and deprive it of oxygen. Deciding to wait until he reached the depot which loomed ahead, it was getting more difficult to see what was actually outside. Ultimately, he hoped to coast to a stop, open the canopy and stay in the cockpit tied into the craft's support system.

■ ■ ■

"Doesn't look like he's got any control," commented Paul.

"If he doesn't, he's going to hit that ore freighter," answered Mike.

Myomerr pulled the rescue shuttle abreast of the two Lancias and watched the stricken Vulcan. "Isn't there anything we can do?" She felt horribly useless at that moment.

As the Vulcan grew closer, the canopy lifted up, followed by a brief puff of smoke, then nothing. The craft, canopy standing open, sailed straight toward the wrecked freighter, certain to be dashed into scrap. "C'mon, buddy," urged Mike under his breath, "eject... C'mon, any time now... *eject* damn you, *eject*!"

"He's trying to stay with his bird for the battery supply to run his suit." Paul looked to his left at the waiting shuttle. "Myomerr, flash your flood lights and move forward..."

"Copy that, Pappy." She moved the throttle forward and the Lancias slid ahead with her as she strobed the shuttle's floodlights. There was no way to know if the pilot had seen them. "C'mon buddy, see the pretty lights? Push the button, out you come..." She switched the color on the lights from white to amber. "Pretty lights coming to help you... get out of that piece of junk..."

They were close enough to see the pilot fairly clearly, and it appeared he was struggling with his harness. Finally wrenching himself free, he stood on his seat, ripping his plugs and lines free from the crippled Vulcan, climbed out and with his legs crouched, sprung off the side of his cockpit like a cliff diver trying to clear the rocks below. The fighter coasted unmanned and crushed itself against the stern of the bulk of the ore freighter, bouncing slowly away, looking like a tumbling, crumpled piece of tin foil. The pilot sailed free above the freighter's hull, waving his arms at the shuttle.

Myomerr nudged the shuttle's throttle forward. "Shuttle Three, the pilot is clear. I'm moving in for recovery."

■ ■ ■

Jack eased himself back into his command chair and relaxed. "I think we should pull out, Walt..."

"We're not quite finished yet, Jack. Another day or two and everything will be one hundred percent shipshape..."

Jack nodded slowly. "I know, Walt, and from what little I've seen, you've accomplished just short of a miracle. I'm amazed. And I'm sorry I wasn't here to help you."

The professor raised an eyebrow "It wasn't me, lad, they didn't do this for me - they did it for you. Let them finish."

"I just don't think we have the time, Walt. That was a pretty close call. My little voice is telling me that carrier will be back. If he's the same one that we ditched in the storm, you can be certain of it. We can't afford to be caught here. You saw how good those pilots were, and that carrier's got to hold at least forty or fifty fighters. They'll go over this depot yard with a fine tooth comb."

The professor nodded, he had learned to trust Jack's intuition. "I see your point. He's been here a few times, and they've launched fighters before, but they never got this close. He probably thought that pirate was us..."

Steele looked over the systems on his command screens and marveled at the extent of the improvements. He paged through the stats and system readouts, shaking his head in amazement over the changes. He reviewed the operational output for the rebuilt engines and the new generators, noting that they stood almost twenty percent above factory-new specifications. "Let's have Trigoss warm up the mains..." his voice trailing off as he realized his mistake; Trigoss was gone. He bowed his head and pinched the bridge of his nose, "Sorry, Walt. Maybe you'd better do this." He began to rise from his command chair.

Walter Edgars was not just any Professor, he held seven degrees including interstellar history, paleontology and psychology, and he knew the best thing for Jack was to get back in the saddle. He put his hand on Steele's shoulder, "It's alright my boy, you'll do just fine. Besides it'll do them good to hear your voice." Jack sighed heavily and allowed himself to slide back into the seat, Alité standing behind his chair. She watched her husband work through the pain.

"Bridge to engineering..."

"Engineering, Toncaresh here, go ahead..."

Jack smiled, happy to hear a familiar name. "Hello, Toncaresh." His voice was friendly, warm. "This is Captain Steele, would you be so kind as to warm up the mains."

"Yes *sir*, Captain!" The ABS's reply was almost jubilant. "How are you feeling, sir?"

"I have a headache my friend... but I'm glad to be vertical again."

"It's good to hear your voice, sir." Jack could actually hear him smiling. "Warmup will be complete in a little over two hours."

Steele pensively rubbed the patch over his left eye socket, "any way to cut that shorter? We really need to pull out as soon as possible."

There was momentary silence before Toncaresh spoke again, a light hiss in Jack's earpiece. "Well, we could shove off on thrust engines while we're warming - those we could light and bring online in about ten minutes... we'd be moving right away. Also, we could warm one main engine at a time, that would cut warmup down to about twenty-five, thirty minutes. The other two we could warm and ignite while under way..."

Jack glanced at the Professor who commented, "Splendid idea, simply right on," he nodded. "Sharp lad..."

Jack turned back to his console and keyed his mic. "Good idea Mr. Toncaresh. Do it."

■ ■ ■

UFW Ensign, Duncan Taylor, was just happy someone was there to pick him up. He marveled at his luck. But where did the shuttle come from? To which ship did it belong? To which *side*? The round, red and gold logo of the flying horse against a rising sun, meant nothing to him, and the name Freedom didn't ring a bell either. But alive, he reflected, was of course, after all, better than dead.

Myomerr was piloting the shuttle alone, Maria part of the fighter patrol, but she found the two ground crewmen assigned to her for rescue competent and eager. Dressed in an atmosphere suit and helmet, one poked his head into the two-seat cockpit. "He's clean, Ms. Myomerr, we're resealed and ready to go."

"Thanks, Dooby," she nodded inside her helmet. "Ask him if he'd like to sit up front with me..." She turned back to the controls as Dooby's head disappeared. Announcing her return to the Freedom while nudging up the throttles, she pulled off her helmet and laid it on the floor beside her seat.

Ensign Taylor stood in the doorway of the shuttle's cockpit. "Excuse me," he said politely, "your crewman said it was alright to sit up here?"

"Sure," replied Myomerr waving to the empty copilot's station, "have a seat."

"Am I a prisoner?" he asked as he sat down. "They took my sidearm."

"Depends on how you look at it..." She realized he was staring at her and stared back at his ice blue eyes, shiny white-blonde hair and chiseled features... He smelled like burnt electronics causing her to wrinkle her nose reflexively. "Do you feel like a prisoner?" She turned back to her controls.

He shrugged, "Not much." He studied her features and wondered what a prisoner felt like. "You're a Ketarian, aren't you?"

Myomerr nodded. "Yep. Why?"

Duncan smiled a boyish grin, "I've never seen one... you... your race I mean. You're very pretty."

368

"Thanks," she replied, "you're pretty cute yourself."

He extended his hand, "Duncan. Ensign Duncan Taylor to be exact. My friends call me Dunk. *You* can call me Dunk if you like..."

She shook his hand. "OK, Dunk. Ensign Myomerr. No second name, no nicknames." She angled toward the stern of the Freedom. "So what happened back there...?"

"I had an electrical fire, everything went dead, the ejection system included. Thank the Gods there was a manual emergency release on the canopy or I'd still be locked in there. I even had to cut through my damn belts."

"You might want to contact customer support about that, sounds like a warranty issue..." She grinned, her canine teeth showing, staring at him again briefly, then turned back to the controls and approached the stern of the Freedom to land.

"Yeah maybe, huh? Wait..." he grinned, pointing at her, "funny." Duncan stared at the open stern of the Freedom as it grew in the shuttle's windshield. "Has this thing been here the whole time?"

"Sure," she answered without braking her concentration. "About four weeks."

"We never noticed it. Hellion, I flew right *over* it and never noticed it..."

The Ketarian smiled, "You weren't supposed to. Bet you never saw our fighters either..."

"Fighters? What fighters?"

CHAPTER TWENTY NINE

FREEDOM, HESPERRIN SYSTEM : *METAMORPHOSIS*

Jack was stretched out on the couch in the quiet darkness of his ready room listening to the healthy rumble of the ship's engines. The only light in the room was provided by the holo-chart hovering above the conference table, a thousand-plus points of light shimmering like diamonds. But he was staring at the green line which ended at the glowing yellow cube at his end of the table. That was home. Fritz stirred where he lay on the couch across Jack's feet. The Shepherd made little noises in his sleep and his paws made running motions. In his mind, he chased noisy seagulls across a warm golden beach, watching them scatter. Then he ran into the surf to play.

Steele shifted his view from the holo-chart to the ceiling and pensively touched the black eye patch Doc had exchanged for the sterile white one. It made him look like a pirate and it would take some getting used to. He would prefer his sight back... without it, flying was out of the question. Doc had said something about how well he was healing but Jack had been too busy thinking about home to listen. He hadn't thought about it for months, but he wondered if his Cobra was still parked alongside of Brian's pickup in the back of the hangar at the airport. He fantasized about the feel of the car on solid ground, how it handled, how it felt and sounded.

Steele was asleep, the holo-chart still on, when Paul, Mike, Brian and Alité, entered his ready room from the bridge. Fritz was awake instantly, poised for defense over his friend's sleeping form. The long-haired Shepherd hadn't spoken much lately, the novelty of it having worn off. He'd reverted mostly back to his instincts and training in recent weeks and most of his memory and distinct personality had resurfaced as reliably as a fingerprint after sanding. Yet, he remained more than he once was and enjoyed his uniqueness. With the sense of discord he'd felt recently from LaNareef, the Shepherd rarely dropped his guard or left his friend's side.

Paul called up the lights after entering but only saw the dog in a relaxed position, the animal's acute sense of smell identifying the visitors as the door opened and before the lights. "Hello," said Fritz quietly, wagging his tail.

"Hello," replied Alité softly.

Mike, Paul and Brian, were studying the holo-chart. "What is it, Pappy?" asked Mike.

"Our route home."

"That must be our solar system," said Brian pointing at the yellow cube at the other end of the chart. Paul nodded in confirmation.

Mike was in awe. "It looks so far..."

"It is," mumbled Jack from the couch, his eye still closed. He swung his feet off the couch and sat up, slowly running his fingers through his hair. "But we'll make it." He rubbed the sleep from his right eye and adjusted his eye patch. "I'm hungry," he announced.

"I shouldn't be surprised," commented Alité, "you've been asleep for twelve hours."

"Awww, not again."

"It's OK, Skipper," said Brian, "you didn't miss anything. It's been real quiet. We're heading into the Hesperrin System soon."

"Since we can skip the trip all the way to UFW Blackmount in Feerocobi for repairs," added Paul, "we can stick to the less traveled routes if we wanted to."

Jack rose and stretched. "I can't focus on this on an empty stomach, anybody else hungry? I'm starved."

Mike grinned widely. "A man after my own heart."

"How ya' feelin' big guy?" Paul asked quietly, as they moved out onto the bridge.

Alité came up on Jack's blind side and took his hand. "I'm OK I guess," he replied. They crossed to the exit and continued down the corridor. "But I can't seem to help feeling a little sorry for myself. I haven't looked at it in a mirror yet... afraid to. And flying's out of the question..."

"We ought to stop and see Doc before we eat," said Alité, changing the subject.

"Geez," groaned Jack, "haven't I spent enough time in sickbay?"

"Just for a minute or two," added Paul. Mike, Brian and Fritz, trailed just behind.

"Alright, fine," sighed Steele. "Let's get it over so we can go see what Marna's got cooking in the galley. I guess my appetite's coming back - that's all I can seem to think about lately."

■ ■ ■

CABL M7 dried his hands on a sterile towel and walked over to where Jack sat, reclined in a contoured chair. "OK, Captain, let's have a look, shall we?"

Jack turned to Alité and the others. "Go wait outside, I don't want you to see..."

She squeezed his hand. "We already have, we're staying." Jack made a face of distaste. "Never mind that," she told him. "Go ahead, Doc." She'd remembered not to call him M7.

M7 removed the patch, opened Jack's sunken eyelids and examined the socket with his micro-zoom optical. The lens extended and produced a faint whir as M7 zoomed in. "Absolutely perfect..." he muttered. He straightened up and backed away. "I'm very good you know," he told Jack. "In fact, I'm exceptional," he smiled, pleased with himself. "It looks like," he said, turning away to a surgical implement caddy, "you're ready."

"For what?" inquired Jack, worried.

"For this, of course." Doc turned back and held up a small cylinder little more than an inch long, between his thumb and forefinger.

"What is it?"

M7 returned to where Jack sat and held out his rubber gloved hand. In it was a small metal cylinder with a tail of wires at one end. During closer scrutiny, Steele saw small rods along its sides and a convex lens wider than the cylinder at the other end. "It's your new eye," the doctor told him. "Temporary of course. We'll get you a more natural one later if you like." It looked much the same as the one Doc had, or even Fritz's, but it was smaller. "It won't stick out like mine does," said Doc. "You'll be able to close your eyes normally."

Jack was getting over his initial fear and studied it carefully. "How does it work?"

"Well, I had to put a small chip in your brain and wire it in," explained M7. "And we put little clips on your eye muscles. They'll hold onto these little rods which control the eye and hold it in." Jack was fascinated and said so. "It'll feel funny for awhile," he continued as he bent over Jack to put it in, "but you'll get used to it."

Using a long set of tweezers, M7 reached to the back of the empty eye socket and plugged the eye's tiny wiring connector into its mate. Jack jumped like he'd been shocked and suddenly realized he was seeing the palm of M7's hand. "Easy, Jack," he breathed. M7 glanced up at Alité. "Hold his head still..." he instructed. She complied and Jack could feel her closeness, which was reassuring. The room moved as M7 lifted the eye and inserted it. *Clikit, clikit, clikit...* One by one, Doc clipped the muscles onto the control rods, creating a great deal of discomfort for Jack. "Done!" he said, straightening up. He pulled a small vial from his pocket, and with it, put several drops of liquid on the eye's lens. "How's that?" he asked, backing away.

Jack blinked, both eyes tearing. "Wow..." he whispered, "I can see!" He stood up, a little wobbly at first and moved to a mirror. It didn't look natural, but it wasn't hideous either. The lens was shaped the same as the front of a real eye but it was all black, looking like a piece of shining, black opal. If he looked real close, he could see the mechanical iris inside. He smiled as the iris moved, "Neat..." He turned around. "Thanks, Doc. Thanks a lot!"

"Well I can only take part of the credit," said M7. "You'll have to thank Hecken Noer, he built the eye for you."

Jack didn't recognize the name. "Who's he?"

"Our new Chief Engineer," said Brian. "He was one of the refugees."

"The guy is brilliant," added Paul. "He's got the engines operating way beyond original specs," he said with an expansive wave of his hand.

"Says he can do our fighters like that too," added Mike.

Steele momentarily forgot his hunger, "Well let's go see Mr. Wizard..."

■ ■ ■

"He was down here earlier," explained Mike as the group stepped off the lift on deck four. "He was tinkering on one of the shuttles." Mike led them through the pilots' ready room and headed for the flight bay.

Jack, walking hand-in-hand with Alité, reflected on how much he'd missed with only one eye and what a tremendous gadget it was that he'd been given. When they passed through the doors into the flight bay, he was absorbed in his thoughts and was caught completely off-guard by the reception waiting for them. A throng of about a hundred people descended upon them, smiling, laughing, arms outstretched, embracing. Alité clung to Jack's hand though they could not see each other through the crowd.

Makeshift tables had been set up and laden with food. There was to be a banquet, right there, right then. Jack was warmed, energized by the hands that greeted him and the smiles that shined on him. Many faces he recognized, the pilots, his bridge crew, the flight crews... but many were new faces. Some of those shone brightest of all.

373

Jack and Alité were swept to the head of the table and deposited like shells on a beach by the surf. The crowd ebbed and found seats, the noise retreating with them. Jack and Alité stood at the end of the long table, the crowd standing quietly at their chosen places, pilots mixed with mechanics, technicians mixed with flight crew. Rank held no importance for this occasion. But old faces or new, they all proudly wore the Freedom's uniforms.

Jack cleared his voice and wiped the wetness from his eyes and cleared his throat, "I um..." he glanced at Alité then back to the faces, "have absolutely no idea what to say..."

There were scattered pockets of polite laughter. Then Ragnaar, halfway down the table, raised his glass. "To honor..." His voice, as large as the man, boomed in the expanse of the flight deck. The voices of the crew repeated the word in unison and drank.

"To Freedom," said Jack, raising his glass. The ritual repeated itself.

"To Captain Steele," said a voice from far down the table.

"Wait!" shouted Jack, holding up his hand. "I... I am *deeply* touched by your affection. In fact, I could never hope to find adequate words to express how much, but I don't want this to be about me. It can't be about me. This should be about all of us... about you. We have all risked our lives for one another..." he thought about Trigoss and the ABS named Mystic. "Some have given their lives..." He raised his glass. "It is to them... and to you, that I toast." He up-ended his glass and everyone else did likewise.

The food was excellent, as was Marna's norm. And as people ate their fill, some departed to relieve others on duty so they might attend and partake in the feast. With a desire to meet the new people and become familiar, Jack strolled about the table and filled empty wine glasses from a carafe he carried, chatting amiably as he went. When he got to Toncaresh, he recognized the voice but could not place the face.

"ABS Toncaresh," announced the young man with the artificial arm. He stood up and shook Jack's hand. "Glad to see you up and around, Captain..."

Jack smiled. "Thanks. It's good to meet the face behind the voice. By the way, how's the arm?"

Toncaresh rolled it around like a ball player loosening up. "Just fine, sir, sometimes I forget it's not real..." They talked for awhile longer before Jack moved on.

Toncaresh elbowed his new friend Marguin, a former refugee who now worked in the cargo bay. "I told you he was different..."

Marguin nodded, "He really seems to care..."

When Jack finally met Hecken Noer, he was not at all as Jack had pictured him; studious and collegiate looking. Instead, he was much older, probably in his early seventies, thin, with an unruly mop of silver-grey hair and matching eyebrows. At first glance, standing there in the long white lab coat, he gave the appearance of what one might picture as the typical *mad scientist*. But the old man quickly put that feeling to rest when he met Jack's gaze. He smiled a broad, warm smile that seemed to round out his face and his eyes danced and sparkled. Jack decided it made him look more like Santa Claus than a mad scientist. The two men shook hands and Jack was surprised he was not as frail as he looked; he had the grip and vigor of a young man. Hecken Noer began with an apology. "I am sorry, Captain, that I could not have done better..."

Jack was a bit puzzled. "With what?" he asked.

"With the eye of course," explained Hecken. "Had to make do for most of it. Basic odds and ends you know... no proper parts or tools. As soon as we have the right bits I'll build you a proper piece." His mannerisms were quick and birdlike, matching his quick halting speech.

Jack half smiled, half smirked. "Let me get this straight," he began, "you built this eye out of assorted spare parts?" He found this fact astonishing.

"No no no. It would not be so crude if I had. I had to fashion most of it."

"By hand...?" said Jack, thinking out loud. "Out of odds and ends... Just stuff you found lying around?"

"Quite." said Hecken Noer with a curt nod.

"Man, I'd love to see what you could do with the right stuff..."

The old man smiled like Santa Claus again, pointing at Jack. "Your own parents could never tell. I guarantee it."

Steele liked him already, admiring his self assuredness. "Thank you," he began, shaking the man's hand again, "for what you've already done. And if you care to make a list of what you need, somehow we'll find a way to get it for you..."

Hecken assured him it would be done.

Jack sat back in his chair and relaxed, watching the crew talk amongst themselves. It was the first moment he had taken to just look around. The flight bay had taken on a much different look since he saw it last, crowded with fighters, shuttles, supplies equipment and parts. Even ground vehicles. "Where the hell'd we get all this stuff?" he asked Alité in a whisper.

"Off of ships at the depot," she answered. "You ought to see the cargo hold... Lots more down there. We're almost full to capacity."

That's when Jack saw him, a shadow between the shuttles in their revetment. *"Voorlak..."* whispered Jack. He felt the Ancient's smile though he could not see his face.

"He says you must be careful when you get home," said Alité.

Jack's head whirled in her direction. "You've *seen* him?"

"Uh huh," she replied, staring at the swirls in her wine glass.

Jack looked back but the shadow was gone. He turned back to his wife and grabbed her hand. "When?"

"When you were in the infirmary," she replied, meeting his eyes. "He came to tell me to have faith, that you would come back to me... "

"What else did he say?"

She shrugged, "We talked..."

"About what..." He was torn between the thought that it felt like there was something she was avoiding, and the fact that she seemed to take his appearance so casually.

"He said things at home are not safe for you. We will not be able to stay, and you should be very careful while we're there. He said you might want to stay but I shouldn't let you." Jack's eyes widened. "He also said," she continued, "I cannot go home. My planet has fallen to severe unrest and local civil wars. There are traitors and spies everywhere. My father fears for the safety of the entire Royal family."

Jack looked down at his hands and back up, thinking about the fact that her brother and sister had been murdered in the life pod they'd been recovered in. He had decided not to tell her unless it became absolutely necessary and up to this point there didn't seem to be any reason to force her to re-live her grief or complicate her life. "Did he have anything good to say?"

She smiled. "He said you would live at a time when I thought you might not, he said it was *important* that *we* had found each other..." she leaned in toward him whispering, *"you and me..."* She sat back again. "He also told me, you were special."

Jack cocked an eyebrow, "Special?"

Alité smiled and ran her finger across his lips. "The word he used was *gifted.* But then again, he wasn't telling *me* anything I didn't already know." Jack smiled at her insinuation, but he wondered what Voorlak had actually meant by that.

■ ■ ■

It was several days later when Jack felt well enough to fly on patrol, that he strolled into flight briefing clad in his flight suit and carrying his helmet. He slipped quietly into the darkened room and sat in the back, wiping the thin layer of dust off his helmet with his sleeve. He was listening to Paul's instructions on patrol pattern and reminders of protocol when a figure in a UFW uniform entered and sat next to him.

"Pardon me, sir," began the young man, "I hope I'm not being too forward, but I was told I needed to talk to you if I wanted to fly..."

Jack looked at him in the darkness. "You're the Vulcan pilot we picked up, aren't you." It was more a statement than a question, Steele knew exactly who he was.

"Yes, sir." He extended his hand. "Ensign Duncan Taylor."

Jack took his hand and they shook. "Good to meet you, Duncan." He eyed the Ensign's human features. "I don't mean to be rude, but are you human?"

"Half," answered Duncan. "My father was human, my mother was Domarist."

Jack had heard of the Domarist and knew them to be intelligent and peace-loving. "If you're half Domarist, what're you doing out here flying a fighter?"

Duncan shrugged. "It's all I know. My older brother was *my* flight leader, and when he was my age, my father was *his* flight leader. I was even born on a carrier."

"Really..." Jack pondered. "Well tell me about your father."

Duncan thought for a moment. "Well I didn't know him very well... he died when I was still pretty young."

"Tell me what you remember."

"OK. As far as I know, he was always a pilot. When he came to the UFW, he had already flown in a military called the United States Navy. I'd never heard that name since, or knew where that was, until I talked to Lieutenant Warren and Commander Smiley. They told me they served there too and explained how you and they came to be out here. It's much the same as I remember my father telling it. The Lieutenant also explained you're returning home. I've always wanted to see where my father came from... meet his people. I've always wondered if they were as dedicated, as selfless as he was."

377

"Some are, some aren't," commented Jack. "About the same as out here I guess."

Duncan seemed to drift off for a moment, then snapped back. "He was killed about fifteen years ago during the battle for Lander's Cluster in the Omnecron Sector. My brother raised me since then." He paused again, searching for the right words. "Look, Captain, I think I know why you're asking all this, you want to know where my loyalties are. And I don't blame you, I would too."

"And?"

"I was doing my job before," stated Duncan. "I took my orders with faith and executed them to the best of my abilities, with intelligence and integrity. But it's obvious to me the Vice Admiral was mistaken. You are no more criminals or pirates than I. In fact, I see the same qualities I saw in my father... and my father was a good man."

"And what if we have to defend ourselves from the UFW before we can straighten this all out?" *If we can straighten this all out,* thought Jack.

Ensign Taylor considered this for a minute, it wasn't something he'd honestly thought of before. "Well, I feel at home here. And you're closer to being *my people* than anyone could ever be. So if you say defend, then I defend. If my brother was here, I think he would feel the same." He pinched his lower lip for a second then continued with his eyes closed, reciting from memory, "Defend what you know in your heart to be right and let no other deprive you of your given freedoms with false claims of what is just or unjust." Duncan opened his eyes again. "A man named Voorlak told me that. I think he was a Wiseman of some kind..."

Jack's eyes widened then crinkled at the corners as he smiled. "Indeed!" *Will wonders never cease,* thought Jack. He adjusted the helmet sitting in his lap and offered his hand to the Ensign. "Welcome to the *Freedom Fighters,* Mr. Taylor."

■ ■ ■

Paul, his helmet tucked under one arm, pulled on his gloves as he walked across the flight deck next to Jack. "Didn't think you'd be flying for a while yet..."

Jack shrugged as he pulled on his own gloves. "I was starting to go stir crazy, I need to get out."

Paul nodded. "Yeah, I know... it'll do you some good. So, you're going to let the kid fly, huh?"

Anyone good enough for Voorlak is aces with me, thought Jack. "Yeah, why not, seems like a good kid. By the way, I didn't see LaNareef at briefing, where is he?"

"No idea," said Paul. "He's acting a little weird too. Do yourself a favor, Jack, keep an eye on him when he's around. Don't turn your back on him."

Steele paused while he slid his helmet on then continued to walk. "What's his problem anyway?"

"I don't know," said Paul, "I just don't trust him." They stopped at the ladder to the cockpit of Jack's Lancia and Paul turned as Ensign Taylor emerged from the ready room in flight gear. "Pretty amazing, huh?"

"What?" said Jack, missing the left turn of the conversation.

"The kid," said Paul.

Jack glanced at the approaching Ensign then back to Paul. "What about him?" asked Jack.

"Well, his dad being Lieutenant Charles Taylor," said Paul, as Jack turned away.

"So? Who's Charles Taylor?" asked Jack absentmindedly as he checked his fighter.

Paul sighed. "Lieutenant Charles C. Taylor, December 5th 1945. He was the Flight leader of Flight 19." He watched Jack's blank look and continued. "A flight of five Navy Avenger torpedo bombers, departs from Ft. Lauderdale Naval Air Station about two in the afternoon for practice bombing and navigational exercises... and disappears over the Bermuda Triangle... A Martin Mariner PBM Flying Boat disappears the same day searching for them. A total of six planes and twenty seven men in a space of about four or five hours... Stop me when any of this rings a bell."

Jack was staring wide-eyed at him now. He had remembered reading that story as well as dozens of others, the topic had always fascinated him. "You're kidding!" Paul was shaking his head no. "Jesus..." said Jack, straightening up. "And he spent his life fighting for the UFW..." he pulled his helmet off and shook his head. "It makes you wonder how many of us are really out here..."

"It makes *me* wonder if these disappearances are more on purpose than by accident," said Paul.

"Because so many of them are military," said Jack, catching up. "Like they're looking for special people..." His voice trailed off, remembering what Alité said Voorlak had told her about him being special.

"Right," confirmed Paul. "Warriors, leaders..."

"What about the regular abductions?" interrupted Jack. "The regular people who get taken away and returned?"

Paul slid his helmet on. "I haven't figured that out yet. Maybe they're trying to figure out how to breed their own warriors. I remember reading about abductees recalling medical exams and even sexual encounters."

Jack put his helmet back on. "Y'know, I always used to wonder about that stuff before... but now, so much makes sense..."

"I know what you mean," said Paul heading for his own fighter.

As Jack climbed the ladder to his cockpit, he decided it would be something to ask the Professor about. If anybody would know more about personal abductions, it would probably be Walt.

■ ■ ■

"Sure," said Walt leaning back in the sofa and lighting his pipe. "I know exactly who you're talking about." He watched the smoke curl away, and Jack came back from the bar with two full drinks and handed one to Paul.

Brian paced around Jack's quarters like a caged animal. "Sit down," said Mike, "you're driving me crazy."

"Sorry." Brian plopped himself onto the sofa on the other end from the Professor next to Derrik.

"You were about to say who," prompted Paul.

"Ah, yes. Well, it's got to be the Acrilee and the Baltec, doesn't it." It was a statement, not a question. "Except the poor sods who get snatched would never know that, of course. They look so much alike, nobody ever notices their physique is different. They just remember the triangular faces, gray-green skin, big black almond shaped eyes... the standard rubbish you generally hear." He puffed on his pipe, the smoke was sweet and aromatic. "Occasionally there are reports on more, but since they may not coincide with what is believed to be the norm, they are discounted as a hoax or a lie, when it's simply a different species."

"I don't get it," said Brian. "From everything I've read, they're either the typical *little green men*, like three feet tall or something, or their tall and really skinny. Which is it?"

380

"Both," said the Professor, expelling smoke from his mouth. "That's just what I was trying to explain to you..."

"Well then," interrupted Mike, "why can't we... you, they, whomever is being abducted, just smack the little suckers in the mouth and walk off? Why are we... they, you know what I mean, why are humans so powerless to resist abduction?"

Walt had ceased his puffing and lifted an eyebrow. "Why did you say we?"

Mike shrugged, "I dunno'."

"I think you do," said Walt, setting the smoldering pipe in an ashtray. "Come here." Mike hesitated and glanced at the others. "Come here, lad," said Walt in a fatherly fashion. Mike rose obediently and moved around the coffee table, where the Professor had him sit on the sofa with his back to him. "Hmmm," said Walt. He inspected the back of Mike's head where the spine connected to the skull. "Ahhh, just as I thought." He parted Mike's hair to reveal a mole about four millimeters across.

"It's a mole," said Paul, moving closer.

"Not bloody likely," said Walt. "It's a homing beacon. Under the skin just beneath it is a control chip about the size of your little fingernail. First abductions are done as children. The chips are to locate and control after adulthood so they can harvest when they're ready. To them, the human male is like a gorilla is to you. Without the control chip, you could simply rip them limb from limb."

Jack cleared his throat. "I'm almost afraid to ask, but what do they harvest?"

"It's harmless really," began Walt, "at least physically. Mentally it scars some people who begin to remember when the chip's power runs low, usually about twenty or thirty years after it's placed. But I digress. They are harvesting genes. Some human, some animal."

"What the hell for?" asked Paul.

Mike leaned back against the couch. "They're sterile," he mumbled, a faraway look in his eyes.

"You're remembering," said the Professor. Mike nodded. "He's right, of course," continued Walt, retrieving his pipe. "They've been around Earth for thousands of years, they're scientists. At first they studied man to understand themselves more fully, grasp their past..." he re-lit his pipe. "Now they've reached their height of evolution, every species does eventually, the same cycle they all take... they're dying."

"Dying?" repeated Jack. "But why?"

"They've evolved to the point where the thirst for knowledge is all consuming. And in that drive for wisdom and knowledge, they forgot themselves, forgot the simple things."

"No children," said Mike quietly.

"Quite," said Walt. "They forgot about sexuality, procreation, enjoyment... Sad actually, a good boff now and again does so much for your general well being. Anyway, they've been using human sperm and eggs to produce their own young, with a few DNA alterations, of course. Then their young adults return to learn and have sex with humans, hoping to create natural offspring no doubt. It's not a bad plan, but it has serious flaws. Mainly, the DNA they're using is their own, and since they have no early DNA maps to work from, from a time they were actually fertile, they produce sterile children. They're doomed to extinction eventually I'm afraid."

"Isn't there anything that can be done?" asked Jack.

"Theoretically yes..." began the Professor. "Unfortunately the key to breaking that chain of events or preventing the chain from initially occurring has been lost over eons and eons of time and has yet to be rediscovered." He paused to stare at the glowing embers in his pipe. "Do you remember when we discussed a place called Base Alpha?"

"At dinner once, I think," said Jack. "Why?"

"Well," began Walt "that's where scientists believe *all life* in the universe originally began..."

"Is that where the *Big Bang* took place?" asked Brian.

Shaking his head, Walt tamped fresh tobacco into his pipe. "Not necessarily. It is believed the *Bang* only formed the stars, planets and universe. We theorize life actually began millions of years after that. It was on one of these original planets that had just the right conditions to nurture life, that it was born. Or placed by the Gods," he added. "In either case, that's referred to as *Base Alpha*. We believe we will find the key there."

"Yeah but with all the different life on all the different planets out here," said Paul, "how could you possibly hope to find the right one?"

"Well it's even worse than that, my boy, there are thousands of planets out there that have died but held life previously..."

"Sounds kinda hopeless to me," said Jack.

"Not quite," corrected Walt, "you just have to think like a detective and look for clues." He re-lit his pipe and savored the smoke before continuing. "You see, everything goes through a cycle; birth, life, death and rebirth.

Planets, continents, civilizations, even solar systems... over different time periods, of course, but they all tie in with one another."

"I'm not sure I understand, Uncle," said Derrik, his brow furrowed. "How did life get to the other planets?"

"Well, plant life existed in one form or another on many planets, but intelligent life started on Base Alpha. By the time the Alphan's civilization had progressed to the point of interstellar space travel, their planet was dying. So they ventured outward, looking for new planets to colonize and preserve their existence. As this occurred, the new civilizations they created went through a degeneration and rebirth process, losing then relearning technology. For instance, when they arrive, they are the most technological beings on the planet. But without trade or manufacturing, they have to cannibalize their technology to survive. They deal with weather, famine and new illnesses until they become accustomed to their new environment. The technology disappears and civilization as they know it must be recreated. From scratch. Personally I believe that's what happened on Earth with Atlantis... The Nazca Lines for instance, correspond with some of our star charts; an early attempt to record their origins and signal possible visitors of their location." He paused to puff a billowing cloud of rich aromatic smoke, watching it dissipate. "Earth will eventually reach the technological level where they can move outward... whether they create it themselves or someone hands it to them."

Walt dropped a pinch more tobacco into the pipe and tamped it down as everyone sat quietly waiting for him to continue. "If you think of each civilization as a pebble and the reaction it causes when you drop it into a pond, you will remember that they produce outwardly moving ripples. Well soon there were three pebbles, then ten, then fifty, later a hundred... all moving out and about. As planets die, others are born and yet again others reborn. The cycle goes on."

"So then you are saying all intelligent life descended from one race, one planet?" asked Paul.

"Yes," was the Professor's simple answer. "We've changed, of course," he waved, "adapting to our unique environments. But we're all brothers under the skin, so to speak."

"And somewhere in there, all those civilizations, the key to the prevention of eventual extinction was lost," guessed Jack.

"For the Acrilee and the Baltec, yes."

"And you truly expect to find Base Alpha?" To Jack it sounded more hopeless than before.

"All we have to do is track those civilizations backwards," said Walt confidently. "The answer will be there."

This was a lot to absorb in such a short time, destroying most of the theories they had been taught and had grown up with. Hell, most people didn't even believe in extraterrestrial life, and here they were, finding out they were even related to it. The pilots sat quietly and sipped their drinks.

Walt glanced at his watch. "Oh, heavens, I'm due on the bridge! I've got to go." He headed for the door trailing puffs of sweet smoke.

"Wait a minute," called Steele, "you can't just dump all this information and run out the door, I have a ton of questions..."

"You're not the only one," remarked Brian.

"Duty calls lads. I'm sure we'll talk more on this later... Oh, by the way," he said pointing with his pipe, "I'm guessing you all have those little Acrilee or Baltec tracking buggers stuck on your heads; go see Doc and have them removed." The door swished closed behind him cutting the cloud of pipe smoke in half.

He was right, except for Derrik, they all had them.

CHAPTER THIRTY

FREEDOM: TONTURIN SPINDLE SPACEPORT, TYREEA SECTOR

The Freedom had been docked at Tonturin for almost a week, taking on supplies and trading some of what they'd recovered from the pirate depot for *Interstellar Trade Credits* or ITCs as they were called; a monetary unit that was constant almost anywhere. From the profits, the crew was paid a comfortable salary and was happily spending it at the hundreds of shops and restaurants on the station.

Tyreea was a quiet sector, rich in trade and completely neutral in UFW/pirate conflicts. Jack compared it with WWII era Switzerland and wondered how that precarious position was mastered and maintained.

Strange dreams plagued Jack's sleep for a week or two after the removal of the Acrilee's homing beacon and control chip, but the truth was not so shocking or uncertain as it would be for someone back home. His mind quickly accepted and regained its normal equilibrium, as did Paul, Mike and Brian.

The four pilots sat in the sand and watched the waves roll in from the artificial ocean, watching Fritz run through the water. "Y'know, I was hoping to be home by Christmas," said Jack, watching a handful of sand run through his fingers.

"Yeah," said Brian, "but who knew that star in the Pitkin System would go super Nova..."

"Or that we'd have to escort that Brugarian freighter two weeks out of our way," added Mike.

"Yeah," interrupted Paul, "but they paid us good money for that."

"I guess for the most part," said Jack, "we're not doing too badly." He watched Ragnaar practice hand-to-hand combat with an invisible opponent, further down the beach.

"So, what did you get her for Christmas, Jack?" asked Brian, changing the subject and breaking the silence. Jack dug a small box out of his jacket pocket and opened it for all of them to see. The large triangular stone sparkled with an intense fire.

Mike let out a low whistle. "Nice rock! Is it a diamond?"

"Well," said Jack, "they have another name for it, but basically yes, it's a real diamond. Think she'll like it?"

"Hell, yeah!" exclaimed Paul, "give it to me and *I'll* marry you!" He made a kiss face and Jack pushed him away as the others laughed.

"Hey!" whispered Mike urgently. "Put it away, here she comes!" Jack stuffed it back in his pocket.

Alité strolled up, a small shopping bag in her hand and Jack gave her a hand as she lowered herself to the sand. She sat cross legged next to him and rubbed her round belly. "Only two more months," she announced, "I'm not sure I can wait that long."

"You're lucky," Mike told her. "Human women carry for nine months."

She shook her head. "I can't imagine it. It must be torture."

"That's what I hear," said Brian. Everybody laughed.

"Merry Christmas," Jack told her. He pressed the small satin covered box into her hand. He had explained the reasons and customs of Christmas about a week before.

"For *me*?" she squealed. "What is it?"

"Open it and you'll find out."

The little box protested with a tiny squeak and her eyes sparkled a curious green as she lifted the lid. "Oh my," she sighed. A tear ran down her cheek.

Jack's heart dropped. "You don't like it..." He should have known better than to try to buy jewelry for a Princess.

"Oh no," she breathed, "it's beautiful."

"But..." He indicated her tears as he pulled the ring from the box to put on her finger.

Alité smiled as he slipped it on her. "I never had a ring before... a Princess is not allowed to wear one until she's betrothed or married." She kissed him. "It's simply the most beautiful thing I've ever seen."

Paul nudged Mike and Brian. "Let's take a walk," he whispered. The three men departed quietly, and Fritz followed them down the beach.

"Now you," said Alité, handing Jack the bag she held.

From it, Jack drew out a robe of heavy blue satin, detailed with dark blue velvet and richly embroidered in gold on the breast pocket and around the cuffs. His initials and a crown adorned the pocket. It was unquestionably the finest robe he'd ever seen. He smiled broadly and held it up, *"Truly* a robe fit for a k..."

"Prince," she interrupted, her eyes now a sparkling azure blue. *"My* Prince."

"Well isn't this sweet..." Sitting in the sand, neither Jack nor Alité had seen or heard LaNareef approach. Jack turned. "No, no, Captain, don't get up. I want to remember you just like this..." a Mercon blaster dangled from his right hand. "You aren't worthy of this woman. You disgust me. You aren't even Velorian." LaNareef raised the barrel of the blaster and pointed it at Jack's chest. Jack had the strange feeling he'd been there before, but in the stress of the moment could not pinpoint why.

"What are you doing LaNareef..?" asked Alité cautiously.

"I am going to kill him," he replied bluntly. "Then I will kill his bastard child..." He pointed the gun at her. "Because in the eyes of the Royal court, you are not really married..."

LaNareef was well out of Jack's reach and rock solid. Completely cool. Jack had no expectations of being able to draw him off guard. He looked around the beach for help but saw no one, the stretch of sand was completely deserted, artificial dusk was approaching.

"And then," continued LaNareef, "I will kill *you*, Princess. Because you are a dirty slut and have disgraced our people. You are a *traitor.*" The hair on the back of Jack's neck stood up and he shifted his position. LaNareef smoothly moved the blaster back to bear on Jack. "Please, Captain, I would enjoy that." He clicked the blaster's safety off. "It would give me great pleasure to kill you in an attempt to attack me." He sighed. "No? Oh well..." He appeared to be thinking for a moment, then added, "You know... perhaps I would let you go if you begged me to spare your life... of course, I would still have to dispose of her."

"Dream on," growled Jack. His fingers dug into the sand, he wondered how fast he could throw it and roll. He worked his other hand out from Alité's grasp.

"Say goodbye, Captain..." said LaNareef coldly. He rested his finger against the trigger.

Jack tensed and held his breath, his hand clutching the sand, unsure how to time his actions.

There was a brief fraction of a second when a large shadow crossed them... Jack's mind raced ahead, all time slowed down. LaNareef squeezed the trigger and the beam of the blaster lanced out... his feet levitating off the sand. The hot crimson streak passed above Jack's head and he could hear the electric sizzle. The couple looked on, as the hapless LaNareef continued to rise from the sand, arms flailing, the blaster dropping to the sand.

Ragnaar snarled, a sound equal to that of a full grown male lion as he lifted LaNareef from behind. LaNareef screamed in agony as the fingers that pierced the muscles of his back squeezed his spine like a pneumatic vice. His cry cut short to a strangled gurgle as Ragnaar's other hand crushed his windpipe.

Raising LaNareef above his head, Ragnaar violently wrenched his helpless victim, crushing and breaking his neck and snapping his spine simultaneously. He tossed the lifeless body into a heap on the sand. "Traitor," he snarled. He turned to Jack and Alité who still sat in the sand, stunned. "Are you alright, Captain? Miss Alité?"

"Fine," said Jack in amazement. He took the hand offered him and rose from the sand. He pulled Alité up with him. "How did you do that, Lieutenant? I never heard you." He wiped LaNareef's blood from Ragnaar's hand on his own pants.

"Practice," said Ragnaar. "I couldn't let you see me either, or he might have known and killed you before I reached him." He leaned over and picked up the blaster off the ground. He straightened up and kicked sand on LaNareef's body. "Honorless trash," he told the corpse before turning away. "You were never alone," he assured them, as they walked across the beach. "Ever." He pointed at Fritz, the other pilots and three of the Freedom's security personnel who ran towards them through the sand.

"As you know," explained Ragnaar, "weapons are not allowed on the station. We knew he would try for you today when one of our security people saw him purchase the blaster from a black marketeer this morning. All we had to do was give him an opening to get him to commit himself..." He handed the confiscated weapon to a security woman from the space station. "Sorry I could not tell you what we were doing..."

Jack wiped the sweat from his forehead. "Don't apologize for success, Lieutenant. Not ever." He extended his hand. "Thanks. I owe you one." The story of the Lieutenant carrying him into the sickbay after the collision flashed through his mind. "It occurs to me that I owe you two...

Ragnaar paused and shrugged, smiling, "Who's counting?"

■ ■ ■

The crew of the Freedom thoroughly enjoyed their time off at the spaceport, recreating, studying or sending messages to family and loved ones.

Slivers of information on InterGal News suggested warring religious factions on Alité's planet had split the population into several main segments. It was thought but unproven that LaNareef might have been a member of a fanatical organization dedicated to the preservation of racial purity on Veloria. Alité had chosen to believe the conflict between their friendship and his strict beliefs drove him to the point of madness. After the Freedom departed, the incident at Tonturin Spindle Spaceport was never mentioned again.

Time came and went and so did the Genesis Gates and systems, mostly unnoticed as the crew strove to maintain and perfect the Freedom. With the aid of Professor Edgar's software abilities and Hecken Noer's hardware wizardry, the Freedom's sensor array improved to exceed even UFW technology and her engines could match the speed of even the newest ships.

The fighter squadron had taken on a confidant and fluid appearance, becoming more cohesive and practiced. As a point of pride, each pilot had his or her own fighter, complete with their names and kill badges listed on the fuselage near the cockpit. Several new pilots had been recruited from the crew and could be seen training daily in the flight bay.

The sectors were fairly quiet and other ships were for the most part, few and far between. From time to time, this uneasy quiet gave Jack a feeling of great foreboding for which he had no concrete reason. Several times they passed warships from one side or the other, hustling off to some urgent destination. But never once was the Freedom considered a threat or challenged. A yellow alert was an occasional occurrence. A red alert was a rarity.

The only sector of any consequence was the Verondo Sector. A UFW convoy stretched for about two hundred miles, patrolled by destroyers and heavily armed gunships. The Freedom's crew counted close to seventy vessels of all sizes. Something monumental was going on and it was uncomfortable for Jack to think about how close it was to home.

A day later they spotted a pair of battered, battle-blackened pirate cruisers which passed at a distance great enough for the Freedom to be invisible to them, but close enough for the Freedom's sensors to be able to see them quite clearly. It would have been possible for the Freedom to steal close enough for a quick fighter strike that would incapacitate or even destroy them, but the Freedom was on a mission. They were going home.

Two days later came the biggest event since their departure from Tonturin Spindle Spaceport... the birth of Colton Thomas Steele.

CHAPTER THIRTY ONE

NORTHERN UNITED STATES: *FROSTY RECEPTION*

The northern half of the United States was blanketed in a late Winter storm, the kind Mother Nature saves up for. It always seemed the worst snows came in the death throes of winter, when it refused to give way to the passage of time and yield to the coming of Spring. If that wasn't severe enough, the broadcaster on the Late News announced, the Arctic cold and heavy snow was causing rolling brown-outs around the Great Lakes where the storm was the worst, something they nicknamed a *Polar Vortex.* Fancy words for a shit-ton of snow.

The Chicago area was covered in over twelve inches of fresh snow and the storm was dumping more with no sign of letting up, the winds creating artistic drifts around every obstacle. The plow crews would have their hands full in the morning.

The Invader was a cross between a shuttle and a gunship. Smaller than a shuttle, it was faster, heavily armored, well armed and specially designed for forays into hostile or unknown territory, capable of holding a crew of three and ten troops or passengers. Presently it held five; Jack, Brian, Mike, Paul and Alité... six if you counted Fritz, carrying them down through the clouds over Lake Michigan. Its dark form and sharp menacing angular lines gave it a particularly evil look.

"Man, this crap is thicker than pea soup." Steele leaned forward and adjusted the range of his forward sensor sweep pattern. "I can't see a damn thing..." he was flying on instruments and 3D image mapping only.

"I sure wouldn't want to be flying a regular bird in this stuff," Brian commented from the copilot's seat.

Jack looked out the cockpit window at the stubby wings covered in ice. "We'd drop like a stone..." he observed. The Invader was flying on a combination of standard flight principles and antigravity. The wings and tailfins were more for steerage in atmosphere than anything else.

"You'll drop free of the clouds in twenty seconds," Mike announced from the navigation and advanced sensor station behind Jack.

"Any air traffic?"

"None. Looks like O'Hare and Midway are both socked in. Everything's grounded."

"Good." Jack pulled the Invader's nose up and level at about a thousand feet from the surface of the mostly frozen lake and nudged the throttles forward. The shoreline was barely visible through the densely falling snow as they flashed over the northern Chicago suburb of what Jack estimated to be Winnetka. A rolling brown-out followed the Invader along the coastline like a strange shadow, streetlights flickering off then back on again as it passed.

The lights of downtown Chicago suddenly appeared through the swirls of white and Steele yanked the throttles back and dropped the speed brakes, banking the Invader through a right-hand turn. Fritz braced himself against Brian's seat to keep from sliding. At a quarter to three in the morning, parts of the downtown area as well as its famous *Rush Street* nightclub district, went momentarily dark. Stout party-goers braving the weather experienced only a momentary inconvenience as the Invader moved on.

The Invader reached the northwestern Chicago neighborhoods in an amount of time that seemed miniscule to Jack. He always considered Chicago, where he'd grown up, to be an expansive city. It seemed so small now. He cut the power to the main engines, leaving the warmers on and maneuvered on the antigravity system only. Reducing the power to the system, he dropped the craft to a height of about two hundred feet and coasted over the houses at about forty miles an hour. Between the blanket of white and the falling snow, he had to look carefully so as not to miss the landmarks he sought. "There it is..." he pulled back on the stick and the Invader slowed. "Anybody awake down there?"

Paul was watching the *Red Eagle* 3D ground-mapping infrared scanning system. "There was a vehicle parked on the street you just passed that had a strong signal, looked like there was someone in it too..."

■ ■ ■

The two Colombian men sitting in the four wheel drive Blazer parked down the street from the Steele residence were arguing when the engine quit running.

"I don't care *what* you say, we don't need to be here! Who the hell would go *anywhere* in *this* weather?"

"Look said the other, Marcus says we sit here so we sit here. Do *you* want to explain to Mr. Vasquez why we didn't stay all night?"

The first man looked at his watch. "But it's *three* in the morning! It's snowing like the North Pole and this character's been missing over a year. If he *ever* shows up, which he won't, it wouldn't be tonight!"

When the truck's engine sputtered and died, so did the conversation. The man behind the wheel attempted to restart it. It refused.

"What's wrong?"

"How the hell should I know?" said the man behind the wheel. "Do I look like a mechanic to you?"

"I don't care what people say about America," grumped the man in the passenger seat, "I hate this place, its foul air, its pale people... I'd rather be back in Colombia, it's warmer. I want to go home.

The man behind the wheel glared at his partner, "Keep whining and I'll send you home alright... in a box! Now shut the fuck up, you're driving me loco!" In his anger he drove the accelerator pedal to the floor and turned the ignition key again. The engine roared to life and he sat back with satisfaction. "Hey! What's that?!" He pointed upwards through the windshield.

"What?"

"That!" he pointed more vigorously, squinting through the gloom and whitewash of falling flakes.

"I don't see anything..." said the passenger with disinterest, his feelings wounded.

"Oh," said the driver, "I guess it's gone now." They sat in silence once again except for the idling engine and the periodic *thwip, thwip* of the windshield wipers.

■ ■ ■

"Think they saw us?" asked Brian.

Steele shrugged. "Not in this stuff. Anything else, Pappy?"

"Just the houses, Jack, nothing else outside. I don't blame them either, it's a good night to be in bed, this weather sucks."

"Tell me about it," he replied, "I lived here for nearly twenty five years." There was a city park a block away, with a playground, tennis courts and a football field. He angled for it, rotating the ship over the ball field to face the way he came, reducing the power to the antigravity system, the ship descending vertically.

Brian extended the landing gear, adjusting its height and sensors for flat unbroken terrain. The Invader settled silently into the snow that covered the darkened football field, the landing feet scrunching in the deep snow.

"Take a blaster, Jack." Paul held out a hand blaster in a shoulder holster about the size of a 9mm automatic. Almost silent when fired compared to the noise of a normal handgun it would be preferable to Steele's favorite bullet-throwing noisemaker.

"Thanks." He slipped the rig on and donned his old leather bomber jacket over his uniform. If someone saw him, he didn't want to look too out of the ordinary. The ship's door hissed as it released and a cold blast of Chicago winter swirled through the door, snowflakes and all.

"Ooohhh!" squealed Alité, shivering. "What *is* that?"

"It's snow," said Jack laughing. "Haven't you ever seen snow?"

"No..." she replied sheepishly.

"Snooowww!" shouted Fritz as he raced past Jack, dashing headlong into the whirling flakes, diving head first into a two-foot snowdrift. He popped out the other side, zooming across the field at a speed that would have surprised a greyhound, parting the snow and leaving skid marks in the undisturbed field of white. Throwing himself down, the Shepherd slid on his back with his feet kicking in the air, mostly disappearing.

"I think it's time for a rubber dog kennel," said Mike, watching in amazement.

"Nah," said Jack casually, "he does this every time he sees the first snow..." He zipped up his bomber jacket and hiked the collar around his ears to block the wind.

Brian handed him a portable comm headset. "Keep in touch."

"Right." Jack kissed Alité and headed off. "C'mon dog," he called softly. The Shepherd righted himself and bounded back.

The only marks in the snow belonged to Jack and Fritz, the falling flakes and wind quickly filling them. When they reached the street, Jack glanced back over his shoulder but could not see the Invader through the swirling white. He crossed the street and walked on, the fallen snow scrunching softly beneath his boots as each step sank halfway up his shins. He stopped momentarily and listened... it was the most silence he could remember hearing in what seemed to be a lifetime, the snowfall making a gentle hushing sound as it fell.

He remembered what Alité had relayed from Voorlak and cut between the houses to avoid the vehicle Paul had spotted on the street. He would cut through the yards and approach his parent's house from the back.

Fritz knew this was no ordinary stroll and walked with absolute silence and purpose alongside his friend. All play had been left at the football field, this was business. He paused momentarily, his enhanced hearing picking up sounds far beyond Jack's range. There was a vehicle with the engine running somewhere... beyond that he heard muffled voices. He decided they were far enough away and posed no threat, so walked on, as did Jack, taking the dog's cue.

Steele motioned to the fence,"Hup." Fritz cleared it with ease, dropping into Jack's childhood yard. Jack followed, the streetlight on the corner in front of his parent's house casting strange shadows through the yard, creating a foreign and sinister landscape. He was suddenly apprehensive, what would he say? What if they didn't live here anymore? It was the first time he'd thought of *that*.

"How's it going, Jack?"

The sudden voice in his ear from his comm made him jump. "I'm fine," he whispered. He moved across the yard and up the back steps to the house, the dog at his heels.

Jack stood at the back door with his heart pounding in his ears and the dog stared curiously at him. "OK," said Jack, staring back. "Give me a second..." He gathered his courage and Fritz wagged his tail.

The knock sounded so tremendously loud he feared it would wake the neighbors. But nothing, no answer. Jack knocked harder the second time, pounded even, and a dog barked somewhere. But nothing. *Damn...* He realized he should have checked the garage to see if the SUV was in it first.

Halfway down the stairs, Jack produced a shadow as the kitchen light came on. He almost slipped and fell scrambling back up the steps to the back door. He fumbled, but quickly pulled the black eye patch from the pocket of his bomber jacket and slipped it over his artificial left eye. "No sense in scaring them half to death," he told Fritz. The dog woofed softly.

The face of his younger sister appeared in the window of the door, her hands cupped around either side of her face so she could see out, her eyes growing to saucer size, her mouth dropping open. But nothing came out. Covering her mouth she backed away from the door in disbelief. Suddenly remembering herself, she clawed at the lock and swung the door wide. *"Jaaack?"* she screeched.

"Hi sis," he replied as nonchalantly as possible.

She threw herself at him, encircling him with her arms. *"Where have you been?"*

"You wouldn't believe me if I told you..."

She dragged him inside, wiping the snow off her bare feet. "Try me..."

"OK... well," he rubbed his forehead, "you believe in UFO's right...?

"Very funny..."

■ ■ ■

The Colombian behind the wheel of the Blazer nudged his dozing partner. "Hey, wake up..."

The other man blinked, rubbing his eyes. "What..."

The driver pointed at the only house on the block with lights on, "Look."

"So?"

"So, they just came on, that's what."

"So?"

"So let's go take a look, stupid!"

"Out there? Are you kidding?" He stared at the swirling flakes and shivered. "You're crazy. You go, I'm staying here."

The driver produced a 9mm semi-automatic handgun from his belt. "Let's go, you lazy slug, or I'll shoot you where you sit."

■ ■ ■

Jack ran his fingers through his damp hair, "It would be easier if I showed you. Where's mom and dad?"

"Florida." Her eyes shifted from his face to Fritz, "What do you mean *show* me? And what happened to your eye? And *what* is that *thing* on Fritz?"

Fritz stared at her, his tail wagging, his right eye glowing green.

"You're just full of questions... Look," said Jack, "get dressed, I'll tell you everything on the way..."

"To where?"

"Florida, where else?"

"Now?" She glanced out the window, "How are we getting there... Sleigh?"

"Something like that. Hurry up, my reindeer are kinda' double parked."

395

■ ■ ■

"Is it him?" asked the passenger of the Blazer.

The driver peered through the dining room window after referring to the photocopy of Jack Steele's photo he kept in his pocket. "Yeah..." He was thinking of the bonus this would bring him. "Let's go get the truck.."

■ ■ ■

Lisa was in her room packing and Jack stood in the living room staring at the tropical fish tank that had been there since his childhood. "How long have they been in Florida?" he called.

"Since late November," she called back. "I stayed for a couple of weeks then came back because I had to work. Y'know you're in a lot of trouble, don't you?"

"So, what else is new? Are mom and dad upset?"

"Upset is not exactly the word I'd use," she called. "More like worried to death..." Lisa appeared a moment later from her bedroom, fully dressed and carrying a canvas duffel bag. "It seems like everybody on the planet is looking for you..."

"Like who?" he wondered aloud.

"CIA," she began, ticking them off on her fingers. "FBI, Military Intelligence, KGB and some drug guy from Colombia named Vasquez."

Jack could understand the CIA, FBI, even Military Intelligence... they'd be looking for Paul and Mike. But... "Why the KGB? And who the hell is Vasquez?"

"I'm not sure," she answered, pulling on her coat. "But those two are supposed to be tied together... something about a missing woman..."

"Who? What's her name?"

"Escobar or something like that..."

"C'mon, Lisa, her full name, *think...*"

His sister frowned as she moved about the house turning the lights back off. She stopped and stood in the kitchen to pull a hat down over her ears. "Martina..." she said slowly, as she opened the back door. "No, that's not it..."

As they descended the stairs to the yard, it came to her. "Marianna, Marianna Escobar! That's it!" She was sure of it.

396

Jack stopped dead in his tracks at the top of the stairs. "Marianna, Maria..." he was comparing the names. "Marianna *Arroyo* Escobar?"

"Yes, that's it!" Lisa frowned again, "Why? Do you know her?"

Jack's face was covered with his hands. "Geeeez! How could I have been so stupid?!"

"You *do* know her then..."

"Yeah," groaned Jack. He tromped down the stairs and followed Lisa out the gate followed by Fritz. The trio turned and headed for the park. He clicked on the comm and called the Invader, "I'm on my way back."

"Roger," came the reply.

"Where are you parked?" she whispered, looking up and down the block.

"In the park," he told her. "Bri, call the Freedom, have Commander Edgars put Lieutenant Arroyo in the brig until we return."

There was a moment of silence. "Maria? But why?"

"You'll have to ask *Comrade* Marianna Arroyo Escobar that question."

"Are you trying to tell me Maria is Russian?"

That was Paul's voice that time, thought Jack. "It sure looks like it, Commander. Lieutenant Maria Arroyo may be a Soviet... KGB."

"A double agent... I copy." The reply was soft, without conviction. *He would be as stunned as I was,* thought Jack.

Lisa looked at Jack and suddenly realized how much he had changed; commanding, evasive, secretive. Not the happy, carefree pilot she used to know. She stopped walking. "What is all this? Commander, Lieutenant? Jack, what's going on? What happened? Are you in the military or something?" She stood with her feet apart and her hands on her hips, something he remembered their mother doing. "I'm not moving until you tell me..."

A hundred feet in front of them, the Blazer slid to a stop in the snow and the doors flung wide, cutting off their path to the park. "Mr. Steele! We need to talk to you..!" The man's voice had a thick, distinctive Latin accent.

Jack shot a glance at his sister, "You said a Colombian drug dealer, right?"

"Yeah..."

Jack grabbed Lisa's arm and spun her around, *"RUN!"* His hand was in his jacket for a millisecond, emerging with the blaster. Hazarding a quick shot as he turned to run, his feet slid in the snow, the bright magenta bolt cleared the roof of the vehicle and bore a hole into a tree on the other side of the street.

The Colombian from the passenger side froze in his tracks. "*WHAT* in the name of Saint Mary, was *THAT*?"

"Get him!" shouted the driver as he jumped back in. He stomped on the accelerator and the passenger door slammed shut of its own accord, the vehicle fishtailing around the corner, knobby tires kicking up blobs of snow. The first man gave chase on foot.

"Between the garages!" shouted Jack, his long strides bringing him closer to his sister. Fritz cut the corner cleanly but Lisa lost her footing and slipped, falling into the snow, Jack so close he couldn't help going down with her. He was better for it, as a bullet thwacked the wooden fencepost above him. *They must be using silencers, I never heard the shot.* He fired behind him without looking and scrambled to his feet. The Blazer slid by, its brakes locked, as Jack pulled Lisa to her feet. He shoved her toward the space between the garages. "Get to the football field," he told her. There was a soft *puh* behind him and a tug on his left arm that spun him off his feet.

"*Jaaack!*"

"Go, go, go!" he yelled. She disappeared in the gap between the garages and he rolled over realizing his left arm was numb. The Blazer slid into a parked car and the driver was spinning the tires in reverse to get out of the ruts he had made in the snow, the other man wading through the drifts between the parked cars and trees along the curb. Jack pulled off the eye patch, half-sighted and squeezed off three fast shots at his running attacker. The blaster had no recoil, so all three caught the man in the same spot just below the ribcage. The sizzling magenta streaks cut him cleanly in half. As the Colombian lay dying in the snow, he knew he should have never left the warmth of home.

Steele struggled to his feet as the driver of the Blazer worked to turn the vehicle around in the drifted snow. Fritz appeared and woofed from between the garages, Jack following him as he hazarded a glance back over his shoulder. There was a dark stain in the snow where he had fallen; when he turned back, the Shepherd was gone.

■ ■ ■

"A little help out here..." The crew in the Invader could hear Jack's labored breathing. *"My sister's coming, watch for her..."*

"Let's go..." Throwing on heavy jackets, Paul, Mike and Brian, grabbed assault rifles off the weapons rack and headed out the door, down the ramp into the cold.

Paul snapped a charge magazine into the pulse rifle and it whined as it powered up, the snow clinging to his hair and the cold biting his cheeks. "God I hate snow..." he mumbled, the white stuff splashing up around the three men as they ran. He activated his mic, "We're on our way, Jack."

■ ■ ■

Fritz had run ahead of Jack to catch up with Lisa and guide her to the ship and they emerged from between the houses, racing across the street into the park. She saw three figures running toward her through the white swirls and slowed her pace in fear. Fritz looked back over his shoulder and slowed. "Come!" he barked, and sped up. She hastened her pace for a second then slowed again, confused at what she thought she just heard.

"Keep going, Lisa!" came the shouts from the men ahead of her. "It's OK, follow Fritz!" She could hear the Blazer behind her, muffled shots and the noise of the strange weapon Jack was carrying. She ran on, past the men with the strange uniforms and odd rifles. One face was familiar but she didn't slow... until she saw the Invader, a bulky gray shadow through the blowing curtain of white. That's when she stopped dead. And stared. Fritz saw this and circled back to get her.

Lisa didn't know much about flying or airplanes, but it seemed abundantly obvious to her, this hulking, vicious looking thing, was not from her planet. Light glowed from what appeared to be the cockpit and further down the hull, an open doorway. Curious, she cautiously ventured a little closer. A woman appeared in that doorway at the top of a short boarding ramp, waving and calling to her in a strange language. Lisa's legs seemed to turn to stone. *It's just a bad dream. I'll wake up soon,* she thought.

Fritz butted her in the thigh with his head. "Go, Lisa!"

She whirled around. "Stop that! Dogs can't talk!" He grabbed her by the sleeve of her coat and dragged her along. She fought but he refused to release her.

■ ■ ■

Jack slid to a stop in the driveway between two houses as the Blazer slid to a stop in the street right in front of him. He saw the muzzle flash out the driver's window and flattened himself against one of the houses, mashing his left arm. A flash of pain shot up his arm like lightning producing stars in his vision. "Ow," he breathed. "That *really* hurt..." Lights flickered on in neighboring houses. The Colombian swung the door wide and took another shot. Jack dropped to the snow and heard the slug strike the garage behind him with a hollow *thwunck*. He wanted to fire back but his vision wasn't clear. He squeezed off two blind shots, flattening the front tire and breaking the back, side window of the Blazer. The Colombian froze in place and snapped off another shot, striking the wall near Jack's head. "C'mon guys..." he groaned, blinking away the stars. He squeezed off a shot that hit the snow at the foot of the driveway with a steaming hiss. Great shooting, Jack, he thought, no driveway is safe with you around.

Jack's vision began to clear enough to see the Colombian advancing up the driveway. "Give up, Mr. Steele..." hissed the voice.

Threads of rapid, neon blue streaks, passed through the falling snow, striking the Blazer. It exploded in a giant fireball, shattering windows in both the houses on either side of the driveway. Except for the crackling of the burning Blazer, there was silence once more. Jack blinked hard, trying to erase the image of the flash.

Half blinded again, he searched the driveway for the Colombian with his limited vision. He pointed the blaster at the advancing shadow.

"Jack!" Brian's voice was a strained whisper.

Jack lowered the blaster. "Yeah... I'm here." He began to see and got to his feet, the driver of the Blazer lying just in front of him, naked, blackened and smoking.

"Come on!" insisted Brian with a wave.

Jack started down the driveway, "I don't know what you guys are *whispering about,* I've heard *tanks* make less noise." He joined Brian at the foot of the driveway and they ran across the street past the burning Blazer into the park. "If that didn't wake these people, nothing will." The four men headed back to the Invader as lights came on all over the neighborhood. There was a siren in the distance somewhere although Steele had no idea how they'd get emergency vehicles through the snowbound side streets.

Clomping up the ramp, Jack lurched through the doorway and dropped himself into a passenger seat as Alité palmed the actuator for the door. "Get us off the ground..." he grunted.

"Give him a hand," Paul told Mike. "I'm going to take a look at Jack's arm." Mike and Brian headed to the cockpit as Alité confirmed the seal on the Invader's door.

Lisa, silent and wide-eyed, sat opposite Jack as Paul helped him off with his bomber jacket. She watched as her brother grit his teeth and winced. Fritz climbed into the seat beside her and watched too.

There was a temporary whine and some vibration as the generators spun up to full power to supply the antigravity system. Lisa's eyes grew wide. "What's that?"

"We're taking off," answered Alité, handing a medical kit to Paul.

Lisa glanced at her then back at Jack and Paul. "What'd she say?"

"Taking off..." said Fritz, annunciating slowly.

Lisa jumped and glanced at the dog who looked back at her, his head cocked to one side in a curious fashion. "Please," she pleaded, "someone tell me what's going on..." She stared at Jack's artificial eye, as black as polished onyx.

Jack took a deep breath as Paul cut and peeled away his bloody shirt sleeve. "Lisa, meet Commander Paul Smiley of the cruiser Freedom. Formerly of the U.S. Navy." Paul nodded as he continued his inspection of Jack's wound. "You've met Brian," continued Jack. "The other guy is Lieutenant Mike Warren, also formerly of the U.S. Navy, he's Paul's wingman." Jack sucked air as Paul cleaned the wound.

"Looks worse than it is," commented Paul.

Jack's eyes watered, "To you maybe."

"Stop being a baby, Jack, it's just a scratch." Paul smirked, "A *big scratch*, but still... just a scratch."

Jack managed a weak smile, "You're a real comedian... But don't quit your day job... *Ow*, take it easy will ya?" Alité sat down next to him and held his hand. Jack glanced at her and saw the worry. "I'm alright," he told her.

"Who is she, Jack?"

"Sorry Lisa; this is Princess Alité Steele. My wife." He turned to Alité. "Sweetheart, this is my sister, Lisa Steele."

Alité smiled and extended her hand. "Nice to meet you."

Lisa's eyes were wide with disbelief as she took Alité's hand. "Um, I, uh..." she closed her mouth, not sure what to say or who to look at. The woman's eyes kept changing colors, and Jack's artificial eye gave her the creeps. There were just too many things to accept and digest and Lisa was having a difficult time wading through it all. She took a deep cleansing

401

breath hoping to clear her mind. "OK wait... let me just take a stab at this..."
She pointed at Alité, "She's not from around here. Am I right?"

CHAPTER THIRTY TWO

FT. MYERS, FLORIDA: *HOME AT LAST – SORT OF...*

Brian had taken the Invader up into the clouds and headed south at a leisurely pace. By the time they passed over Kentucky, they were out of the cloud cover and so was Lisa. It took Jack that long to outline the events of the past year and how things came to be. Lisa listened to most of it in intense silence, only stopping her brother on occasion to clarify something. When he finished, Lisa leaned back in her seat and looked down at Fritz who had fallen asleep, his head across her lap. Her fingers stroked his left ear and her thumb ran back and forth along the steel skull cap that covered the right side of the Shepherd's head. When she looked back up she was smiling. "Wow," she breathed, "It's a lot to digest... I feel like I'm in some sort of science fiction movie. I'm here but... I don't know, I still feel like I'm dreaming this." She shook her head trying to clear away the disbelief. "Boy, I sure would've liked to have seen some of it."

Paul had found a temporary translator disc in the medical kit and taped it behind Lisa's left ear. When Jack and Paul had returned to the cockpit, Lisa and Alité were sitting alone talking girl talk.

Jack had pulled a fresh tunic from the crew locker and stood between Brian and Mike at the controls while he buttoned it and pinned his rank pips to its collar. "Any problems?" he asked.

Mike shook his head. "Not really. Had a couple of nosy Air Force birds but this thing is a little stealthy, we lost them."

Jack looked out through the cockpit perspex. The Invader had flown back into cloud cover over southern Georgia, and beads of moisture raced across the windscreen. Mike and Brian were flying on imaging instruments. "We're clear of the mountains," said Jack. "Why don't we drop below the clouds..." Without answering, Mike adjusted the craft and it began a gentle descent. As they dropped free of the greyness, rain slashed across the sky, pelting the Invader and creating a familiar noise. The pilots glanced at one another and smiled little smiles, the kind one makes when remembering something pleasant.

"Sounds nice," said Paul. It was funny about the little things, how much you could miss them.

The heavy overcast soon gave way to broken cloud and the rain stopped abruptly. Stars were visible through the holes in the clouds, but the sky would soon begin to lighten in the east. "How do you want to do this, Jack?" asked Brian.

Steele pinched his lower lip. "Approach low over the Gulf, drop me, Lisa and the dog on the beach and come back for us after dark."

Paul shrugged. "A good a plan as any, what time do you want for pickup?"

"Hmmm, how about ten o'clock?"

"A lot of people will still be awake..." reminded Brian. "Midnight might be better."

Jack nodded. "Midnight sounds good."

"MacDill Air Force Base just picked us up," announced Mike.

"Swing out over the water, drop below five hundred feet," instructed Paul. The Invader banked hard and dropped four thousand feet in a matter of a few seconds, the distant lights of Tampa disappearing below the horizon. Brian followed the terrain at two hundred feet until he reached the water where he swung back south to follow the coastline.

The Captain of the shrimp boat below almost fell overboard as the Invader passed directly overhead. "Bobby! Bobby! Get the camera! Get the camera! Quick!"

The first mate looked up lethargically from his chores. "Why? What'd you see Jim?"

The Captain searched the empty sky down along the coastline, the same way he would do for the rest of his life. "Never mind... forget it."

Streetlights flickered off and winked back on along the beach as the Invader passed, but very few people were awake to notice. The sky in the east was beginning to lighten. "Slow down, Bri," coached Jack, "Let me see..." Brian eased the throttles back and cut the engines, using the antigravity to continue cruising. "There...!" pointed Jack. "The surf shop! Slow down, the house is only a few blocks..."

Brian eased back the power and the ship slowed, dropping to less than a hundred feet. "We've got company coming," announced Mike. "A Coast Guard boat's got us on radar and there's a couple of F-16s nosing our way..."

"Find it fast," added Paul.

"There it is," said Brian, angling the ship over the beach.

"Lisa!" called Jack. "You've got about thirty seconds, we're here!"

"Already?"

"Yep." He slung the blaster rig over his shoulder and pulled on his uniform jacket to cover it. He decided not to wear the bomber jacket because of the bloody hole in its left sleeve. He grabbed a comm unit and clipped it on his ear.

"They're almost on top of us, Jack..." While Mike held the controls, Brian jumped up to vacate the pilot's seat to Paul who hastily belted himself in.

"Alright let us out..." Alité opened the door without extending the ramp and Paul dropped the ship to mere inches from the sand without using the landing gear. "See ya' later..." Jack kissed Alité and jumped to the sand as two F-16s whistled overhead. "Uh oh," breathed Jack, looking up. Fritz jumped, then Lisa. They ran towards the house as the door of the ship began to close, the F-16s splitting into a *Y* in the distance, banking sharply to make a return pass. The Invader lifted slightly and turned slowly to face the advancing fighters and the open water.

■ ■ ■

"This is Major Sutton, United States Air Force. Unidentified craft do you copy? Please identify yourself..." Sutton had already instructed his wingman to call for additional aircraft. *"Unidentified aircraft, this is American airspace, please identify yourself or I will be forced to shoot you down."*

"Drifter, this is Wet Willie..."

"Go, Wet Willie..."

"Major, there are two more birds on the way, and we are cleared to fire over water. I repeat, over water, clear to arm and fire."

"Copy Wet Willie, clear to fire over the drink."

"Hello, Air Force," responded Paul on their frequency. He flipped the switches for the main engine burners and adjusted the forcing cones for maximum thrust, the Invader coasting out over the water. "Commander Paul Smiley, United States Navy, don't shoot."

"Navy? You are not displaying an IFF beacon... A full identification please," insisted the Major. "And if you don't mind me asking, what the hell *is* that thing?" The F-16s passed overhead to the left and right of the Invader, disappearing from view over the houses. Two more F-16s appeared in the broken clouds at about six thousand feet, flying a protective CAP.

405

"No beacon - Black OPS exercise," lied Pappy. " And you wouldn't believe me if I told you, Major... it's classified."

■ ■ ■

Jack, Lisa and Fritz, huddled at the foot of the steps to the sundeck of his house, watching. Jack could see the burner rings inside the Invader's engines turn from a dark cherry red to a bright pink and the tails of the forcing cones as they narrowed. "Heads down," he instructed. The trio ducked and covered themselves as the F-16s passed overhead and the Invader accelerated away, first on antigravity then igniting her main engine burners as she passed low over the first of the waves breaking on the sandbars. The water split beneath her down to the sandy bottom with a boom, sending a sheet of water and sand over a hundred feet into the air on either side of her. Thunder boomed and rolled out across the Gulf of Mexico, the Invader easily outrunning the noise.

"Holy *shit*!" squeaked Lisa, peeking. In a blink, the Invader was nothing but a brilliant speck of light low on the horizon, a trail of churning water and mist the only signs of her departure. The F-16s gave chase, igniting their afterburners and creating a sonic boom in the distance. They would have as much hope of catching the UFO, as a Piper Cub would of catching *them*.

Lisa could barely see it as it climbed straight up into the morning sky. "Good God," she whispered, how fast *is* that thing?"

Jack shrugged. "It's supposed to be able to do about Mach 20 in atmosphere... that's about fifteen-thousand..."

"Miles an hour?"

Jack nodded casually, "Yep."

Fritz cocked his head. "Ssshh, people coming," he whispered.

Lisa thumbed towards the dog, "That's going to take some getting used to..." she whispered. They huddled back down as two men in business suits ran from between the houses onto the beach.

"I *told* you!" insisted the first.

The second was watching the F-16s through a pair of binoculars. "I don't see anything but the Falcons, Tom."

"I'm telling you, there was something else. It looked like it was on the beach..."

"Well, look," said the second, "if there was something here, it didn't leave any marks..."

406

"C'mon Frank, I saw *something*, maybe it was a helicopter..."

Frank shook his head. "There's not a helicopter alive that could outrun an F-16."

"Well it *was* kinda' bulky." He made gestures with his hands to approximate a shape.

"You're not trying to tell me you saw a UFO, are you, Tom?"

"Well I..." he saw the other man's expression. "Ahem, I, well, no. No, of course not. No. Definitely not." He turned and walked back toward the street. "Let's go get some coffee." They disappeared between the houses back the way they came.

"Neighbors?" whispered Lisa.

"Not unless some new ones moved in," said Jack. "It's Saturday, right?" His sister nodded. "Mmmm," nodded Jack. "Suits before six in the morning, on a Saturday. My guess is alphabet soup..."

"Alphabet soup...?"

"FBI, CIA, NCIS, NSA... whatever." He stood up. "We'd better get inside." He searched his pockets as Lisa brushed herself off. "Damn," he growled, "I left my keys in my bomber jacket, guess we'll have to knock."

"Your eye," said Lisa.

"Oh yeah..." he paused on the bottom step searching his pockets for the eye patch. "Also in my bomber jacket. Got any sunglasses?"

"Yeah sure, because I need those all the time in the middle of winter in Chicago..."

"Yeah..." snorted Jack, "maybe they won't notice..."

Lisa laughed loudly. "And pigs fly, right?"

Jack stood ready to knock at the sliding glass door into the kitchen but froze. This was home, and for a second, it was as if the last sixteen months hadn't happened. But they had. And suddenly he felt like he didn't belong there anymore, a foreigner in his own world. A stranger at his own home. He backed away from the door.

"What's wrong?" asked Lisa.

"Uh, well, maybe we should wait a little bit, it's awful early..."

"Oh sure!" she retorted. "It's OK to wake *me* at some ungodly hour, but you're too chicken-shit to wake mom and dad!" She pushed him and he bumped the door, making it rattle. "Knock, you weenie!" The family dog barked from inside the house and Fritz barked back out of reflex.

"Now look what you've done!" said Jack, backing away from the door again. He grabbed her by the arm and put her in front of the door. "You talk to them first," he told her, "my eye... you know." He moved out of view.

She smirked. "Yeah, sure. Right. Your eye." The curtain moved and her mother peeked out. The curtain closed again. "What am I supposed to say?" hissed Lisa.

"Break it to them gently, I'll stay out here..." He pulled the comm unit off his ear and slid it into a pocket inside his jacket.

"Now, how am I supposed to do that...?" Lisa spun toward the door when she heard it begin to slide. "Oh, hi, mom!"

"Lisa? What are you *doing here?*" Lynnette Steele slid the door wide to let her daughter into the house. "How did you get here?"

"Funny you should ask me that," said Lisa casually as she stepped past her mother, tossing her duffel bag on the floor.

■ ■ ■

Lynnette jumped up off the couch. "He's here? Why didn't you say so in the *first* place?!" She moved forward, "Where is he?"

Lisa stepped in front of her mother to head her off. "Just a minute, mom. Yes, he's here. But he's changed..."

"Changed how?" Kyle's expression was one of anticipation, but he remained calmly seated on the couch.

"Different, maybe that's a better word, he's *different*..."

"He's hurt, is that it?" said Lynnette.

"No. No, he's not hurt... he *was*, but he's all healed now." *Just don't squeeze his arm,* she thought. "He's fine, honest."

Kyle rose from the couch. "Well, let him in, girl! Why is he standing outside?"

Lisa raised her hands. "OK, OK! Just don't stare at his eye..."

"What's wrong with his eye?" Asked Lynnette, almost in tears.

Lisa thought how she might explain it. "Umm..."

"What?" Her mother tried to get around her.

Lisa held her. "Wait, mom..." She sighed, there was no easy way. "His left eye isn't real, and it might be a little scary..." *OK, a lot scary,* she thought. She saw the tears rolling down her mother's cheek. *Dammit Jack,* she thought, *I hate when you make me do this stuff.* "It's OK, mom, he can see

408

fine, it's just not a real eye." Lynnette pushed past her daughter and ran to the door, peering through the glass.

Always in control, Kyle moved casually to the door and stood next to his wife. "He looks fine," said Kyle quietly, resting his hand on Lynnette's shoulder.

■ ■ ■

Jack stood motionless on the sand halfway between the water and the house, watching Fritz splash happily at the water's edge. The dog had been eyeing the surf and Jack had decided to let him play. The water was fairly cold and Fritz was only getting his legs wet, but he was having a terrific time. The broken clouds were giving way to clear sky, the eastern horizon behind them turning a rosy shade, casting slivers of color between the houses and across the sand. Jack drew a deep lungful of the fresh air and could almost taste its substance. *What a beautiful morning,* he thought, *absolutely outstanding.* How he missed this.

When he glanced up at the sky, he saw the three-quarter morning moon hanging there; pale, cool, quiet. Looking like it had been painted into the sky. It beckoned to him and he could feel its pull. And he knew. This would always be his home, but out there was where he belonged. Where he was destined to be.

"Jack..." Jack spun around and the Shepherd stopped playing, turning toward the house. Kyle and Lynnette stood at the rail on the sundeck and Lisa stood in the sliding glass doorway to the kitchen, waving him in.

Homecoming was full of hugs, tears... and stares. Jack had to grit his teeth and Lisa thought his eyes would pop out when their mother hugged him across the wound on his arm. But he made it through. His parents must have dismissed the tears in his eyes as the result of the emotions of the moment.

Lynnette couldn't help herself. Lisa had said his eye looked odd, but she couldn't have imagined it like it was if she tried. And poor Fritz, he looked like a dog version of Phantom of the Opera with a small camera lens stuck to his face.

Jack and Lisa had a few moments alone as Lynnette made breakfast and Kyle showered. "I don't get it," whispered Jack, "they haven't asked me a thing. How much did you tell them?"

"Not much," replied Lisa.

"So you didn't tell them about..."

"Are you *nuts*?" she hissed. "I don't want to end up in a rubber room!"

"Stop exaggerating," said Jack, "they wouldn't do that."

"They sure as hell wouldn't *believe* me," she sassed.

"Mmm, you're probably right."

"There's no probably about it," said Lisa quietly. "If you want them to *believe* this story, you're gonna' have to show them concrete evidence."

"You're just hoping to see the Freedom for yourself," said Jack sitting back on the couch and switching on the big-screen TV.

"Damn right," confirmed Lisa. "But you know I'm right. They won't believe it unless they see it. Not with all that's happened. They'll think you're nuts or on drugs or something."

"Alright," said Jack calmly, "it's settled then, a midnight tour it is."

"Breakfast...!" It was not a call anyone in this family was likely to miss. Eggs, bacon, pancakes, milk, juice... the whole fanfare. And nobody made it better. It smelled spectacular and Jack's mouth was watering long before he sat down at the breakfast table.

"Man, this is great," said Jack, loading his plate.

"My Lord," said his mother, "don't they feed you? I mean, wherever it is you've been."

"That's one thing we do well, is eat," he replied. "I just haven't eaten since about seven last night."

"And where was that..?" said Kyle carefully.

"And why are you so pale?" asked his mother. "You used to be so tan."

His father waved at her to be quiet. "That's not important Lynn." He never took his eyes off Jack. "So what happened, son? Exactly... Where have you been and why has it taken so long for you to come home? Your eye, the dog..." he glanced down at Fritz who sat quietly next to Gus the family dog. "What's happened?"

Jack was seriously hoping Fritz wouldn't feel the need to speak anytime soon. "Well," said Jack, "I'll tell you what I can, but some of it will have to wait until tonight..."

"Why tonight ?" interrupted his mother.

The doorbell rang before Jack could respond and his father rose from the table to answer it.

"Where's my car mom?" asked Jack, between forkfuls.

"In the garage. Your father and I had to go get it from the airport. Why?"

"Just curious..."

Kyle Steele walked back into the kitchen with a man dressed smartly in a blue-gray suit and Jack's stomach filled with butterflies. He looked like a Fed. Jack had not removed his jacket, his first instinct was to reach inside and produce the blaster. He resisted the urge. "Dad?"

"Son, this is Agent Phil Cooper, FBI. Phil, this is my son, Jack Steele." Phil Cooper stepped forward and extended his hand. Jack remained seated, stone-faced. "He's here to help you, Jack," prompted his father.

Jack rose slowly, taking care to prevent his jacket from dropping open and revealing the blaster. He shook hands with the agent, a short, curt shake, then sat back down.

"The scariest words in the English language," commented Jack, "I'm from the government and I'm here to help..."

"Hey!" shot his father, glaring at him, "that was uncalled for..."

Lynnette set another place at the table and Phil joined the family for breakfast. The Agent ate happily and quietly for some time, studying Jack as he ate. Jack ignored him. "You were in Chicago last night," said Phil, after some time, "weren't you?" He glanced at Lisa and smiled. "It was easy to figure," he added. He watched Jack's face but there was no reaction. "Yeah," he continued, "it seems Jack Steele and body counts are synonymous."

Jack looked up from his food and cleared his throat but said nothing. His father had stopped eating and was staring at him, his mother looked pale. The only one that seemed unaffected was Lisa. "You know," continued Cooper, "those two guys you left in the snow were Vasquez's men. He won't be happy about that."

"Don't know the man. But I suppose that's his problem, isn't it..." said Jack sarcastically, still eating.

"Hey kid, I'm not condemning you. Honest." He took a swig of milk and wiped the white mustache off his upper lip with a napkin. "In fact, in my opinion, you did the world a favor. But there's something curious, see..." He lit a cigarette and watched the smoke curl away. "The guy in the driveway is still alive." He watched Jack's eyes narrow. "And my men tell me, he keeps babbling something about some kind of lightning gun or something. The other guy... Christ," he breathed, "they faxed me pictures, he was burned in half..."

"Nice breakfast talk..." interrupted Jack, eating. He waved his fork, "And if you don't mind, I'd prefer you not to smoke in my house."

"Their vehicle was destroyed beyond recognition," continued Cooper, snubbing his cigarette out in his half-eaten scrambled eggs. "And there was a

411

small amount of radiation of undetermined origin. Just what the hell did you use?"

Jack met his gaze and held it. He took a deep breath and let it out slowly, thinking. Stone faced and without blinking, he reached in and drew out the blaster from under his jacket. Cooper was unmoved. *He'd be a good Ruge player,* thought Jack. Ejecting the power cartridge into his left hand, Jack held the weapon out in the palm of his right hand. "I used this. I suppose a lightning gun is actually a pretty fair description..."

Cooper picked it out of Jack's hand and examined it, turning it over and over. It was about the size and shape of a 9mm semiautomatic pistol but lighter than it looked. Kyle leaned over and stared at it too. "This is it? It feels like a toy..." said Cooper.

Jack snorted, "Hardly." To his surprise Cooper handed it back.

"How does it work?" asked his father.

"Well I took one apart once..."

"And?"

"And I learned I should never take one apart again," he chuckled.

"Don't be a smartass..."

Jack shook his head, "I'm not, totally a true story. It's actually called an Ion Pulse Laser Blaster. It operates on a burst of intensely focused light. That's the total extent of my knowledge of this thing..." he slid the power cartridge back in and re-holstered it. "That and how to reload it."

"And how did it come into your possession?"

"Hmm," Jack smiled, "interesting choice of words, Mr. Cooper. I'm sure you have a hundred questions, but if I told you, I doubt seriously any of you would believe me. So, if you can all wait just a few hours until tonight, I will be able to answer all your questions and explain absolutely everything." He drained his juice glass.

"Why, what happens tonight?" asked Cooper.

"It'll be easier to show you rather than just tell you," explained Jack.

"What could be so unbelievable?" asked his father. The phone rang before Jack could respond and his father rose to answer it. "It's for you," he told Cooper.

Cooper came back and sat down at the table after a short phone conversation. He stared at Jack. "It seems the B-25 Sweet Susie, the one you disappeared in, has turned up..."

"Do tell..." said Jack sitting back with a wry smile.

"Really..? said his father. "Where?"

"Right back at the hangar where it first took off from," answered Cooper. His eyes never left Jack's face. "Would you know anything about that, Jack?"

Jack smiled innocently. "Who me?" he shrugged. "Maybe..."

"Funny thing is," announced the Agent, "it seems it simply dropped from the sky earlier this morning... right through the roof of the hangar of Miles Aviation. Destroyed the plane, the hangar, and a partly restored P-38 Lightning parked inside."

Oooh, bonus points! "Geez, that's too bad..." he replied unconvincingly.

Cooper eyed him suspiciously. "Yeah, you look really broken up about it. How'd you do it?"

"Tonight," said Jack, pushing his chair back. "Midnight." He was tired, his left arm aching. He wanted, *needed* some rest.

"You know there are a lot of people who want to talk to you, Mr. Steele..." said Cooper standing, "FBI, CIA, ATF, NCIS... I could go on..."

Jack was unmoved at Cooper's posturing, "Please don't." His arms were folded casually across his chest.

"Maybe we should talk about protective custody," he said drawing out a pair of handcuffs slowly. "Give us a chance to straighten things out, the FBI can protect you..." He laid the cuffs on the table. "It would be best if you did it voluntarily..."

"Best for who...? You?" He glanced at his dad and back to Cooper. "See what I mean dad? They're here to help... what a crock. They thrive on using people. I wouldn't have been in the mess in the first place if it wasn't for the *helpful folks* in the government."

"I don't want to have to do it the hard way." Cooper shifted but froze, blinking in disbelief. With a momentary blur of motion, Jack had the Ion Blaster pointed at him, still sitting calmly. It was as if he hadn't moved at all.

His parents stared at him silently, blinking. Kyle wasn't sure he had actually seen him move.

Jack raised an eyebrow, "So if it doesn't go your way, you'll bully people. Nice. I've got news for you, you really don't want to get into a pissing match here, Mr. Cooper. You will lose. That ballistic vest you're wearing might as well be made of tissue paper - and you've seen what this thing can do. So how about you take your hand off that Glock, so I don't have to mess up the walls of my house with your guts..."

Cooper let his hand drop to his side, then leaned forward, his hands on the table. "Kid, you have no idea what you're up against, how much trouble you're in... there's a *price* on your head. You *need* the FBI's help."

Jack laughed hard, "What I'm up against? You pompous ass... you have no idea what I'm capable of. You saw what happened to the last two guys that tried to collect on that," he added flippantly. "And as far as one branch of the government protecting me from another branch of government - I can't believe you can actually say that with a straight face. It's quite possibly the dumbest thing I've ever heard." He stood and slid the blaster back in its holster. "Let me be perfectly clear, Mr. Cooper, I don't need your help, *or* the help of any government agency..."

Cooper straightened up and shrugged. "So you want to live the rest of your life looking over your shoulder?"

"Cooper, you're starting to bore me. You're in so far over your head, you can't even see the light of day... and you don't even know it." He glanced at his parents but did not turn away from Phil Cooper. "Dad, if you value him as a friend, keep him away from me until tonight." Jack walked out of the room followed by Fritz and Lisa. "I'm going to get some rest."

CHAPTER THIRTY THREE

COVERT INCURSION: GULF OF MEXICO

Ensign Myomerr pointed the nose of the Invader at the planet, the Gulf of Mexico her targeted entry zone. "Are you gentlemen ready?"

"All set, Skipper," called Dooby from the back, checking his harness.

"Fifteen-hundred miles to coordinates," stated Ragnaar, activating a secondary sensor screen.

"Thank you, Lieutenant." She reached forward, flipping the shields on, the hum of the shield generator spinning up." We'd better hustle it up, we're running late..." she added, shoving the throttle forward.

■ ■ ■

Lisa dragged a lounge chair from the other side of the sundeck next to her brother, "Where are they, Jack?" She dropped into the chair and kicked her feet up.

Jack checked his watch, 12:15. "I don't know, Lisa." He leaned back on the lounger and scanned the sky over the Gulf, Fritz strolling around on the sand inspecting shells and other things washed up on the beach. He glanced over at his sister, "They'll be here," he added confidently.

"Can you see them yet?" she asked.

"Not yet. Believe me, you'll notice their entry. It'll be hard to miss. But I can see the Freedom..."

"Really? Where?"

Jack pointed up at the full moon. "There, see that little rectangular shadow on the left side? Can you see it?"

"I think so..."

"That's it."

"Hmm, it must be pretty big if we can see it from here..."

Kyle, Lynette and Phil Cooper stood in the house at the sliding glass door watching Jack and Lisa. "What do you think they're looking at?" asked Lynette.

"Good question..." mumbled Cooper staring at the night sky over the Gulf of Mexico.

"What do you suppose he's waiting for?" asked Lynette, stepping away to refill her coffee cup.

"I wish I knew," answered Kyle. "But in a minute I'm gonna' go out there and get a straight answer out of him if I have to shake it out of him..."

"Easy, big fella," said Cooper. "We don't know what kind of mental or psychological pressures he's dealing with. Let's let him play it out. Maybe when nothing happens, he'll come to realize that he needs our help."

Kyle raised an eyebrow. *Was that a reference to a Stockholm Syndrome of some sort?* He was starting to think his son was right - while Jack rested, he'd had to stop Cooper from calling in other agents. He'd begun to realize what Lisa had said about Jack having changed, was true. They were deep changes, he had a command presence that was unmistakeable, and Kyle felt a sense of fearlessness that was almost palpable. While always a fairly tough kid, his son had grown into a man that he would consider extremely dangerous if forced to fight. As a parent, he felt no fear for himself, his wife or his daughter, perceiving a protected family status. However, he did not get the sense that this special status extended to anyone outside that small circle. With that in mind, Kyle felt the need to convinced Cooper that forcing his way on Jack would end in disaster, in more ways than one.

■ ■ ■

It was a pleasant night and Jack was thoroughly enjoying it, a gentle breeze dancing through the palm trees around the deck and a set of wind chimes on someone's house somewhere up the beach. The gentle tinkling notes made Jack's eyelids heavy as he drew in the wonderfully fresh, unfiltered air.

"Look!" shouted Lisa, sitting bolt upright, straddling her chair, pointing to the horizon.

Jack's eyes shot open just in time to see the tail end of what looked like a shooting star coming straight down. "That's them!" he said with a smile. "It stands out if you're watching for it..." The light had disappeared below the horizon and he pulled his comm from his pocket as he stood up, fitting it into his ear.

416

Cooper and his parents had seen his actions and filed out onto the sundeck. "What's going on, Jack?"

"Our taxi's here, Mr. Cooper," said Jack flippantly.

"I don't see anything, Jack," said his mother.

Thunder rolled gently through the cloudless night sky from somewhere out over the Gulf. "Give it a minute."

"Look, son," said his father, aggravation dripping from his voice, "I think we've had just about enough of this, it's going on twelve-thirty..."

"Patience, dad..." retorted Jack, calmly. A few moments passed where the only sounds were the breeze and the surf rolling in. "There!" he pointed. A faint, rosy glow appeared on the distant horizon, reflections dancing on the water. Glancing up and down the beach, reassured him most of the houses were dark, their occupants asleep. Thunder rolled again, louder, closer than before.

"What is it?" Asked Cooper.

"You *government* types," prodded Jack, "would probably call it a *weather balloon."* He keyed the comm unit, "Steele to Invader, back it down or you'll overshoot."

"Copy, Skipper." Myomerr dropped the atmospheric speed brakes and yanked back the throttle and Ragnaar toggled off the main engines as the throttles hit the zero mark. The dark ship coasted toward the beach on antigravity at over two-hundred miles an hour.

"Set it right on the beach," instructed Jack. The blue flare of the braking jets reflected brightly off the water, their soft whooshing audible over the gentle Gulf breeze. The shadowy profile of the Invader grew out of the darkness like a dragon, breathing fire. Looking at the blank faces behind him, Jack smiled to himself with righteous satisfaction. "Invader, adjust your gear settings for soft, uneven terrain."

"Invader copy, sir." Ragnaar input the commands into the computer and the auto-controllers extended the gear to anticipate sinkage and the need for auto-leveling.

Kyle scratched his chin. "Some kind of hovercraft..." he observed, unsure of his estimation.

"You could say that..." commented Jack, overhearing. "And while it *can* hover, you'd be incorrect. Thanks for playing..." he joked.

"Hovercraft don't have landing legs," observed Cooper. His hair was standing up on the back of his neck. "You've been on a ship, haven't you? That's why no one's been able to find you..."

"Very good, Mr. Cooper," smiled Jack, shooting him a glance. Phil Cooper smiled back but he looked pained, not pleased. Jack wondered if he had figured it out yet.

"That would explain the uniform," whispered his mother.

"But what country?" whispered his father. "I've never seen a uniform like that..."

The small group watched in silence as the Invader coasted to a stop, turned, and crabbed sideways as it reached the beach. Jack was aware of a distinct humming as it approached, a familiar tingling washing over his body. *Probably the antigravity generators,* he thought.

Settling to the sand, the humming subsided as the antigravity generators spun down. A flush armor panel on the side of the hull popped outward, sliding up over the top of the hull, revealing an inner waist door. It hissed as the seal released, the door swinging inward and folding out of the way, a boarding ramp extending from a slot under the doorway. Ragnaar's hulking frame almost filled the open doorway, red light pouring out past him, casting a long shadow down the ramp and onto the sand.

Jack knew exactly who it was without seeing his face, Fritz darting past and up the ramp, brushing past the Lieutenant. "Sir," he saluted. Jack returned the salute and was aware of the others crowded close behind him, filled with curiosity and apprehension.

"Sorry about the delay, sir," began Ragnaar, "we had a few minor problems..."

"That's alright Lieutenant." Jack turned to the others. "Let's get everybody aboard..."

Ragnaar frowned, his features hidden in the shadows, "I wasn't aware we would have passengers, sir."

"Is it a problem, Mr. Ragnaar?"

"No, sir," he replied backing out of the doorway.

"All aboard..." encouraged Jack, gesturing up the ramp. He ushered everyone up the ramp except Agent Cooper who stood at the bottom, one foot on the sand, the other on the ramp. "Go or stay, Cooper, makes no difference to me," he shrugged, "but I would've expected you'd want to see this through..." Phil took one step up and paused, undecided.

Steele pursed his lips and folded his arms across his chest. "You can't possibly tell me you're scared... I'm not going to kill you, Cooper; we're going for a joy ride. We'll be back before daybreak." Phil Cooper nodded and strode up the ramp without speaking. At the top of the ramp Jack gave the deserted beach one last scan before palming the actuator, closing the door behind him. Phil Cooper sat next to Kyle and Lynette, studying Ragnaar and his unique features. Despite his size, he looked human enough, *sort of.*

Lisa smiled wryly as she strolled past to see who was in the cockpit. "It's not nice to stare..." she whispered at Phil Cooper. She returned as wide-eyed as her parents after meeting the Ketarian pilot, Myomerr.

"Dooby," said Jack, "find the med kit and get everyone a translator disc, my sister will give you a hand."

"Yes, sir." He turned to Lisa, smiled gregariously and stuck out his hand. "Hi, name's Dooby, good to meet you. Didn't know the Skipper had a sister."

She shook his hand and smiled at the young man with no hair. "And I didn't know he had a crewman named Dooby. So I guess we're even."

Jack stood in the doorway of the cockpit, his back to his passengers, talking to Ragnaar and Myomerr as the Invader lifted off the beach and sped across the open expanse of water. "So what was the delay?"

"The ship's been on yellow alert most of the day, Captain. There's been a lot of traffic through the far end of the sector. The freedom has patrols out as we speak..." He paused to adjust the input for the navigation computer. "Commander Smiley said *better safe than sorry.*"

"Roger that..." added Jack, nodding.

"Did I hear the name Smiley?" Jack turned to find Agent Cooper directly behind him. "That wouldn't be the missing Navy pilot, Paul Smiley, would it?"

"The same," said Jack. "Mike Warren is with us too." He motioned to the seats, "Better buckle up, Phil."

"What about a woman named Marianna..."

"Maria Arroyo," interrupted Jack. "She's with us too. I had her placed in the brig last night when I found out her real identity." He shook his head. "I didn't like it though; she's been a good friend. I'm sure we've got quite a discussion in store for us when we get back."

"We're not going to a ship that floats on water are we..." It was more a statement than a question, obvious that Phil was uncomfortable with a realization that he was reluctant to accept.

Jack smiled as he and the agent buckled into their seats across from each other. "No, Phil, we're not."

"Ascending...!" called Ragnaar from the cockpit.

The floor tilted up and pushed them all into their seats, although the artificial gravity system vastly reduced the effects of the acceleration into space. Once out of the planet's atmosphere, the cabin gravity stabilized to normal and it was comfortable to move about.

Jack drew his father into the cockpit and pointed out through the perspex at the moon which seemed extraordinarily large. The rectangular shadow on the center of the moon growing rapidly. "I've been out here, dad, in space. UFOs, the Bermuda Triangle, Atlantis... they're not just myths..."

Kyle's sharp eyes were studying the rectangular shape in front of the moon. "That's a ship isn't it..."

"Yeah, dad, that's the Freedom, that's *our* ship."

Phil Cooper, Lynette and Lisa, peered out the Invader's slanted side windows, watching the ship grow larger.

A flight of four Lancia fighters met and passed the Invader, looping around behind it and sliding up parallel, bracketing, two on either side, escorting it back toward the Freedom.

Lynette sat with a white knuckled grip on her seat as she peered out the window, eyes glued to the fighters pacing the Invader. "Oh my God," she whispered, "we're in *space...*" She swallowed hard; this was the never ending darkness she'd dreamt about. And the reason her son had felt so far away. *Space.* That was something that had never occurred to her. She would have never made that connection, not in a million years.

"It's OK, mom," whispered Lisa, her face pressed against the window, staring at the tapestry of stars spread across the sky.

On either side of the Invader the fighter escort broke off, arcing gracefully away just before final approach.

Lining up on the flashing runway markers that started on the Freedom's fantail leading through the blue haze of the stasis field, Myomerr expertly coaxed the Invader toward the open stern. The stasis field washed over the ship as it passed through, the skid plates on the landing gear thumping the deck solidly before neutral buoyancy of the antigravity let the Invader slide along on a two inch cushion of blue light. Firing breaking jets, Myomerr steered over toward the base of the flight tower, shutting down the systems and letting the craft settle to the deck.

"What kind of ship is this?" Kyle asked his son, the antigravity generators, engines and blowers audibly whining down, each with their own sound.

"Well it started out as a Raider Class cruiser," began Jack, palming the door actuator. "But it's been so modified, it's actually a cross between a Liberator Class cruiser and a light carrier. Physically we're a little smaller than a carrier though."

Kyle raised an eyebrow as a wash of flight bay air surged through the opening door, smelling like electronics, lubricants and hot metal. A cacophony of sound flooded the interior. "So it's a military ship..."

Jack cocked his head, "Yes and no, dad. Military type, but it's actually privately owned."

■ ■ ■

After watching the four Lancias land and a couple more launch, Jack explained the various jobs, functions and equipment around the flight bay. There was a fighter in every revetment now, as well as in the cargo hold below. They used the cargo elevator to bring fighters up and down as needed for repair or make-ready. He pointed out some of the new Cyclone fighters they'd recovered from the Geo Zee salvage depot. The wide-eyed group got a tour of the ship, meeting on duty crew members and getting explanations on each section and its functions. Lynette was particularly struck by how all the crew members, no matter how different or frightening they might look, were extremely polite and respectful, especially toward her son.

"Are there other Earth people out here?" asked Cooper as they walked down a long padded corridor. Bulkhead doors swished open and closed automatically as they passed through.

"Sure," replied Jack, "more than you would think... and in many cases their descendants."

"Human descendants?" Asked Kyle.

"Tons. And mixed races," replied Jack. "We're all basically the same, but like home there are different colors, cultures, features, religions... But being more culturally and socially advanced, they're a little less concerned about those differences out here." Steele thought about the pirates, "Of course there are exceptions to every rule, even out here..."

"Like what?" asked Phil Cooper, loosening his tie.

Jack shrugged, "Good and evil, what else. It seems some things are a constant no matter where you go." He paused as he listened to the comm in his ear. "I've just been informed, they've arranged a light snack in the ready-room off the bridge. It's this way," he motioned.

"What's *your* job here, Jack?" Asked his mother. The door to the bridge slid open and Jack strolled through followed by his parents, Phil Cooper, Lisa and Fritz.

"Captain on the bridge," announced Walt Edgars.

The bridge crew saluted from their stations, Steele reciprocating with a polite smile, "As you were, gentlemen."

"Officers are waiting in your ready room, Captain," announced Raulya.

"Thank you, Lieutenant."

As he turned for his ready room, his mother caught him by his sleeve. "This is *your ship?"* she whispered, none too quietly.

"*Our* ship," he corrected her, "I'm just the Captain."

Even at the late hour, the galley crew had produced an ample buffet for the guests. Over fruit, wine and cheese, the guests met the pilots of the Freedom's fighters. Agent Cooper spoke in depth with Paul and Mike, learning that not only had the B-25 been returned, *sort of,* but their F-18s had been returned, intact. They'd left them on the runway skirt at the Jacksonville Naval Airbase.

Lynette was chatting with Brian, Lisa with Myomerr, and Jack and Kyle were speaking with Professor Edgars when Alité entered, looking radiant, her eyes a vivid, piercing blue. In her arms, she carried a small bundle.

"Mom, dad," interrupted Jack, "I would like you to meet someone special," he beamed. "This..." he slid his arm around his wife's waist, "this is *Princess* Alité Steele... *my wife*." Lynette blinked, not sure she'd heard him correctly. He nodded and pulled her closer to Alité, as tears welled up in her eyes. "And this," he said, gently uncovering a little of the bundle Alité held, "is *your grandson*. Colton Thomas Steele."

Little hands reached out for the finger Lynnette extended, his eyes a curious emerald color. "My God, he's beautiful..."

Kyle looked proudly down at his grandson. "He's a great looking kid, Jack..."

Lynnette looked up cautiously at her son. "We're not going to get to see him much, are we? You're not staying I mean."

"I'm afraid not, mom."

"But why?"

"Because we belong out here, I can see that now. All we could think about when we left, was how to get home," Jack looked to the pilots who nodded in agreement. "Now it's all about what comes next out here..."

"Things are happening out here," explained Paul. "Bigger than us, bigger than Earth, and we have a chance to make a real difference..."

"Without them," added Alité, "worlds could fall. Like mine..."

The door to the bridge swished open and Ragnaar's form filled the doorway. "Sorry to disturb you, sir, that remote sensor we placed out near Mars just picked up two UFW cruisers entering the sector. Liberator class. And they're making a beeline for Earth!"

Jack pulled his comm unit out of his pocket and slipped it over his ear as he jumped out onto the bridge, followed by everyone in the ready room. *"This is the Captain, Red Alert! Repeat, Red Alert - this is not a drill!"* Someone on the bridge palmed the alarm button and lights wet to red as the alarm klaxons blared throughout the ship. *"All hands to battle stations! All hands to battle stations!"* Steele turned to Paul. "Go, go, go! I'll join you as soon as I can." Paul Smiley, Mike Warren and Brian Carter sprinted out of the bridge and pounded down the corridor bathed in red light.

"Captain!" yelled Raulya, "All guns *manned and ready!"*

Jack reflexively checked his watch, barely sixty seconds had passed. The floor vibrated as fighters launched from the decks below them, their engine flares arcing away from under the nose of the Freedom on the vidscreen. He keyed his mic, "Bridge to tower, do we have a Zulu ready?"

"Tower, that is affirmative, bridge."

"Stern-launch that gunship," ordered Jack. "Walt, keep the Moon between them and us."

Jack turned to leave and halted in his tracks. "Raulya, tell Myomerr we're taking the Invader to the surface, full arms load. She's in the second seat, and I'll need gunners..." The floor vibrated again as two more fighters launched from the Freedom. *They're getting even faster* he thought. He kissed Alité and ushered his family with Phil Cooper toward the corridor. "Walt, how many birds do we have out...?" he called over his shoulder.

"Those last two make eight so far...!" Jack was at the bridge door when Walt called him back. "Jack! Incoming comm!"

He turned and strode back, standing next to his command seat. "On screen." A video comm insert appeared on the big screen imposed over the live feed of the system spread before them.

"Well, well, well," said Jack. "Captain Kelarez..."

"I thought I might find you here," said Vince Kelarez.

"What can I do for you, Captain?" asked Jack casually. "Or should I say, *what can I do to you?* As you can see, we're not in the same shape as when you last saw us."

"Yes I see," he replied, "quite a difference," he smiled.

Or was it a sneer?

"You should be congratulated, Captain Steele, your ship is probably the first I've ever seen to come out of pirate territory in better shape than it went in." He sighed, "But I digress. There have been changes, my friend. I am a Captain no longer." He pointed to the pips on his collar.

Jack nodded. "Rear Admiral. Congratulations."

"Yes, well, it seems a certain carrier commander followed an unknown cruiser into an ether storm and disappeared in pirate territory. They are still missing, by the way. This left a vacancy... I was chosen. Right time, right place. That and I suppose not being stupid enough to fly around in an ether storm," he said deadpan.

"And now you've come to repay me?"

"In a manner of speaking," replied Kelarez with a smirk. "We're here to apologize."

"Excuse me?" snorted Jack. "You're joking..."

"No he's not," said a second voice.

"Second signal coming in, sir," said Petty Officer Stacell.

"On screen," waved Steele. *What is this, a convention?* The screen flickered and a second video comm insert appeared next to the first. *"Gantarro?"*

He nodded and smiled, "Commanding the cruiser Bowman. Good to see you Jack."

"Good to see you too, Gant. We heard some horrible rumors - thought you might be dead."

"Almost. It was close. The Princess Hedonist is gone though. Damn pirates... Listen, there will be enough time for stories later. I've squared everything Jack, it's all on the level with the UFW now. Your rank, crew and ship have been completely and properly recorded at the UFW Directorate on Tanzia. No more screw ups..." His face grew more serious. "We need you, boy. Things are heating up out here. You'd be assigned to Rear Admiral Kelarez's task force with me, and you'll all receive full back pay from the day you launched the Freedom. She's been classified as a Jump Carrier. How about it, are you in? A little pirate bashing?"

Jack raised one eyebrow and looked over at Walt. "Commander, recall all fighters and have the gun crews stand down..."

■ ■ ■

Captain Jack Steele stood with his parents, Phil Cooper, Lisa and Alité at the base of the Invader's boarding ramp. Fritz took one last run through the water along the beach before it was time to go. "It'll be getting light soon," commented Jack. "We'd better go before someone notices this thing." He kicked a toe-full of sand on the ramp.

"Do you *have* to go?" asked his mother.

"They really need us," said Jack. "The pirates are getting stronger."

"I want to go too..." volunteered Lisa.

"Stay here, Lisa. Besides," Jack winked, "you guys have a new winter home..."

"Can I drive your car...?"

"What? No."

"Please...?"

"Still *no. No to infinity,*" he smirked. "I'd rather teach you to fly this thing," he thumbed at the Invader.

"Really? You will?"

"No," he grinned, "*you wish.* Well..." he shrugged, "maybe... later." His eyes moved down to the electronic notepad about the size of a laptop, tucked under her arm. "You going to remember how to set that up...?" he whispered. She nodded almost imperceptibly.

He strode over and took Phil Cooper by the elbow and they stepped away from the others. "Phil, I'm not going to pretend it was a pleasure..."

"I understand," he nodded.

"But some day maybe I'll get a chance to read the *total work of fiction* you're going to label as a *report* on this, I'm betting it'll be an amusing read..."

Cooper shook his head, "I have no idea how I'm going to deal with this... I think I'm going have to look up an old friend who worked with Project Blue Book and get his input first."

"One last thing," said Jack quietly, shaking Cooper's hand for the benefit of his family. "I'll be back from time to time, and I don't expect there to be *any problems.* I'm putting their safety *personally* into your hands, understand? Nod and smile Phil," he added, squeezing his hand a little

425

harder. Getting the response he was expecting, Steele continued, "Good, because I think you realize the size and magnitude of the *shitstorm from hell* I can rain down upon anyone who hurts them, could very literally obliterate a city." He released the man's hand, smiled and stepped away, "Take care, Phil," he waved.

Hearing the Invader's antigravity generators initiate, Fritz ran past the group and up the ramp, pausing in the doorway to look back over his shoulder, "Let's go!" he barked.

Jack laughed at the wide-eyed open-mouthed expressions of his parents. "Yeah," he gestured, "I knew there was something I forgot to tell you..."

After a quick explanation and a final round of hugs Alité and Jack backed up the ramp waving as they went. "Give `em hell, son," called his father.

"Be careful," waved his mother, tears streaming down her face. "And take care of each other..."

"And the baby!" shouted Lisa, fighting back her own tears.

The ramp retracted, the Invader lifting off the sand with the door still open. Alité and Jack stood in the doorway, clutching the grab-rails, leaving his parents, sister and Phil Cooper standing on the beach near the water's edge. *"WE'LL BE BACK!"* shouted Jack, *"I PROMISE!"* He watched as the shore slid away underneath the Invader and refused to close the door until the shore was completely out of sight, the water glittering below as the sun neared the edge of the horizon creating a rosy morning glow.

Contemplating the proverbial meaning of life and its strange twists and turns, Steele's head and heart were torn between his home and family, and his new life and new family. Thankfully it was a quiet and uneventful flight back to the Freedom, Alité silently holding his hand and leaning comfortably against him without clinging. She knew enough to leave the silence unbroken, void of useless chit-chat. He was struggling between the old and the new and anything she could say or do at that moment would only serve to muddy the process of sorting through his thoughts. Jack was grateful for the time alone with his reflections and her gracious comforting support.

EPILOGUE

JUMP CARRIER FREEDOM: *THE HUNTED BECOMES THE HUNTER*

The UFW ships Archer, Bowman and Freedom cruised through the Piralenin System, separated by about a hundred miles from one another in a Delta formation, the Freedom flying lead. Being Liberator Class cruisers, the Archer and Bowman were heavy on ship firepower but only had two light fighters apiece, used more for scouting than anything else. The Freedom on the other hand, now had eighteen birds, having acquired the six Cyclones from the pirate salvage yard at Geo Zee. Had they more time, who knows what else they might have recovered. It was certainly a place worth revisiting for more than one reason, but that was not first task on the hit list. Among other things that weren't first on the list, would be a visit to the UFW Blackmount Station in the Feerocobi System... though not for repairs. Supplies, crew, pilots and more fighters were en route to be transferred there, waiting for the Freedom to arrive. In her current configuration, she was fully capable of carrying almost twice the fighters and pilots she now held. They would probably retire the Warthogs and get some beautiful, shiny new Vulcans... at least that's what Jack was hoping for.

Jack Steele strolled casually up the padded corridor headed for the bridge, Fritz pacing along at his side. Using an electronic notepad, the Captain was reviewing the logs and service records for the fighters and pilots that were now running almost constant patrols. The battle weary Warthogs were showing their age and he had delegated the new pilots to them for lighter duty. Even with the upgraded electronics installed and the power plant improvement by Hecken Noer's people, they could not come close to the performance parameters of the Lancias or the Cyclones. The floor vibrated beneath his feet as a pair of Cyclones were launched out into space, which meant birds would be coming in through the stern for recovery. He slid his fingers across the screen, flipping pages as he walked, watching the statistics update live as he turned to a new page. *Nothing sighted* was the message from the incoming patrol.

"Bridge to Captain Steele..."

Steele activated his earpiece, "Steele, go ahead, bridge."

"Sir, you have a secure incoming comm signal..."

"Thank you, on my way..." he tucked the notepad under his arm and trotted up the corridor, the Shepherd pacing him effortlessly. Reaching the bridge, the doors slid open as he neared without having to slow his pace. "I'll take it in my ready room," he announced, turning right and passing thru the door into his office. The lights were low and the holo-chart was still on, tracking their route, navigation notes hovering in the air near some of the plotted lines and points of light. He dropped the electronic notepad on the sofa and grabbed a bottle of water out of the little fridge below the table. Plopping into his chair behind his desk, he ran his fingers through his hair then entered his password on the flat keyboard for the communications service, the glass surface blipping musically as he typed. The picture on the screen went from the blue UFW Directorate logo to a live video screen. The InterGal News came on briefly before being replaced by a vid-cam picture. "Lisa?"

"Hiya, Jack!" Lisa waved at the screen on her end in Ft. Myers, Florida. "It works!"

Jack nodded and waved back. "Have any problems getting it set up?"

"Not really, the on-screen directions pretty much walk you through everything. Dad hooked it into the satellite dish... I wasn't sure how that was going to work, but it does!"

"I'm not sure either, something about backtracking the carrier signal to the satellite itself, and using it to transmit while the dish receives..." he shrugged "As long as it works I don't need to understand it," he grinned. "Picture's not perfect, but..."

"But it's not bad, either - seems to have a little delay though."

"Yeah, well it's going a loooong, way," he chuckled. "What's the weather like today?"

"Eighty degrees, a couple clouds and a nice breeze. Mom and dad went out for a walk on the beach..." She sipped a soda. " I was watching the InterGal News on this thing the other night, they were talking about some of the latest Pirate strikes... are you guys doing OK?"

Jack nodded, yeah, we're hunting in Piralenin right now, kind of a detour, but it's been quiet so far. UFW has transferred us some new pilots and birds, we just have to go get them. Probably be about four weeks before we get there." He took a sip of water from the bottle he pulled from the fridge. "Any problems? Phil Cooper or anybody else been nosing around?"

428

Lisa shook her head. "All quiet..."

"Good, but keep your eyes open..." He could see the mottled, red brick back wall of his office, in his home in Ft. Myers, behind her. "OK, one more thing you need to know..." he directed her to the doorway of the office where an electronic thermostat was mounted to the wall, its display glowing green, the temperature shown on it. She had turned the communications tablet in that direction so the camera was pointed toward her and he could see. "See the two buttons on it to adjust the temperature?"

"I see them," she nodded.

"OK, don't do anything yet, just listen first. You're going to push them both in and hold them, while repeating exactly what I say. After the last word, which is *end*, release the buttons, OK? Don't say anything else." Her back to the comm-tablet's camera, he could see her nod. "Here we go, push them in and hold them; *Six, Six, Charlie, Oscar, Bravo, Romeo, Alpha, Four, Two, Seven, Sierra, Oscar...end.*"

Repeating exactly as she was told, she released the buttons as directed. A female voice came from the thermostat control, "Programming command code accepted, voice pattern not recognized... please state your name..."

Lisa looked back at the comm-tablet with a puzzled look and saw her brother nod. She turned back to the thermostat. "Lisa Steele."

"Hello, Lisa Steele, do you wish to add your voice pattern to the command system?"

Lisa looked over her shoulder at the comm-tablet, and her brother nodded again. She turned back, "Yes, I do..." The voice walked Lisa through a set of steps before logging off. She turned around, hands on her hips and looked at the comm-tablet, "OK, big brother... what did I just do..?"

He grinned, "Just say your command code out loud..."

She shrugged, "Alright... *All dogs go to heaven...*" Something inside the red brick wall at the back of the office clunked, or was it a clank? It sounded metal and heavy making her jump. She wanted to back up and run, but her curiosity begged her to investigate. The bricks in the back wall showed an uneven toothy edge on two sides as a three foot wide section of the wall moved evenly inward, carrying the framed painting hung on it along with it for the ride. The darkened opening grew deeper as the section of the wall disappeared inside. In a brief moment, lights winked on inside and she could see the brick wall on tracks at the back of a small room, the floor and crown molding in the office unmoved, part of the door frame. The floor and ceiling in the next room were at the levels of the office's moldings, the rails for the heavy door imbedded in them. "What the ffffuuu..." she mumbled open-mouthed, walking forward to peer into the room. "Holy shit, Jack, there's a whole armory in here..." The room was six feet deep and fifteen feet wide, loaded with various types of firearms, ammunition, water, dried foods, canned foods, blankets, a little worktable built like a shelf into one end, a small flat-screen TV, cable access, a laptop... almost everything one could need in an emergency. From her place at the doorway she turned to look at the comm-tablet. "You planning for the end of the world, *or what...?"*

He shook his head. "No that's in the basement..."

"The *WHAT?!"*

He started laughing, "Kidding, *kidding.* There's no basement. No, that's just my little zombie survival room." He sipped his water. "You can close yourself inside, it has battery backup, solar power, fresh air system, supplies and defenses. It was built to withstand most tornadoes or hurricanes, a fire... almost anything except something like a tidal wave. It seals pretty well, but I don't think it would seal out something like that."

She shook her head, "Wow... just wow..."

"Just remember," he added, "if you have to go in there, take the comm-tablet with you, don't forget it. Unplug the laptop connection and plug it into the comm-pad. Also, if you turn the flat-screen on, you can get security video and audio feeds around the house." He sipped his water. "To close it up when you're done, step out and say your command line again, the rest is automatic."

She stepped back, said her command line and watched the door come smoothly back toward her, the bricks fitting back together like a puzzle piece. The action on the door locked with the same clunk as when it opened, and it was done. She studied the wall for a moment, blinking, trying to distinguish the outer edges of the door; it was difficult if not impossible to notice, even if you knew what to look for. She turned back to the comm-tablet and sat back down in the chair. "Pretty amazing..." She shifted in her seat, thumbing toward the thermostat. "What if someone tried to tamper with that thing?"

Jack shook his head, "Don't even joke about that, it wouldn't be pretty." He didn't elaborate any further, changing the subject. "You might not want to show this to mom and dad unless you absolutely have to... they probably wouldn't understand." He held up his hand to halt the conversation and activated his earpiece. "Steele here... Roger, tower, copy that. On my way..." He turned his attention back to the screen. "Gotta go..."

"Problem?"

"Nah, I'm scheduled for a patrol... probably be a couple hours of empty space, stars and boredom..."

THE END - *FOR NOW...*

Other books in the series...

Book 2 - WINGS of STEELE - Flight of Freedom

Book 3 - WINGS of STEELE - Revenge and Retribution

***Coming in 2016* - WINGS of STEELE - Dark Cover**

ABOUT THE AUTHOR

Jeff Burger was born and grew up in Chicago, Illinois, moving to the Gulf Coast of Florida at the age of 28, where he still lives today with his German Shepherd, Fritz. Jeff returns to Chicago on a regular basis to visit family and friends.

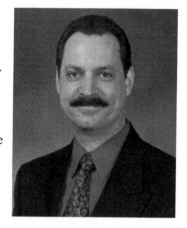

Originally drawn to law enforcement like his father and uncle, Jeff's extremely creative nature drove him toward a rewarding career in photography, illustration, design, marketing and advertising.

Jeff's choice in career and life in Florida have offered some truly unique experiences which he continues to enjoy. A certified NRA Instructor, Jeff has worked with civilians, Military Personnel and Law Enforcement Officers from many agencies. This has afforded him the opportunity to regularly handle and become proficient with firearms of all types, new and vintage, from all over the world.

An affinity for aircraft and flying have provided many opportunities to fly with talented civilian and military pilots in a wide selection of fixed wing and rotary aircraft. While Jeff finds jets to be supremely exciting, nothing beats the sublime sound or primal feeling of a piston-driven Rolls Royce Merlin V12 in a vintage P51 Mustang.

For more information about the author, additional Wings of Steele content, events, future novels, or to join my mailing list, please visit:
www.wingsofsteele.com

77613937R00259

Made in the
USA
Columbia, SC